**Garry Kilworth** was born in York in 1941, but has travelled widely around the globe ever since. He began his writing career with science fiction, which he still does, but has since been attracted by various forms of fantasy and supernatural writing. He is especially fascinated with the folklore, myths and legends of cultures which flourish beyond his own native shores, finding a universality in their rich tales.

# SHADOW-HAWK

*Garry Kilworth*

ORBIT

An *Orbit* Book

First published in Great Britain by Orbit 1999

Copyright © Garry Kilworth 1999

The moral right of the author has been asserted.

A CIP catalogue record for this book
is available from the British Library.

ISBN 1 85723

Typeset in Sabon by M R
Printed and bound in Great Britai
Mackays of Chatham plc, Chatham, K

Orbit
A Division of
Little, Brown and Company (UK)
Brettenham House
Lancaster Place
London WC2E 7EN

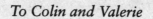

*To Colin and Valerie*

# Contents

# Glossary

**Apu Lagang:** The world of spirits.

**Badang:** A forest ghost.

**Bajang:** An evil spirit in the form of an animal.

**Basir:** Priest-shaman in some Dyak tribes, often dresses as a woman.

**Bezoar stones:** These form in the intestines of monkeys and are found by Dyaks to sell to Chinese medicine shops.

**Bomoh:** Malay witchdoctor or spellmaker.

**Bukit Kaca:** The glass mountain.

**Burbur:** Dyak porridge.

**Datu:** Malay prince.

**Geruda:** Malay for 'eagle'.

**Indera Bayu:** 'Divine wind' – a magical bird owned by Princess Moonshade, which can cure sickness with its songs.

**Iskander:** The Far Eastern name for Alexander the Great.

**Junips:** Tiny demons with hairy bodies and huge genitals.

**Kaseteran:** Kingdom of the ghosts.

**Korwar:** Carved wooden statues with a real skull inside the head.

**Lidah bumi:** Tongue of the earth, a mythical plant.

**Long Bali Matei:** The river of death.

**Long Malan:** A river in the land of the dead.

**Moonday:** The day a Chinese baby is shown to relatives and friends and is acknowledged to be 'alive'. Since infant mortality rates were once high, a baby was kept away from the world for a month after the birth – if it died during that time it was as if it had never been born.

**Orang-utan:** Malay for 'man-of-the-forest'.

**Palang:** Small rod inserted through a Dyak's penis.

**Pampahilep:** Tree spirits who take the shape of beautiful men and women and seduce lost people into madness.

**Parang:** Malay machete.

**Pelesit:** Cricket-shaped demon.

**Penanggalan:** 'The one who pulls out' – witches who drink the blood of their prey, getting at the blood supply by opening their victims up and drawing out their innards.

**Pengilipur lara:** Storyteller or 'eliminator of worries'.

**Pirogue:** Dyak canoe.

**Polong:** A bottle imp.

**Prahu:** Malay river and sea craft.

**Ruai:** Communal verandah of a Dyak longhouse, roofed but open at the front, where all the tribe gathers socially.

**Rumah:** A longhouse usually on stilts, consisting of a single row of rooms, sometimes stretching to hundreds of yards in length, in front of which a wide communal ruai runs. A longhouse is a single building housing a whole tribe.

**Semangat:** Soul.

**Tuai rumah:** Dyak longhouse chief.

**Tuak:** Iban rice wine. The name changes depending on the Dyak tribe, but for simplicity this novel uses 'tuak' as the generic name for Dyak rice wine.

**Tuan:** Form of address to a European.

**Ulu:** The hinterland, the interior of Borneo.

# Pantheon

**Amei Awi:** A Dyak agrarian creation god.

**Antang:** Mahatara's hawk, who carries the soul of sacrificial food up to his master to eat.

**Asai:** God of pioneers, whose honed shin bones can cut down trees.

**Bujang Sembelih:** The throat-cutting demon.

**Burung Une:** Amei Awi's mate.

**Durga:** Goddess of death and disease.

**Hantu Air:** The sea spirit.

**Hantu Ayer:** The freshwater spirit.

**Hantu Kuang:** The ghost with a hundred eyes.

**Hantu Puteri:** The lovely girl spirit

**Hantu Uri:** The placenta spirit, responsible for trouble after the birth of a child.

**Jata:** Son of Mahatara and the lord of the crocodiles: he has the red-faced head of a crocodile and the body of a man.

**Kilir:** Demi-god who accompanied Iskander (Alexander the Great) to Kalimantan. (The Malay legends say that the Greek ruler reached their lands.)

**Lilang:** A demi-god, 'parter of the waves' and brother of Tempon Telon.

**Mahatara:** The supreme god of the Dyaks.

**Mang:** The goddess who brought darkness to earth.

**Membang Kuning:** The spirit of the sunset.

**Rajah Angin:** King of the wind.

**Rajah Hantuen:** King of the ghosts.

**Rajah Jinn Hitam:** King of the black jinn.

**Rajah Jinn Peri:** King of the fairies.

**Rajah Naga:** King of the sea-dragons.

**Sangiang:** Demi-gods who once dwelt on earth until men learned to use iron, then they fled to the clouds.

**Santang Sisters:** The seven daughters of Mahatara who direct the fate of mortals. They take turns in patrolling the skies over the forest, flying around on golden brooms.

**Sengalang Burong:** The war god of the head-hunters.

**Tempon Telon:** The ferryman who conducts the souls of the dead to heaven.

# PART ONE

# The White Rajah

# 1

The old rajah knew he was dying: he had seen a strange bird flying across the mouth of the Sarawak River. Witnessing the sight through one of the lattice-work windows of his white palace, he needed no bomoh to tell him the meaning of this omen, which could have been interpreted by a four-year-old child. Surprising to some, the rajah was not depressed about this state of affairs for he had been ill over a long period. Death, while not perhaps a blessing, was at least welcome.

The bird had been green and red in colour, flying as straight as a blow-pipe dart. These refinements told the rajah that something else was happening out there in the vibrant world. Something else was occurring which would be of benefit to his region of the sultanate which was ostensibly ruled from Brunei, but was in practice virtually autonomous. He sent for one of the Malay princes, Ahmed Rimah, and asked him to describe what was going on in the world outside the palace grounds.

'My lord,' said the prince, in a quiet voice, 'it is market day in the city. The people have come from far and wide –

Sea Dyaks, Land Dyaks, Chinese and Malays – they are bartering for goods, selling their wares, cheating each other.'

'And on the rivers?'

There were dozens of rivers like brown snakes writhing through the jade forests of Sarawak. Their banks were shared by red orang-utans and reticulated pythons, their waters by crocodiles and mosquito larvae. The surfaces of these meandering waterways, ruffled by frequent rapids, were human playgrounds for trade, travel and occasional war.

'The rivers are quiet, my lord.'

Breezes lightly lifted the prince's cream silken pantaloons and yellow brocaded tunic as he stood there wondering what was in the rajah's mind. The prince had a tightly wound turban of green silk on his head with an enormous ruby brooch pinning it fast to his black hair. Below this turban a small frown marred his smooth, pale-skinned countenance. Harsh sunlight rarely touched the delicate complexion of Prince Ahmed's face.

'The sea? What of the sea?'

Again the prince's eyes were troubled. He did not know how to answer. In the end he decided upon the truth.

'There is a yacht cruising through our coastal waters. I am told it flies the flag of the British Navy.'

'Ahhhh,' murmured the rajah, sinking back on to his soft cushions. 'Please send for its captain, Prince Ahmed. I must speak with him.'

'Might I be permitted to know why you wish to see this British captain?'

'No, Prince Ahmed, you may not.'

Allen Starke stood on the deck of the *Monarch*, watching the coast of Sarawak slip by to starboard. Starke's face was lightly scarred down one side and he held his right arm tucked into his waist. These were the only indications of the hideous wounds he had received in India several years earlier, in 1840. Lieutenant Starke, as he was then, was riding with a message when he was caught in withering crossfire.

For many months Starke trod water between life and death. Eventually the ferryman decided death did not want him and left him to wash up on the bank of the living. Once he had recovered enough he returned to England, to his younger cousin Harriet's house, where she nursed him back to complete health. It was to Harry that Starke had announced his intention of travelling the world to try to find himself. Harry had instantly demanded to accompany Starke on his search for his destiny, saying that England was dull.

'You could leave me here, Allen. In which case I would die of boredom amongst flower gardens and old aunts, while you go off with a guilty conscience. On the other hand, you could earn my eternal gratitude by taking me with you,' Harry had said to him.

'But Harry, you know how shocked everyone would be. Ladies just don't go traipsing around far-flung countries. Apart from the danger, how will you find a husband when you've been halfway around the world with your cousin?'

Both cousins knew there were no romantic feelings on either side, nor would there ever be. Starke was a confirmed bachelor and, though she was very fond of him, Harry had no wish to share a life with him as his wife, only as a companion. Harry was not a beautiful woman. In fact, many unkind mothers of pretty girls called her 'dark and plain'. She also had a fiery personality, too full of enthusiasm for the wrong pursuits. She loved riding fast unmanageable horses and tramping in the Cumberland hills. Most men of her class liked their ladies to be ornaments who sang prettily at the piano and painted water colour pictures on the lawn.

At twenty-eight, Harry was past making a 'splendid match' and the best she could wish for was a husband who loved her. Hopefully, the right man would see her fire and enthusiasm as assets, but he was not the sort of man she would meet in the drawing-rooms of Surrey. Finding a husband was not her reason for wanting to accompany her cousin however – she was not that eager to place her future in a stranger's hands – but Harry craved excitement in her life. Travel helped satisfy that craving, especially travel outside Europe, in the more exotic regions of the earth, where more or less anything could happen.

'I don't want to be Fanny Price, of Mansfield Park,' she told her cousin, 'I want to be Harriet Glendenning of No Fixed Address.'

'You saved my life,' he replied, exaggerating things just a trifle for the benefit of the shocked aunts, 'so how can I refuse you, Harry?'

During the time that he convalesced in Surrey, the death of his father provided him with enough funds to purchase a yacht. It was a sleek racehorse of a craft which cut an elegant figure on the water. Because this vessel had belonged to the Royal Navy it had the same privileges as a man o' war and was authorized to fly the white ensign. Starke had decided that although he been permitted to live, his military years were over, and he determined to set out and search the world to find a new purpose for his life. He set sail for Ceylon by way of Aden, cruised around the Maldives for a month or two, then went on to Singapore. He found the 'lion city' full of merchants and tradesmen, most of them expatriate Chinese. In search of more exotic company he moved on and so circumnavigated the Malay peninsula and cruised to Borneo.

Now he was sailing along the coast of Sarawak. Here he knew lived three races – Dyaks, Chinese and Malays. He knew a little about the latter two, but he had needed to look up the word 'Dyak' in his books. It seemed the Land Dyaks were split into several tribes – Kayan, Kenyah, Kejaman, Skapon, Berawan, Sebop, Punan, and many more – and they lived inland, in longhouses controlled by chiefs and paramount chiefs. Only the Iban were known as Sea Dyaks. They lived on the coast and were different in appearance to the Land Dyaks who lived along the rivers. The Iban were raiders, a fierce people, often hostile.

'There's a boat coming out, Cap'n,' said the helmsman, John Keller, a red-headed seaman. 'A royal canoe by the look.'

Starke looked up to see that Keller was right. There was a canoe with a thatched roof. Starke could make out a figure sitting on a carved chair in the centre. The canoe was rowed by what appeared to be Dyak Indians. Starke had already encountered some Sea Dyaks sailing prahus, pirates who tried to board him. He blew them out of the water with his six-pounder cannons and two swivel guns mounted fore and aft.

'I see them now, Keller, thank you.'

'Aye, aye, Cap'n.'

Though his eyes were sharp and keen, Keller was the only real troublemaker on board. Allen Starke intended to leave Keller in some foreign port when the time came. He was the cause of much unrest within the crew. Most of the others would have been happy to knock Keller on the head and tip his body overboard in the middle of the night, but Keller was handy with his fists. It would have taken more than one of them and they were not yet a cohesive enough unit nor sufficiently confident of one another's willingness to remain silent afterwards.

Starke knew that if Keller remained on board the seaman would eventually disappear one dark night – or someone else would be killed by his hand.

Starke ordered Rediman, the first mate, to take in sail.

Soon the canoe was alongside and a Malay dignitary came on board. After declining refreshments, the man said he was Prince Usop. He was armed with a kris, a wavy-bladed dagger, and was wearing a colourful sarong and a red velvet jacket trimmed with silver which had large buttons made of hornbill beak. Usop was Prince Ahmed's older brother and the crown prince but, unlike his younger sibling, Usop was extremely ugly, and had a humped back. The prince pointed to the beautiful Santubong Mountain on the mainland and said in good English, 'The Rajah of Sarawak requests your presence at a feast this evening. Will you come, sir?'

Starke thought about declining. There were treacherous people amongst the local rulers. However, at the last moment an impulse urged him to accept.

'Yes, thank you, I'll be there. I shall come in one of my boats, so you have no need to wait.'

The prince bowed and left. He did not sit down again but stood in the stern of his prahu, looking back at Starke's yacht the whole while until he reached the shore.

Starke waited for the flow tide and then went upriver in one of the ship's four boats. He took with him six of his crew, armed with muskets and cutlasses. Keller had given Starke a problem. If he took him along, he might cause some incident and ignite a riot. If he left him behind, there would without doubt be some kind of fight. He decided to take him, but made the sailor steer the boat to keep him occupied. Starke had made sure Keller was also without a weapon of any kind.

Harry remained on board. She had gained considerable respect amongst the crew for her doughty character. During the pirate episode she had remained on deck the whole time, not getting in the way, but determined to watch the battle. In her slim white hand had been a rather large pistol. It had been given to her to use on herself, if the battle had gone the wrong way, but she had no intention of committing suicide for such a silly thing as protecting her honour. She had used it to shoot a Dyak pirate between the eyes as he clambered over the gunwales.

She had now been left in charge of the *Monarch*. If Starke did not return she was supposed to order the rest of the crew to sail the yacht to Singapore. She was just as likely to take the craft up the Sarawak River and lay waste to the city. In her way she was as much a rebel as was Keller, only her intentions were good, whereas Keller's were at best dubious.

When Starke reached the royal jetty he found a large gathering of Malay princes waiting for him.

'Keller, you will accompany me,' said Starke, 'the others remain on the jetty. I want no trouble. You will wait for my direct orders before doing anything at all, is that clear?'

The boatswain nodded briskly. 'Aye, aye, Captain.'

'Keller,' went on Starke, 'keep your mouth shut and your fists in your pockets. I'm taking you with me only because I don't trust you back here. If you give me any problem whatsoever, I'll shoot you dead. Do you understand?'

Keller growled, 'Murder, Cap'n?'

'Out here there are different laws and no one cares about the rights of villains, Keller.'

The seaman shrugged and nodded sullenly.

The Malay princes, Ahmed and Usop among them, clustered around the two Europeans and bustled them towards the palace. Starke was taken through marble halls to a cool room in a high tower. Here he was ushered into the presence of an old man swathed in cotton, lying on a bed of silk. The old man was as shrivelled and wrinkled as a brown lizard. Starke could see that the spark of life within the man was all but gone. His breathing was quick and shallow, his throat pulsing like that of a reptile suffering from too much sun. There was not much time.

A gnarled, crooked hand, devoid of any flesh, beckoned the captain closer to the bedside.

'You are Allen Starke, the Englishman?'

Starke raised his eyebrows. 'You are well informed, sir.'

'You are Captain of the *Monarch*?'

'I am indeed.'

'I have heard of your exploits against the Sea Dyak pirates in my waters,' said the rajah, his voice like dry leaves rustling in the breeze. 'You have done well. Those pirates are a plague on my country. Do you think you could rid these waters of them for good and all?'

'I don't know,' said Starke, sensing an important announcement. 'I could – but why would I wish to risk my men and my yacht to do that?'

The crowd of princes were standing in the doorway, watching and listening intently to every word that was spoken. Keller was standing a little way off from the bed, his eyes flicking from one face to another, gauging the mood of those participating in this drama. Keller was a liar, a thief and an all-round scoundrel, but he was a survivor and no coward. No matter what his captain's orders might have been, if trouble started he was going to fight his way out of that room. Where was the sense in doing anything else?

The old man continued. 'The leader of those pirates is called Lingore, a vicious cutthroat who thinks nothing of using a live baby as a flag hanging from his mast. He is an evil man, who lays waste to villages and destroys my prahus. The datus,' the old man waved a bony hand at the Malay princes, 'can do nothing about him. They are helpless and only fit for court intrigue and plotting against each other.'

'I understand,' said Starke, 'but shouldn't you be resting, instead of telling me these stories? You seem very ill to me, sir, and I advise you to get some sleep.'

The old man, his head like a fleshless skull, gave out a husky laugh. 'I am not only ill, I am dying. I shall be dead before the morning. This is what I have to say to you, Captain. If you rid the waters of these pirates, then I wish you to be the next rajah in my place. Promise you will be the scourge of this blight and you shall rule Sarawak for Sultan Omar Ali of Brunei. I have sent word to him and already have his approval. I offer you a kingdom, Captain Starke, in exchange for your promise.'

There was a gasp from the doorway. The princes began chattering amongst themselves like starlings. Keller, unarmed at the orders of Starke, looked around him for a handy weapon and decided upon an ornamental Dyak sword which hung on the wall behind the bed. Keller calculated he could have that weapon in his hands within three bounds. He remained poised on his toes, ready to make the leap forward if the princes came on.

'Quiet,' cried one of the datus. There was immediate silence, for the voice was that of Prince Usop, the crown prince. 'Let my uncle the rajah finish his words.'

'Thank you, Usop,' said the rajah. 'But now I am simply waiting for an answer to my question.'

Allen Starke sat for a moment or two contemplating the old man's offer. He had little doubt he could get rid of the pirates, given time. If he could not do it with the *Monarch* he could send for a larger ship to do the job. The question was, did he want to rule a foreign land? If he undertook this task it would be lifelong. There would obviously be much opposition from the princes in the doorway – and others, no doubt. Furthermore he had no idea of the enormity of the task, what it might entail, and whether or not he was being tricked into something much more complex than appeared on the outside.

'I'm sorry,' he said to the rajah, 'I need more information – and you are very weak.'

The skeletal hand waved away the concern for his health.

'A man who is dying is beyond rest,' said the rajah. 'What do you wish to know?'

'Why me – an outsider?'

'It is precisely because you are an outsider that I wish you to take my place. There are three races here – the Chinese, the Malays and the Dyaks. During my lifetime the Chinese merchants have become rich and powerful in their own right. The head-hunting Dyaks also need a ruler who will look after their interests as well as those of the Malays and the Chinese. If I appoint anyone else – Malay, Chinese, Dyak – there will be jealousy, rivalry and riots. In short, there will be a blood bath. You, as an outsider, can look to the interests of all groups, without having any particular bias or prejudice.'

'I understand that part of it now, but how do you know you can trust me to act as you wish? Englishmen are as fallible as any other race. We have our share of greedy, brutal despots who would milk a country dry. What makes you so sure I am not one of those men?'

The rajah came off his silken sheets and grabbed Starke's collar, pulling the captain's ear close to his mouth.

'This is not a rich country. There are some individuals who have money, jewels, fine clothes, big houses, but the kind of wealth that warps men into lesser creatures cannot be found in Sarawak. Even so, I would not hand over my kingdom to just anyone. There are sorcerers here, people who can see into a man's soul. I have consulted those who can foretell the future,' he whispered hoarsely. 'You are spoken of as a man with integrity and justice in his heart.'

Starke lowered the rajah back on to his bed of silk. Behind the bed was a huge Persian carpet: a wall-hanging. In corners of the room were ivory ornaments, vases of solid gold, ebony chairs and jade carvings. Yet, it was as the rajah had said, the country itself was relatively poor. It had gold and antimony mines, but these did not produce the kind of wealth that made men rich overnight. If Sarawak was to become great it would be a slow process, through hard-gathered trade, and perhaps would never happen at all.

'I accept your offer,' he said, solemnly. 'I'll do my best to rid the South China Sea of pirates. I hope I shall prove as wise a ruler as my predecessor.'

There were several intakes of breath from the princes in the doorway at these words. The rajah smiled, faintly.

'Good,' he said. 'I announce you as my heir. My grand vizier, Muda Hassim, will take care of you.'

Starke looked up to see that a powerful-looking man had forced his way through the knot of princes into the room. He was accompanied by guards, who immediately took up positions around the room and pushed the princes back, clearing the doorway.

Allen Starke nodded towards Keller and the pair of them joined the princes, who had now moved outside the room, as more of the rajah's personal bodyguards began to press them towards the stairs of the tower.

On the way back to the boat the two Englishmen were jostled by the Malay princes.

Prince Ahmed said to Starke, 'You will not last very long if you come back here.'

'Why are *you* making threats, brother?' asked Prince Usop. 'I am the next in line – it is me who has been robbed.'

'No one is safe,' cried another prince. 'Your uncle had no children. We all have a claim.'

Starke turned to them and said, 'That's precisely why the rajah wishes the next ruler to come from the outside, so all this petty squabbling will cease. I'll tell you now that when I return it'll be for good. Once I'm ruler I shall suppress any insurrection with utmost firmness. You all heard what the rajah had to say about all the races having an equal interest in this fine country of yours. Let the silly quarrelling amongst you come to an end and let us have peace here.'

With that, Starke jumped into the boat and ordered his men to cast off. The mariners rowed downriver to the sea with great energy, mistaking their captain's intense silence, and Keller's high excitement, for signs that all had not gone well at the palace. The seamen thought they were about to be chased back to the yacht by prahus full of armed men from the city.

When they reached the yacht and Harry came to greet her cousin, Keller could hold back no longer.

'They've made him a king,' he cried in a wild excited voice. 'We'll all be rich!'

'A king? What's this?' said the boatswain. 'Is that the truth, Cap'n? Have you been crowned a king?'

'I've been offered the sultanate of Sarawak by the present rajah, who is unfortunately dying. This doesn't mean you'll all become suddenly very wealthy, despite Keller's outburst. If you remain with me, you will no doubt find a comfortable life here, but I don't intend to enrich my own people at the expense of others.'

Despite these words, Keller was irrepressible. He believed that Starke was merely playing the English gentleman, saying what he thought people wanted to hear. Keller could not conceive of anyone who would not take advantage of this windfall. Who would it hurt? Only a bunch of natives. Why, you took what you could in this world, and left the leavings to the poor. Of course they were all going to be made rich. It was his good fortune to be on Starke's yacht when the gods were smiling.

Harry spoke to her cousin in his cabin, privately.

'Is this true? You're going to be the next rajah?'

'Yes, Harry. I have accepted the old rajah's offer. I have promised to rid the area of the pirates, but I think that was just a sop for the Malay datus. They believe it should be one of them, you see, which I suppose it should. Nevertheless, we'll set about hunting for the pirates tomorrow.'

'I'm very happy for you, cousin. I'm a bit sad too. I thought we were going to have more adventures.'

'There's adventures to be had in this land by the fistful, Harry. The interior is full of Dyak head-hunters. The mouths of the rivers are inhabited by Chinese merchants who are all trying to outdo each other with regard to trade. And the city is teeming with Malay princes who will no doubt try to assassinate me at the first opportunity. Oh, there'll be plenty of excitement for you here, Harry. This is a colourful exotic land, full of Eastern mysticism and magic.'

'Oh, good – just what I've always wanted – and not a disapproving aunt in sight!'

**2**

The Chinese pantheon is and always has been a confusing muddle of deities. There are three main philosophical religions stemming from three teachers: Lao Tzu (Tao), Buddha and Confucius. In addition, there are many other divinities, from kitchen gods to shepherd boys, to rocks, trees and the odd dragon-shaped passing cloud. Fishermen pray to Tin Hau, goddess and protector of all seafarers; students make offerings to Wan Chung, who sees to it that they garner knowledge; and soldiers show obedience to Kuan Ti, red-faced god of war.

There is a great deal of sorcery and magic entangled in the Chinese religion, and also side-religions like Feng Shui, the art or science of exploiting the environment to its best advantage. Joss, however, is the main goal of all devotees of the many and various Chinese gods. Joss is luck, without which even the most enterprising merchant could fail to make his fortune.

The Malays of Sarawak are Islamic, praying to Allah.

Once away from the coast, however, the Dyak gods, multitudinous and strange, hold sway.

The morning after Allen Starke returned to his yacht a leaf fell from the 'Tree of the End' in Islamic heaven. It bore the name of the rajah, who consequently drew his last breath the moment the leaf left the tree. The rajah ascended to the seventh of the seven levels of heaven, arrayed like the upper floors and balconies in a mosque, all under the same dome.

In this paradise he found cool streams, beautiful gardens, lawns and orchards with delicious fruit on the trees. Here sherbet was brought on golden trays by high-breasted maidens. Above the mosque 70,000 angels sang for the soul of the rajah, who had found true peace at last in his heaven.

At the same time as the rajah expired, a Dyak tuai rumah in the Ulu, the interior of Borneo, died from fright. He had been out in the forest hunting moonrats with his blow-pipe when he saw a spectre huntsman, a corpse with moss all over its body which continued to hunt game even though dead. This chief of a Kayan longhouse, Mayok by name, dropped stone dead at the sight.

This action on Mayok's part annoyed the third of the Santang Sisters, one of the seven daughters of the Dyak's supreme god, Mahatara, since it was her job to direct the fate of mortals. She skimmed over the body on her golden broom and stared at it in disgust. She had not given permission for the death and the chieftain's soul was therefore at great risk. It hovered near the body, not knowing what to do or where to go. She left it there, unguided and bemused, to teach the chieftain a lesson.

Mahatara's hawk, Antang, later came sweeping through the trees when it came across the freshly dead man. Antang, the shadow hawk, immediately fell on the loose soul and carried it up as food to Mahatara. The supreme god of the Dyaks was pleased with his hawk for finding such a morsel when the owner had not been a sacrificial offering.

Mahatara had a staple diet of chicken and pig spirits, but it was nice to eat a human soul for a change.

When, after searching the rainforest high and low, the rest of the Kayan longhouse found the chief's corpse, some of his tattooed skin had already been eaten away by forest creatures, small and large. The Kayan warriors sensed something was very wrong with the death. The look of utter terror stamped on the chief's face was enough to tell them he had witnessed one of those sights which should not be seen by any mortal. The chief's wife was already dead, but he had a son, also called Mayok, who had just become a man.

Mayok had an enemy in one Danta, the son of the basir, or priest-shaman. Danta was ambitious and Mayok, being the son of the current chief, was in his way. Here was a chance for Danta to get rid of his rival. It took but a moment to sow the seed of mistrust and fear into the hearts of those in the longhouse.

'You must leave the village,' they told Mayok, excitedly. 'You will bring us bad luck. Your father's death was too strange to be normal. You must take the wrath of the gods with you, and leave the longhouse for ever.'

Mayok, like any Dyak, believed he would die if sent out into the Ulu without support of his longhouse.

'Do not do this thing to me,' he cried, almost in tears. 'Let me stay amongst my people.'

But the Kayan people, incited to a pitched state of terror by Danta, were adamant. Mayok was tainted. He had to go. No one could take the chance of displeasing the spirits of the rice field and putting the harvest in jeopardy. It was nobody's fault if Mayok died. They gave him his blow-pipe, his father's parang, and sent him on his way. The tattooed youth, dressed only in a loincloth, began a long trek through the rainforest towards the coast. On the way he stole a canoe from a neighbouring longhouse, for one cannot travel swiftly and far in the rainforest without using the rivers.

He camped the first night by some rapids which he knew to be swarming with demons at the foot of their waters. It was said that these rapids were such terrible killers you could collect a jugful of eyes amongst their rocks. Some of Mayok's friends had been drowned at this very set of rapids and, even though he was anxious to be far away, Mayok dragged his canoe several hundred yards across land rather than risk running the swift waters.

Mayok was so sick at heart the first night he cared nothing for the supernatural world. As soon as the sun went down, Mayok missed the ruai, the deep communal verandah of the thatched, ironwood longhouse, behind which were the individual rooms of the families. On the ruai everyone would gather and exchange stories and news of the day, as they worked at various crafts: weapon making, weaving, plaiting fish traps. It was on the ruai he had begun courting the girl he wished to marry. She would now go to someone else: another young man who brought her a head.

That was another thing! Mayok stared out into the darkness. Alone and unprotected by his clan he would be not only the prey of supernatural creatures, but also a prime target for young men of other tribes. Like Mayok, they were head-hunters, who would not miss the opportunity to prove their worth. He slept fitfully, his blow-pipe with its speartip close to his side. In the morning he was on his way again, letting the current carry him downriver, towards the sea.

At noon Mayok stopped the boat to light a fire with a bow and tinder. Once he had a burning twig in his hand he was able to remove the leeches which had gathered around his throat like a necklace of bloated wobbling beads. He had collected these from leafy branches stretched shoulder high across the river. Burning the leech made it remove its jaws from the skin, otherwise the head would be left behind to turn septic.

It was while he was removing the leeches from his neck that he heard just the faintest of puffs. Mayok immediately fell sideways, into the water, as he was struck in the head by a dart which he knew to be poisoned with the sap of the ipoh tree.

He thrashed for a while in the shallows and then lay motionless, still keeping a grip on his blow-pipe. His head was floating in the water, as if lolling and lifeless. Once in two or three ripples, half his mouth was above the surface, which was when he snatched a quick breath. It was beyond his understanding why he had not been paralysed within seconds. But he was not stupid enough to stand up and ask why the hunter had failed to poison his dart.

After a while two men emerged from the rainforest. They were Skapon Dyaks, hostile to Kayans. Once they saw that the Kayan was dead, they talked to each other. One was drawing his parang from his belt.

'This is my head,' he said to his companion. 'It was my dart which killed him.'

'I helped track him down,' protested the other man. 'It was me who took the message from the Kayan, Danta.'

So, Danta had further betrayed him! Mayok knew that this would have been without the sanction of the rest of the longhouse. His own childhood friend was a traitor and a murderer. Mayok could hardly bear it. Danta had played with him under the longhouse, they had swum together in the river, they had reached manhood as one.

The two boys, unusually, had gone through their manhood ceremony at the same time, lying on the ants' nest as was expected of them, allowing themselves to be bitten in a thousand different places, without showing they were in pain.

Then they had to separate and go off into the forest alone, to live for twenty days without society. Those twenty days had been difficult enough. Now Danta had forced Mayok out completely, to place him for ever at the mercy of warriors like these two Skapon head-hunters.

'I am not going to help you take a head back to our longhouse,' continued the disgruntled second man. 'If you want it all to yourself, then you will have to do the work yourself.'

With that, the second warrior trotted off into the rainforest, leaving the first man.

Mayok blessed Mahatara for this piece of good fortune. However, he was still about to be decapitated. He could not see the other warrior and had to rely on sounds to help him locate his opponent. He heard the soft tread of bare feet on mud, as the man came to the edge of the water. Then there was a pause. Mayok guessed the Skapon was mentally preparing himself for the task of chopping off another man's head with a parang.

At that moment a kingfisher flashed across the river, through the bars of sunlight piercing the rainforest. The bird brushed the water, then the leaves of a tree. It was enough to distract the Skapon, sensitive to his moment of victory.

Mayok rolled sideways and thrust upward with the spearpoint of his eight-foot-long blow-pipe. The iron harpoon head buried itself in the Skapon's tattooed belly. Mayok wrenched sideways to throw the warrior off his balance in the mud. He was unsuccessful. The other man was very strong, a seasoned hunter and warrior, and he slashed downwards with his parang, chopping the blow-pipe in two pieces, the smaller half remained hanging from his abdomen.

'I'll kill you!' screamed the man in pain and anger.

The parang came swishing close to Mayok's ear.

The Kayan youth, now in terror of his life, drew his own parang. He was still sitting awkwardly in the mud, unable to regain his feet. He swung the parang horizontally over the mud and severed the Skapon's leg at the ankle. The wounded warrior fell thrashing to the ground, screaming in the fear and horror of losing his right foot. His eyes showed that he could not believe he had been bested by a raw youth. How had that happened to a middle-aged warrior who had taken six heads?

Mayok followed up his advantage very quickly, regaining his feet, then swiping with the broken blow-pipe. The hardwood stem struck the Skapon on the temple, knocking him senseless. Mayok leapt on the body and with two quick chops removed the man's head from his torso. Then the youth staggered back, a sob of relief and shock in his throat, to stare at his handiwork.

The mud was running with blood.

Mayok picked the severed head up by the hair and threw it into his canoe. When he reached up with trembling fingers to his head, he found that the poisoned dart had buried itself in his thick hair, without touching his scalp. Carefully removing it, he thanked the river spirits for saving his life. The dart was indeed poisoned with the deadly sap from the ipoh tree, which only took a few seconds to paralyse the creature it penetrated.

He thought at first about returning to his longhouse, to show them that the gods were not against him, but he knew Danta would not allow him to live even for one night. So he got back in his canoe and prepared to cast off, still pointing the bows towards the coast. The last thing he saw before the current took him swiftly downriver was the face of the Skapon who had set off home, framed by the leaves of a bush. The warrior had obviously heard the screams of his friend and had returned.

Too late, for Mayok was almost instantly beyond the eighty-foot range of the Skapon's blow-pipe, even if that hunter did have the stomach to fight a youth who had so easily killed his friend.

Mayok had some thought about getting to the coast, where he had heard he could ask for an audience with the rajah. He had never been more than a few miles from wherever the longhouse was situated before now. Longhouses change their location, but always within a certain region. Though he knew the river would lead him to the sea he was lost, especially in his spirit, which was most confused of all. Mayok had some vague idea of asking the rajah to intervene, so that he could return to his longhouse and live out his life as a Kayan.

When night came, Mayok found himself a place to sleep under a tree. He was very afraid. Being alone and lost he was at the mercy of any number of supernatural creatures of sky and forest. He prayed to Tempon Telon, one of the Sangiang and ferryman of the dead. Two more of the Sangiang, Tempon Telon's brother, Lilang, and his friend, Asai, were also invoked by the youth, who believed in covering every corner. Lilang was powerful with water and Asai, the god of pioneers, could chop down trees with his sharpened shin bones. Once the prayers had been offered, with the sacrifice of a monitor lizard, the only thing he could catch, Mayok felt a little safer.

Sometime in the middle of the night he was woken by someone entering the leafy forest glade. Startled, he leapt to his feet, clutching his parang. In the moonlight he saw a tall handsome woman coming towards him. She had a little smile at the corner of her mouth. While he stood and trembled, she came to him and began to stroke his tattooed shoulders, crooning all the while. Then she took his free hand and led him to a mossy bank, indicating that they should lie together and make love.

Mayok was still muzzy from sleep and he wondered whether he were dreaming. But this all seemed so real, not at all like a dream. He allowed the woman to run her hands over his body, arousing him. All the while his head was becoming clearer. Just as he was about to enter this beautiful creature, he remembered the stories from his mother and father.

'If you are ever lost in the forest,' they had told him, as all Dyaks tell their children, 'beware of the pampahilep.'

The pampahilep were tree spirits who, in the guise of tall handsome men and women, found lost tribespeople in the forest and made love to them, causing their victims to fall ill or to become insane.

Mayok jumped to his feet in fright and swiped at the woman with his parang. The blade passed right through her body without harming her, as it would through mist. Yet in that instant her features turned to fury and she faded from his sight. She had indeed been one of the pampahilep and Mayok had had a lucky escape.

Mayok took his canoe and turned it upside down, crawling into the near pitch darkness beneath, with the Skapon head for company. Here, surrounded by a wall of wood, he felt a little safer, even though the confined darkness was worrying to him. He decided he would not be lured from underneath his shell by any sounds. It was best to remain there until the morning light.

While laying in the blackness he remembered the story of Mang, the goddess who first brought darkness to the earth.

Mang had been consuming a sacrificial feast left for her by a chief called Lejo when he suddenly returned. Her long hair got caught in the trees and she was unable to take flight, but Lejo fell in love with her instantly, she was so beautiful. He too was a handsome man, for an earthling, and she consented to lie with him. First, however, she returned to Apu Lagang, the world of spirits, for fresh raiment.

On her way back to earth she collected enough darkness in a milk-basket (the Dyak weaving being so fine and tight as to contain liquid) to cover her and the man while they made love. Some of this darkness later escaped when a curious child crept into her bedroom and made a little hole in the milk-basket reeds with his finger. Mang, on noticing the infant, got up from her bed and put him outside. When she opened the door, the darkness which had seeped from the milk-basket poured into the world.

The people ran screaming, this way and that, for they had known only sunshine and light until now. Many of them went to pray to Mahatara, as the darkness spread like a fine dust, settling in every nook and cranny of the world. Mahatara took pity on the frightened people. He banished the darkness for twelve hours of every day. Now it goes reluctantly, not leaving all at once, but dragging its heels like a child on its way to bed, until its thin shadow has finally vanished.

Many days after leaving his longhouse, Mayok reached Kapit on the mighty Rejang River.

Allen Starke sailed up and down the coast in the *Monarch*, ruthlessly culling the Iban pirates. There was no lack of interest on their part either. One morning, Starke faced up to fifty prahu, some of them armed with swivel guns. But he was a good seaman and outmanoeuvred this small fleet, sweeping back and forth on its outer edges, sinking a prahu here and a prahu there, until they saw how useless it was to face this sleek, graceful craft and made a run for the nearest rivermouth.

Starke had now effectively broken the pirates' hold on coastal waters. Many of them fled up the rivers to inland waters, where the Land Dyaks eagerly waited to even old scores. It was said that for a while a trail of headless corpses stretched from the shores of Sarawak to the Ulu, the heads having been taken to decorate Land Dyak longhouses all along the Rejang, Miri and Skrang Rivers.

Lingore, the pirate paramount chieftain, managed to escape evasion, but most people thought he would be wise to remain in obscurity for the rest of his life.

Allen Starke went back to the city on the Sarawak River, to be officially invested as Rajah of Sarawak. In the quiet hours he had been learning a little of the local languages, especially Malay. He still did not know the name of the city, so on landing he pointed to it and asked what it was called. The grand vizier, believing that Starke was pointing to a domestic cat licking its paws in the middle of the dusty road, told him it was a kuching, a pussy cat, then shrugged his shoulders and moved on.

'Kuching,' repeated Harry, standing by his side. 'What a pretty name for a city.'

When Muda Hassim later learned of his error he did not correct it. This would have been very bad manners. If the new rajah believed the city was called Kuching, then Kuching it would stay. The instruction went out, far and wide, and it would be many years before Rajah Starke learned of his mistake. By that time the old name of the city had been forgotten and, in any case, the people of Sarawak had a lively sense of fun. They enjoyed retelling the story of how 'cat city' got its name.

Rajah Starke rejected the palace as a home and instead settled on a bungalow on the edge of the Sarawak River. Harry kept house for him there, though that merely entailed giving instructions to servants. Much of the time she was out and about, first mostly in Kuching, but then taking to visiting the longhouses along the rivers.

She found the Dyak people fascinating, never tiring of watching them dance the hornbill warrior dance, with its graceful movements which were so hard to copy. Whenever she arrived at a longhouse and asked permission to enter, a baby would be thrust into her arms to coddle. This was the Dyak way of welcoming a woman, to show her they trusted her even with their young. Harry learned the languages, slowly but surely, and once she could converse a little the people opened their hearts to this white woman.

There were those, gentleman travellers from England, who began arriving once they learned a white rajah was ruling Sarawak, who voiced their disapproval of the behaviour and freedom given to Harriet Glendenning – even if this were the Orient. Starke took little notice of them. So far as he was concerned Harry could do no wrong.

'Apart from her gallivantin',' said one critical visitor, 'she wears men's clothes.'

'She wears pantaloons and shirts because they are more suitable in this climate, in the type of terrain through which she travels. Leeches, my dear sir, are apt to get up and under a woman's skirts,' replied the imperturbable rajah. 'Something tight around the ankles, above thick socks and stout shoes. Something tight around the wrists and around the neck. There are leeches out there you'd not believe. They'll suck your body dry of blood within a few hours.'

The visitor went to bed that night feeling shocked and horrified. Not because he had learned about various types of leech, from tiny thread-like leeches that attached themselves to lips and tongue when drinking from rivers, to the foot-long beast which the rajah had thought fit to describe to his guest in detail. No, not because of that, but because the rajah had talked about his cousins 'skirts' in such an open manner. Queen Victoria would have been outraged to hear such language.

When the travelling gentlemen discovered that Rajah Starke was incorruptible and that he was not going to exploit the country in order to make himself and others rich, they gradually dwindled away. In the end the worst of them stopped coming and only honest gentlemen, families, teachers, missionaries and genuine tradesmen remained to assist the new rajah in his duties.

During the first week of his rule, Rajah Starke had fallen desperately ill. Once again it was Harry who saved him. She found him wandering the bungalow in the middle of the night, clearly perplexed and confused. Recognizing by his pallor that it might be something he ate, she forced salt down his throat and made him sick. He vomited some vile-coloured liquid into a pan, which she had the foresight to retain and show to the vizier, Muda Hassim. This liquid turned out to be poison.

Already the Malay princes were at work, doing what they did best, poisoning their way to power.

'I suspect the crown prince, Usop,' said the grand vizier. 'We must have him assassinated immediately.'

Muda Hassim was a Malay prince too, and though his loyalty to his former rajah's heir was unquestionable, his methods were much the same as those employed by the rajah's enemies. It was court intrigue, beloved of all the princes, who were adept at plotting and doing away with their rivals. They used magic, poison, assassination and all the under-the-cover ways known to man to achieve their ends. The more cunning and underhand the deed, the better they thought themselves for it.

'I know two men who will do the work,' continued the vizier, while Starke and his cousin stared at him in horror.

'They are to be found in the Chinese quarter. They are experts with a pillow and a red-hot poker . . .'

'We can't stoop to their methods,' said Starke, finding his voice at last. 'You must see that, Muda Hassim?'

'Why not? Your own King Edward II died in such circumstances, so one of your new teachers told me. A poker inserted up the anus leaves little tell-tale marks – not one that would be noticed by relatives. We must choose a good embalmer, one who can hide any scars. Give me your leave to arrange this thing and it shall be done before one week is out.'

'I can't. Apart from my abhorrence of such a deed, it wouldn't serve my ends. I'd lose all the respect of the other princes.'

'My esteemed lord,' said the vizier, 'the other princes will respect you enormously for it. They will realize you are one of them and not to be trifled with. Even amongst the ordinary people your esteem will rise like a river in flood.'

But Starke was adamant. There was to be no murder. There was not even any proof that the crown prince was to blame for the poisoning. It seemed likely, but that was not evidence.

Once he was well again, Starke called the datus to the palace, to the great hall where he held court and dispensed justice. He could not use the bungalow for such duties, it was too small and lacked the proper intimidating atmosphere for such functions. The princes came in fear, knowing that at least one of them was responsible for attempting to murder the rajah. Starke told them what he thought of them.

'You are fat and lazy creatures,' he said, 'who have had too much of the good life. Have you nothing better to do than plot against me and against each other? Don't you consider such activities to be a criminal waste of a man's time on earth? Why aren't you out there trying to better your country? Look at the Chinese! They're so enterprising. They make themselves rich, it's true, but they also enrich Sarawak with their trade. I'd rather you were merchants than idle princes.'

They came to him afraid, but his speech made them furious. Who did he think they were, to suggest they should become shopkeepers? There was royal blood in their veins. They had pedigrees. This was what became of appointing a commoner to the position of rajah. He had no conception of what it was like to be of noble and royal blood. He was an ignorant man.

They told him as much, as they choked on their indignation.

The rajah retorted, 'A noble lineage is nothing without a noble spirit to go with such breeding. If you are indeed princes, then you should develop princely ways. It is to be expected that your behaviour should match your blood line.'

After the meeting, Prince Ahmed fled to the hinterland, believing that although nothing had been said to him, his plot to murder the rajah had been discovered. It had indeed been the younger Ahmed Rimah, not the crown prince, who had poisoned Starke. Being the creature he was, the sly prince thought he had been found out and would be murdered in his bed, or some devious way would be used to kill him and make it look like an accident. He did not rule out magic, for how otherwise could the rajah have survived the poison if no sorcerer was involved?

The other indolent princes remained sullenly silent and watched the progress of Ahmed from the wings.

Now, at this time, most of Starke's sailors were still looking after the *Monarch*, though one or two had been given posts of responsibility under the new rajah's command. The troublemaker, Keller, had actually left Starke's service, with two shipmates. Keller, Johnson and Blake, had set up a trading station just beyond a fort Starke had ordered built at Kapit. They had made themselves comfortable on providing some of the materials needed by the builders of the fort.

Starke, knowing he had to stay in Kuching to handle the other princes, sent for Keller, who came down the river by prahu to meet with the rajah.

'Prince Ahmed Rimah is gathering some men about him,' said Starke. 'He seems intent on rebellion. We must move swiftly. I want to hit him before he attacks the city. Are you prepared to lead a force of Dyaks against this troublesome datu?'

'Can I take Johnson and Blake with me?'

'You may take whomsoever you wish. I shall also supply you with muskets. Cannons will be of no use to you, since you have to travel fast and light. Ahmed is gathering his men around the slopes of Gunung Santubong. I suggest you recruit some of the Iban tribesmen. Try to stop them taking heads, but I appreciate it's a little early for us to have any effect so far as this part of their culture is concerned. If you can't stop them altogether, then at least try to limit it.'

'The Iban?' said Keller, surprised. 'Aren't they Sea Dyaks? Pirates?'

'Not all of them and in any case we must use warriors where we find them. We can't go rooting about in the interior for Land Dyaks. We must move quickly.'

Keller shrugged. 'What do I use to pay them?'

'The currency the Dyaks use consists of beads imported by Arab and Chinese traders. It's the small black beads they treasure the most, called lukut sekala, but there are also blue and yellow ones, and some with stripes. I'll give you a variety to make your payments from. Some of them prefer to use Chinese jars and brass gongs as currency. Whatever they ask for, tell me and I shall supply it.'

'And I'll have plenty of powder and ball?'

'As much as you require.'

Keller, a pain in the neck on board the *Monarch*, was really quite useful to Starke in situations like this. Keller was a naturally aggressive man, a man of bitter character, who liked nothing better than a fight. The ex-seaman turned tradesman went off with Johnson and Blake and persuaded several longhouses of Iban to follow him up the peninsula on which Gunung Santubong stood. Despite what Starke had said to him, Keller promised the Dyaks they could have as many heads as they could take.

Keller trained a dozen of the Dyaks in the use of muskets. Johnson and Blake were in charge of this small force, which was used to block the main pathway down from Gunung Santubong, where Prince Ahmed and his Malays had their hideout. Keller took the rest of the Iban up on to the mountain. They managed to track the Malays easily, for the prince and his forces were not used to living in the jungle, while to the Dyaks this was home.

The Malays were ambushed in their camp in early morning. A big red sun was just rising above the dark green of the trees. The peak of Gunung Santubong had begun to glitter in its rays. Parrots were waking with raucous shouts that would alarm anyone not used to their harsh cries. Insects were buzzing, whistling and whining. The heat of the night was folding into the heat of the day. Keller suddenly gave the signal.

Darts flew into the waking Malays from the surrounding trees like a swarm of deadly hornets flashing through the bars of sunlight. The victims, some washing, some rising from their beds, began dropping in twos and threes. There were those who staggered a few paces first, swatting at the dart which stuck from their skin, then crashed to earth like a felled tree. There were those who dropped the instant they were struck. There was no panic or screaming. It was all too quick for that.

'My God,' said Johnson, appalled. 'It's a bloody slaughter.'

Keller was stunned more by the cold efficiency with which it was carried out than by the scale of the massacre.

'Well, they had their chance.'

What he meant by that, Blake or Johnson had no idea. There had been no call for a surrender. No offering of terms. Keller had just let the Iban have their way.

Prince Ahmed managed to escape this onslaught with seven of his royal guardians, but they simply ran headlong down the main path, to be met by a line of muskets. The firelocks roared flame and ball, and Prince Ahmed, being in the front of the retreat, was the first to die. A musket ball took out his teeth and smashed through his spinal column. Others went down around him, one or two of them hit in the back as they tried to run.

Only one of the escaping Malays survived to be taken prisoner. One or two others, who had remained where Keller had ambushed the main party, also lived. These were herded together and given to the Dyaks, who took them into the forest.

Keller and his two friends then witnessed the gory spectacle of the Dyaks decapitating the corpses.

'Bloody savages,' murmured Johnson. 'There ain't a civilized godly man amongst 'em.'

Keller shrugged. 'What does it matter, eh? They're dead bodies, only so much meat. They can't feel nothing, can they? It don't matter to them that they're losing their heads. Let the Iban have their fun, I say. The harm's already done.'

Keller paid off the Iban in beads and jars, and then returned in triumph to Rajah Starke. He took with him the body of Ahmed Rimah, as proof of the prince's death. Starke was suitably impressed by Keller's speed and efficiency.

'You did well,' said the rajah, handing Keller his payment in gold. 'My congratulations. Where are the prisoners?'

Keller's expression remained bland. 'The Dyaks don't take prisoners,' he said. 'It was a massacre. There was just four of 'em left afterwards. Muda Hassim's got them.'

'You couldn't control your warriors?'

'I ain't their chief. We yelled at 'em, but that just seemed to make 'em more excited. We was lucky they didn't turn on us in the end, for givin' 'em lip.'

Starke nodded grimly, but caught in a trap of his own making.

'Any time you want someone turned off,' said Keller, 'just send a messenger to me.'

'I may indeed have to use you again, to hunt down the perpetrators of serious crimes. There's no system yet in place for policing the territory. If a man commits a heinous misdemeanour, he simply disappears into the forest. We've got to make sure such criminals don't continue to go free after such crimes.'

'I'm your man. Sounds just like my kind of work.'

'A rape was committed on a woman in her own house just yesterday. The culprit was a Chinaman, who ran away to the forest. I want you to find him and bring him back, alive if possible. I'm told he went up the Kemena River.'

'If he's still alive, I'll find him all right.'

On his way out of the bungalow, Keller ran into Harry, who was gardening.

'Hello Miss Glendennin',' he said, touching his hair at the front. 'You're looking very tasty today.'

At first Harry was not sure how to take this expression, which for all she knew might be a compliment. However,

Keller's leer left her the impression that it was something quite unsavoury. She gave him a half-smile and continued to weed between the oliander shrubs. She did not like Keller and saw no reason to encourage him any more than necessary.

Keller left the bungalow feeling soured. Who did she think she was, this high and mighty strumpet? One day he expected to be in a position to put her in her place. Until then he satisfied his hatred by imagining those slim pure-white arms and legs entangled with his own weathered limbs. Not that he had to wait to satisfy his lust. He could have all the women he wanted from amongst the native girls, most of them prettier than Miss Harriet Glendenning, and all a darn sight more willing.

## 3

The busy streets of Kuching made Mayok feel nervous. This great city frightened him, with its ox carts and horses, and hundreds of people bustling here and there. There were Indian and Arab tradesmen with turbans woven, surely, from the skins of multi-hued snakes. Women in purdah, wearing masks as fine as the webs of jungle spiders, their mysterious eyes shining, glistening, bright with secrets. Grim-faced Chinese, men and women, driving hard bargains in the arcades. And Malay dandies wafting by in clouds of perfume and colourful robes.

Mayok had decided he would not go and speak with the rajah after all. The old rajah was dead. In his place was some kind of albino creature from far across the seas, quite foreign to someone like Mayok. There were one or two others, and a woman, with the same fish-belly pale skins. They were beings from another world. Mayok was too shocked by the rajah's appearance, too frightened of him to approach him. The rajah and his retainers were surely ghosts from the land of the dead.

Even though some of the Dyaks Mayok spoke with told

him the rajah was a good man and would listen to stories of injustice and put them right, Mayok still could not summon the courage.

Instead, the young Kayan sold his canoe for a handful of beads and bought tuak and got drunk. When his beads were all gone he went to work for a Chinese laundry, washing clothes in the river. It was women's work. It was not befitting a warrior and a hunter.

This distressed Mayok enormously. However, he could not hunt for his food in town and in any case his blow-pipe was broken. If he wished to eat and drink, he had to do some sort of job. The only people who would employ him were the Chinese clothes-washers.

He was paid in rice and tuak at the end of every day: just enough to get him through to the next day. It was a terrible cycle, a trap which enabled him simply to eat and drink, and nothing more, offering a bleak future. It meant he could not really escape, unless he went back into the forest. Half-drunk on tuak most of the time, he slipped down to the level of an alley cat. Needing more and more alcohol, he went to work at night for a man who sold Chinese medicines, helping to grind down the bones of tigers, prepare the genitals of deer and cut the gall bladders from live venomous kraits, cobras and coral snakes.

It was while he was staggering around half-drunk in the dusty market place one day that Mayok literally bumped into one of the strange newcomers with the pale skins. Mayok had been drinking as usual and was weaving between blankets and stalls piled high with fruits all the colours of the rainbow. There were sweets of lurid hue also, and monkey meat, and a knife seller with all his wares in a neat shining line in the dirt. Fortune-tellers and soothsayers, roadside physicians and even those who claimed to be magicians, clutched at his arm and offered their services for payment. One such man was so insistent he would not let go.

Since Mayok had no money these people were wasting their time and he wrenched himself angrily from the man's grasp, only to stagger into a cluster of dentists and doctors, pulling teeth and smearing balm on sores. Extricating himself from these monstrous people Mayok decided he needed some water and headed towards the river, away from the frenetic energy of the market place. It was then he walked head-on into a white man.

'Where d'you think you're going?' snarled the man, whose red-stubble-bearded chin was thrust an inch from Mayok's nose. He pushed Mayok in the chest. 'Watch where you're walking!'

Mayok did not understand the man's sounds. He looked into eyes the colour of pale sea water. Then he glanced at the man's head. It appeared to have been stolen from an orang-utan. The man had hair the same colour as the man-of-the-forest. This was astonishing to the simple Kayan, who until a few weeks ago thought the world a leafy kingdom full of ordinary Dyaks, who all looked like proper human beings should look.

Again the creature in front of him made angry sounds.

Another Dyak, leaning against a stall, told Mayok what the sounds meant. Mayok began to get angry. Who was this creature to speak to him as if he were a slave? Mayok was a chief's son, brought to terrible circumstances by the will of the gods. Yet he was still entitled to be treated as a man among men.

Yet, a moment later, the pale-eyed man seemed to have changed his character, like a snake sloughing its skin. This man was now all smiles and pats on the shoulder. This man spoke to another Dyak, who said, 'Kayan.'

Pale-eyes nodded on hearing the only word which Mayok

understood. He made those funny sounds again, with his mouth, just as if he were talking. The Dyak said, 'He wants you to go with him. He wants you to be a guide and hunter. He will pay you many beads for this.'

'Why does he want a guide? And he looks strong enough to do his own hunting.'

'These white men like to have things done for them. This one has to go into the forest sometimes, to hunt other men. He has killed many Malays and cut off their heads. Sometimes he hunts Dyaks and Chinese. He does this for the rajah.'

'What have these men done to be hunted like animals?'

'They have broken the laws of the rajah. I too am this man's guide. It pays many beads. This is the way the white men do things. When they cannot carve life out for themselves they pay others to carve it instead.'

'It is a very strange way to live,' replied Mayok, 'but it is better than washing dirty clothes which smell of sweaty men and women, or scraping tigers' bones for Chinese charm cures. Tell this pale-eyes I will help him do these things.'

The pale-eyes laughed on hearing the other Dyak's sounds and scratched the head he had stolen from an orang-utan. He touched Mayok's shoulder again, before walking on.

Thus Mayok became a guide and hunter for one of the strange newcomers.

Mayok found he did not have to do very much at first. He simply waited around the market place. However, when some crime was committed, like a robbery, murder, or the rape of a woman, then the red-headed pale-eyes sent the other Dyak, who was an Iban, for Mayok, and about six of them would go hunting the bad man, or bad men, depending on the nature of the crime. Sometimes the Dyaks were allowed to kill those they hunted, and keep the heads, but on other occasions they took the men back to Kuching.

The first time he went out on a manhunt Mayok disgraced himself. He had noticed the blow-pipes carried by the white men, made of iron and wood. He had thought them strange-looking, but politeness prevented him from enquiring further. When they came across a party of Sea Dyak pirates, everyone was agitated, gesturing, waving their weapons. What he saw next was the white men lifting their blow-pipes to their mouths. Then there were some ear-crashing noises and long flashes followed by acrid smelling smoke. Several pirates fell to the ground.

Mayok yelled in great fright and dropped his parang. He ran off into the forest. He had seen roaring, flame and smoke coming from the end of the white men's magic blow-pipes. They had puffed thunder and lightning from between their lips like monsters from the world of darkness and death. Mayok was mortally afraid of these supernatural beings and wanted to hide from them.

The other Dyaks, laughing, found him afterwards, jammed and trembling in a tree-hole. They explained about the iron blow-pipes. It was still some time before Mayok could come to terms with what they told him. He was jittery every time a white man turned their face towards him, which of course they did often, to tease him. Each time he flinched, expecting a mouth to spout noise, flame and smoke, and strike him dead where he stood.

In between hunts Mayok was taught a little English by Johnson. Mayok was told this was necessary if he was to remain a hunter of men. There was time off now, too, to return to the forest and make himself a new blow-pipe.

He went back into the trees and selected a long hardwood straight branch which he trimmed down to a required slimness. This seven or eight foot length of wood he hollowed out over a number of weeks with a boring tool. The hole through the branch had to be very straight and the fashioning of it took a lot of skill. Afterwards he rubbed the outside with hornstone and the inside with fine sand, until the finish of both was smooth to the touch. Finally he fitted an iron spearhead to the end of his new weapon.

The darts were made of bamboo, eight inches long, with butts of elder. There were darts for hunting and darts for war, different from each other. Then fresh sap from the ipoh tree was gathered and boiled down to a dark-brown paste with an acrid taste. It was only dangerous in the blood stream. This poison paralysed the nervous system of animals within seconds.

Once he had a new blow-pipe Mayok began to feel more like a real warrior again. It was true he had no longhouse to govern, like his father had done, but he was seeing many things which would have terrified his people. Yet he was not frightened. He had become very sophisticated. Sometimes, when he had a significant dream, he would go to the market place and find a soothsayer. Here he could pay the man with a Chinese pot to have his dream interpreted. The soothsayer would take a white chicken and, holding its legs, circle Mayok's head before slitting the bird's throat and sprinkling blood in the dust.

Once he had his fortune told.

The old woman told him, 'You will become very rich and powerful – even more powerful than the white men who have come here – and you will go back to your longhouse in triumph.'

Mayok was very excited by this prophecy, and being young and eager he asked when this would take place.

'We do not know this yet. Time is difficult to foresee.'

'I need it to be soon,' said the youth, 'for I am growing old quickly.'

The soothsayer smiled at him with black teeth.

'How impatient are the young,' she said. 'You will return to your tribe when the gods are ready. It may be tomorrow, or you may be an old man with a long beard before it happens, but you must believe me when I say that it will make no difference to your feelings. They will be the same whatever age you are.'

He bought the old woman a pig for her prophecy, for she was not a Malay, but half-Chinese and half-Dyak. She was delighted with the payment. It was more than she had asked for, but Mayok desperately wanted her prophecy to come true, and thus thought to keep the bearer of that prediction sweet. It was not so much that he wanted to become rich, but he desired to return to his people in triumph. On that day he wanted to challenge Danta to mortal combat and kill his childhood friend.

Mayok began to temper his drinking habit, only getting drunk on tuak twice a week. He found he needed to keep a clear head in case the tuan with the red hair and pale eyes wanted him. There seemed to be a lot of lawlessness in the early days of the new rajah, for many of the Malays wanted the rajah dead. There were many plots, many rebels who became renegades, many chases through the forest which ended with the death of the prey.

There came a day when Mayok had to kill his first white man, which was a strange experience for him.

Six European sailors had jumped ship at Singapore, stolen a Chinese junk, and had sailed to the Sarawak coast. Here they had come across an Iban longhouse. The Iban took pity on the starving sailors and fed them and gave them beds for the night in one of the rooms of the longhouse. The mariners rewarded the Iban by raping two young girls, looting the longhouse, and then escaping in the junk to a landing place further down the coast. A runner from the longhouse had made the journey to Rajah Starke's bungalow and made his people's complaint. The rajah had been incensed. He told his sister:

'It's bad enough to have to keep order amongst people who break the law because they know no better, but to have Europeans importing such crimes is monstrous. I want these men hunted down and brought to me. It's time to impress upon the local population that I'm impartial with Occidentals and Orientals alike.'

Keller was called to the palace, where all the business of the rajah took place. When he learned what he had to do, Keller collected his head-hunters together. He had men from several tribes now, outcasts mostly, who could not return to their longhouses for some reason or another. They were Iban, Kayaks, Kenyah, Berawan and Sebop. This small group often questioned other Land and Sea Dyaks. The Dyak saw things while they were hunting which would be of use to Keller and his two cronies, Johnson and Blake. Once the information was in Keller's hands, the party would regroup and set off in pursuit of the wrongdoers.

The European sailors had been spotted by some Sea Dyaks heading along the coast towards Brunei. Keller gathered his trackers and hunters together, some twenty or more, and set out after them.

'Thieftaker General, that's me,' said Keller, grinning, to his shipmate Blake. 'I'm like that Jonathan Wild, the London thieftaker. I've got it made here. I get paid by Starke for hunting down people I can rob first.'

'You got to be careful,' warned Blake. 'If Starke finds out what you're doing, he'll send you packing.'

'Dead men can't tell tales,' Keller growled. 'And our Dyaks ain't got the wit to say anything.'

The first night the group were out the three white men shocked Mayok by stripping off and bathing naked in the river. This bothered all the Dyaks, who were quite prim about total nudity, even though they often wore nothing but a loincloth. Mayok was, however, fascinated to see that Keller and his two friends did not have palangs through their penises. Not all Dyak tribes used the palang either, but Mayok was a little sniffy about those who did not, believing them inferior men.

The palang is a small rod made of bamboo, bone or hardwood, driven through the end of a warrior's penis. The ends of the palang have knobs or points, or even sometimes blades, attached to them. This sensible device is pierced through that sensitive part of the anatomy at a fertility ceremony. Its purpose is to increase the pleasure of the woman during lovemaking.

The Borneo rhino had a natural palang which obviously satisfied his mate and at some time in the past a Dyak had watched the device in action and had later tried an artificial one with good results. There were some men who had two palangs, obviously great lovers, and were much sought after by the young maidens in their longhouses. Mayok was not one of these philanderers, but he did have a single palang.

'What are you starin' at?' cried Keller to Mayok, as the red-haired man left the water. 'Keep your eyes to yourself.'

Mayok knew a little English now. He stumbled off into the forest, embarrassed and confused by this verbal attack. In consequence he spent the rest of the night on his own, not wanting to join the others at the campfire in case they mocked him. That night though, because he was alone and vulnerable, Mayok was visited by the omang: stumpy forest gnomes. He knew they were omang because their feet were on backwards. They asked Mayok for rice, and he gave them as much as he could from the pouch on his belt. The omang took it without a thank you and disappeared back into the forest.

'Where have you been?' asked the man on sentry duty, who happened to be a very grouchy Johnson. 'You boys slip off into the jungle without a by-your-leave!'

Mayok, who almost ran back to the camp once the omang were gone, understood enough to know he was being questioned about his absence.

'I get lost,' he lied. 'This no my forest.'

'You better not tell tuan Keller you got lost – he pays you as a tracker, boy. Go on, get some sleep. I'm going to wake Blake soon, and he's not a gentleman like me.'

The three white men never went to sleep all at once. One of them always remained awake and on guard. Mayok and the other Dyaks knew this was because they were not trusted. He hastened to find himself a place to sleep, away from a termites' nest, in a natural hollow formed by the buttress roots of a great tree.

Mayok was happy to be within company again. He had learned of more horrors of the otherworld while in Kapit, from a Malay woman there. She had told him of supernatural fiends like Rajah Jinn Hitam, the king of the black jinn, who could send animated hostile shadows to his victims, causing pain and death. And Hantu Kuang, the ghost with a hundred eyes, from whom you could never escape once he had you in his sight. Or Bujang Sembelih, the throat-cutting demon of the forests, who could slit a resting man's neck through to the spine, while two others sleeping on either side heard nothing, and only discovered his terrible handiwork when they woke in the morning.

Such horrors, piled on the Dyak spirits and demons of the forest, were enough to give a boy heart failure.

The next morning Mayok woke to find the sun shooting rays through the canopy on to his face. He jumped up, startled by his own fear. In fact, camp had been struck, and the other Dyaks were preparing to move out. One of them asked him why he was so sluggish and he told the man about the gnomes. The Dyak nodded, sympathetically, with perfect understanding.

'You are lucky they did not carry you off,' he told Mayok. 'I saw a hawk flying backwards this morning. If there is no red sunset tonight – if Membang Kuning ignores the end of the day – then I think we are all in trouble.'

With this sober piece of information in mind Mayok made ready to leave.

The party travelled past a rumah that morning. The occupants, Kenyah Land Dyaks, were questioned by one of the trackers. He was told that they had not seen the sailors Keller was seeking, but they had heard some strangers had landed on the shore just half a day's run away. The tuai rumah of the longhouse was thanked and the party continued.

Finally, they came to the edge of the rainforest and Mayok could hear long lines of surf booming down the beach. The ocean opened up before him as he stepped from the tree line. It was breathtaking. A great blue desert of water melted into the blue sky in the very far distance. Looking back over the path they had come, a hundred shades of green swept like waves, up and down, until they swamped a distant range of hills.

The hunting party was in a wide curving bay with a rock like a humped man just a hundred yards out in the water. They saw the junk beached further along the coast. At first Keller and his party thought the sailors had been caught by the tide, but when they reached their enemy, they found the men drunk on tuak they had stolen from a longhouse they had raided. The sailors tried to put up a fight, but it was a one-way slaughter.

One sailor ran up past the high-tide mark, trying to reach the forest. He was slow and labouring, due to the hot sun and the drink he had imbibed. Mayok followed him. On the edge of the tree line the man turned and aimed a pistol at Mayok. The small weapon belched noise and flame. Something burned past Mayok's cheek. Then the man started fiddling with his pistol, trying to reload it. Hopelessly inept in his drunkenness, the sailor dropped the weapon and started to run again.

Mayok lifted his blow-pipe to his lips and puffed.

The dart hit the sailor behind his left ear. The man slapped at it, as if trying to swat a mosquito. Then he turned and gave Mayok a hurt look, before staggering a pace and falling flat on his face in the sand. Mayok had killed his first white man. It gave him nightmares for several days afterwards.

# PART TWO

# Singapore Jack

# 1

A year after Allen Starke had been made Rajah of Sarawak he offered the country to Queen Victoria's government in Britain, to turn into a colony. The offer, to the rajah's great relief, was rejected. Had they accepted, Sarawak would have been flooded with opportunists from Britain: people he would have had no direct control over. He had done his duty as an Englishman, but from the moment he heard the rejection Starke considered himself a naturalized Sarawakian.

He remained the sole power in Sarawak and, fortunately for its people, the man chosen by the old rajah was not one who let this power corrupt him. Starke and Harriet set about improving the country's economic condition, and raising its status in the Far East. One of the first things he did was to forbid the Dyaks to take heads. This order was among the few they ignored. They continued to decapitate their enemies. When they were caught at it, they took the rajah's rather patronizing and hurt reprimands on the chin, promising never to do it again, but of course when the opportunity arose, they did.

'They're like children,' he grieved, speaking to Harry about the practice abhorrent to men from the West. 'But it's not a child's game. What are we going to do about it?'

Harry said wisely, 'It'll take more time and patience than you think, Allen. It's deep in their culture. I doubt we'll see an end to it in our lifetimes. We'll just have to register our disapproval, administer the law, and hope to make an impression.'

Those missionaries who arrived from other parts of the world tried to influence the Dyaks too, but Starke did not altogether approve of wholesale conversion of the natives. He felt that if at all it should be a gradual thing, coming in by degrees to those who genuinely wanted it. He did not want it rammed down their throats like so much porridge. Thus he limited the number of missionaries coming into the country, much to the indignation of the various Churches in the West.

One Sunday he was in his bungalow, musing on such problems, when he was aware of shadows around the house. He looked up just as the French windows burst open and several figures came striding into the room. One of these figures was a large tattooed man, naked to the waist, with a scar across his face. His hair was cut in a fringe at the front, but was long and straggly at the back, falling down past the nape of his neck to his waist. In his hand he had a Dyak sword. He was an Iban, a Sea Dyak, and Starke had a good idea as to the man's name.

'Lingore?' said Starke, in the Iban dialect. 'Have you come to take tea?'

Through the open French windows Starke could see the bodies of two of his Dyak house guards lying on the lawn. He had no doubt the others were also dead or severely wounded. The attack had obviously been swift and merciless. If he had heard any cries, amongst those given out by raucous parrots and other birds, they had failed to arouse any alarm in him.

The paramount pirate chief, who had spent the last year hiding out, was impressed by the rajah's nonchalance.

'You know who I am? You speak my tongue?'

Starke settled himself comfortably in a chair, as if the pirate chief were really here on a social visit. His mind was working nineteen to the dozen. Harry was out visiting a sick Malay woman, so he did not have to worry about her. The only other person in the bungalow was a houseboy, who was at that moment in the kitchen, eating his midday rice-and-chicken meal.

'I *guessed* who you were. There have been reports of you coming out of hiding. And I have your description, from one of my Dyaks. As to speaking Iban, I spend two hours of an early morning every day learning the local languages. I seem to have a gift for it. So, what have you really come here for? To kill me?'

Lingore looked around the room. His men were now standing quietly by the door, watching for any intrusion. The royal bungalow had a garden leading down to the river. The pirates had obviously come down the river by canoe and had simply moored up at the end of the lawn. At first they were a little nervous, but they began to relax when all they could hear were the birds in the garden bushes, and the distant sounds on the river.

'Yes,' said Lingore, taking a chair opposite the rajah. 'I have come to kill you. Just as you have killed many of my men with your cannons. This is a bad thing you have done to me, but now I will take my revenge.'

Starke took a cigar from a carved wooden box on the table and lit it, blowing out the smoke in a satisfied way. He offered the box to Lingore, who also took and lit a cigar. They sat and puffed, staring into each other's eyes.

Rajah Starke said, 'I would expect you to be angry with me. I have indeed broken the back of your power base here. I shall continue to fight you and your kind. There are still pockets of pirates, here and there, which I intend to root out. My vessel is well armed, as you know, and we can do the job. Your people do not stand a chance. Why don't you just surrender, throw yourself on my mercy, and I will see what I can offer in the way of mitigation.'

Lingore grinned broadly, his big-boned face registering his amusement. There was one startling gold tooth in the front of his mouth, which flashed in the sunlight coming through the bungalow window. Starke could not help but admire the muscles on this man: they rippled with every movement of his body. In his huge hand Lingore balanced his sharp Dyak short sword.

'You are a very funny man, Rajah. If I kill you now, which I am going to do, I will be free to do as I wish in future. You know that once you are gone the Malay princes will never allow another white man to take your place. They will then continue to squabble amongst themselves, poisoning each other, murdering their rivals, while I am left to pillage in peace.'

Starke nodded. 'I'm impressed. I knew you to be a good fighter – perhaps a great warrior – but I had not expected you to be intelligent. A brute of a man, I thought, who can bully others into submission, but with a lizard's brain. How wrong I was. I really am quite overwhelmed. Have you had an education?'

'I knew a Chinese from Singapore, who taught me how to think in your way . . .'

'Look,' said Starke, quickly, 'why don't we have a whisky with this cigar. If it's going to be my last, I should like it to be the best I ever smoked. Whisky and cigars go together, as you probably know. Have you ever tasted good Scotch?'

'Of course,' replied Lingore, grinning. 'You think I only rob native boats? I have overcome European vessels too, in my time, and taken what they have to offer. Let us drink to each other's health, and then I'll kill you.'

Starke suddenly called out in English, 'Badu, two whisky glasses on a tray, then signal my Dyak guards!'

Lingore leapt to his feet, brandishing the sword.

'What was that? What did you say?'

The rajah switched back to Iban.

'Calm down,' replied Starke, having gambled on Lingore not knowing English. 'I merely called my houseboy and asked him to bring some glasses. See, here he is now. Put the tray down on the coffee table, Badu, thank you. You may continue with your duties in the kitchen.'

'Yes, tuan,' murmured the young man, trembling as he placed a tray with two glasses on the coffee table. 'Thank you, tuan.'

The houseboy left the room accompanied by one of the pirates. The youth looked very scared, but all he had to do was tug a cord which hung from the kitchen ceiling. He did not even have to do it surreptitiously, for the cord was also the switch which worked a mechanical ceiling fan. After the cord was pulled any suspicious Dyak would witness the fan swishing back and forth, wafting cool air in the room, and dismiss it as a wonder of modern science.

However, Starke had anticipated attacks on the bungalow and had installed a pulley-and-weight system in the roof. When the same fan cord was tugged, weights dropped and cords tightened, sending a flag up a pole attached to the gables.

Ignoring the threat the hovering Lingore posed, Starke calmly got up and went to his drinks cabinet. He took a brass key from his pocket and opened the cabinet, taking out a bottle of Scotch. Then he filled the two glasses on the table to the brim and offered one to the pirate chief.

Lingore's weapon was lowered and he took the glass.

'You are hoping to get me drunk, so you can overpower me?' laughed Lingore.

'Would that be possible, with your pirates standing at the French windows, ready to rush in and cut me down? Besides, I have a bad arm. I was wounded in India.'

'You might think the risk worth taking.'

'Oh, yes, I might. Then again, I might think the whisky will dull the pain when you cut off my head. I think I like the second reason better. It makes more sense.'

Lingore's gold tooth flashed again. He took a sip of the whisky. Starke could see that Lingore was enjoying this chattering back and forth. The pirate obviously gained pleasure from being in control of a situation which was distressing to others. Occasionally Lingore asked of his pirates guarding the doorway, 'Is there anyone out there?' and received a negative reply.

The two men sat opposite each other for the next three-quarters of an hour, talking about life in general. Starke was right in his assessment of the pirate chief. Lingore was highly intelligent and was probably starved of conversations such as the one they were having at that moment. They were on their third whisky when the Dyak guards arrived and began battling with the pirates out on the front lawn.

'You betrayed me!' cried Lingore, jumping to his feet.

'How could I betray you? I owe you no allegiance,' replied the rajah. 'Tell your men to lay down their weapons and I will offer you leniency for your crimes.'

'Never!' bellowed Lingore. 'I shall kill you now!'

The pirate swung at the rajah with his blade. Starke leapt backwards, out of reach, as an oil-lamp standard was severed by the blow. He was about to reach for the whisky bottle, to use it as a weapon, when someone came into the room from the kitchen end of the house. It was a tall, lean white man. The intruder levelled a pistol at Lingore and pulled the trigger. There was a boom, a flash, and the pirate chief fell dead, clattering over the coffee table and then sprawling across the carpet.

When the Iban pirates saw their chief was gone, many surrendered their arms. Some of them ran towards the river, pursued by the guards. Others were lead meekly away to be locked up. Rajah Starke shouted a few orders to his men, called in his houseboy to thank him profusely for his good work, then turned to the visitor who had saved his life.

'Sir? I don't know who you are, but I thank you from the bottom of my heart. Lingore was determined to take me with him on his journey to hell, but you foiled that plot. Your name, sir, that I might thank you properly?'

'Lord Randolph Braiks,' replied the man, coming partly to attention and offering a strong hand to shake. 'Some people call me Singapore Jack. You may have heard of me?'

The rajah had indeed heard of Singapore Jack, the near penniless nobleman from England. Lord Braiks was well known in the Far East for his madcap ventures. His estates back in Shropshire had been left in ruins, through no fault of his own. (His father had lost heavily at gambling.) There was some idea of Lord Braiks making himself rich in the Orient, then returning to England and restoring them.

He was a slightly unsavoury character – one of those opportunists Starke felt Sarawak would be better without – his reputation being sullied by a number of dubious schemes which had gone wrong and cost the lives of others in his party.

There was one story that a sumptuous and magnificent pavilion had been lost to man in the jungles of Burma, close to the town of Yenangyaung, on the banks of the Irrawaddy. This fabled pavilion was supposed to contain treasures left behind by Iskander (the Eastern name of Alexander the Great) to be guarded faithfully by the Pyus, Shans and Mons who inhabited the region. Singapore Jack had raised an expedition and led a party to search for the fabulous treasure of Iskander, only to lose half his men to disease and snake bites, and hostile Burmese.

There was another tale that the impoverished lord had travelled the Silk Road until learning in Samarkand that a priceless parchment had been stolen from the Temple of The Seven Veiled Virgins and spirited away to Siam. Singapore Jack traced the document to some Portuguese traders, who had then taken it on to Macau, one of their colonies on the Pearl River in China.

The swashbuckling aristocrat gathered together some riff-raff from the Singapore waterfront, hired a junk, and attacked a Portuguese trading vessel which he believed to be carrying the manuscript back to Europe. It was not. The ship contained nothing but China plate and rhubarb, the latter being prized for its supposed medicinal qualities and unobtainable in Europe.

'Lord Braiks,' said Starke, a little less than enthusiastically, 'you were just in time to save my life.'

'I'm glad of that, sir. Think nothing of it, or if you do, remember I have a favour to ask. It was all purely fortuitous in any case. I was already on my way here when I saw the Dyak guards running towards the bungalow and I guessed there was trouble afoot. Pleased to be of assistance.'

The aristocrat smiled. He was around thirty-five years of age, dark haired, and with deep brown eyes the colour of the Skrang River. He had that lean chiselled look which many women thought handsome. The ladies also liked the way he moved with a lazy, fluid grace, as if born to liquidity. His mouth was their only disappointment, most finding it too small and tight. However, the nobleman, like the rajah, was not greatly interested in women or what they thought of him, so it was all a bit of a waste.

Starke said, 'I am eternally grateful. So, what brings you to Sarawak? We have no lost treasures here.'

Again, that silky smile. 'Ah, well as to that, I wouldn't be so sure if I were you. However, actually I'm here at the instigation of the Geographical Society of London. They've agreed to partly fund an expedition. It's my intention to chart a route from Kuching, through Kalimantan, to Bandjarmasin on the south coast of Borneo. If I should come across some treasure on the way, why then that'd be a bonus, wouldn't it?'

This caused the rajah a moment of anguish.

'You may have saved my life,' said Starke, 'but I won't have my people exploited, Lord Braiks.'

'Call me Jack, everyone does,' replied the lord, languidly. 'My dear, sir – may I call you Allen? If I've saved your life I should be counted a close friend, even though we've only known one another a very short while.'

The rajah nodded.

'My dear Allen – by the way, I love the way you say *my people*. It makes you sound like some deity. Anyway, Rajah Allen, my good friend, I am not in the least interested in exploiting anyone. Any fortune to be had is out in the rainforest somewhere. And I'm not going to rob your Dyaks either. I say, may I have a glass of this whisky, it looks very good. Malt whisky, eh? Nothing but the best for the Rajah of Sarawak.'

'Purchased with my own money,' answered Starke, pouring the lord a glassful. 'Listen, if you go blundering about in the rainforest looking for buried treasure you're likely to lose your head. You know the Dyaks are head-hunters? I can't take responsibility for you.'

'I'll sign a bit of paper.'

'There are some strange things go on in the Ulu,' continued the rajah. 'Here in Kuching, and the other towns, we're fairly civilized. It's civilization that keeps the darker side of this country at bay. Inside the barriers, beyond the tree line and the riverbank, you'll find sorcerers, ghosts and demons, and all manner of bizarre entities.'

Jack took a sip of the whisky. 'You believe in these things?'

'Here, I don't have to, but when I'm in the Ulu I'm not so sure of myself. Oh, yes, we're sensible Christian men, raised in the understanding that the supernatural world is for children and primitives to believe in. However, it's not so easy to shrug these ideas off when you're stumbling around in half-darkness, and odd things begin happening. I have to go into the Ulu to see the Land Dyaks sometimes and I always go in full of a confidence which evaporates with the going down of the sun.'

'Good, you believe in the supernatural. So do I, to a certain extent. If I didn't, I wouldn't go chasing after half-dreams and myths, would I? Chin-chin, yam sing!' With these words the aristocrat swallowed his whisky in one gulp.

Later that day, Jack sat down to a meal with Starke and his cousin, Harriet. It had been Harry who insisted that Jack stay to dinner, once she had heard the story of the rescue and had met the famous Singapore Jack. Her cousin was more inclined to think that the houseboy was the hero of the hour, but, though Harry secretly agreed with this view, she had fallen instantly in love with Singapore Jack and love is a ruthless passion.

Badu's reward was a profuse thank you and several gifts, but Harry's attention was reserved almost wholly for the handsome English lord.

'Jack? May I call you Jack?'

The English lord regarded the cousin of the rajah, smiled, and placed a large tanned hand on her small white wrist. He had no tender feelings for this woman, but he always enjoyed making ladies feel special. It put a sparkle in their eyes and they became beautifully animated. This young woman was not at all pretty, but she had an enthusiasm for life which intrigued him and which he admired. Such energy and fire deserved his full attention and he was pleased to give it.

'Of course you may, Miss Glendenning.'

Jack was one of those men who made women feel they were the only person in a crowded room. This particular room was hardly full of people, but Harry sensed that Jack's attention was all hers. She burned inside with fiery joy. It was her understanding that Lord Randolph Braiks was not interested in marriage and had never pursued a woman beyond friendship, but that did not deter Harry in the least. In fact, he presented a challenge which she was willing to take up with vigour.

'Please call me Harry – after all you did save my cousin's life. I feel you're part of our family now.'

The rajah winced and Jack caught the expression. He laughed at Starke's discomfort. 'I don't think your cousin agrees with you, Harry. I think he wants to keep his family free of footloose, wandering Jacks.'

'I think,' said Starke, 'I would like to hear what our friend is planning on doing once he enters the Ulu. You have a scientific purpose?'

'Are you asking in your position as rajah, or as an acquaintance?' Despite Jack's earlier flippant speech he was not going to use the word 'friend' to a man who so obviously disapproved of him.

Starke placed his knife and fork carefully on his plate and nodded to Badu, who was hovering near to the table. The houseboy realized a private conversation was going to take place and excused himself, heading towards the servants' part of the house. However, unknown to the people in the room, he remained in the hallway, just within earshot of their conversation.

'Both, I suppose,' replied the rajah, once Badu had left. 'As an ordinary man I'm curious, but as rajah I feel I have a right to know what you plan to do in my country.'

'My main purpose, as I have already told you, is one of exploration. Pathfinding. Europeans may have come through, from the south, or have travelled up from the north and reached the far coast, but none of them have charted their progress. My purpose is to chart a route across the interior of Borneo. I'd like to provide other expeditions with a mapped path from here to the south coast. At the same time I'll be studying the flora and fauna, and the topography.'

'Sounds like an immense task,' interrupted the rajah.

'I'll do the best I can. No one expects me to do a thorough job. This is the first expedition of its kind in Borneo. My party will gather what information it can, of the difficulties of the terrain, and leave it to others to do a more meticulous and exhaustive study.'

'And this treasure you mentioned?'

Singapore Jack grinned.

'That's just a little something to spice up the journey. I'll tell you about that too, but I don't want it to go any further than this room. I have a reputation as a level headed, sensible man . . .'

The rajah knew enough of Lord Randolph Braiks to know this was irony, but he remained silent on the subject.

'You have my word and I know Harry will say nothing.'

'It was in Sumatra,' began Jack, 'that I heard the tale of the seven heads. You may dismiss what I'm about to tell you as incredible, not worth an instant's consideration, and you'd probably be right. But I've seen things, heard of things, which the average man would find unbelievable, unthinkable – yet I know them to be true. For instance, when I read the words William of Rubruck wrote in 1254, "They also told me as a fact that there is a province of Cathay, and at whatever age a man enters it, that age he keeps," I knew there was a country of the young. I'm as sure of it in my heart as I know you are sitting opposite me now.'

The candles flickered in their holders as a light breeze wafted up from the river and through the open French windows. Beyond the south bank of the river there was a desert of darkness. Out there was the Ulu, broad, dense and deep, with nothing *but* foliage and darkness to hold it together. It was five hundred miles from north coast to south coast, but they were long, wide and dangerous miles, through unknown rainforest full of deadly snakes, insects and leeches that could drive a man mad, crocodiles, leopards and, perhaps the most alarming of all, hostile tribesmen.

'One day, when I am rich – for there is no purpose in searching for this land and entering it poor – I shall seek out the country of the young – but wait, I began to tell you of the story of the seven heads.'

He paused and took a sip of wine. Harry was looking at him with wide eyes. Starke still appeared sceptical.

'Somewhere out there, in the rainforests of this country of yours, Rajah Starke, is a region I call the Kingdom of the Sun Bear, because the clans in that quarter of the forest hold the sun bear sacred. In the Kingdom of the Sun Bear there are seven heads which once belonged to the first chiefs of the most ancient tribe of Dyaks – the Punan of Kalimantan – one of the oldest races of people on this earth. Not only were these men tuai rumahs, but also basirs, sorcerers in their own right.

'It is said that possession of these seven heads will lead to untold riches.'

The English aristocrat took another casual sip of his wine and leaned back in his chair, waiting for the reaction.

'You are serious?' asked Starke.

'Very serious. You should not be so incredulous, Rajah. You yourself said there are things which go on in the Ulu which ordinary men would find inconceivable. Such ordinary men have no imagination. You and I are the extraordinary ones. We go out into the world and seek what is not supposed to be there. If you had told someone, before you left England, that you were going to travel the Far East to become king of an exotic country, what would they have said?'

Harry laughed. 'They would have said he was mad.'

'Precisely.'

'But I didn't leave England to become a king,' pointed out Starke.

'No, but you knew you were looking for *something*. Isn't that just as bad? To chase rainbows? To believe that some wondrous destiny awaits you, if you only have the courage to let go of ordinary life and seek it?

'We venture forth on paths others do not see. You've found the treasure at the end of your particular path. Do you honestly believe you were not foreordained to be rajah? Was it pure accident, or was it fate, which put your yacht in the South China Sea at the very moment the old rajah was dying?'

Starke looked uncomfortable and Jack knew that he had hit a vulnerable area in the rajah's self.

'What do you propose to do?' asked Starke.

'I'm deeply interested in discovery – of new plants, new animals, new rivers, new tribes – and I shall be making notes, sketching and painting, as these things unfold themselves during my trek into the interior.

'I hope to bring back samples, of the soil, of mosses and ferns, even creatures if they're not too big and I can catch them. The pursuit of knowledge is just as important as the

pursuit of riches. To explore! To discover new worlds! But,'
here he paused for effect, 'if the opportunity presents itself
I shall of course investigate this legend of the seven severed
heads of the ancient Punan chieftains. Why not? No harm
can come of it, surely?'

Starke nodded thoughtfully after this speech.

'As to that, I have always regarded the search for treasure
as a futile occupation, but you have other more respectable
reasons for entering in the Ulu. You say you are a member
of the Geographical Society?'

'The Geographical and a number of other societies. They
are a source of funds for my journeys. I give them what I
can in return. There are a number of artefacts in private and
public curio collections – the British Museum to name but
one – with my name underneath them.'

'What?' said Harry in an amused voice. 'Singapore Jack?'

Jack laughed. 'No, of course not. "Lord Randolph Braiks".'

'And are you leaving right away?' asked Harry.

'I need to rest a little first, catch my breath. I've been travelling constantly for about two years now and it wears a
man down. As soon as I'm fit again I shall begin to get
organized.'

Harry said, suddenly, 'I want to go with you. I can make
notes and sketch. Doing water colours on the lawns of
provincial England was not to my taste, but painting parrots
in gorgeous colours – why that's a different thing altogether.
I'll show you some of my line drawings of riverboats . . .'

She stood up, intending to leave the room.

Both men were startled by her outburst. Jack regarded
her in a puzzled way. Starke looked horrified.

'What's that, Harry? Say it again, so I know I can trust
my ears.'

Harry sat down again, realizing she was going to have to
fight her corner with vigour.

'I want to go with Lord Braiks, into the rainforest. Oh, I don't know whether this astonishing story is true or not – I don't really care one way or another, except that it would please Lord Braiks if it were. I want excitement. I want adventure. To go into the Ulu. Has it ever been done by a European woman before?'

Jack wore a wry smile. 'Not to my knowledge.'

'Precisely why I cannot allow you to do it now,' Starke said, sounding as firm as a rock. 'It's unthinkable. I'm sorry, Harry, you'll have to put this wild idea out of your mind. I'm sure Jack would agree that an expedition of this sort is very dangerous. Taking a female along would be out of the question. Why I have grave reservations about letting *anyone* go in there, who is not a native and able to take care of himself.'

'I wish you would think of me as a man, sometimes Allen,' she replied fiercely, 'instead of a woman.'

'But how can I? You *are* a woman – a lady.'

'Yes, but I'm not some delicate eighteen year old. I'm a mature woman – a spinster if you like, though I hate that word. Being older and unmarried entitles me to some sort of freedom of choice, to do with my life as I see fit. Why do you think I came out here with you? It was partly in order to be free of all the restrictions of English society. Yes, I wanted to be with my cousin, Allen Starke, Rajah of Sarawak, but I also hoped for adventure. Why should you men get all the glory? I insist on going, cousin Allen. Please don't try to stop me.'

'It would be very wrong of me to let you go. Think of what our friends and relations would say at home, if anything should happen to you! Where would I hide my head?'

'You need have no fear of their approbation, out here in the sweltering jungles of the East.'

'And what about my own conscience?'

But even as he said it, Starke knew that he would have to

give in. Harry was a strong-willed female. Out here, in the East, there was no society to check her, as there would have been back in England. As she would say, there were no disapproving aunts. No one to forbid her to go to balls at Almack's Assembly Rooms – not that she would care a wit if they did. There was no Princess Esterhazy or Countess Lieven or Lady Castlereagh in Borneo to castigate and ostracize wayward young ladies. Her aunts, maiden and married, would have had heart attacks of course, if they had known what Harry proposed to do, but they were far away and because of the distance, impotent.

Despite the tough opposition from her cousin, Harry prepared for the expedition with her usual enthusiasm, buying suitable clothes for the rainforest, and purchasing all manner of things she thought she might need in there. One object she was particularly proud of finding was a waterproof pen, ink and paper set. She doubted she could send any letters back, but she wanted to keep a record of the expedition. It gave her something to do, an official job: the chronicler of the journey. She had to agree to obey Jack's orders in all things while in the Ulu, but she did that readily, in order to obtain her cousin's blessing.

Singapore Jack had more discussions on the subject with Rajah Starke, without Harry being present.

'I need one or two good men,' said Jack. 'I understand some of your sailors might be willing to join me. Someone mentioned a seaman called Keller?'

Starke pursed his lips. 'I wouldn't take Keller if I were you. He's not particularly stable in a confined party, under tight leadership. I use him to hunt down criminals, but only the worst kind of criminals. He has a tendency to go too far. I have to be sure they are guilty before he goes looking for them, because he rarely brings one in alive.'

'The man sounds a positive menace,' said Jack.

'He is – a born troublemaker – I'm thinking of getting rid of him myself. I couldn't let you take him.'

'Wouldn't want to,' replied Jack.

They settled on two other mariners. Ferguson, the boatswain, and Kitts, the carpenter. These were suitably steady characters, who would assist Jack with handling the Dyak porters and boatmen. The two men would be contacted and sounded out.

'Now, I have to tell you this, Jack,' said Starke, 'and I want you to take it seriously. Harry is very precious to me. If anything should happen to her I don't know what I would do. At the very first sign of fever or faint heart on her part, I want you to send her back. I'm relying on the fact that it will be so hard out in the Ulu she will want to return within the week. Do not persuade her otherwise. Send her home to me.'

'Allen, I shall look after her as if she were my own wife,' replied Jack, solemnly. 'Believe me, the first sign of weakness and I'll pack her in a canoe with Ferguson and several good Dyaks and return her to you.'

'Thank you, Jack. I'm relying on you.'

Leaving the rajah, Singapore Jack took a ferry across the river to the town on the other side. Once in its dusty streets, amid the hum and bustle of the population, he felt happy. This was a world he loved, this Eastern paradise. The people here had fire in their footsteps. They were a bright, animated folk, swift in their movements, quick to smile, quick to laugh. How many times had he paused on the street in thought, only to have someone immediately say to him, 'Are you lost? Can I help?'

How long would one of these dark-skinned people stand on a London street before someone asked them if they were lost and needed help? For ever, that's how long, thought Jack. They could fall in the gutter and die on a London street and no one would take notice of them.

And there was so much colour and verve in their lives. The whole town was a swirl of colour, of bright chatter, of greetings and laughter. Here too, many races lived and worked in relative harmony. Of course there was the occasional fracas between people of different races, but it was never the race that was at the root of the trouble. It was usually money, or land rights, or something fairly solid. Something the rajah could apply his mind to and settle with good judgement.

Jack loved all the temples, the mosques, the new Christian churches, huddled together. There was always the scent of joss sticks wafting from some open Chinese doorway, or perfumed air from an Indian temple. There were the sounds of the muezzins calling from the minarets, calling the faithful to prayer at various times during the day.

Then there were the ubiquitous markets, never really closing, simply dying down to an ember at night, flaring into a blaze the next morning with the rising of the sun. Wares from all over the East: Japan, Hong Kong, Singapore, Bali, Siam. Things useful and things decorative. He could spend all day in such a market and not be bored, just wandering amongst the stalls, looking and admiring.

It was while he was doing so that he noticed a Dyak who seemed more than usually aware of him.

He went up to the man and greeted him.

'Where are you going?'

'Over there,' the Dyak replied, with a nod of his head.

Jack did not really want to know the man's real destination, nor did the other have any intention of telling him. This was simply the normal exchange of greetings between strangers in the street. It meant nothing more than 'hello' or 'good day'. Just as in Britain one would say, 'How do you do?' and expect to receive the reply, 'Very well, thank you.'

This Dyak, taller than average, had broad shoulders

tattooed with tribal designs. Dressed in a decorative loin-cloth, there were woven bangles of raffia around his arms and the calves of his legs. His feet were bare. Black hair was cut in a fringe at the front, but fell like a dark waterfall down his back. At his waist he wore a Dyak short sword, adorned with human hair and the feathers of hornbills. These swords were often quite old, being passed down from generation to generation.

'Ah, you do speak English,' said Jack.

'Yes, tuan,' replied the Dyak, warily.

'What's your name? How do they call you?'

'I called Mayok.'

'You look like a Kayan. Am I correct? Are you Kayan?'

'Yes, tuan.'

'Well, Mayok, I am looking for good men to come with me into the rainforest.'

'What for you go rainforest, tuan?'

Jack did not want to go into his reasons for entering the Ulu in depth, so he used his usual excuse, which those natives who had come into contact with English gentlemen understood.

'I go hunting butterflies. I'm interested in beautiful but-terflies.' Jack flapped his arms in what he thought was a good imitation of a butterfly fluttering around some bushes.

The Dyak laughed at him and shook his head.

'No, no, tuan. Mayok got one-time job. You find other Dyak for hunt butterfly.'

With that the young man strode off into the thick of the market place populace.

Jack stared after the man, who was tall and stately for a Dyak Indian.

Pity, thought Jack, he looked a good man. Strong, honest features. Nothing sickly about him. I have a feeling we shall run into each other again, that fellow and I.

## 2

There were certain waterfront taverns in Kuching where the riff-raff gathered. Many of them were fashioned of spare timber on rickety jetties at the river's edge. Keller was in a tavern one night, with six or seven of his cronies. They were seamen who had drifted over from Singapore harbour having jumped ship for one reason or another. Keller seemed to gather such human refuse around him like dung gathers flies. They were sitting on a bench at an open glassless window, watching a cock fight take place.

'Ten ringgits on the white rooster,' said Keller to a bearded man at his side.

'I'll take that wager,' replied the other.

They watched as the white bird was thrown into a ring of men along with a red one. Both birds had artificial spurs of honed metal attached to their feet. The fight was short-lived. There was a flurry of dust and feathers, a lot of noise, much of it from the Dyaks who were staging and watching the fight, and when the ring parted the red cock lay in a pool of its own blood. Its feathers fluttered pathetically in the breeze from the river. The winning cock was being preened by its owner, who was obviously well pleased with the result.

The bearded man looked sour as he handed over the money to Keller, who took it with an air of indifference.

Behind the jungle on the far side of the river, the sun was going down as a huge red plate into a bubbling cauldron of foaming blood. It was a magnificent evening, one of those only found in certain corners of the earth. Even for men like these such a sight was awesome in its peacefulness and beauty.

It was true the mosquitoes were coming in, and one or two large armour-plated bugs, the size of a man's fist, began flying in to investigate the light from the oil lamps, but the men were used to these irritating distractions. They swatted at the mosquitoes and kicked at the big bugs which clattered on the floorboards. Someone was cooking meat in the corner of the room, its smell attracting stray cats and dogs.

Keller settled down on the floor to a game of cards with some squatting Dyaks. He played for beads, rather than hard currency. It was not that he could win a fortune, but he found it fun to outplay these simple creatures from the rainforest. Every so often he would turn his head and wink at his men, who would laugh uproariously, before laying down a winning card and scooping up the beads. The Dyaks played with a kind of earnest terror, frightened of making an error and looking a fool. Their faces were creased with the effort of concentration.

It was while Keller was throwing beads into a large kitty that he felt a tap on his shoulder. A young Malay was standing there, looking very nervous. Keller raised his red eyebrows.

'You want a game, fellah? Come on in, sit down.'

'No, I don't want to play cards, I wish to speak with you,' said the Malay boy, who was dressed in western clothes. 'Can we go into the next room?'

Keller was surprised at the fluency of the boy's English, then he recognized him as Starke's houseboy.

'What's your name?' asked Keller.

'I am called Badu.'

'You work for Rajah Starke?'

'Please,' the youth looked around him, even more nervously than before. 'I wish to speak privately. Do not tell everyone here where I am from, or I will get into trouble.'

Keller shrugged and without a word to the Dyaks squatting on the floor, he threw his cards into the middle and stood up. The other players stared at him with puzzled looks and play ceased altogether for a few moments, before they realized he was not betting any more. Then they bent their heads again, taking a bead or more from the lap formed by their sarong, and muttering something to themselves before placing their bet carefully with the others in the middle of the circle.

There was a back room, where the Chinese proprietor slept. The doorway was surrounded by thorny vines. This was to protect the sleeper within from any penanggalan – witches who fly in through the darkness. To make themselves lighter and so be able to travel faster the witches leave their bodies behind, only the head attached to the oesophagus and the entrails dangling from the other end of the food pipe. They soar through the night air. Being close to the river and the jungle, the Chinese owner of the tavern was sensitive to such horrible creatures.

Penanggalan means 'the one who pulls out'. These witches dissected their victims to get at the vital organs, ripping them out of the body. They sucked all the blood from the heart, lungs and liver. But they had to stitch the body back together again before dawn. If they did not, the witch died with the rising sun.

The thorns were nailed in an arch around the door frame in order to catch and entangle the witch's trailing intestines. Such garlands of thorns were considered enough to deter any penanggalan from even contemplating the sleeper as her victim, making her pass on to more accessible prey within the walls of less well defended houses.

The Chinese proprietor of this establishment was living proof that such a witch had never entered his room in order to decapitate and disembowel him.

Inside the small room was a single bed, the frame of which was criss-crossed with rattan to form its springs.

'Well now,' said Keller, sitting on the bed. 'What's all this, Badu?'

'I have some information,' whispered Badu, 'which I can sell to you for a price.'

'What sort of information?'

'It will enable you to find untold riches.'

Keller thought about this for a moment, wondering whether this was a trap set up by Starke. He knew he was not the rajah's favourite servant and that for less than two pins the rajah would send him packing. However, untold riches were not to be sniffed at and dismissed lightly. He probed further.

'Look, I may be a bad man in some ways, Badu, but I ain't a thief nor a murderer. If this has somethin' to do with killing the rajah for them Malay princes, or robbing the palace or whatever, then I'm not your man. I don't hold with such things,' he said, sanctimoniously. 'Them jealous datus can do their own dirty work, so far as Keller is concerned.'

'No, no, you misunderstand me, tuan. This is just something I hear, from the man they call Singapore Jack. He stay to dinner with the rajah and tell him something about treasure. I can give you this information – for money. I am a poor man. I wish to go to Singapore or Hong Kong and I need the fare.'

'Doesn't the rajah pay you, boy?'

'Of course, but I need more. I need lots more.'

Keller realized the youth had grown greedy in the rajah's service. It happened to some native servants. Even though they might be well paid, they wanted more and more water from the well, seeing it to have an inexhaustible supply. This young Malay had obviously heard stories about others of his kind who had gone to Singapore and made their fortune.

Badu was not a particularly weak young man. It was just that he had been exposed to something beyond his control. He had no inherent mechanism for dealing with this hunger for 'things' which civilization had exposed him to. He found himself yearning for more and more possessions.

'Untold riches, eh?' said Keller. 'Come on then boy, out with it.'

'You pay me some money first,' Badu said. He was not that green. 'Then I tell you.'

No beads or Chinese pots for this young man. He wanted hard cash. Keller offered him thirty ringgits.

'Take that,' he told the Malay, 'and if I think it's worth any more after you've told me, why then I'll up it a bit.'

Badu looked suspiciously upon this promise, but realized he was not going to get any more money until he came across with at least some of the information.

'Have you hear of Singapore Jack?'

'I've heard of him – some toff adventurer, eh?'

'Well, he save the rajah's life yesterday. Pirates come to kill the rajah, and I fetch help. On they way the Dyak guards see this man going to the bungalow. It is Singapore

Jack. He kills Lingore with his pistol, just as the pirate chief go to kill the rajah with his sword.'

'Fair enough,' replied Keller. 'Sounds like you saved the rajah's life too.'

'I am rewarded for this, but then when Singapore Jack is staying to dinner, he tells a story . . .'

Badu repeated the tale of the seven heads of the ancient Punan chiefs in the Kingdom of the Sun Bear.

When the story had been told, Keller, who had in the beginning no intention of giving Badu any more money, actually doubled the thirty ringgits, at the same time as extracting a promise.

'Look, this is a lot of money,' he said, waving the ringgits in front of Badu's nose. 'I'm givin' you this partly 'cause your information is good and partly to knock a bung in your mouth. It means you can't talk to no one else. Not a word. You mention this to another living soul and I'll come and cut your head off myself, you understand? You know I'll do it, too, don't you? I've killed men just 'cause their breath smells, so don't you even think of crossing me, boy. You hear?'

Badu was quite sure he would not breathe another word about the seven heads.

Keller said, 'I think I'll join this little party of Singapore Jack's.'

'No, no, I heard the rajah say not to ask you. Rajah Starke say you bad man and no good for expedition.'

Keller's temper flared and he cursed violently before saying, 'Oh, he did, did he?'

Badu recognized the danger signals in Keller. It was likely that the seaman would go to the rajah and accuse Badu's master, thus getting the Dyak into serious trouble. He saw that a little diplomacy was needed.

'I think rajah cannot do without you, for his hunter, so he tell Singapore Jack these things.'

Keller nodded. This made more sense to him. Starke needed a good hunter to go after malefactors. Keller had proved to be the best. So of course the rajah would try to keep him.

'Yeah, that must be it, boy. On your way then. Not a word, mind, or I'll cut out your liver and eat it.'

After the young Dyak had gone, Keller sat down with his friends and ordered a drink of rum. He was deep in thought. This business sounded far fetched, but then everything in the Orient was stranger than back in England. Things happened in the rainforest of Sarawak the folks back home would not believe. So far as Keller was concerned, it was a godless country, full of pagan savages, where chaos and darkness stood a good chance of throwing its demons in the path of ordinary men.

Godless, to Keller, meant unChristian, not a place without gods. There were plenty of those around. But they were unholy creatures, more ready to do you harm than help you. Keller had a healthy respect for the local deities. His mother always told him not to mock those things which he did not understand. Keller took this advice quite literally. He did not understand the Dyaks themselves, let alone their religions, so generally, though not always, he treated them with respect.

If someone back in England had told him the same story that Badu had told him, Keller would have put it down to too much drink and an overactive imagination. Out here he was inclined to believe such a tale. Here there were sorcerers and magicians, whose powers were manifold. Keller had seen demons extracted from a man's throat. Demons that reshaped themselves into snakes and lizards, then wriggled away into the undergrowth. He had seen a polong, a bottle imp the size of a garden slug, sucking the blood of a man through a wound made by its constant companion, the pelesit, a demon with the shape of a chirruping cricket, who crawls into men's orifices backwards. There was the Malay bomoh prince, talked about by all as a magician, and Chin Hua, the Chinese sorcerer and shapechanger. Keller had seen the latter at work and had listened to witnesses of the former.

Keller could not dismiss these, and other strange things he had witnessed, with a wave of his hand.

'What's the matter with you tonight?' asked Johnson. 'Cat got your tongue?'

'No, not unless it's a clouded leopard,' replied Keller, who had seen the beautiful skin of such an animal for sale in the market earlier in the day, and when he asked where it had come from he had been told, 'The country of the Punan'.

All this was, of course, lost on Johnson.

'What's that supposed to mean?'

'It means, my bully boys, I'm gettin' together a band of men to go with me into the rainforest. Deep in, to places we've never been before. It'll take months, maybe a year, but when we come out we'll be richer than Croesus.'

He changed the story to suit the intellect of his men. Keller told them the seven heads were crammed with gold coins and jewels, that when they found them all they had to do was smash the skulls and walk away rich men. The waterfront scum lapped it up like cream from the top of milk. Their eyes shone with the avarice of men who wanted wealth without hard work.

'We're with you, Keller,' they cried. 'Show us the way.'

Little did they know but they were going to work harder than they had ever worked in their lives before.

Harry was busy planning her trip into the Ulu. She was taking Lidah, her Malay maid, with her. Lidah was as excited as Harry. She was part Dyak and had been brought up in a longhouse but, her father being a Malay, her mother did not get on with the other women in the longhouse and eventually went seeking the father in Kuching. Now Lidah was going back into the rainforest under the protection of Singapore Jack. If she ran into some of her relations, she could not be ordered away.

Harry's dark locks lay on the floor of Harry's bedroom, as Lidah cut away, giving her a short hairstyle.

'How sad this is,' Lidah said, 'all your fine hair!'

'It will only get in the way on the trip,' replied Harry, firmly. 'It'll get tangled on thorns, like those witches' intestines you told me about.'

'I think it is sad. I like your hair.'

'Well, I liked it too, but one must be practical.' Harry turned her head this way and that, studying herself in the mirror. 'I think I make a more handsome boy than I did a pretty girl, don't you think?'

'Tuan Jack will not love you with short hair, missy.'

Harry sighed. Her first burst of passion had gone and she was seeing with clearer eyes. It did indeed seem that Jack was only interested in her as a good friend. She ran her fingers through her short locks. 'Well, as to that, I doubt he would look at me in that way even with long hair. I'm resigned to being best friends with him, Lidah. It seems to be my lot in life to be "best friends" with the men I meet. Not that I'm eager to marry just any man, you understand. I am probably too picky for my own good.'

'You are nice looking lady,' replied Lidah, seriously. 'I think tuan Jack be lucky to get you.'

Harry laughed and said brightly, 'So do I. Now, tell me one of your stories, Lidah. I do find them fascinating.'

'Like the one where my name come from?'

Some days previously Lidah had told Harry where her

Malay name came from. 'Lidah' meant 'tongue' in Malay and she had taken it from a mysterious, mythical plant called lidah bumi, which meant 'the tongue of the earth'. The earth holds all knowledge of all time and it has as its mouth the lidah bumi plant. She told Harry that if she ever found one of these plants, to put her ear to its leaves and listen to what the earth had to say.

'Yes, but a longer one.'

Lidah was something of a storyteller, or pengilipur lara as the Malays call them. Pengilipur lara means 'eliminator of worries', because a skilful storyteller can make you forget your problems and give you another world and time to live in for hopefully the length of the tale.

'There was once a great Malay king of Indrapura, whose name was Mengidera,' said Lidah, while combing Harry's hair. 'When still the crown prince his father had forced him to marry a queen from a neighbouring country. This queen had already been married to two kings and had outlived them and swallowed up their territories in her own. The old king had hoped that his son would be heir to all three kingdoms.

'One day King Mengidera was out hunting in the rainforest and became lost in a faraway and dark area. Towards evening he happened to stumble upon a cabin made of rattan, half-hidden in the leafy growth beneath the canopy. Needing shelter for the night, he knocked on the door. It was opened by a beautiful young woman who was rubbing her eyes as if she had just woken up.

'Aware that this lovely girl might be a pampahilep, the king questioned her.

'"Have I just woken you up? Do you sleep during the day?"

'"Always," replied the young woman. "Ever since a spell was put on me by a wicked queen. I wake only during the dark hours and sleep during the light. My semangat has been stolen."

'The king was disturbed to hear that the girl's soul had been stolen from her. It meant she was not only confined to the night, but would be weary and unable to travel far. He expressed his sorrow and asked if he might sleep the night in the cabin.

'The girl allowed him to enter. Inside he found simple fare, but the girl did her best to make him comfortable. She told him she would sit up and watch over him, while he slept.

'"Who was the queen who stole your semangat?" he asked.

'The girl then uttered the name of his own wife.

'Without revealing who he was, King Mengidera then enquired as to the reason why the queen had imprisoned the girl.

'"She said I was too beautiful and that I might entice her husband away from her."

'"And that is exactly what has happened," said the king, "for in the short while I have known you, I have fallen in love with you."

'When the king returned to his palace, he confronted his queen and ordered her to restore the girl's soul to its rightful owner. The queen refused, thus showing the king how wicked she was. The king called in his court magician, who did the deed instead. Then the king sent his soldiers for the girl, whom he married and placed over the wicked queen.'

Harry raised her eyebrows, but then remembered that Malays could have more than one wife.

Lidah said, 'There, isn't that a romantic story?'

Harry was not so sure. She was a woman who did not trust beauty so much as other feminine attributes.

'Well, it sort of has a happy ending, if you aren't the first wife of the king.'

'No one should be sorry for a wicked queen,' said Lidah, teasing Harry's hair with a comb. 'She is lucky her husband did not beat and kill her.'

'Is she indeed?'

# 3

Badu knew his treachery had been discovered when an owl flew in the open window and snatched a piece of meat from his fingers. Everyone knows the owl is in love with the moon, because he sits and stares at it longingly, every night. The moon governed all night demons, who used the besotted owls as messengers to those about to be punished for evil deeds. Since demons are friends of wickedness, they perform this service for evil-doers, warning them of retribution.

Badu hastily packed a bag and left the bungalow of the rajah. The unhappy houseboy ran towards a jetty on the river and managed to take a ferry out to a large Chinese junk, moored on the far bank of the Sarawak awaiting the outgoing tide.

'Where are you bound?' asked the boy. 'Are you going to Singapore?'

A seaman on the deck leaned over the rail and stared at the Malay boy.

'First we go to Java,' said the man.

'Take me with you. I have money.'

The boy showed the seaman a leather pouch and jingled its contents.

'You must speak with the captain,' replied the Chinese, sailor, his single tarred plait gleaming in the light of the moon. 'He is with his cousin, in the medicine shop in Kuching, and will be back on board at midnight.'

'May I wait on the ship until he comes?'

The sailor shrugged and pointed at the scrambling net over the side of the craft. Badu leapt on to this and climbed up on board the junk. Once the ferry had gone, he breathed more freely. The night air was suddenly quite sweet. He looked up at the moon and felt a rush of guilt.

'I hope my master will forgive me,' he said. 'I merely wish to become wealthy.'

The sailor, who had been busy with the rigging, laughed on hearing this.

'Don't we all, little man – don't we all?'

Singapore Jack was gathering together stores and goods for his expedition. At midnight he found himself in a knife store. Like all Chinese shops in Kuching it was still open, even at this late hour, if there was a customer. A lamp burned fiercely inside the cluttered store, in which there were not only knives of every kind, but sacks of rice, dark bottles of some unknown liquid, a small, rat-catching dog which lay with its head on its paws watching Jack's progress over the boards, rice-flour sieves hanging from a ceiling which seemed to stretch upwards into an infinite darkness, and brass weighing scales.

Whenever Jack went into one of these rambling stores, which seemed to have more corners than the universe, he was amazed at the amount of junk and space there was inside. The Chinese were hoarders. They saved every bit of string and wrapping that came their way. They slept amongst their treasures, in their vast wood-plank shops, on rattan beds with a meat cleaver or a parang at hand. You could sell them anything, so long as you sold it cheaply enough to allow them a resale profit. There was always the smell of dried mussels about their establishments.

Jack sniffed the air and smelt the mussels now, mingled with the burning oil from the lamp.

'I want half a dozen kris knives,' he told the man, 'and two dozen parangs.'

'Yes, sir. You go jungle, sir?'

'I might be going into the forest. What makes you ask?'

'I have other man come to me for knives. Man with red pigtail they call Keller. He want gunpowder in sealed jar. Lots of gunpowder jar. In jungle, gunpowder get wet pretty damn quick, so I know he go to jungle. Everything wet in jungle. Ground wet, trees wet, even air wet. You go jungle with Mister Keller?'

'Oh,' said Jack, 'Keller is out hunting malefactors again, is he?'

'No, Mister Keller he go deep. He look for Dyak treasure. Everyone hear this on the river. I think he come back with no head. You stay here, mister. You keep head on shoulders.'

Jack's eyes narrowed. Keller had gone into the rainforest to look for Dyak treasure? It sounded suspiciously like the sailor had got wind of Jack's expedition. There was only one place he could have got his information, because Jack had been extremely tight-lipped until now. Was it possible the rajah was mounting his own expedition, in opposition to Jack?

Jack paid for the knives, which were wrapped in oily sacking for him and tied with hessian string, then he made his way to the rajah's bungalow.

It was one o'clock in the morning when he reached the dwelling. A light was still burning in the rajah's study, where a figure was bent over a writing bureau. Once Jack was on the lawn, amongst the oleander shrubs, several Dyak guards came out of the darkness and challenged him. They were much more vigilant since the pirate attack and had been doubled in numbers.

'I must speak with the rajah,' he said, and anticipating their next words, 'tonight. I must speak tonight, not tomorrow morning or next week. Tell him Singapore Jack is here.'

One of the Dyak guards went to the window of the bungalow and spoke to the rajah, who looked up and stared out into the darkness. The rajah murmured something and the Dyak returned, to lead the fuming Jack through the French doors of the house, and into the study where Starke sat dressed only in a sarong.

'Forgive the informal dress, Jack,' said Starke, 'I had not expected callers at this time of night.'

Jack calmed down a little on hearing these words, realizing how rude his interruption was. However, he was not going to be deterred from his purpose.

'I wish to know if you have sent Keller into the rainforest to find the seven heads I told you about!'

The rajah's amiability deserted him and a frosty look came over his features.

'My dear Jack, do talk sense. I don't believe in the existence of your silly "seven heads" so why would I send someone like Keller to look for them? I'm being very patient with you, trusting you with the life of my cousin, because you seem a strong man, if a little unreliable. I owe you my life. You have a bee in your bonnet and it seems the only way to get it out is to let you mount this expedition. I don't expect you to come back with anything more than a new species of leech.

'But I do expect you to come back. You have been into worse terrain and returned unscathed. That does not mean

I approve of such quests. Harry craves adventure. This expedition should cure her of that for all time and I'm hoping she'll find out sooner rather than later that she has made a mistake in going with you, and agree to be sent back here to me.

'Is it reasonable to think I would send someone chasing after whimsies? I think your expedition will be of benefit to us, if you make maps, chart the interior, catalogue the fauna and flora you discover on route, and gather information on the tribes that live at the far reaches of my kingdom. But as to these heads, why, they are just a foolhardy sideshow.'

Jack slumped down in one of the study's leather chairs.

'I'm sorry, Allen, I should have known better. Keller has somehow found out about my expedition. He's gone in ahead of me.'

'Ah,' said the rajah, looking serious. 'That explains the absence of my houseboy. Badu has absconded. I've no doubt he sold the information to Keller, then ran away.'

Jack shrugged and sighed. 'Well, there's nothing I can do about it now. I'll just have to bring my expedition a little further forward, that's all. We'll just have to move on a pace and try to beat Keller to the punch. Damn the man. I was looking forward to a leisurely stroll through the rainforest, not a blasted race.'

'So when do you plan to leave?'

'Probably next week. Tuesday I think. Can't see us being ready before then.'

The rajah moved over to the window and looked out on the lawns which flowed down to the river. Jack knew Starke was about to say something important because he had his hands linked behind his back. The rajah always took this pose, whether consciously or unconsciously, before he made an announcement.

'Jack,' said Starke, not turning from the window, 'I'm going to insist you take someone else with you. He's been into the Ulu before and he knows its ways . . .'

'I've got good guides and trackers – good pathfinders – in my Dyaks.'

'No, he's not a pathfinder, exactly, although it'll depend on where your expedition takes you, as to whether he knows the area or not. But he knows the nature of the rivers, which plants and animals are friendly and which are not, where to sleep, and all that sort of thing. You might get this information from your Dyaks, or not, but you won't have to rely on them. You can't always expect to communicate with the natives to any degree of accuracy. They have their own ideas and they seem to be immune to certain insect bites which we would find extremely painful. All that sort of thing.

'No, the chap I'm thinking of is a European – actually he's not – but he's an extremely competent and practical man. He knows how to survive in the wilderness. I'm not saying you need a nursemaid, but I'd feel happier about Harry going with this man along.'

'And who is this mysterious non-European white?'

'His name is Christopher Colenso. He was a South African colonist. He made the trek through the Ulu from the southern coast of Borneo to the north coast, here. He's a rather dour, abrupt sort of man – probably his Yorkshire ancestry – but that might make him a better companion in the rainforest. You don't want some bright chatty socialite, do you? I would appreciate it if you would take him along, Jack, for Harry's sake.'

Jack made a gesture of reluctant acceptance with his hands.

Kit Colenso was the younger brother of John Colenso, Bishop of the newly formed Natal Province in South Africa.

Bishop Colenso had raised a storm of controversy in South Africa with his books which seriously questioned certain aspects of the Old Testament, such as the myth of creation. Bishop John Colenso was a low church man, apparently appointed in error by high church men who had not thoroughly checked out his beliefs.

Once they found they had a viper in their nest, the high church men sought for reasons for getting rid of John Colenso and installing another bishop in his place. The Colensos were gritty folk, however, and the incumbent would not budge. His brother Kit, an ivory hunter and confidant of Mpande, the King of the Zulus, was something of an embarrassment to the bishop. Kit Colenso had married a Bantu girl and lived with her in his own kraal. She had died shortly after the marriage, trampled by an elephant herd that had charged through the kraal, but that did not take away the fact that Kit Colenso had 'gone native' in a rather shocking way for a churchman's brother.

John had not asked Kit to leave Africa – in fact he had begged him to stay – but Kit had felt that he was doing his brother's cause no good by remaining there. The death of his wife had broken his heart in any case, and he could not bear to be around the sights, sounds and smells which reminded him of her. Her death had been something in the nature of poetic revenge by the tuskers Kit had hunted and he was no longer able to pursue that profession without a feeling of guilt. He could not shake the strange idea that his ivory hunting had somehow brought about his wife's death. She had been as beautiful as a leopard and had owned a great wit. His love for her had been vast.

That was all several years ago. Now Kit Colenso was firmly established in the Far East. He hired himself out to Chinese gold prospectors and Malay traders who wanted to go into the Ulu for whatever reason. He had once taken a

Malay prince called Rakota to a Kenyah longhouse, but when he saw that the prince merely wanted to plunder the Dyaks, to strip the longhouse down to nothing but bamboo water jugs, he refused to take him back again, leaving him to wander at the mercy of his victims.

When the old rajah had been alive, Colenso had assisted in killing a chieftain of some Ilanun pirates who had their base on Talang-Talang island. Rowing out alone from Cape Datu, he had planted a gunpowder bomb in the pirates' camp and blown several of them to smithereens. The chieftain had escaped the blast and sought out Colenso on the mainland. Armed with two krises the pirate had come at Colenso in a tavern. There followed a knife fight, at the end of which the Ilanun pirate chief lay on the floor of the tavern, his blood draining through the gaps in the boards to the ground below the stilts.

When he received the summons to the rajah's bungalow, he obeyed it reluctantly. Kit had little use for what he saw as jumped-up Indian army officers. He respected the rajah as a man, but Kit Colenso was not amenable to authority.

Calling at the bungalow, he passed a plain-looking woman who was cutting flowers in the garden. She was wearing some sort of gaudy yellow silk dress, which looked awkward on her. Her short-cropped hair was tied around with a velvet ribbon. There was something coltish in the way that she stood.

She looked up as he passed and smiled. 'Can I help you?'

Colenso glowered. If he had little use for rajahs, he had even less use for their families. He saw colonial women as leeches, sucking the good life out of a place they did not make the effort to understand. He wondered if this were the rajah's wife, though he had heard that Starke was unmarried. Perhaps his sister? He had seen the rajah once, and there were certain resemblances.

'I don't think so,' he replied, curtly. 'I'm looking for the rajah.'

Harry, in her turn, did not like to be glowered at by strange glum-looking men with hard features. The smile left her face instantly. She regarded the thick-set blond man, shorter of stature than either her cousin or Jack, with some distaste. He was wearing a shirt made of coarse nankeen cloth and canvas sailor's trousers. On his feet were rope-soled yachtsman's shoes, the worse for wear. Who did he think he was, dismissing her as one might dismiss a young schoolgirl? She thought him rude and ill-mannered. Even if he was some rough sailor from her cousin's yacht he might have been more polite to her as a person.

'If you're looking for the rajah, I might be able to tell you where to find him. I happen to live here.'

'I can see you live here, you're mightily at home, miss whatever-your-name is. Personally, I couldn't care less whether you lived in Timbuktu or Middle Wallop. Now, if you'll excuse me, I'll get about my business.'

'I wonder what business you have with a gentleman,' she retorted, 'since you appear not to be one yourself.'

'If it's any business of yours, I was sent for,' came the hot reply. 'I didn't ask to come, and I certainly didn't ask for a garden-party chat with a spoiled sister of the rajah.'

'How well informed you are,' she answered, haughtily. 'You seem to know all about everything, yet you have it wrong. I am not the rajah's sister. The rajah has no sister.'

A bit put out, all he could answer was, 'Who are you then?'

'No one grand, but then again, not one who likes to be shouted at as if she were a hoyden.'

'Huh!' he muttered, and left her with her scissors and trowel, to nod to the house guards.

One of the guards took him into the drawing-room of the

bungalow, where he found the rajah and another man whom he recognized immediately as Singapore Jack.

The rajah extended a hand. 'Mr Colenso. Thanks for coming. Do you know Lord Braiks?'

'I know Singapore Jack,' replied Colenso, shaking the rajah's hand, then that of the other man. 'I haven't much time for titles.'

'Ah, a man of the earth,' murmured, Jack, seemingly not at all put out by Colenso's manner. 'Well I haven't much use for 'em myself, so we'll get on famously. Somehow I expected you to have an "ee bah gum" accent, Mr Colenso. I was told you had a solid Yorkshire background. In fact you speak like a gentleman, but with a rather clipped twang. That's the South African connection I presume?'

'I suppose,' replied Colenso. 'It's not important, is it?'

'Not in the least.'

Once they had drinks in their hands, they settled down to talk business. The rajah let Jack explain about his expedition, not holding anything back. The rajah then asked Colenso if he would be prepared to join Jack on his trek into the Ulu. Jack explained the main purpose of the expedition, then, seemingly as an afterthought, told Colenso about the legend.

'The seven heads of the ancient Punan chieftains,' muttered Colenso. 'I've heard of the myth. I'm not in the business of making judgements. I'm a good shot with a rifle, I can show you how to live in the Ulu, and where I know some of the landscape. If that's what you want, that's how I earn my living.'

'That's exactly what I want. Someone like myself, in case something should happen to me. Two good men are better than one in these circumstances. If I fall sick, or something more serious happens to me, then you can take over. In the meantime, your advice will be invaluable. I won't necessarily take it, but I'll listen to it with interest.'

'So there'll just be the two of us?'

'And some seamen loaned to us by the rajah, here. Plus the Dyaks of course. Oh, and Harriet, the rajah's cousin.'

As Colenso's eyes were widening and he paused in order to find some reply to Jack's revelation, Harriet was passing the room. On hearing her name she obviously thought it all right to enter and present herself. She was clearly enjoying the horrified expression on Colenso's face.

'Yes,' she said, sweetly, 'the rajah's cousin, who will be part of the expedition into the interior.'

'You must be mad,' he told the two men facing him. 'You can't take a woman in there.'

'There are already women in there,' Harry pointed out.

'Not namby-pamby women with soft hands and liable to swoon at the sight of an insect. You know there's deadly snakes in there, and scorpions, and spiders as big as soup plates? You'll be screaming every few seconds.'

The rajah smiled. 'You obviously don't know my cousin, Colenso. She is the one in this household who chases the snakes out with a broom and picks the spiders out of the bath with her bare fingers. I think you'll find she's tougher than she appears at first sight.'

'And what's all this to Mr Colenso?' asked Harry of Jack and Starke.

'He's coming with us,' replied Jack. 'I need a good companion.'

'I'm a good companion,' Harry said, with some heat. 'We don't need him.'

The rajah intervened. 'Mr Colenso is going because I asked Jack to take him. If he doesn't go, you don't go, Harry. I don't often put my foot down with you, but I will over this matter. It is of no interest to me whether you hate one another at first sight, as you seem to do. You will have to get along for purposes of the expedition. If you wish to leave on Tuesday . . .'

Harry's eyes widened and brightened. 'Tuesday? We're going Tuesday, Jack?'

Jack nodded. 'If I can pull everything together by then, we'll be on our way.'

She turned to face Colenso again. 'You'll see how wrong you are, Mr Colenso. I'm no swooning lily. And I'm not going to let the likes of you ruin the most exciting moment of my life. If you will excuse me, gentleman, I shall finish my packing.'

Once she had swept out of the room, in a rustle of silks and stamped velvet, the rajah sighed and shook his head.

'She's been packed for a month,' he said. 'But it was a good exit.'

Colenso ignored the remark. He had other things to think about now.

'Look,' he said, 'have you picked all your Dyaks yet? I'd like to have a hand in that.'

Singapore Jack took out a brass snuff box and took a pinch.

'I thought I had, but if you want one or two more of your own men, by all means bring them along. You're travelling at the rajah's expense, and since he's a fairly wealthy man I'm sure he won't begrudge another canoe. What do you say, Starke?'

'Take as many Dyaks as you want.'

'Well, as Jack says, one or two will be enough. They're men who've been with me a couple of years. I trust them.'

'What are they?'

'Ngaju Dyaks. They came up from south Kalimantan with me. They know the interior.'

Once he had left the bungalow, Colenso sniffed the air of

Kuching, smelling the scent of casuarina trees. He loved
Borneo almost as much as he had loved Africa. And
Sarawak was so full of colour and light. It was different in
the Ulu, of course, where the light was filtered by the green
canopy. Often one was stumbling around in near darkness
because the trees were so close together and the foliage so
thick around them. Size was important in the rainforest.
You had to be big to push others out of the way and find
the best light. The tualang tree reached a height of three
hundred feet with a ten-foot diameter base. The rafflesia
flower, the largest bloom in the world, measured one metre
across.

The rainforest was bountiful. There was no other word
for it. There were nearly a thousand different varieties of
orchid alone, lush-petalled, with soft-breathing blooms.
There were insect-eating pitcher plants as large as a man's
foot. You could drink from them after the rains and swallow a bit of protein in the bargain. Hiding amongst the
canopy were birds of every hue, ranging from kingfishers,
to trogons, barbets and woodpeckers, not to mention the
hornbill, so prized for its 'ivory' beak. Thundering about
the undergrowth were rhinos, deer, scaly anteaters, sun
bears and orang-utans. Eagles and falcons fell upon lesser
prey, scampering about over and under the roots of trees,
beneath the ferns and leafy vines.

It was good he was going up into the covered mountains
again, into the hidden, mysterious valleys. He was looking
forward to the shallow rivers which spread their fingers
over the rich dark earth inhabited by a million creatures. In
the Ulu there were handsome tattooed warriors with blow-
pipes and swords, who might flit by you close enough to
touch your coat, yet remain a shadow. It was a lost world of
green foliage severed occasionally by golden blades of
sunlight. It was waiting to be discovered. But only for a

moment. It did not remain found for long, closing in on itself, changing its face, growing out of recognition by the day, by the hour, by the minute.

# PART THREE

# Into the Ulu

# 1

Tempon Telon, the ferryman for the dead, was aware that a party of seekers had entered the rainforest. He knew from experience that such seekers carried the reek of death about them, as a moonrat carries its stink. He polished his great canoe, covered in elaborate carvings of bones and skulls, lovingly rubbing oil into the ancient forgiving wood. Its craftsmanship was superb. Besides the bones and skulls, there were other symbols of death carefully wrought into the hull, which was made from the first tree which had ever grown in the world. These were deadly snakes, the crocodile, the clouded leopard.

Tempon Telon glanced across the river of death to the land of souls on the other side. Those he had already ferried to the far bank were drinking palm wine. Once he had someone to take over, Tempon Telon would join them for a cup or two. He was fond of drinking with dead souls. Occasionally a living spirit – that of the dead person's priest – would accompany him both ways. It was the priest's job to travel with the soul and then relate its adventures to the rest of the longhouse on returning.

He and the priest would talk about death, which made the tricky journey shorter than if the ferryman had been alone.

As the ferryman was working on his canoe a great hornbill flew down from the trees and perched on the gunwales.

Tempon Telon looked up. 'Ah, Sengalang Burong, you have seen the new travellers too?'

'I have indeed,' said the hornbill, who was none other than the war god of the head-hunters. 'There is bound to be trouble.'

The hornbill looked across the river of death and saw a familiar figure, a soul who was drinking wine and laughing with comrades, a warrior retelling stories of past battles.

'Is that Radin I see there?' said the war god. 'My old friend?'

The ferryman looked up. 'It is indeed.'

The great hornbill shuffled his claws on the gunwales, making Tempon Telon wince, for the ferryman did not want his precious canoe scratched, but at the same time good manners would not allow him to protest.

'I remember,' said the hornbill, 'how Radin won the Battle of Betong. It was a glorious fight and I was given so many sacrifices afterwards my stomach was as tight as a drum. I was belching and burping for a good month or two. Radin took so many heads at that battle he had an image carved of me and put in his longhouse, where the men celebrated their victory.'

'Not a wise thing to do,' murmured Tempon Telon, oiling around the war god's claws, as that distracted deity reflected on past glories. 'What happened?'

'Well, as you know, they should have abandoned the longhouse after the celebrations, as well as removing my image. But Radin was a bit overconfident in those days. Of course my presence, even as a wooden carving, was too powerful. Men began falling dead as if they had been turned to statues.

'Radin realized what was wrong and took me out into the forest and left me there.'

'Wise, very wise.'

'But he still did not abandon the longhouse. He was very attached to it. The spot was pleasant, having clear clean water running nearby and a rich soil. So his people stayed where they were.'

'Very foolish.'

'Of course, my presence, even as a shadow, was still in the dwelling and his people began to fall sick and die. I couldn't stand it. Radin was one of my best warriors. So I sang to him, trying to get him to leave. One night he woke and struck at my shadow with his sword. The very next day, while walking in the forest, he found my wooden image, in two halves.

'Radin realized what he had done then and he took his people out of the diseased longhouse.'

'They come to it in the end, but they need a lot of encouragement.'

'Quite.'

A strange shapeless shadow suddenly moved up beside Sengalang Burong just as he finished his tale.

'My, my,' said Tempon Telon, 'this is turning out to be quite a gathering.'

The intruder was Rajah Hantuen, king of the ghosts.

'I have just seen Rajah Jinn Peri, the king of the fairies, and he told me of the newcomers. I think the population of my kingdom is about to expand. The more ghosts I get, the more powerful I become. I shall soon be more powerful than Sengalang Burong here, if my luck holds out.'

'You will never be more powerful than me,' replied the bird-shaped war god. 'I am power itself . . .'

And so an argument ensued, as it often does amongst the gods of the rainforest Otherworld. It was their one intellectual sport. Later, they drank tuak together, from bamboo cups, and praised one another's prowess.

Keller's party numbered thirty, including Dyaks and one Malay boy called Budrudeen, who had joined the expedition at the very last moment, just as it was leaving Kuching. They went in four canoes, which upset a half-Chinese sailor because four is such an unlucky number in Canton where the man was born. The number 'four' in Cantonese is the same as the word 'death' and this man would have gladly paddled a canoe on his own if it meant they could continue in five craft, instead of four. Keller would not hear of it and laughed at the superstition.

By the third day they were on a tributary of the Kerang River, going southeast. It was a narrow waterway, which wound alarmingly through high banks and tall trees. Already the rainforest had turned to jungle and had closed in around them. It was a kingdom of leaves – broad, narrow, succulent, dry, wide, flat, puffed – leaves, leaves and more leaves. They dripped green, hanging over the riverbanks like figures in mourning. They reared up like surprised green ghosts, reeling back from the water's edge. They trailed and slithered like the longest of long snakes, climbing up cathedral-high trees with buttress roots that spread themselves wide enough to form small caves.

In the canoes there was always one man at the front, to watch for rocks and floating dead trees, and one man operating a steering oar at the rear.

The man at the front would flick his hand, back and forth, warning of any obstacle in their path. He would be the first to see or hear any rapids. It was because of noisy rapids that it was no use shouting his warnings. The signals had to be visual and acted upon swiftly. The lookout's eyes had to be sharp, his ears primed, his reactions quick and fluid.

Mayok was behind Budrudeen in the last canoe. The Malay youth was obviously not used to hard work. By the middle of each day he could only manage one stroke to everyone else's three. Mayok was the only person who noticed this and he kept quiet about it. He could see Budrudeen was in distress. He also knew that if Keller realized they were carrying a passenger, the Englishman would drop that passenger off on the bank nearest to the small convoy.

'You must build up your strength,' he whispered to the Malay youth. 'Or you will be found out.'

'I know,' whimpered Budrudeen, 'but it's hard. I have never paddled a canoe before. You must help me.'

'I can do nothing.'

When they stopped in the evening, Budrudeen could hardly get out of the canoe. Mayok could see that his legs were stiff from kneeling and that his arms were so weak they could not lift him from the sitting position. Mayok, despite his previous negative reply, helped the boy by lifting him under the arms.

Unfortunately, Johnson saw what was happening.

'What's the matter with him?' demanded the sailor, pointing at the Malay.

'Cramp,' replied Budrudeen quickly. 'Just a touch of cramp. I'll be all right when I've had a walk round. It's my calf muscles.'

The Englishman snorted, but said nothing further. Quite a few of the men got the cramps in the canoe, from sitting awkwardly, and from sweating too much salt.

'Thank you,' Budrudeen whispered to Mayok. 'Leave me to walk around.'

Even so, when Mayok let go of him, Budrudeen almost collapsed on the ground. By supreme strength of will the Malay youth kept his feet. He stood, swaying for a few minutes, then staggered off into the jungle. Once he was out of sight of the others he made noises, as if he were going to the toilet. One of the other sailors said something and there was laughter.

Budrudeen had only been allowed to join the expedition on the understanding that he was to cook for the white men. Most of the Dyaks fed themselves, with fish or game they caught themselves, certain roots, edible leaves and fungi, and some of the rice. Budrudeen had been a good cook since he was ten years old. He could make dishes which were palatable to European taste, while the Dyaks produced food the white men considered indigestible. Keller was pleased to have someone along who could make them hot meals. It was hard work.

Mayok felt very sorry for the young man and wondered why he had come on this trip.

Later, he asked him. 'You do not seem to like the river and the jungle.'

'No,' admitted Budrudeen bitterly, 'I do not. I hate the leeches and the biting ants. I am afraid of the big spiders and the snakes. I would rather be in a house where these things can be swept out with a broom.'

'Then you should have stayed behind, in Kuching.'

'I could not,' answered the other, but his voice faltered and he did not embellish on it.

Mayok at once deduced, correctly, that Budrudeen was running from the law. If not the law, then the wrath of the rajah, which was the same thing. He could see it in the youth's eyes. There was terror there, and guilt, and a look of delayed shock. The young man had done something very bad. He was running away. This was why he had joined the expedition at the last minute.

'What is it you have done?' asked Mayok. 'I only ask because you seem to need to speak to someone about it.'

'Nothing. Nothing at all,' whispered the youth, fiercely. 'Why do you ask such things?'

Later, Mayok showed him how to make a bed out of saplings, bending them down, using vines to anchor the natural hammock to the trunks of trees. The bed, off the ground and out of the way of night crawlers, was nice and springy. Budrudeen appreciated the gesture. Finally, Mayok rubbed some sap from a special tree on to the anchor ropes and around the base of the saplings.

'So the ants will not come.'

'Thank you,' murmured Budrudeen gratefully.

It was on the third day that he told Mayok what he had done.

'I have to tell someone. Can I trust you?'

'Yes.'

'If you mention it to anyone I shall deny I said it.'

'You may tell me. I shall tell no one else.'

'I murdered my master,' whispered the youth, almost in tears. It was obviously the first time he had put the deed into words, for his tone wavered. 'He was very cruel, to me and to his wife. I have been his slave since I was eight years of age. My cousin sold me to him when my father and mother died because of the volcano exploding on top of our house. My master used to burn me, very often, with a hot iron bar, to make me work quicker and harder.'

Budrudeen lifted his shirt and showed Mayok some hideous scars on his belly and back.

'Even when his wife worked too slow for him, he would take a cane and lash her about the legs and head. He was a very cruel man. I wrestled the iron bar from him three days ago and struck him over the head with it.'

'Are you sure? Are you sure he was dead?'

'I think he must have been – I hit him very hard.'

'Good,' said Mayok. 'Such men deserve to die. I think the rajah will give you a gift for killing such a man.'

'No, the rajah will hang me.'

Mayok still thought this was unlikely, but he knew the youth would not listen to him.

'Where are you going now?'

'I shall try to get to Sabah. I have an uncle there, who lives at the foot of Mount Kinabalu. He will hide me from the rajah. You will not tell the red-haired tuan about this?'

Mayok said, 'I told you, I will tell no one. Do you think I am not a man of my word?'

The Dyak was secretly pleased that the Malay youth had done something terrible. It was selfish but the crime had bound them together as friends. Since leaving the longhouse Mayok had not been able to talk to anyone about private matters. He had to keep everything inside him, like a swollen bladder that was never allowed to relieve itself of its contents. Now he had a friend, one bound to him by a confidence. It felt good.

Also, he could unburden himself of some of his own worries and fears, as well as listen to those of another and be able to offer comfort like a brother. They exchanged confidences when out of earshot of the others, discovering many mutual problems.

Mayok was just eighteen years, while Budrudeen was sixteen. They were only just finding their way in the world of men.

Keller was very pleased with himself. He felt he had stolen a march on one of the hated 'nobs' who had plagued his life since he was a child living in a hovel in Yarmouth, Norfolk. To Keller, anyone in a superior position was a nob and he had spent much of his time kicking against that authority.

The first person he had ever physically struck was the landlord who threw them out of their hovel after his father was tragically drowned. It had felt so good he continued to strike out when the opportunity arose.

Keller's father had been an honest fisherman, a crew member of a fishing vessel that went missing in a storm in the North Sea. Keller had been six years of age at the time. He could remember standing on the quay with his mother, waiting for the fishing fleet to come home. It had been a dark, louring sky that evening, with black clouds rolling through the murky grey overhead. The wives and families always came out to watch for the boats in those days, their hearts in their mouths. Fishing was a dangerous business and the sea had no mercy.

First there would be the black dots on the horizon, appearing one by one. Gradually they would take the form and shape of a fishing smack. On this day the sails were straining in a stiff wind, and the boats were climbing and falling into deep troughs of water. It was difficult to number them in such weather, but the women stood, some with children in hand, their tattered shawls wrapped tightly around them and laboriously counted the craft as they drew nearer the quayside.

Then Keller remembered the women wailing hysterically when they came up one boat short. His mother's fingers had tightened dramatically around his own, as she moaned along with the others. Though her grip was hurting him he made no sound himself. He was too terrified, scared stiff by the caterwauling from these drab, shabby fishwives. It seemed to him that one of those stories about old women turning into witches during the dark of the storm was coming true.

There was worse to come, for, as the boats were recognized, the wailing of some of the women ceased. In the end, there were only four women crying, and one of them was his mother. Her shrieking had reached such a pitch it hurt his ears to listen to her. Finally, he had broken away from her grip and run and hidden in a warehouse amongst the sacks of flour. His heart had been racing and his head spinning. When his mother found him, several hours later, her dirty red hair was streaked with premature grey. She had grown many years older.

'What will happen to us, child?' she had sobbed, clutching him to her breast. 'We'll starve or end up in the workhouse.'

'I'll go to sea, Mother,' he had told her, 'and catch some fish, like father.'

At that his mother's face had turned from a loving, pitiful expression, to one of terrible fury.

'You will *never* go to sea,' she said.

Of course, he did go out, just as his father had done, when he reached twelve years of age. By that time they had been thrown out of their house, such as it was, and had spent years living rough. They had gone from farm to farm, picking fruit and vegetables in the seasons. In the winter his mother gutted fish for a farthing an hour. She had died in the hedgerow one January night in a severe frost. He found her, stiff and cold by his side, the following morning and just left her there for the parish authorities to deal with, having no money to bury her.

That was when he was ten. By the time he was fifteen he was a hardened sailor, thief and troublemaker. Thrown off the fishing smack by a captain who could stand his insubordination no longer, he walked to Liverpool and took a job as a deck hand on a four-masted schooner. There followed one ship after another – runs to Botany Bay, the Americas, the West Indies, and other exotic places. Finally a friend got him on board Allen Starke's yacht, the *Monarch*, and here he was in Borneo, looking for the treasure which would make him rich for life.

'I'm going to take one of the Dyaks out to get some meat,' he told the other white men, 'You keep sober.'

They had, of course, brought some tuak with them, which they were busy guzzling. Keller knew that it would not last long. Once it was gone he was determined not to let them barter for any more at the longhouses on the way. This lot had no real sense of purpose, as he had himself. If he had not been leader of this expedition, they would likely all die in the jungle.

'And treat the Dyaks right,' he warned them.

'Why?' asked Blake, who was used to ill-treating natives, wherever he was in the world. He looked on it as a white man's sport. 'It's only a bit of fun.'

'Because, you dim wedge, we need them. This ain't the town, where you can go back to your bed in lodgings. You treat 'em badly and they'll run off and leave you stranded. You want to be without guides in this mess?'

He waved his arm to encompass the luxuriant growth around them. It was a maze of vines, tree trunks, shrubs and creepers. A man could get lost five yards away from the river. There were eerie sounds which broke the stillness every so often. When the evening came, crickets set up such a din you could believe you were close to a sawmill. Some creatures let out high-pitched whistles, others whoops, still others cold barks. If you did become lost you would go mad within a few days.

'You help 'em to look for sago while I'm gone.'

The sago plant was the staple food of the Dyaks when they were in the rainforest. Blake shrugged. He did not even know what a sago plant looked like. So far as he was concerned, the whole undergrowth grew out of the same seed. Nevertheless, he went along with Dyaks, hoping to get a pot shot at wild pig or something more substantial than vegetation.

On his foray Keller took along an Iban who was proficient with a blow-pipe. His own hunting weapon was an old Brown Bess musket, a smooth-bore firelock which he had won from an army deserter in a card game. It was a good gun but it fired such a large ball it mangled any bird smaller than an eagle. The blow-pipe hardly ruffled the fur or feathers of the prey. Keller bowed to its superiority as a hunting weapon.

The Iban's name was Raki and he was the same man who had first spoken to Mayok in the market.

Raki led the way along the riverbank. He could hear, in the distance, the chattering of what he called 'leaf monkeys'. Keller followed closely behind him, almost as careful as Raki not to make a sound. Raki was dressed only in a loincloth, so that none of his clothes could catch on bushes or trees and give him away. Keller was too concerned about leeches to go naked, but he had stripped down to long-sleeved shirt and canvas trousers. He had boots on his feet, while Raki was barefoot.

Raki chanted under his breath, a prayer for hunting with a blow-pipe, until they came to a wide part of the river. Here any sound would carry. He motioned for Keller to remain very quiet, then he crept forward stealthily. The monkeys were up in the canopy. They were eating fruit, the skins and pips of which were raining down on to the forest floor. Raki inched forward a few more paces and went down on one knee in a hunting crouch.

Slowly, he raised the eight-foot-long blow-pipe to his lips, after inserting a dart in the mouth-piece. It was, to Keller, an extraordinarily unwieldy and quite heavy weapon, yet the pipe did not waver, even though it was only anchored by both the Iban's hands at the mouth, pressing it tightly to his lips. There was the merest puffing sound and one of the monkeys shrieked loudly. Raki stood up and began weaving about at the base of a tree, keeping an eye on his prey. The poison took effect and the monkey fell crashing through the foliage, to land at the Iban's feet in a pathetic floppy heap of gangly arms and legs. The dark fur on its back contrasted sharply with the white front fur.

'Meat,' he said, grinning at Keller. 'You eat good tonight.'

'Yeah, well, I think the men would be better pleased with a deer or wild boar. They ain't used to eating monkey meat.'

'No find deer or boar. We find monkey.'

Keller had to admit this was true. You could not pick and choose in the rainforest. You took your opportunities as they presented themselves. Raki was busy slitting open the monkey's stomach and feeling inside.

'What are you doin'? What're you looking for?'

'Bezoar stones.'

Keller's interest was aroused. Maybe these creatures ate diamonds or something from the riverbed. Even amber would be worth a bit.

'What are them – *bezoar* stones?'

'Monkey has them in gut. You see!' Raki withdrew his hand triumphantly from fingering an intestine. He came out with an egg-shaped pebble. It looked worthless to Keller.

'What do you do with it?'

Raki said, 'Chinese man use them for medicine. We sell them to him for beads.'

'Oh, that stuff,' murmured Keller, disgustedly. He had seen inside the Chinese medicine shops. They would sell you anything which came from an animal, inside or out, especially if it was rare. 'Gall stones, I'll wager. So much rubbish, if you ask me. Still, if you can get beads for it, that's fine with me. I'm all for getting something for nothing.' He took out a hunting knife. 'Now we've got to skin and cut up this monkey, before we take it back to camp. I'm going to tell the men it's venison.'

The two men skinned the monkey and jointed the meat. It was hard work, despite using a parang and a hunting knife. Cutting through raw sinews, tendons and muscles was no easy task. Once they had it jointed, Raki wrapped the meat in broad leaves and tied them up with strips of bark. He and Keller then set off on the walk back to camp, alongside the river.

Some way along the river, where the water deepened slightly, Keller stopped to drink. He bent down at the water's edge and was about to put his lips to the clear swift water, when a dark shadow made him jerk back. In another moment a crocodile's head came up and the jaws slammed together inches from the mariner's face. Shocked by the suddenness of the attack, Keller fell backwards and rolled away from the water's edge.

The crocodile had not given up on its white meat. It came on in a peculiar swaying run up the bank, remarkably quick for such a short-legged creature. Its jaws were slightly open, ready to snap shut again with a piece of Keller inside them. Keller unslung his loaded musket and levelled it at the reptile.

'NO!' cried Raki.

But it was too late. Keller pulled the trigger. There was a boom and a flash from the Brown Bess. The crocodile took the shot down its open throat. It rolled on to its back and thrashed there, its tail lashing at the undergrowth. Within a minute or two it lay still. Keller was jubilant.

'Wey-hey! Did you see that! Beggar nearly got me. But I put him to rest instead. Is the meat any good? Can we eat it?'

Keller turned to look at Raki.

On the Iban's face was a look of pure horror. He stared at the crocodile with great fear in his eyes. The Iban fell full length, like a chopped tree, on his face in the mud. He held his head with both hands. He was trembling from head to toe.

Keller knew that something was really wrong. He had never seen Raki act in this way before. Once, when Keller had killed a wild boar, Raki had danced with him around the body. What could possibly be wrong with the Iban? It was only a crocodile. Surely Dyaks would be pleased to get rid of the creatures which stole their babies.

He turned the Dyak over, using the butt of his firelock as a lever.

'What's up with you?' he roared, aggrieved that Raki should be acting this way.

Raki opened his eyes and stared up at Keller's angry face.

'This is a bad thing,' he whispered.

'Why? It's only a croc!'

'This creature is sacred, tuan. This is a holy creature to the Dyak peoples. Mahatara's son, Jata, is the lord of the crocodiles. In the Underworld they are real people and the servants of Jata, tuan. They only change to crocodiles when they come up here for short time, to swim in the real world. Jata will be very very angry we have killed one of his men.'

Keller had mixed feelings. On the one side he was not sorry he had killed the beast which had so nearly decapitated him. On the other side, he regretted upsetting his Iban. Keller was truly fond of Raki: as fond of anyone as Keller could ever be. He greatly admired Raki for his skill at tracking and hunting. There was not another man Keller knew who could stalk prey like Raki. Unlike most sailors, Keller looked on the primitive fears of natives as quite real issues, to be respected. He understood that a man who had been raised to believe a crocodile was some sort of divine creature was not someone to be laughed at.

'Look, what's done is done. I can't help it now. If this Jata is angry, then we'll just have to make a sacrifice to him, see? You'll know best what to do. Now get the monkey meat and we'll be gettin' on. There's nothing we can do here.'

Raki got to his feet still shaking. 'Yes, tuan.'

He stared at the dead crocodile without remorse. What vicious creatures they are, he thought. Savage as sharks. Of the same spiritual clan, no doubt. Cold-eyed, cold-blooded brutes, with not a feeling in their ugly bodies not directly connected to thoughts of blood and the smell of raw flesh. They had the emotions of a log. They would kill you without a reason. How strange the Dyaks should choose this creature, above all others, as sacred.

'We'll work this out, Raki. You just wait. It'll be fine.'

Raki was inconsolable. He trailed after Keller back to the camp with a heavy heart. Keller walked into the camp and told the whites that there was deer meat for supper. They grunted appreciatively and called Raki a 'fine hunter'.

Raki did not feel like a fine hunter. He sat down with the other Dyaks and they saw by his expression and demeanour that something was badly wrong. He wondered if he dare tell them. Even the Malay, Budrudeen, considered the crocodile to be untouchable. The Malays believed that the crocodile had two pairs of eyes: one for the open air, the other for under the water. Likewise they had two stomachs, one for normal food, and one in which to hide the clothes of their human victims.

Children who fell into the rivers and drowned changed gradually into crocodiles, first growing a tail and then so on until they developed a crocodile's head and jaws. Killing a crocodile was like killing your brother's son. If the victim was a female they sometimes turned into a kind of mermaid, woman from the waist up, with a crocodile's lashing tail. It was thought that tigers came from crocodile eggs. If the hatched infant dived into the river it became a reptile, but if it ran off by mistake into the jungle then it grew fur and stripes.

Yes, even the Malays believed that if you shot a crocodile, harm would come to you and your family.

In this case, the party with Keller counted as his family. Raki knew that if Jata found out this Englishman had killed one of his servants, he would feel justified in taking revenge on Keller by killing one of *his* servants. As a servant of Keller, the one with the red-haired white man when the trigger was pulled, Raki counted himself the prime quarry of Jata.

The Iban lay all the rest of that night, shivering and staring out into the darkness. He was watching for the red-faced one, waiting for him to come up from hell and take a few heads.

## 2

John Grigg and Hut Potgieter were two mariners who had found their way over to Borneo from Java. They were deserters, both from the Dutch Navy. Grigg was British by birth, but had a Dutch mother and had been pressed into service while visiting his relations in Holland. The two had jumped ship together at Surubaya, crewed for an Indonesian trading vessel, which they again left on being recruited by Keller in Kuching.

Already these two men were becoming dispirited with the expedition. Like the other white men on the trip they had been bitten innumerable times in countless places by vicious insects. Potgieter especially hated the humidity of the jungle, which gave him prickly heat rash under his arms and between his legs. Grigg had trouble with a fungal infection, which the damp and dankness of the jungle did not help. They were appalled by the leeches, which they squashed between thumb and forefinger, leaving the head of the leech to fester. Even before Keller had told them about the crocodile they were thinking of desertion.

'You awake?' whispered Grigg to Potgieter.

'How can I sleep with mosquitoes as big as vultures flying into my ears?'

Grigg sat up. He stared around the camp site. There was a fire in the middle, which all the sleepers avoided. It had been lit for cooking and to keep away wild beasts. The guard was on the other side of this fire, sitting with hunched shoulders and staring out into the forest. The two Dutch seamen were nearest to the river, where the canoes were beached.

'Let's take a boat now,' whispered Grigg. 'I've had enough of all this. It's only a few days back to that little town – what was it, Skrang?'

'Can we find our way?' asked Potgieter, fearfully. 'Who's going to watch for dead logs in the water.'

'We just paddle with the flow of the rivers. We're bound to hit the sea sometime. Don't worry, we won't do it all by night. Once the day comes, one of us will take the watch on the prow. In the meantime, we'll just have to take the risk. Come on, follow me.'

Grigg began to snake his way down the bank to where the canoes were at rest. After some hesitation, Potgieter followed him. The two deserters were lucky that it was a white man on guard that night and not one of the head-hunters, whose ears were more sensitive to foreign sounds. As it was, the man on watch was far more interested in the noises of the jungle than the crack of a twig down by the river.

Screened by a fence of sandlewood trees, Grigg and Potgieter took the canoe nearest the water, easing it down the bank into the flow. Once they were in the craft they let the current take it a hundred yards downriver before picking up the paddles. There was a full moon above, which shone through the leafy arches overhanging the river's edge. They slipped along, through the mottled shadows, as if on a river of dreams. Grigg felt rather satisfied with himself and was quite unworried by the dangers.

Paddling through the gentle, rippling waters, they kept their eyes and ears tuned for rapids. Although the moonlight shone on the water while they were in the wider parts of the river, the overhanging foliage hid the surface completely on the narrow sections. It was while they were in one of these tunnels of leaves that a flying fox skimmed over their heads, then cut through the canopy to create an eerie shape against the moon.

Potgieter let out a sharp cry of fright. This sound startled Grigg, who dropped his wooden paddle. The paddle floated away ahead, was taken in towards the bank, and fetched up amongst some driftwood on an island forming an oxbow lake.

'Now look what you've made me do,' he growled at Potgieter. 'Pull in to the bank.'

By chance, the two men were going the same way as Keller and Raki had gone earlier in the night. In consequence they were passing the spot where Keller had shot the crocodile. When Grigg stepped out of the canoe, in the shallows, he could see what looked like a pale-coloured log. Then he saw that it was not a log at all, but the body of a creature. It lay belly up on the bank, its legs stiff and standing proud from the carcass. Grigg, on seeing the corpse, walked over to it and nudged it with his foot.

'Look,' he said, 'here's that croc Keller told us about.'

Potgieter stared and nodded from the safety of the canoe. 'What of it?'

'Think, man. We're going back with nothin' to show for this little jaunt except mosquito bites. What say we skin that beauty there. Crocodile skin's worth somethin'. Valuable. We could sell it to some Chink to make boots out of. Take the teeth too! I've seen croc teeth on sale. Make a necklace with them. What d'you say, Hut?'

'I don't know,' replied Potgieter, nervously. He stared into the blackness of the jungle. 'What if Keller finds out we've gone before morning? He'll be after us. Shouldn't we just get on?'

Grigg began paddling towards the bank. 'Naw, listen, you told me you worked a Norway seal-hunting ship. You must know how to skin things. You have a go at that beggar, while I try to get his teeth. We'll make somethin' of this bloody jaunt yet.'

So, despite Potgieter's concerns, he found himself skinning a crocodile on the bank of the river. The moonlight flashed on his hunting knife as he worked more feverishly than he had ever done on seals. It was true he was skilled at this sort of thing. A crocodile is not a seal, but Potgieter had been cutting dead creatures to pieces most of his life, including whales, and he knew how to wield a skinner's knife.

Grigg on the other hand had never pulled teeth from anything. He had knocked a few out, with his fist, in drunken brawls, but that was entirely different. In the absence of a pair of pincers, he was having to prise the teeth out with a parang, and it was not an easy business. By the time Potgieter had almost skinned the beast, Grigg had only six teeth.

'These'll do,' he muttered, the sweat pouring from his brow. 'It's the skin what's important.'

Just as they were rolling up the skin, to put it in the canoe, a silence fell on the night.

'What's that?' whispered Potgieter.

Grigg was uneasy too, but he hated to show it. 'What's what? The noises have stopped, that's all. Probably some wildcat around.'

'Crickets don't stop for wildcats.'

'Well, whatever. Look, let's get this thing in the canoe. Help me with it, it's bloody heavy, man.'

They dumped the crocodile skin in the boat and then climbed in after it. Potgieter tried shoving off from the bank with his paddle, but with the extra weight the bottom of the canoe was caught in the shallows. Grigg got out and began pushing the boat, sliding it across the shingled bottom to deeper water. When the craft finally reached a depth where it bobbed freely, he prepared to climb in again.

At that moment a creature came out of the jungle. It ran as swiftly as a charging bull, first thudding down the bank, then into the shallows, its two pale feet splashing through the water. It was huge and ghastly to look at, having the body of a man and the head of a reptile. Its eyes burned white-hot with rage, as it thundered towards the two men, intent on malice.

Potgieter let out a high-pitched squeal, like that of a terrified pig. Facing the monster, he knew they were going to be torn apart. The other man had not yet seen what was coming, though he had heard it, and was trying to climb into the canoe. Grigg had snagged his trousers on the gunwales and was having difficulties in getting aboard. Potgieter panicked.

The Dutchman started paddling, but his friend still had hold of the boat. Potgieter, now insane with fear, chopped at the other man's fingers with the paddle, forcing him to let go. Grigg stumbled backwards in disbelief, astonished that his friend had deliberately attacked him and was leaving him behind to die. Potgieter set off upriver, heading for the widest stretch of water. So terrified was he that he missed the water several times, catching crabs with every other stroke.

Grigg had now turned to face his assailant. Having seen the horror which faced him he knew he had no chance of survival. He screamed long and loud, causing havoc amongst the sleeping creatures of the jungle, who echoed his terror. They added their own terrified voices to his shrieks. Then the monster was upon him and he lifted his arms to attempt a defence. It was a futile gesture, as one of the arms was torn from its socket.

Potgieter was twenty yards distant from his shipmate when the creature from the jungle struck. He saw it rip Grigg's arms from his torso. Then, with Grigg's high-pitched whimpers still piercing the night air, it struck again. Its long jaws opened and swept sideways and upwards, decapitating him at the base of his neck. Blood fountained upwards, as Grigg's heart, still racing with terror, pumped it out in forced spurts. The seaman's body simply folded and dropped into the water. The stump of the neck kept spouting blood and gore into the current. This offal was swept away downstream.

From the creature's jaws there came the sound of a coconut cracking under pressure.

Potgieter almost choked on his terror now, but somehow managed to keep paddling. For reasons known only to itself, the creature did not follow him, but simply stood in the water staring as the Dutchman got further and further away from it. Potgieter battled against the current with superhuman strength, putting as much distance between himself and the creature in the shortest time possible.

The beast's shape was caught in the moonlight. Potgieter saw that it had the body of a naked man, perhaps eight feet tall, but its head was long and flattish. In his blind fear all Potgieter could think of was that the murderer had a circus clown's upturned boot on his head. He stared horrified as the sole parted from the upper to reveal rows of sharp steel nails running along both top and bottom edges.

Potgieter somehow managed to get back to the camp.

Without bothering to moor the canoe he ran up the bank. It floated away on the current. He ran into the camp yelling like a madman. Sleepers leapt from their beds, reaching for rifles or blow-pipes. Keller was on his feet in an instant, hunting knife in his hand, the blade flashing in the moonlight. Potgieter fell at Keller's feet, blubbing incoherently. Gradually, with some rough coaxing, his story came out. Keller was predictably furious with both men.

'You stole one of my canoes?' he thundered. 'You ran off without a by-your-leave?'

Potgieter confessed their desertion.

'I'm sorry,' he groaned.

'I ought to hang you now,' cried Keller. 'Lookit, the canoe's gone downriver again. We'll have to get that back. You're a bloody fool as well as a thief and a deserter.'

When Potgieter started to describe the 'creature' which had come out of the jungle, Keller believed him but thought him a coward. It seemed to the party leader that the man's terror had got the better of him. If Keller had been present when some beast had pounced on Grigg and had torn him apart, then that beast would have paid with its life. It was when Potgieter drew the shape of the man-like monster in the dust by the fire that the Dyaks gasped and drew back. Until now they had hardly been able to follow the Dutchman's gabbling, his accented English being difficult to understand at the best of times.

Raki cried out, 'It is lord of crocodiles!'

'What are you saying?' yelled Keller, trying to keep control of the situation.

Raki was insistent. 'It is Jata, son of Mahatara, come to take revenge for death of crocodile.'

The Dyak turned to Potgieter.

'His head – what colour?'

'I don't know,' sobbed the Dutchman. 'It was dark – it was moonlight.'

'Tell me what colour! Think!'

The Dutchman, bowed and shivering, still on his knees and surrounded by his fellows, seemed to genuflect. He thought very hard about the incident. Then he straightened his back and spoke the word.

'Red – I think it was red.'

Raki turned to Keller again. 'There – I tell you, tuan. It is Jata. He go looking for the servant that never come home to him in the Underworld. He find his servant, dead and with no skin, laying on the riverbank. He also find two others, running with the skin and teeth of his poor servant. Jata very angry and make his kill. He will make more, you will see.'

Keller made no answer. Instead he broke open a powder jar and loaded his Brown Bess with fresh ball and dry powder. Then he motioned for Johnson and two of the European sailors to follow him.

'Come on, we'll get that lost canoe back.'

One of the sailors said, 'What if this . . .'

But Keller cut him short. 'Either you come with me, or I shoot you dead,' he said, bluntly. 'I'll have no mutiny here – and that goes for you Dyaks too. You hear me? The rest of you men,' he indicated the whites, 'you keep your muskets trained on them natives. If they try to run for it, shoot them down.'

Keller was acting in accordance with the principles of navies and armies throughout the world. A sense of strong leadership had come over him and he knew that any subaltern or captain would have acted in the same way. It was necessary to keep a firm hold on his leadership. These were imperial qualities he was showing and he had every reason to believe they were sound.

The four men went off in a canoe, downriver. Before long they came across the headless body of Grigg, wavering in fast-flowing shallows. Keller merely glanced at it and passed on by, making no comment. Finally, they came to the lost canoe, caught in some protruding roots on the bend of the river. Keller and Johnson boarded it. He ordered the other two to paddle the first canoe back to camp and then followed in the recaptured craft. On the way he threw the crocodile skin overboard, into some deep water. It sank away, out of sight.

'I'm not going to have my Dyaks run off,' he said, by way of explanation to Johnson.

On the way back, past the spot where Grigg's body lay in the rippling waters, Keller stared at the bank. The skinned body of the crocodile was nowhere to be seen. It was as if something had lifted the monstrous carcass and carried it off.

'Somethin' ate it,' he murmured to himself. 'Some big cat or other.'

He mentioned as much to Raki when they arrived back at the camp: said he had seen the tracks of such an animal. The Dyak nodded, clearly not believing it, but not wishing to argue with the tuan. They struck camp almost immediately. Someone asked if they were going to give Grigg a Christian burial.

'You goin' back for the body then?' asked Johnson.

The speaker volunteered no further comment.

# 3

Back in Kuching, Singapore Jack and his party had been delayed longer than he had intended. A new war had broken out between the rajah and the pirates. The death of Lingore, their paramount chief, had confounded the Ilanun pirates for a while, but they soon reorganized. A new chieftain emerged, a Dyak called Usman, who now appeared to be even more formidable than Lingore had been in his time.

Usman had gathered together a fleet of a hundred war prahus, roofed canoes ninety feet long, each with some seventy rowers. Some of the warriors would stand on top of the roof for fighting purposes. These craft were swift, their crews merciless in battle, and they plundered up and down the Sarawak coast, looting and burning villages. They massacred women and children along with the men. Among the towns they sacked were Sussang on the Kuluka River, Palo, Mato, Bruit and Ingan. They attacked local and even international shipping which tried to use the rivermouths where they held sway. They swept down on any easy prey in their hordes and destroyed it. Prince Usop, the rajah's adviser on the pirates, estimated that there were around twenty-five thousand men living off piracy along the Borneo coast.

The nearby Sultan of Sambas, Starke's neighbour on the other side of the mouth of the Sarawak River, was at his wits' end. His country was being ravaged all along the coast, and some villages inland, by the constant attacks of the pirates. Many of the pirate prahus had swivel guns, which could devastate local canoes, armed perhaps with an ancient smooth-bore flintlock, but more often than not they were carrying just swords and spears. Hundreds of people had been killed, many women raped and left to be eaten by ants, disembowelled or with their throats cut, children had been taken from their families to be sold as slaves.

'We've got to do something,' said Starke to Jack, 'and we've got to do it *now*.'

'But I'm due to take my expedition into the jungle today,' agonized Jack. 'We're ready to start. Harriet is champing at the bit and so am I.'

'I need your help,' replied Starke, flatly. 'Yours and Colenso's. I've got a fleet together of sorts, which includes my yacht and the East India Company's steamer, the *Nemesis*, which I've hired for the battle. I need commanders on the prahus. I'm going in the *Lion*, but I want you in the *Tiger* and Colenso in the *White Ant*. With 150 prahus we need to maintain tight control.'

'What about the rest of them?' sighed Jack, giving in. 'It'll take more than just the three of us.'

'I have my Malay princes. Many of them don't want to fight at sea, they're not sailors, but several are willing. Prince Subtu for one. And Prince Usop. I want to swoop down on those rivermouths and destroy the pirate fleets as we find them, before they can get together to form an armada.'

Jack resigned himself to another few days, or even two weeks, of delay. Harry told him he need not worry.

'I'm sure two or three weeks in the Ulu is nothing. One wrong turn, one broken canoe, and Keller will have lost all that he has gained. I don't suppose he took half the amount of medicines and stores you're going to take. From what I know of him he has not got your organizing abilities. His own inefficiency will slow him down.'

Jack thought perhaps that this was partly true, though he did not have such a dim view of Keller's abilities as did Harriet. He cheered himself with her words though, telling himself that he drove himself hard and could travel faster than any other man in the same circumstances. He had to take the others with him, of course, but that was part of the challenge, to inspire, to lead, to get the best out of men.

The rajah's fleet sailed in on a calm and serene evening to the main pirate bases at the mouths of the Kaluka and Sarebus Rivers. They arrived at dawn to find the bases empty. Somehow the pirates had got wind of the attack and had moved further up the coast to the Rajang River. Rajah Starke was determined to break them this time and followed with his unwieldy armada of Malay and Dyak craft, with his yacht the *Monarch* and the steam ship *Nemesis* covering their flanks.

Again, the pirates were one jump ahead, and had left the Rajang before the arrival of the fleet. As they moved along the coast the Ilunans gathered up their own craft and were gradually building a fleet comparable in size to the armada chasing them. This was just what the rajah had hoped would *not* happen. Usman was finally run to ground at the mouth of the Baram, where a mighty night battle took place which was illuminated by rocket flares from the *Nemesis* and the *Monarch*.

The pirates were overwhelmed. The *Nemesis* had thirty-two pounders, loaded with canister and grape shot. They blasted the enemy to pieces. They blew them out of the water with round shot. When the pirates, who had bravely attacked the steam ship and yacht in their solid but inferior prahus, where sent reeling back towards the coast, they were chased by the rajah's prahus and desperate hand-to-hand fighting took place.

Both Jack and Colenso received minor wounds in the battle, as they each commanded ten prahus. By morning the pirates were in disarray. Many of them had beached their craft and had gone running into the interior. They were chased by Dyak warriors eager to get heads. Local tribes, finding the pirates in the jungle, hunted them down as mercilessly as the pirates had sacked their villages. There were hundreds of decapitated bodies scattered over the region, among them that of Usman's.

There was a great deal of joy amongst the rajah's fleet, for having yet again smashed the pirate fleets. It was a problem that would always be with the rajah during his rule, but such lessons as the one he had taught the pirates that day would not go unheeded. Prayers went up to Allah from the Malay craft and to Mahatara from the vessels containing Dyak warriors. They sailed home to Kuching in triumph, flags flying, masts covered in banners.

For his part, Jack was just pleased the whole affair was over. He had lost the tips of two fingers in the fight and he counted himself lucky. There were wounded men without legs and arms, some without their sight. Others had horrific injuries caused by musket balls and Ilunan straight-bladed swords. Many of them would not live beyond a few hours. This was not Jack's forte, this warring. He did not mind danger, but of a different kind, battling against the elements and the landscape.

Three days after the war with the pirates, Harry was in a canoe travelling down the Baleh River. She was bitterly disappointed to be in Kit Colenso's canoe and not Jack's, but she said nothing to either of them. Jack had simply said, 'You will travel with Colenso, Harry,' and that was that.

For his part, Kit Colenso had ceased to be argumentative. In fact he all but ignored the woman who wore men's clothes. When something needed to be said, he spoke to her plainly enough, without any of his usual gruffness. But there was no social chatter, and she did so want to point out things in her excitement.

For instance, there were literally clouds of butterflies along the banks of the rivers, of many varieties and colours, seemingly scudding around without a purpose. Birds swooped in to feast on these multi-hued snacks. She tried to classify these birds, but most of them came in and went too fast to identify.

Those she could catalogue were the kites, hawks and eagles, perched on bald trees with broken limbs. They were usually about a yard or two from the top of the tree, still as statues, waiting with watchful eyes for the end of the world to roll in. She recognized the Brahminy kites with their brown-flecked, white bibs; and grey-headed fish eagles, and crested serpent eagles; and once she thought she caught sight of a changeable hawk-eagle. She tried to sketch these creatures in her notebook, but the canoe was unsteady and the rowers sped her past.

Harry actually needed to concentrate on something other than her back and buttocks. After three days in a boat her body was bruised and aching in many places. The canoe continually bounced and smacked on the fast-flowing river. It came down hard enough to make her teeth rattle. Contrary to what she expected, the hull of the boat was not rigid but flexed and moved the whole time with the buffeting of the waves and the occasional bottom strike. This movement rubbed her sore in places she dare not mention to anyone but Lidah. There was also always water in the bottom of the craft which caused the rubbing to chafe. They were travelling eight hours a day, sometimes nine, and she was weary beyond her normal endurance. Only the ignomy of admitting failure stopped her from asking to be sent back to her cousin in Kuching.

The river itself was a source of interest, without the animals, insects and birds. It was ever-changing, from narrow straits with white water curling up its banks, to wide stretches with low scrubby islands in the middle. Here and there she could see a jam of dead branches beginning to turn into such an island, as they wedged themselves together, gathered mud from the flow, and looked set to build themselves to stability. Sometimes the water was clear and she could see a pebbled or muddy bottom: at others it was murky and deep-looking, with swirling eddies and snaking currents.

They were passing through a stretch where the foliage hung like witches' hair over the banks when she suddenly saw something which made her squeal.

'Look! What's that?'

It appeared to be a colourful ribbon of flesh gliding through the air towards her. She instinctively ducked and the ribbon passed over her and landed in a tree on the far bank. It wrapped itself around a branch. Now she could see it was a snake and she shivered involuntarily.

'Paradise-tree snake,' muttered Colenso from the front of the canoe. 'It won't hurt you.'

'But it was flying.'

'Gliding. They glide from tree to tree. It's harmless.'

Harry gritted her teeth and stared at the sweaty shirt-back of this infuriating man.

'Did I ask whether it was dangerous?' she snapped.

He still did not turn round, but kept his eyes forward.

'You screamed. I assumed it was because you were afraid. In my experience a scream usually comes from a frightened person.'

'I did not scream.'

'It sounded like a scream.'

'It was a squeal of surprise, not of fear.' She continued haughtily, 'I understood you were an expert on animals. If so, you seem to know little about the female of the *homo sapien* species. Women make all sorts of high-pitched noises, most of them nothing to do with the emotion of fear. You should make a study of them before you make such swift and rash comments.'

'I don't think I shall. It would bore me.'

'You prefer orang-utans and gibbons?'

He made a slight nodding motion with his shoulders and head.

'They are certainly more interesting.'

'It explains to me,' she said, more sharply than she really intended, 'why you are still a bachelor.'

He muttered something back, which she could not catch, since the river had become very agile at that point and the canoe was again crashing up and down, jarring her back-bone.

'What?' she cried over the noise of the rushing water. 'I can't hear you.'

'I said,' he yelled, 'I have been married – once – but I expect you have always been the same waspish spinster you are today.'

She made no reply. His cruel remark had numbed her tongue. He had stung her as surely as a hornet. Mortified, she sat in the bottom of the canoe and allowed the tears to fall down her cheeks. Lidah, sitting behind her and seem-ingly careless of the jolting ride, did not see the tears for their faces were wet with spray anyway. But she did see her mistress's colour and knew something was wrong. The Kenyah girl stroked and massaged Harry's neck with her strong slim fingers, hoping to send the hurt away to some other less troublesome region.

A few moments later Colenso glanced behind, but soon had his face to the front again.

They fetched up that night by a traditional Kejaman longhouse, an elongated hut on stilts. The rooms were at the back half of the oblong shaped dwelling and there was a long covered verandah at the front. The whole village lived in this one building, the individual family rooms separated by thin wooden walls. All rooms opened on to the verandah, where the occupants gathered for social and other activities, such as weaving baskets or making fishing nets.

After beaching the canoes, Jack went to talk to the tuai rumah, to ask if they could stay near to the longhouse. There would not be rooms for all the visitors, but some could stay in the longhouse as guests. The chief turned out to be a friendly man, who accepted gifts of beads and tobacco. It appeared that there was a large guest room on the end of the longhouse and those not able to share this could sleep on the verandah.

Jack thanked the tuai rumah profusely and was presented with the unavoidable cup of tuak, which he downed in one.

Once the formalities were over, Jack escorted Harry up the steps to the guest room. She found she had been given a small area in the corner of the room, separated from the rest of it by a split-bamboo screen.

'It's the best I can do for you and your companion,' said Jack. 'We're all piled in here together.'

'Jack, this is luxury after the last two nights camping in the forest and you know it. As for Lidah, why this is home to her. She was raised in a longhouse.'

'Yes, but you weren't, and you won't be able to escape the snores of the men. In the forest I could put you fifty yards away, but we're right on top of each other here. Men sleeping in a confined place like this can sound like a sty full of pigs. I don't even like it much myself.'

She assured him she would be fine. Then she went down to the canoes to carry up her pack containing, among other things, her sleeping blanket. Lidah had already unloaded their stuff and was preparing to take it up to the longhouse. One of the men would have done it for them, if Harry had asked, but she did not want to be a passenger on this expedition. If she was going to retain any self-respect she had to look after herself.

While the two of them were lugging their belongings across the dirt yard, where the occasional piglet ran squealing into a bunch of scraggy chickens, scattering them noisily, Kit Colenso came up to her. He looked a little grim and she wondered what she was in for this time.

'Miss Glendenning,' he said, 'I apologize.'

She was thoroughly taken aback, having expected more rebukes from him.

'For – for what?'

'For that last remark I made in the canoe. It was not – not very gen—'

She interrupted him. 'Gentlemanly?'

'I think I was going to say *generous*. I've never claimed to be a gentleman.'

'Just the same, I'm sure you were right. I am a spinster, though I don't consider myself to be an old maid. And I have been told before that I can be very sharp tongued, though I hope I'm not a shrew. In short, Mr Colenso, I don't think you have said anything for which you have to apologize.'

He gritted his teeth. 'Damn it, accept my apology!'

She realized he had probably agonized over this meeting for the last hour or so. That glance backward in the boat had told her at the time that he was feeling guilty. He had stewed since then, waiting for the opportunity to speak to her.

She decided to accept his apology gracefully.

'I do – thank you. But this does not make us friends.'

'You're damn right it doesn't,' he said, briskly, and swept past her, heading towards the canoes.

Lidah said, severely, 'He is very bad-tempered that man. He should speak to you more nicely. Tuan Jack would not like to hear him curse to a lady like that.'

'No, he wouldn't, Lidah, but I think Mr Colenso has very rough manners, from living too much alone. Or perhaps he picked up the habit of swearing in Africa, where they thought it normal? I understand his brother is a Church of England bishop.'

'His brother a bishop of the English Church?' cried Lidah, raising the eyebrows on her round cheerful features. 'Then he *definitely* not supposed to curse in front of ladies.'

'Oh, we mustn't be too prim about these matters, or we'll turn into Fanny Prices, Lidah. That's the very worst thing that can happen to a lady explorer you know, to become a Fanny Price. It would end a promising career in a moment.'

'Fanny Price? I think you tell me about her before. You say she was a missy too-nice-for-words, yes?'

'Much too nice. Priggish is probably a better word. It prevented her from doing things that I find quite jolly. She was what we explorer ladies call *homely*. There is nothing worse in the world than becoming homely, Lidah, you mark my words. Otherwise our fate is not in our hands.'

'Fate is in the hands of the seven Santang Sisters, missy, who ride the night on golden brooms. They say if we die, or if we live, or who we not marry and who we marry. They fly around our heads and tell us what we should do.'

'I should like a ride on a golden broom,' sighed Harry. 'To glide through the night airs! Seven sisters on seven golden brooms! I imagine it is quite cool up there, above the trees. And there would be no mosquitoes or other annoying insects. Or leeches. Yes, I think the Santang Sisters have a nice time of it.'

Lidah was a bit shocked. 'They are goddess, missy. Not ordinary ladies like us.'

Harry tried to look admonished.

Once she had sorted out her bedding, Harry joined the others on the ruai of the longhouse.

Outside, the evening was closing in. There were frogs and cicadas in their thousands, filling the air with their songs. Something screamed alarmingly, far out in the jungle: prey with a predator at its throat. Monkeys who hung around the longhouse hoping to steal scraps were screeching at one another. Birds of all sorts hooted and hollered, warning each other of the limits of their territory, threatening those who trespassed.

'Isn't it noisy out there?' Harry said to Jack. 'I always thought the forest would be a quiet place.'

'Noisier than a city,' he laughed. 'But different. You probably find the rumble of carriage wheels and the call of the watch more comforting.'

'No, no. There are predators out in the streets of London far more dangerous than those in the jungle. I like it here. Oh, yes, there are deadly snakes and I've yet to meet a sun bear or a clouded leopard, but I prefer my dangers not to be in the form of scallywags. Animals are more predictable than men.'

He laughed. 'What about the leeches?'

'Well, I have to admit I find them loathsome in the

extreme, but they're part and parcel of this leafy world I love, so I have to put up with them. I felt the same way about cockroaches as big as seashore crabs, when I first arrived at the bungalow, but I got used to them in the end.'

Jack shook his head in admiration. 'You're a fine lady, Harry, there's no doubting that.'

He left her then, glowing in the warmth of his compliment.

That evening they were entertained on the ruai by warriors dancing the hornbill dance, with graceful movements none of the white men could emulate. The Kejaman warriors used their swords to re-enact battles mythical and real, as their dancing carried them into the realms of old but not forgotten wars. The women too, bare from the waist up, danced with sinuous, serpentine movements, proving their own agility and litheness.

Harry was given a succession of babies to hold, none with any form of towelling, and she was terrified that one of them would do more than urinate on her pantaloons. However, she realized it was an honour to be trusted with the young of longhouse and she stared down into their gleeful features, chucked them under the chin, and did all those things a woman was supposed to do with the infants of doting mothers.

A great deal of tuak was drunk by the men.

By midnight, most the men, and Lidah and Harry, were exhausted. Harry's soreness needed some balm she had brought with her and she retired to her little corner of the guest room to apply it before the men came in to sleep. The split-bamboo screen was very shakily put together and there were many gaps in it. When they eventually came into the room they were not as rowdy as she had expected them to be. Before long the whole lot of them were fast asleep and, as Jack had warned, snoring.

Lidah did not come to bed for a very long time and Harry

suspected her companion of morality which would have had Fanny Price spinning in her grave.

In the middle of the night, Harry woke with sweat trickling down her neck. She sat up in bed with a start, wondering where she was. It took her a full minute to remember. She was in the longhouse of the Kejaman. Around her, snuffling, snoring men filled the room with their fetid breath. It was sweltering, stifling in the room. Mosquitoes droned around her head and tickled her skin when they alighted on her flesh.

She felt she had to get out, into the fresh air.

Lidah was asleep beside her. Harry climbed over Lidah without touching her. Cockroaches scuttled out of the way and found narrow cracks in the floor. A toad as large as a man's fist hopped into a corner. There was a scrabbling sound in the rattan matting, which came from rodents of some kind. From the walls came the clicking chatter of geckos. The whole room was shared by wildlife from the riverbank and from the forest: an aspect of jungle life to which Harry was becoming used.

Rather than negotiate steps between the men to reach the door, she slipped through the glassless window on to the ruai. There were a few more bodies there, deep in sleep: the Dyaks who had been unable to find room in the guest house. She did not feel she could pace up and down on the verandah, so she went through the doorway, down the steps, to the dirt yard below.

A pig came trotting over to her and sniffed the edge of her shift.

'I've no food for you,' she said, breathing in the night airs deeply. 'Sorry.'

The pig went off, disappointed. It lay down amongst others underneath the longhouse. There were chickens there too. They were quieter than Harry imagined they should be. Even the forest was silent. It was, she admitted to herself, a little eerie. Somehow she did not feel afraid. Instead, she felt adventurous, and wandered down towards the river, being careful where she trod for there were snakes abroad in the dark hours.

There she sat on the bank, watching the dark waters carry driftwood to an unknown destination. Even as she sat and watched she saw the snout of some creature – snake, lizard or perhaps even an otter – cutting the surface of the river, moving away from this intruder from the world of two legged flightless animals with no fur or feathers.

She remained on the bank, cooler at least than the hot stuffy guest room in the longhouse, and went into a reverie of sorts, dreaming of past, present and future. Suddenly, Harry became aware of someone sitting beside her. It was a man. She had not noticed him arrive. He simply seemed to appear. He smelled of incense and myrrh and other sweet perfumes of the orient. The skin on his round face was damask, completely without blemishes and, even stranger, without a trace of perspiration. Its texture invited touch.

'Who are you?' she asked, drawing away from him.

He seemed not in the least disturbed by her manner towards him. Dressed in dark flowing silks, with a black turban, there were golden sandals on his feet. Then he smiled and she noticed that he had the whitest teeth she had ever seen. His face was certainly very handsome – olive and handsome – with light brown eyes that twinkled whenever he looked at her. It appeared that he was quite happy to sit near her and say nothing.

'Look,' Harry said, 'I had no idea someone else was staying with the Kejaman at this longhouse. No one has mentioned your presence and you were not at the dancing. I think you should give me your name, don't you?'

'My name?' he said, in a deep husky voice. 'Oh, as to that, it's Rajah Hantuen.'

'You are a king?' she asked, raising her eyebrows. 'What is a rajah doing, travelling the forest alone? You *are* alone, I take it.'

'Oh yes, very much alone. I always travel alone. I am a solitary person, always have been and always will be. Which makes it so nice that you are sitting here, idling away the night hours, staring into the swirling waters of the river. It is an activity I enjoy myself, but it is so much better to be able to share it. I can sit beside you and no longer feel quite so lonely.'

'Do you not have any subjects?'

'Why, hundreds of thousands, but they do very well without my constant presence.'

'What is the name of your country?'

'They call it Kaseteran.'

'I do not believe you are a rajah,' Harry said, after thinking it over carefully. 'What would you be doing in the jungle at this time of night? I think you just dress up that way to fool visitors. You're taking advantage of my inexperience. You should be ashamed of yourself. I'm just a callow woman. No credit can be had from playing your games with me.'

'You wish me to prove it?'

His white teeth flashed again and their brilliance blinded her for a moment.

'All right then, prove it.'

He reached out and took her hand. A few moments later they were walking through a dark forest, denser even than the rainforest through which she had already come. The trees and bushes were planted so close together that there was no space between them. Yet they seemed miraculously to part as she moved through the foliage, opening an adequate path for her.

Another aspect of this forest disturbed her. She could see no light coming from above. What light there was appeared to be internal, coming from no particular direction, simply in the atmosphere. Consequently there were no shadows. If she saw the shapes of things it was because she sensed them rather than pictured them. The whole place had a strange brooding ambience, not oppressive, but somehow torpid and listless.

'Where are we?' she asked her guide. 'Where have you taken me?'

'This is the kingdom of which I spoke – my kingdom.'

'But there's nothing here but trees.'

'Wait, you are too impatient.'

He led her suddenly into a clearing on the edge of a wide stretch of water.

'This is Kaseteran,' said Rajah Hantuen. 'This is the land I rule.'

Harry stared about her. There was nothing terribly spectacular about the landscape, though much of it was interesting. Some magnificent trees standing on the edge of the water reached upwards like massive grey pillars. These trees had ugly human faces carved into their trunks, into the great boughs which overhung the water. As Harry stared at them, the lips moved on these faces. They were talking to each other, or to nothing, she could not tell. Their eyes stared mournfully out at the active world, as if full of longing for real movement.

An occasional sigh escaped the mouths of these faces as below them a root reached out, dripping soil and mud, waving and groping like a hairy white tentacle. Clearly the tree was trying to walk, but there was no concerted coordination between its individual roots, which floundered helplessly.

Amongst the branches of these trees sat black owls, also with human faces, staring bleakly at the sky. Once in a while one of these creatures would take off and swoop down to snatch up a lizard or a rat, also wearing the face of a man or woman, running from one hole in the earth to another.

Around the clearing, grey clutches of waving bamboo formed screens behind which some unknown activities were being performed. In the distance were the dark shapes of mountains forming a ragged wall around this eerie world. The lake water shone black, like wet slate, and was perfectly still: so still it appeared you could walk upon it and not wet your feet. There was a cold feel to the air, to the ground, to every aspect of the grey scenery.

There were many weird shapes here which should have frightened Harry, but simply struck a chord with her sympathy.

There were severed human heads, with long flowing hair, floating around in the dim atmosphere. They trailed their black locks behind them like diaphanous veils, making brush marks in the sand. Someone had cut away the eyelids, so their bulging orbs were left staring at Harry in a frightful manner. Long pale tongues hung out of wide toothless mouths and trailed in the dust when the head drifted too low to the ground. The expressions on the faces of these heads were apt to be dour and moping, as they used their large ears, flapping slowly like the wings of big birds, to steer and drive themselves along.

One of these grisly objects paused to stare at Harry.

'Do I know you?' pleaded the head, in a piteous voice, as it rolled the vile reptilian tongue into the back of its throat. 'Please, are you my cousin?' The damp swollen grey lips on the face of the head pouted. 'Can I kiss you, my cousin?'

Rajah Hantuen waved the head away and, with a troubled look on its features, it floated out over the grey sand of the long wide curving beach.

Harry was vaguely aware of an unearthly music in the air and saw, amongst some low bushes, human shapes dancing to the rhythm of this macabre melody. While she was watching this dance she felt wet flesh touch her bare feet. Looking down she saw more clammy creatures in the shape of human beings, kissing and licking her feet with cold tongues. Their complexions were ghastly, of sickly hue, grey-green, as if some horrible disease were creeping through their flesh. She drew back, alarmed at their obsequious behaviour, and wondering at it all.

Rajah Hantuen ordered the wraiths back and they left her, their eyes shining with tears.

'They just want to touch you,' he told her, 'because you are from the real world.'

'I believe you are king of this place,' Harry told him, 'and I would like to go back now to my friends.'

He made no objection, but took her hand and led her back through the dark forest. Before very long she was standing on the bank of the river where he had first appeared to her. It was just becoming light, the sun glaring red through the tree tops.

Lidah found her there just a little while later.

'Where have you been?' cried her distressed Dyak companion. 'I've been looking everywhere.'

'A man came,' answered Harry, in a faraway voice. 'He called himself Rajah Hantuen and he took me through there – I think . . .' Harry pointed vaguely at the rainforest. 'We went to his kingdom. It was a very strange place, Lidah.'

Lidah's eyes opened wide and she muttered something that sounded like a prayer.

'You come with me, missy, into the river. I want to bathe you quickly.'

'What for?'

'To wash away the stink of the ghosts. You have been

with Rajah Hantuen, king of the ghosts. Did any of the corpses kiss you on the lips? Did they try to chew at your hair? Did any ghost attempt to touch your feet?'

'Some licked my feet with their cold tongues, certainly, but no harm came to me.'

Lidah shuddered. 'We must wash away their spittle, before you are consumed. It will make your feet turn black and the rot will creep up your body like fungus up a tree. Come quickly, missy, come quickly. Rajah Hantuen! Oh, my, you have been to the land of ghosts and we must clean you thoroughly before you waste away to nothing. Oh, my! Oh, my! Thank goodness they didn't kiss you, for they would have sucked the life from your body. Are you sure they didn't run their fingers through your hair? Are you absolutely sure . . .?'

# PART FOUR

# The Cave of Rajah Naga

# 1

Keller and his men were beleaguered: chased from dawn to dusk by Jata, who attacked more of the unhappy group before they came to the foot of a mountain. There they hid their canoes in amongst the foliage and rocks, travelling overland in an attempt to stay away from the rivers. In this way Keller hoped to leave Jata behind. His Iban told him that Jata would not stray far from the big rivers and lakes, his habitat.

Indeed, Jata receded into the jungle, falling back to where the rivers were widest and strongest. But the travellers were left in no doubt that he waited for them to come down from the high country, where the tributaries of those lazy meandering rivers were born, gushing from the ridges and ledges above.

Avoiding rivers did not protect them from attacks by other demons. Bujang Sembelih, the throat-cutting demon, cut a smile in the neck of one sleeping head-hunter, leaving his companions on either side untouched. Durga, goddess of death and disease, killed one of the seamen with a terrible fever. Junips, those horrible little jinn with hairy bodies and swollen genitals, ate the eyes out of another man who got himself lost.

Then a great storm threatened the Ulu, coming on a strong wind from the north, bringing with it tumult and turbulence to air, land and water. Rufous-backed kingfishers fled along sultry backwaters as black rainclouds tumbled over one another in their eagerness to get to the mountains, where they could shed their heavy load. Lightning flashed like messengers between clouds as the monsoon weather moved inland. There was no space between horizon and cloud base, since the tempest joined earth with heaven during its progress south.

Every bird movement meant something to the Dyaks. Each flight, whether straight or weaving, was some portent or other. Some of them preferred not to move when they saw evil omens in such things. While Keller was tolerant of these beliefs he could not allow them to endanger his expedition.

'We can't just sit on our arses,' he said. 'I'm as willin' as the next man to be careful, when it comes to superstition, but damn it, every bit of bloody cloud has got some sort of message here, ain't it? Well, there's a limit.'

He was, however, cautious about overtaxing his men physically, and he made frequent rest stops. One of these was halfway up an enormous mountain covered in beautiful flowers and greenery. If you transported that mountain to middle England, the shires would be in raptures about it. As it was, the seamen and Dyaks alike looked on its steep jungled sides with distaste.

'We need to rest up,' said Keller. 'Gather ourselves together a bit. I'm tuckered out myself, so I expect most of you are too. We'll hole up in a cave until the storm has gone.'

The mountain was wholly green, with no rockface showing through, even up to its peak. Foliage dripped from it, hung from it, like ragged green curtains. Keller managed to find a cave on the south side of the mountain, partly hidden by vines. He urged his men to enter.

Just inside the low, wide opening there were korwars on short posts. These took the form of large sacred wooden heads carved by priests and shamans. The wood was rotten, fungi rimmed hollow eyes and open mouths. Grass grew like hair from nostrils. The surface of each head was pitted with termite and woodworm attacks. The expressions on the faces were mournful. They stared out with swollen eye-sockets and pouted with thick lips at the curious Europeans.

The Dyaks drew back on seeing the korwars, wondering who had placed them there, and for what reason. Keller asked Raki what was the problem with these carvings.

'They are someone's ancestors, tuan,' replied the Iban warrior. 'Inside all wooden heads is real bone skull, from an old dead warrior. Someone wish to guard this cave, or warn people not to go in. I think we should leave.'

'Listen to that thunder outside? You want to go out and face a storm? We got no choice. We stay here.' As he spoke, Keller put a powder cartridge down the barrel of his fire-lock. He rammed this home and then followed it with a ball. Next he put some powder in the priming pan. Finally he looked up again, at Raki. 'I'll shoot the man who tries to leave, in the back if I have to. We've got to stay together.'

The Dyaks understood he was serious. In any case they were in need of rest. They dropped the loads they were carrying and fell across them, exhausted. Some of the white men were already asleep. Though he too was tired, Budrudeen, who had no astrolabe to calculate kiblah, asked Keller, who owned a compass, to point the way to Mecca for him. The young Malay then fell on his knees and began to pray.

When he had finished his prayers, Budrudeen joined the

others, who were all fast asleep. There were scorpions and cave spiders all over the walls, but everyone was too fatigued to worry about such trivial creatures. At that moment they would have slept on the backs of crocodiles.

Later, a loud crack of thunder woke Budrudeen. He lay for a moment and listened to the crackle and fizz of lightning, the consequent snarl and snap of thunder which followed and, in the silences, the sound of water pouring from the heavens in torrents, forming a waterfall over the mouth of the cave. He then realized Keller had been wise to choose a cave up on a slope, where they would not be flooded and drowned in their sleep.

'You cannot sleep?'

The voice was that of Mayok by his side. The Dyak too had been woken by the noise outside. Budrudeen shook his head. 'Not through such a storm.'

Just then a cave spider scuttled near the Malay, who slapped at with his sandal.

Mayok grabbed his wrist. 'No, you must not kill a spider.'

'Why not? It might be poisonous.'

'Not that one. In any case, it was a spider who made the world we live in.'

'Allah made the world.'

Mayok shook his head. 'No, no. It was like this. A spider came down on a silken thread from heaven and built a web between the stars. This web caught a piece of coral, and coral, as you know, grows and grows. It grew flat and round like one of the mats the women weave for their rooms in the longhouse. On to this mat fell a slug and a worm and these two creatures brought with them soil from heaven, which they carried around and dropped in several places on the hard coral surface.

'Then a seed blew in from nowhere, to grow the first

tree, from which Tempon Telon later carved his canoe. From the branches of this tree dropped a giant crab, which burrowed and tunnelled all over the place, making mountains and valleys, and great shallow basins. When the rains fell they filled the basins, to make lakes and seas, and from the mountains came the rivers, which cut their way across the landscape.

'Once the rains had been, other seeds began to grow and flourish, until the whole earth was covered with forests. Up sprang sago plants, bamboo shoots, mango trees, grass to feed the pigs, and many more kinds of harvest.'

'What about the people, like you and me?' asked the Malay, interested in spite of his own beliefs. 'When did they come?'

'Why, once the earth was flourishing with game and produce, two spirits, a female and a male, who saw this garden which no one owned, came down to live in it. They made lots of things out of wood: tools to work with, kitchen utensils to cut fruit and stir soup; mats to sleep on; blowpipes with which to hunt game. One of these wooden tools fell into the female spirit's loom and out of the tangle of threads fell two roughly hewn heads.

'The two spirits did not like the look of the two heads, so they departed from this world, leaving it to their wooden progeny. The two heads mated and their offspring had shoulders as well as a neck and head. And later, when the offspring mated, their children had arms, and so on, until finally the humans were born with a body and two arms and two legs. Gradually, through the generations, the parts of the body had begun to grow more flexible, and could be moved at will. The first two real humans, made of flesh, were called Amei Awi and Burung Une.

'These two had such long arms they could reach up to heaven and pull themselves out of reach of the earth. This they did, but not before parenting eight earthly children and four lunar children, to live on those separate worlds. The eight earth children were faced with a mountain to climb. The first two went right to the top and their ancestors became the hard workers, who do all the manual chores like agriculture and building houses. The next two managed to get three-quarters of the way up and their ancestors became artisans, making sandals, fishing nets, weaving mats. The next two only got halfway to the top and they became the hunters. Finally, the last two did not start the climb at all and they became kings who sat around talking all day long, discussing important issues and making decisions.

'In the meantime Amei Awi cut a branch and peeled away the bark. The chippings and peel which dropped to earth turned into dogs, chickens and pigs. Burung Une gave birth to some more people, who could not speak a word. These people eventually went out to sea, to harvest the fish, and once they had eaten the fish they found they could talk, but not in the same language as the hunters and farmers.

'Once all this was done, and there was no more work for Amei Awi and Burung Une, these two gods settled down deep into the soil, to encourage the crops and fruit trees to grow. Every year we make sacrifices to these two deities, so that we have a good harvest.'

Budrudeen nodded. 'We Moslems don't believe in such things, but they are interesting to hear. You said that some of their children went to the moon. What happened there?'

'The most lovely of the lunar children was the full moon. Among others she beguiled owls with her beauty. However, her brother, the crescent moon, became very jealous of all the attention she was receiving, and he threw hot burbur porridge into her face, scarring her beauty. You can see those marks if you look very hard – they are dark patches on her skin.'

It was while the two young men were talking, that something arrived to block the light from the front of the cave. There was the sound of flapping, of huge wings, then a creature with blue scaly skin dropped lightly from the sky, to rest on the mountainside directly in front of the cave. It was so large it blocked out most of the light. Mayok gave a yell of fright, which woke the rest of the men in the cave.

'What in Christ's name is going on?' cried Keller. 'Can a man not get some rest in his own bed?'

It seemed not. The Dyaks had jumped up and were wailing about an attack by 'black jinn', the demons of their world. One or two of the white sailors had grabbed their muskets and were loading them quickly, their faces pale with fright. Budrudeen had thrown himself in a corner and was shrieking about retribution. Keller, now perceiving that it was day outside, yet little light was entering the cave, also rose from his bed.

Keller saw the need to gain control of a situation which was rapidly deteriorating into anarchy.

Rajah Naga, king of the sea-dragons, was taking advantage of the monsoon rain to travel to the land. His ancestral home was in Pusak Tasik, his palace in the deepest part of the ocean. Here he presided over all sea-serpents and sea-dragons. Rajah Naga was a very handsome god, with a body covered in blue scales, a dozen giant flying-fish fins which he used as wings, a fine head with white silken cat-whiskers some two yards long that hung from either side of his broad nostrils, and massive claws on each of his four feet. Handsome indeed, was he.

Rajah Naga very much disliked having dry scales and the only time he could leave his home on the bottom of the sea was when there was a good deal of rain falling. So it was at the moment and so it was that he had arrived on the mountainside. From here he planned to survey the top of the rainforest, simply to sit and wonder at its greenness, its abundant growth, watching the eagles circle in the sky and the hawks flashing down through the canopy.

Although he gave no indication of the fact, he was aware that there was a clutch of mortals inside the cave. He could smell the delicate scent of human flesh. Although humans were not his staple diet, Rajah Naga was not averse to a morsel or two of such meat. He thought he would remain outside the cave until some of these creatures emerged. Then he would feast on them, recalling old times, remembering past repasts.

Keller was not prepared to discuss the nature of the beast which blocked their path to freedom. Whether it was a dragon, or a black jinn, or some previously unknown species of real animal was immaterial to him. The fact was it was large, it looked very dangerous, and it was in their way.

'What are we goin' to do?' asked Johnson. 'We can't blast that monster out of the way with muskets – it's too big.'

'What I'd give for a six-pounder cannon,' muttered Blake. 'I'd blow a hole through that belly wide enough to crawl into.'

Keller said, 'Well, we ain't got no cannon. Johnson's right about the muskets. We could wait until it goes away – it's too big to get in this cave – but that might take a week. We've got Lord Howd'y'do on our tails. I need to steal a march on that Singapore Jack and get to the heads before him.'

'So what's the plan?' asked Blake.

'Caves nearly always have other ways out, besides the obvious one. We've got to find one of 'em. We'll follow this as far as we can go. Maybe branch off if we have to. Johnson, you've got the lamps. Light two and give one to me. I'll take the lead and you take the hindmost.'

The Dyaks looked frightened when they were told they were going into the cave. Indeed, Rajah Jinn Hitam, king of the black jinn, lived in a cave just such as this one. If you went too deeply inside, you never knew what might lie in wait for you. On the other hand, they saw that there was little point in offering themselves as sacrifices to Rajah Naga, who was known to be fond of human flesh, providing he did not have to put himself out too much to get it. They were in a troubled loop.

Once the lanterns were lit and Keller was organizing the line, Mayok at least felt a little better. Keller, for all his character faults, was a good leader. He instilled confidence in his men. They saw him take things in their stride and they too began to wonder whether indeed there was anything to fear.

'All right,' he said, holding up the lamp, 'I'll lead off, the rest of you follow. Now I'm told by Raki that they'll be cave racers down this tunnel. That's a white snake, but it's blind and harmless, so don't go shootin' at it, or yelling blue murder. It won't hurt you. The rest is just bats, spiders and scorpions, and you've already been to bed with them.'

With that he started the line forward, going slowly and carefully. He was wise enough to know there might be pits which dropped away to nothingness.

Instead of growing narrower, the cave got wider. Stalagmites and stalactites began to leap up in front of the lamp's beams. In the walls of the cave were recesses which held all kinds of natural architecture, from stone curtains to shapes vaguely resembling creatures of the earth. It was a spooky and challenging environment, but not particularly dangerous.

They drew further and further away from the main entrance, yet the air still stayed sweet, and there was a breeze blowing through. This told Keller he had indeed chosen correctly. There had to be at least one further opening somewhere ahead. He hoped it would be far enough away from that brute outside to escape its attentions.

Although the breeze remained, the air grew warmer. They seemed to be descending, rather than rising or staying on the same level. Keller remained hopeful that the ground would rise again before long, leading them to an exit passage. Then, as they came to a great cavern, taller than thirty men and wider than a fallen tree, he heard the sound of chinking. Someone was ahead of them, working stone against stone.

Keller immediately doused the lamp and motioned for Johnson to do the same.

Once the lamps were out the dark snapped in around them and for a few moments they were blind. Then a faint light began to creep in, from the far side of the cavern, which had been masked by the light from the lamps. Keller motioned for the men to squat down and put his finger to his lips. Then he touched Raki on the shoulder and the two of them went forward.

They kept close to the wall of the cavern, using the stalagmites as cover. Keller noticed that a stream ran through the middle of the cavern, draining into a lake near the source of the light. Around this lake, and up on the rocks above, were small stocky figures, completely naked. They were little men, covered in coarse hair. Their noses were flat against their faces, with large nostrils, and their mouths were lipless slits above their sharply pointed chins. Most of them seemed busy with chunks of stone, which sparked when they struck it. Keller realized they were making flint tools, or weapons.

These creatures could not have been more than two feet high. They had tiny eyes, which shone red in the light. Keller noticed that the light source was a hole in the cavern roof, from which dangled many vines. The little creatures went up these vines, carrying basketfuls of sharpened flints on their backs, to return a little while later with an empty basket. They slid down the vines again, their hands smoking with the friction.

Suddenly, one of the creatures sniffed the air, his head jerked up, and he ran a few paces forward. Keller noticed with revulsion that the dwarf's feet were pointing backwards. In fact, all their feet were back to front. The sniffing one stared out into the darkness, his tiny eyes registering suspicion.

'Omang,' whispered Raki, fearfully. 'Gnomes, I think you call them in your country.'

'We might call 'em that, but I ain't ever seen one before,' said Keller. 'Has that one seen us?'

At that moment the gnome in question raised a hairy, muscled arm and pointed dramatically in the direction of their hiding place. The creature began squealing like a pig. The rest of the omang, a hundred of them a least, dropped what they were doing to stare at the squealer. Keller decided to reveal himself.

He stood up, musket under his arm, and began to walk forward.

'Hello,' he said, holding up a hand in the universal sign of peace, 'I just want to talk.'

With remarkable swiftness, so quickly that Keller did not see it happen, the omang in front of him whipped out a stone knife and threw it. The weapon went spinning through the air and had not Keller moved his head a fraction, an instinctive gesture, it would have struck him in the eye. Instead, it grazed his cheek, and then glanced off a stalagmite.

Keller was incensed.

'You bastard!' he growled.

He raised his Brown Bess, aimed, and pulled the trigger. The weapon kicked against his shoulder. Inside the cavern the sound of the shot was tremendously loud. It was followed by an horrendous noise – the sound of the omang screaming like monkeys – then silence. With the smoke and smell of the gunpowder in his nostrils, Keller walked forward.

He found the dead omang, a hole in its chest, by the edge of the lake. Its mouth was open, revealing rows of small blunt teeth. A horrible stink came from the corpse, worse than the stale sweat of a sickly orang-utan. The omang probably smelled that way in life. There was a throwing axe clutched tightly in its stubby-fingered fist. Presumably it was going to follow up its first attack with another. Keller had killed it just in time. The rest had fled. The cavern was now empty of them and the vines had been withdrawn.

'Over here!' he called, as he heard the others scrambling to get to him. 'Raki, come and look.'

The Iban was indeed the first man on the scene. He stared at the omang, his eyes wide.

'Don't tell me,' Keller said. 'I've done a wrong thing.'

Raki shrugged. 'I don't know. I would have killed him too, tuan. They are magical people, but not to be trusted. They steal babies to eat and poison the river water with their piss. If you can kill one, so be it. But we have no way out of here now. The rest of them have taken up the ropes. We should have caught a live one and held him for hostage.'

'So, what do we do now, Keller?' asked Blake, in a disgruntled tone. 'What big ideas have you got in that head of yours?'

'I'll put a gun butt in that big head of *yours* you talk to me like that,' snarled Keller. 'You keep a civil tongue in your mouth, Blake. Let me think . . .'

As he was thinking there came a plopping sound from the lake. The omang were dropping things into the water from above: lumps of faeces among other objects. Larger lumps of more solid material began to fall. Screams began to filter down from above, but whether human or not Keller was unable to tell.

'Quickly, fill the waterskins,' cried Keller. 'They're poisoning the lake.'

The men quickly did as they were bid. They were already quite thirsty. Of course, in their panic they had not thought of the stream that fed the lake, but then for all they knew the omang could find a way of polluting that too. Once they had water in the skins, they stared at the things being dropped from the hole above. Pieces of human remains. They were cutting up bodies and throwing them down. The screams increased in intensity, then suddenly ceased. Clearly the omang had human prisoners and had been dissecting them alive, with those primitive stone cutting tools they had harvested from the cavern.

Mayok reached into the water and pulled out a whole human arm. He showed it to Raki. The Iban nodded.

'Tuan, this is an Ilanun pirate. I know the tattoo from this arm. The omang have captured him – maybe more. They cut him to pieces. See, there is private parts, floating on the water, and I see foot at the bottom of lake . . .'

'All right, all right,' moaned Blake, having a very pale pallor to his cheeks, 'we can see what they are.'

Nothing happened for the next hour, while Keller and Raki searched the cavern for another way out. There was none. They had come to a dead end. Raki said he wanted to look in the lake for some reason. He dived in amongst the floating body parts and went under. They watched him swim downwards, through the green water, until he disappeared from view.

Then something took their attention away from the diver. A single vine was suddenly dropped from the hole above, to dangle there. Temptingly. The omang were inviting brave climbers to take their lives in their hands and try to scramble up to the hole. One of the Dyaks began shinning up the rope immediately at the speed of a spider going up a wall. He almost made it, despite being pelted with stones, before they cut the vine and he fell down into the lake.

'Bastards!' yelled Johnson, angrily, shaking his weapon. 'I'll cut off your feet and stitch 'em on the right way round if I catch one of you.'

He looked round his group for approval of his jest, but no one was in the mood for merriment.

However, an omang hung over the edge of the hole and began hurling insults and oaths at Johnson. Neither creature could understand the other's language, but Johnson's tone had obviously communicated his contempt of the omang. Now they wanted to fling a few obscenities his way, for good measure. Then the warty gnome disappeared from view again.

Johnson took careful aim at the hole above with his musket. Then he yelled, 'Just show your bloody eyes, goblin, and I'll shoot both of them out.' He remained with his musket pointing at the hole, waiting for a glimpse of his tormentor. He was rewarded by a thickly thatched head poking over, as the same omang prepared to trade insults again. The people below could see its tiny eyes glinting.

Johnson was a good shot, having been a poacher back in England. His weapon boomed in the echoing chambers of the cavern. The ball took the top of the gnome's head off and sent bits of skull and brain raining on his fellows. The limp body slipped forwards and fell, through the hole, to land with a heavy *crumph* at Johnson's feet, on the lake edge.

'Bloody goblins,' he muttered with some satisfaction, rolling it away with his foot. 'How'd'you like that, you blasphemous little hairy bastard?'

'Send another one of the Dyaks up the rope,' whispered Blake to Keller. 'See what happens.'

At that moment Raki came to Keller. He had dived into the subterranean lake and swum around under water, looking for an escape vent. Raki was very pleased with himself. He had discovered their way out.

'I find a hole at the bottom of water,' he said. 'One man must go through this hole to see if there is cave on other side.'

Keller said, 'You hear that, Blake? You often get potholes where the water's broke through from an underground river. Could be there's a tunnel on the other side.'

'We send somebody through,' insisted the Iban.

'How about *you*?' asked Blake, sneering, and pointing at Raki. 'You seem to know all about it.'

'No,' Keller said, 'he's a good swimmer, but he's not as good as you or Johnson. Whoever goes to look must stand a chance of getting back out again, or we lose another man. I want you to go, Blake.'

'Me?' cried the seaman, incredulously. 'You won't get me at that lark, Keller . . .'

Despite his protests, Blake found himself with a rope tied around his waist, standing on the edge of the lake in his longjohns and minus his boots. 'Remember, two sharp tugs on the rope and I want you to pull me out quick,' said Blake, shivering. His eyes were dark with worry. 'If it gets stuck, don't pull too hard. I might be jammed in the hole, or caught on some rock projection. Send Johnson down for me, if that happens. Three yanks on the rope mean I've got through and need some time to set things up.'

A tinder box was wrapped into a waterproof goatskin parcel and this was tied to Blake's waist. A firebrand was similarly wrapped and strapped to his chest. He wanted no extra lumps on his back which might get caught on underwater crags.

Blake dived into the cold water. The shock of it knocked all the breath out of his body. He had to surface again for another draught of air. When he had refilled his lungs he went under once more, this time somewhat acclimatized to the coldness of the water. Down and down he went, much in the same way a penguin swims under the sea. He had done this often in the navy, when it was feared a ship had been holed. It had been the job of seamen like him to check the hull.

Deeper and deeper he went, looking for the hole in the position Raki had said it would be. Far below, the visibility was almost nil. He felt along the bottom, churning up sediment and making it even more difficult to see. Then, by sheer luck, his hands found an edge and he knew he had the rock hole. With his lungs beginning to ache he swam through and upwards, hoping those on the end of the rope did not allow it to tauten and so prevent him from reaching any air the other side.

He broke surface sooner than he expected, coming up into darkness. Sucking in air he felt exhilarated. He had done it. What was more he could feel a slight breeze on his left cheek, which meant the outside air was getting into the cavern from somewhere. He hauled himself out of the water and gave three quick yanks on the rope to tell them on the other side that he was safely through and they could send another man.

He then unwrapped the tinder box and brand, and lit the latter with the former. Soon there were shadows dancing on the walls of this new cavern, which seemed to be mainly fashioned of white limestone and glittering quartz. Finally, he tied the end of the rope to a stalagmite and waited.

Soon afterwards Raki broke the surface, heaving for breath. Another man was through. It was not so difficult with the rope in place. A man did not even have to be a good swimmer, but simply needed to pull himself along the rope. There was the psychological advantage of knowing that there was air on the other side.

Despite that, one of the Dyaks panicked and got his ankle entangled in the rope halfway through the hole. To those above it was if they had caught a great fish on the line, which jumped and jerked for over a minute before it was still. There was nothing anyone could do for him. He swallowed water and drowned before the next man reached his trapped body. They left him there, simply feeling their way along his clammy corpse, past his round staring eyes, to the next part of the line.

When half the men were through, those remaining wrapped the weapons and goods up in the waterproof packs they had taken into the jungle and ferried them under the lake to the other side on pull-through ropes. Once the belongings were all on the other side, the second half of the group began to go.

Finally, all the men were through, bar the poor fool who had panicked.

'Right men,' said Keller, having unwrapped and lit more firebrands, 'let's be having you.'

The big red-headed seaman marched on, keeping to what appeared to be a track running alongside the underground pool. Eventually he led his men to a foliage-covered hole, and then out into the blessed sunshine, which poured through the canopy. Keller felt rather exhilarated. He had outwitted one supernatural foe and had beaten two others to reach this point. Jata had been left far behind now; Rajah

Naga had failed to thwart his plans; the omang had been defeated. Keller felt he had a right to feel self-congratulatory and did so without any false modesty.

'I shamed them,' he murmured to himself. 'I shamed them into submission.'

## 2

It was while they were camping on the bend of a fast river that Mayok saw his first penanggalan. It was the middle of the night. The sound of the rushing river and Budrudeen complaining of the mosquitoes had kept him awake. Now the Malay boy had fallen into a fitful sleep, but Mayok was still alert. He got up and went to sit by the dying embers of the fire, feeling uncomfortable with his unknown surroundings. Although born with the jungle all around him, except for his initiation ceremony he had barely spent a night out it in before being exiled. A longhouse was the place to be once the darkness fell.

He sat and poked the ashes with a twig, brooding on the nature of his fate. If Danta had come to him and said, 'Let me be chief instead of you,' Mayok might have conceded. Danta had been his best friend, after all, and sacrifices had to be made for one's friends. But his friend had become his arch-rival and had stolen the chieftainship from him, then sent men out after him to kill him. Mayok sighed in unhappiness.

Just at that moment a shadow passed between the moon

and the river's edge. Mayok was startled. What bird would fly around in the darkness? Then the movement was to his right, away from the river. He stared at an oxbow lake, left behind when the river had moved further away, like a snake shedding its skin. There in its waters he saw what he believed was a great jellyfish, like one of those he had seen washed up on the beaches to the north.

A giant jellyfish? he thought. But this is the river. There are only such things in the sea. He was about to stand up and take a closer look, when he realized the image was *on* the surface of the lake, and not beneath it. It was then he looked up and saw the *thing* hovering above the still waters. What he had seen was a reflection of a floating head.

What he had taken for the trailing tentacles of a jellyfish were in fact the hanging intestines and organs of a witch. Aghast and trembling in fear, he recognized the head, with its horrible slit of a mouth, long shaggy unkempt hair, tiny piglike eyes, and needle-sharp teeth. Here was a penang-galan's head, with windpipe attached, and all her disgusting innards and organs trailing along the ground below her. The slimy guts of the creature were leaving a track of slick bodily juices, as a snail leaves its shiny path, all over the campsite.

Mostly the penanggalan seek women just after childbirth, they being helpless and weak, with fresh blood to offer. This one, however, just seemed to want to cover the camp area with its ooze, not bothering to enter bivouacs, nor wake the sleeping men. It even ignored Mayok, so intent was it on drifting over every section of the camp. Finally, it smiled at Mayok, a ghastly leer, and then made off along the river, carefully avoiding any thorny trees, prickly bushes or hooked brambles.

The witch's residue stank.

Mayok sat and shook violently from head to foot, knowing he had witnessed what few men on this earth have seen.

He knew also that he was a lucky man. The witch could easily have descended on him in his state of funk and ripped open his stomach. That had not been her purpose though, and he wondered why. When he looked around the camp, everything was dripping with the clear scum she had left. It would all have to be washed off, before they set out again.

There was no point in waking the others. They could do nothing about the disgusting ooze until the morning.

In the next few minutes, something more dangerous than the visit of a witch occurred, which threatened the camp with an even greater danger. The witch's slime had attracted a marching colony of inch-long ants, thousands of them, which now flowed into the camp like a black shadow. The ants fell to eating the penanggalan's residue, devouring cloth and biting human flesh in the process.

'Up, up!' cried Mayok, first in Kayan, then in English. 'Up on feet! The ants are here.'

He sprang to his own feet, running through the sticky mire, shaking each man. Some were already awake, crying out in pain as the sharp acidic bites went through their skin. Men leapt to their feet and ran down to the river, jumping into the fast-flowing waters, which were fortunately only centimetres deep. Keller had woken the white sailors, leaving the Dyaks to Mayok. Everyone managed to reach the river safely, each slapping at the others to get rid of the few ants which clung tenaciously to their bodies, the mouths sunk into their flesh.

Men pinched ants from their eyelids, lips and nostrils: the tender painful places, including their genitals and anus. They worked assiduously to rid themselves of the pests. Individual bites were painful, but a mass of them, in the groin, under the armpit, was excruciatingly agonizing. Men moaned and gasped as they scraped ants from the recessess of their bodies.

Back in the camp, the great ants were everywhere, feeding on the odious fluids of the witch, ruining equipment and clothing in the process.

'What *is* that stuff?' asked Blake. 'I never felt it raining that digustin' mess.'

'Must have come from the trees,' Keller replied, looking up. 'Some kind of sap . . .'

They could do nothing but watch, as their camp was destroyed by a rippling shadow, knowing that they would lose more than a night's sleep before the morning came.

Many miles away, in the camp of Singapore Jack, two witches this time had left their tell-tale blanket of slime. Here, although Jack had posted a guard, he had not been quick enough to rouse the sleeping forms. One man was left behind in the rush to the river, to be eaten by the ants. They could hear his screams as the ants covered his body, making a black writhing shape on the ground, until Harry could stand it no longer.

'I'm going to help him,' she said, her tone revealing her distress. 'I *have* to help him.'

Before she could be stopped, she stepped out of the water and into the vast dark flow of savage ants. Both Jack and Colenso tried to follow her, to pull her back, but swarms of ants immediately flowed up their bodies, blinding them, so that they were useless to her anyway. Both men plunged back into the river, to wash the vicious creatures from their skins, before trying again. A man could be driven mad within a minute by such a terrible multitude of bites.

Jack could not help himself screaming, almost as loudly as the man dying in the camp, and Colenso flailed at himself wildly until his two Ngaju Dyaks took him in hand, and scraped away the ants with the edges of their hands.

There was no need for Colenso and Jack to try again.

Everyone stared, first in horror, then in amazement, as Harry walked through the ants unharmed. They flowed around her feet, obviously seeking some way past them and up her legs, but seemed unable to make any progress. One or two ants dropped from the leaves of trees, on to her shoulders, but she dealt easily with these, nipping them as someone would their lice.

Only Lidah knew what was happening.

'It's the ghosts,' she murmured, enigmatically.

Harry managed to reach the poor beset figure, still writhing on the ground. All his outer skin was now gone and the ants were feeding on the red-raw flesh beneath. His eyes had been eaten away, so that he was blind, and she knew that the ants were inside him too, probably feeding on his lungs and stomach, working their way into other tubes. There was nothing she could do to save him. To end his agony she picked up a parang, brushed the ants from it, and then hacked through the man's neck. She kept on chopping until he was quite dead, then she let the weapon fall to the ground.

Going back the river, with the ferocious insects still milling around her, desperately trying to get at her but frustrated by her feet, she burst into tears.

'I had to kill him,' she said. 'He was in such pain. I had to cut off his head. It was horrible.'

Jack held her in his arms against his chest, cradled her head in the hollow of his shoulder, let her weep for the death of the man, and for her own actions.

'I'm so proud of you,' he said. 'That was a very brave and unselfish act. To go to him and attempt to save him was heroic enough, but I never thought you would have the courage to end his misery in the way that you did.'

'I could not stab him in the heart,' she sobbed. 'I did not ow how – I might have made the situation worse.'

'The parang is a slashing weapon,' Colenso interrupted.
'It's not made for stabbing. You did the right thing. The
fellow would have thanked you from the bottom of his
heart. Any man would . . .'

'So proud of you,' Jack repeated.

Afterwards, once the ants had gone and Harry had
calmed her nerves, they assessed the damage. It was bad.
Stores had been devoured, tents had been ruined, equipment
had been soiled. There was still speculation as to why
Harry, alone amongst them, should have been regarded by
the ants as so unpalatable she was repellent to them.

'I'm not sure I find it flattering,' she said to Jack. 'I
thought I had quite delicate skin. I would have considered
myself tastier than any of you, to ravenous insects. The
mosquitoes feed on me enough.'

'It must have been something you put on your feet,' Jack
replied. 'No doubt you smeared them with some ointment
or other which repelled the creatures.'

'I don't remember putting anything on them.'

'What about something on the ground earlier? Did you
walk through any particular patch of grasses, or pools,
which might have left a residue on your feet?'

'None at all, that I remember.'

But it was Lidah, when they were alone, who provided
the answer.

'You were in Kaseteran, the kingdom of ghosts, where
they licked your feet, missy. That's why the ants would not
go up your legs. You have magic feet from the tongues of
the ghosts.'

That was possible, thought Harry. An invisible barrier
formed by the dried spittle of the ghosts. It was a disgusting thought, but this had saved her life. Rajah Hantuen
must have foreseen the future, knew the ants were goin‹
to descend upon the camp, and had provided her wi‹

protection. Had he chosen her for a reason, or was it just chance that they met on the banks of the river that night, when she had been led to Kaseteran?

It was all speculation, and the leisure of conjecture could not be wasted on wondering about what had passed. Any time she had for such a luxury was concerned with the future. It appeared to look somewhat better after this night. She had seen something in Jack's eyes that had not been there before. Her actions had aroused within the reserved and unemotional aristocrat some feelings of tenderness towards her. He had seen her real worth and had been vastly impressed. It might not yet be love, but Harry was ever hopeful that such feelings were not too far over the horizon.

Indeed, Jack came to her again, later in the day, before they broke camp.

'That was a splendid thing you did.'

'It was horrible,' she said, remembering her actions with distaste.

'Splendid because it was so horrible. You were completely unselfish. I've never met a woman like you, Harry.'

His eyes burned, fierce and bright, as he spoke the words.

'I – I, thank you, Jack. I'll take that as a compliment.'

Suddenly, Jack took her by the shoulders, one large hand on either side. He held her at arms length.

'Harry, I've never said this to another woman before, but I think – I think I would like us to have an *understanding*.'

Harry's head began to swim. What was Jack saying? That he loved her? That they should become engaged? That he wanted to marry her? What did he mean? It was unfortunate that he was always so vague when it came to things like this. In the past she thought she had recognized signals, only to discard her hopes on meeting him again at a later time. She felt dizzy.

Harry put her confused thoughts into words. 'What are you trying to tell me, Jack?'

'Oh, I can't be too precise at this moment, can I? We're in the middle of an expedition. I must remain single-minded, clear-headed. You must know what I mean about an *understanding*. We'll go into it more once we reach our journey's end.'

'Must I? I suppose I must.'

He laughed, delightedly.

'Can I take it that's a "Yes"?' he murmured.

'If you like . . .' She was still a little confused.

'Good. See you later then.'

He released her from his firm grip, without ever having held her in his arms, or kissed her. She revised her thoughts yet again. Perhaps he meant he wanted her as a companion, a secretary perhaps, a personal assistant? Someone close, but not too close, in an unromantic situation.

Kit Colenso now came to congratulate her on her act of courage.

'Well done,' Colenso said, somewhat gruffly. 'You acted where the men just stood around.'

'I'd rather forget it, you know. That poor man was being eaten alive.'

'Well, I feel rather ashamed. Still, you did have some special thing about you, which we did not. You had some sort of protection.'

'I suppose I must have,' she answered, not wishing to give anything away. She was sure he would ridicule her if she told him about Rajah Hantuen. 'I think it was a balm Jack gave me, which he purchased in Singapore.'

'Good old Jack,' muttered Colenso.

She bristled. Conversations with Kit Colenso always seemed to turn to quarrels. 'You don't like Jack very much do you, Mr Colenso?'

Kit Colenso shrugged. 'He's all right, but he has too much flamboyance for my taste. I have nothing against him. I would not choose him for a brother, but then I would not choose very many men for that.'

'Who would you choose, supposing you had a choice?' she asked, suddenly intrigued. She was thinking of the bishop in Natal, and whether he had any other brothers at home.

'Either of the Ngaju Dyaks who travel with me. They are both men of quiet reserve and strong loyalties. I would trust either of them with my life. They are noble men, without the need for a title to proclaim it to the world.'

'They didn't rush to save the man who was being eaten by the ants,' she retorted.

'If it had been me, or either one of them, they would not have hesitated,' Colenso snapped back.

She was unimpressed. 'So, they select whose life they save?'

'They would have been giving up their own lives to reach that man. He was not well known to them. If it had been a matter of simply *risking* life and limb, they would have helped him, but it was not. It was sheer suicide. A man should be prepared to throw away his life for his best friend or brother, but not foolishly abandon it for someone he hardly knows.

'You were really quite stupid to do what you did. You were not only tossing away your own life, but also those of Braiks and myself, for we could not have let you die without trying to save you. What would the rajah have thought of us then? You, and the two of us, were very, very fortunate. Without that balm you say you had rubbed into your feet, we should all be dead.'

'Stupid, was I?'

'Very,'

'Well then, Mr Colenso, we know what you think of me. Be so kind as to go and attend to your own affairs, if you please. I have things to do.'

He glared, shrugged his shoulders, then left her to it.

Rajah Starke paced the floor of his bungalow. There had been no word back from the expedition, which had been out many days. He had expected Harriet to be back by now, telling him how terrible it was in the jungle, and how glad she was to be home safe and sound. There was no sign of his cousin, and no messenger had arrived to inform Starke of the expedition's progress. Not that he had asked for one to be sent, because he had truly expected Harriet to return within a few days, or two weeks at the most.

He could not bear to think what his relatives and friends back in England would have to say about him, for letting Harriet go on this expedition, but that was the least of his worries. It was Harriet herself for whom he was most concerned. To think of her either in pain or distress made him moan audibly in despair. He loved her dearly, in his way, and he would never forgive himself if she failed to return.

Outside, the sun was shining, throwing down the harsh midday light it is wont to do in the tropics. The river was busy as usual, with trade and passenger vessels ploughing up and down its grey waters. Along the banks were merchants and fruit sellers, their wares adding bursts of colour to the dark green of the grass. Kuching, and indeed Sarawak and its neighbours, was flourishing now that pirate activity had been curbed.

The brigands were not gone altogether, of course. There were still pockets of them, at riverheads and on some of the islands, but their power base had been smashed and their effect on trade was small.

Similarly, Starke had little to concern him regarding the

Malay princes. The datus were not completely cowed, but if they plotted against him it was with fearful hearts. Starke knew they still pored over their books of poisons at midnight, and spent candlelight hours working out devious plans for his death and disposal, but for the moment their schemes remained at the theory stage, the princes having lost the courage to turn them into practice. They were, fortunately, very jealous of one another, as well as envying the rajah, so when such evil schemes were near fruition, they would inform on one another. Starke would call in the culprits and say sternly, 'I know what you're up to.' Bags would be packed, plotters would run off for a while to Brunei or Sabah, and everything would go quiet again.

One of the datus was an elderly man by the name of Issam, who was known as the bomoh prince. He was supposed to be a sorcerer and a soothsayer, hence his nickname. Issam was not one of those who regularly conspired against the rajah. He was an old man, a respected one, and he had no use for rulership. Life, the bomoh prince said, was complicated enough without grasping for the last straw of power. Rajah Starke suddenly decided to send for this man and speak with him.

Prince Issam arrived at midnight. He was a tall man for a Malay, and could look Rajah Starke directly in the eyes. There was a stately air about Prince Issam which impressed Starke. All the princes were of course raised in the belief that they were special, privileged people with a right to a stab at kingship, but their bearing was often spoiled by the petulance and sullenness which revealed their jealous, greedy souls. Prince Issam showed none of this brooding nature. He was respected by all who knew him for his honour and integrity.

'Rajah,' he said, 'Muda Hassim said you wished to speak to me.'

Starke, who had been roused from his bed, stared at the prince.

'I asked for you at midday. This is midnight.'

Issam was not at all put out by this statement.

'I imagined that there would be only one reason why you would wish to see an old man like me. You have heard of my powers as a bomoh and wish me to use them for your purposes. If these skills are to be employed, it is best to use them at the magical hour. No one takes a sorcerer seriously when the sun is shining and the birds are singing. We need the right atmosphere, the right vibrations, and the middle of the night is the time when such things are at their best and darkest.'

The prince walked over to the French doors and flung them open, startling the guards on the verandah.

'Look at the stars,' said Issam, staring up at a sky which can only be found in the tropics, 'how they encrust the blackness of the night.'

He turned to face the disturbed rajah. 'You have a bright star missing from your life and you wish to know how she is faring – is that not so?'

'I feel a little vulnerable standing here in my nightshirt,' said the tousled-haired rajah. 'Do you mind if I change into some suitable clothes.'

'As you wish,' murmured the prince, who was wearing a long black gown and white silk turban. 'I shall make myself as comfortable as I am able on your English furniture.'

When the rajah arrived back in the room, a few minutes later, the bomoh was squatting on the carpet.

'I'm afraid I prefer it down here after all,' he said. 'I find your sofa too lumpy for my old bones.'

'At least let me get you a cushion.'

'No, no, your carpets are quite thick. Now, let us get down to business . . .'

'Look,' said Starke, interrupting the elderly prince. He squatted down on the carpet opposite the old man. 'I admit I did think of asking your advice, but I'm not sure I approve of all this wizardry – the black arts as we call them.'

'Ah, you don't say you don't *believe* in them, just that you don't *approve* of them?'

'Well, you spoke of atmospheres when you first came in. I am sure we are all influenced by such things. The human mind is just as capable of delving into the paranormal, as it is into the secrets of mathematics and science. I believe the mind to be infinite in its resources. Given the right conditions, the right owner, it can do things undreamed of by unimaginative men.'

As he was speaking, the rajah was aware that his Dyak guards had moved away from the house, on to the vast lawns which surrounded the bungalow. He knew the presence of the prince disturbed them. They were as frightened of magic as they were fascinated by it. They had no trouble whatsoever in believing that it existed and they were men of intelligence. An unbelieving westerner was tolerated for his scepticism, but he was regarded as a fool.

'Do you wish to know about your cousin's welfare, or not?'

Starke swallowed any remnants of incredulity and nodded hard.

'Yes, please tell me if she still alive and well.'

The wind blew the chiffon curtains. They were like flimsy ghosts dancing on the edge of the room. From garden, rainforest and river, the scents and sounds of the night outside were carried into the living-room. Perfumes of blossoms, the sound of tree frogs and crickets, the half-light and the brilliance of the stars framed by the doorway, all went towards enhancing the atmosphere in the room. Starke knew that he was about to experience his first taste of Oriental magic.

Issam said, 'You must not mind my accoutrements.'

He produced a small skull, perhaps that of a monkey, and placed it on his right hand. On his left was a carved wooden bowl, filled with tiny bones and the heads of dried flowers. In between these items he placed a copper mirror, highly burnished, so that Starke could see reflections of the ceiling on its polished surface. There was no frame around the mirror, but its edges were etched with strange symbols, which appeared to shimmer like the heat waves of a mirage on hot sands.

Issam began chanting. Starke could speak both Malay and several Dyak tribal dialects, but he could not understand the language which came from the mouth of this royal bomoh. He felt his skin prickling at the sound, which he guessed was like no other tongue on the face of the earth. From its rhythms it sounded like a litany, but he knew there were no responses required from him, nor was he able to give any. As he listened, sometimes staring into the bomoh's eyes, sometimes down at the copper mirror, the wall of the room began to recede.

Starke was not too frightened by this. He knew that the prince had gone into a trance and that he himself had followed into that same vague area between reality and illusion. The two of them were now floating, drifting on the carpet, which had no solid floor beneath it. They existed, it seemed, in a half-lit netherworld, with no boundaries. Then, as he watched in wonder, he found they were in a courtyard, white in the gentle moonlight, with founts falling on all sides. It appeared they had been transported to another garden, somewhere in time and space, woven from the words which still flowed from Issam's lips.

The bomoh reached forward and lifted the copper mirror, holding it up before the rajah. At first he saw only his own reflection, but his features wavered and changed, and soon he was staring at Harry. She was moving around a rainforest camp, looking reasonably healthy. He watched as she went to a pot hanging over a fire and filled a wooden bowl with some soup. This she took to an ill-looking Kit Colenso, who had to be propped up by a Dyak servant, in order to be spoonfed by the rajah's cousin.

'She is well,' he said, relieved. 'Harry is well.'

In that instant the courtyard shimmered violently and Starke found himself whisked through the half-light, back into the room where he had begun his journey.

'You should not have spoken,' said Issam, gathering up the tools of his trade. 'I should have warned you not to speak.'

'I broke the trance?'

'You ruined the spell. But I think it does not matter too much. You saw your cousin, just as I did. She seems to be coping with life in the jungle better than some of the men who took her there.'

'Colenso, I am told, suffers from recurring malaria.'

'It is so.'

Starke sighed. 'Well, if the mirror is to be believed – and I am perfectly prepared to believe it, even though there is a strong possibility that it might be hypnostism – it does not appear she is going to return as quickly as I had hoped.'

'I have no reason to hypnotize you into thinking your cousin is alive and well.'

'That is true of course. You have nothing to gain.'

The prince stood up and prepared to leave.

'If you wish to follow your cousin's progress, please do not hesitate to call on me again.'

Starke nodded. 'Tell me,' he said, after a little more thought, 'how is the expedition itself faring, generally? Do you know? Have you followed them with your farseeing mind?'

The bomoh said, 'There are two expeditions. You are

aware of this. Both are under the scrutiny of the rainforest gods. Both are being harassed, with obstacles being placed in their path by the supernatural elements of the jungle. Men are falling foul of these deities and are dying because of it. Had they been scientific expeditions, I doubt the gods would have showed themselves. But science is not the object. These men are out to discover one of the secrets of the Otherworld. They have to expect interference from beings of that world.'

'But why would the rainforest gods – and the mystic beings who come under their rule – wish to prevent such expeditions from reaching their goal?'

'I can think of a number of reasons, but mainly it comes down to two.

'Firstly, this has become a quest, and no quest should be expected to be made easy by the gods. The rewards for success of such expeditions are very great indeed, therefore the path to those riches must be made extremely difficult. Such quests must improve the spirit and the mind, as well as the purse. There is no spiritual gain, no mental progress, if the path to the goal is without pain and sacrifice. The greater the treasure, the greater the problems and obstacles on the way.

'Secondly, the gods do not like incursions into their domain, by strangers who do not fully understand its ways, nor believe in their existence. They are naturally going to be out of humour with those ignorant of their culture.

'If these reasons are not enough, it must be remembered that, as with humans, the gods do things for sport. To scatter impediments in the path of men hacking and blundering their way through the greenery, unlike the natives who trip lightly through the lacework of shadows and sunlight, is a game that is played by gods and preternatural creatures of the forest alike.'

Rajah Starke nodded. 'Do you think they stand a chance of coming back alive – all of them?'

'Not all of them. Some have already died. It depends on whether they learn as they progress.'

After the bomoh prince had gone, Starke sat in his study and brooded. Harriet was fine and well, if the copper plate was to be believed. He did believe it because he now felt it in his heart. A great weight had been lifted from him and he was able to concentrate on matters other than the welfare of his cousin. However, everything in the garden was not rosy. She was still many miles from home, going deeper into the Borneo rainforest with every day, and the likelihood of her falling ill, or being bitten by a poisonous snake, or cracking her head on a rock in some remote rapids, was still a possibility.

He had to hope and pray that she continued as she was, in good health and with her strength of spirit intact.

**3**

Kit Colenso had a form of recurring malaria, given to him by the African mosquito, which, as its name implied, revisited him from time to time. He had it now, during a short stay by a quite beautiful waterfall where the monitor lizards worshipped the sun like jewelled kings, laying their yard-long bodies out on dry rocks. There were fresh-water turtles gliding through the pool beneath the falls, which had attracted the party and persuaded them to pause in their journey. Turtles were a good source of food for such a large group.

Also, around the waterfall, there were clouds of butterflies. Singapore Jack wished to catch a number of these and classify them. A particularly wonderful specimen – large, emerald-green and black, with a peculiar wing shape not seen before – he called the 'Rajah Starke'. He also discovered several new types of rhododendron, one of which he called 'Harriet'. Two of the Dyaks returned after a hunt and reported seeing a rhinoceros. Jack immediately set out after this creature, but failed to locate it.

While Singapore Jack was busy with his naturalist duties,

Colenso was sweating and shivering it out under the shade of a bivouac. Harry herself was suffering from a mild form of dysentery, but she saw that Kit Colenso was in a much worse state than anyone else in the camp and felt it incumbent upon her to nurse him. He shivered violently and overheated by turns.

All she could really do for him was provide cold compresses when he was hot, and a blanket when he was cold. She was slightly resented by the two Ngajus, but they saw she was not to be prised from what she saw to be her duty and eventually accepted her presence.

Kit Colenso did not know her. He stared up into her face and called her a number of different names during the time she nursed him. Women he had known, she supposed. Perhaps one might even have been the wife he had hinted at. Sometimes he looked at her softly with his feverish eyes, and spoke to her lovingly. At other times he seemed angry, accusing her of various things. Nothing really serious. Things like forgetting to wake him for a hunt, or for not putting enough honey on his porridge. She guessed he was, in those cases, a youth or child and berating his mother or sister for these terrible crimes.

One night he was tossing and turning, muttering in his sleep. He was having the sweats and there was no cool water to hand. Harry picked up a bamboo pitcher. The Dyaks fashioned these at each stop, throwing them away when they vacated the site. It took them but a few minutes to produce a few jugs, cups and pitchers out of bamboo stalks several inches in diameter. Harry then walked down, through the sleeping bodies of the men, past the guard, to the water's edge.

In the night she could see the eyes of tree and grass spiders, luminous in the starlight, glittering from under root and leaf. She knew that if she lifted one of those large succulent leaves which lapped like tongues around her feet, it would be covered in enormous hairy spiders. They were so numerous and ubiquitous they no longer bothered her. Had she been a little girl again she would have seen the twinkling eyes as belonging to garden fairies.

She filled the pitcher then turned to go back. In the starlight, however, she saw that a smooth trunk of a tree had fallen across the path. Trees were always falling in the rainforest. It was one of the most dangerous aspects about the place. They were the equivalent of fast horse-drawn coaches back in Britain. Walking under unsafe trees or crossing a busy highway were similar exercises. What surprised her about this tree was that she had not heard it come down. Usually there was a crashing of branches, as it tore down boughs of other giants, on its way to earth.

This particular tree was about as thick as her own torso, with dark markings. She shrugged and was preparing to step over it, when she noticed with some consternation that it was moving along the ground, very slowly. A tingling went through her body and the hair on her scalp itched with alarm.

She stepped back, her heart beginning to pound, as she realized that what lay across the path before her was a reticulated python. It was a monstrous reptile and she did not wonder that Borneo people believed in dragons. Slowly, slowly it slid across the path, its head and tail hidden in the foliage on either side. Once its tail did appear, then disappeared again on the other side of the path, and it was finally completely back in the undergrowth, she guessed it had been over thirty feet long. It was a long while before she was able to make her feet move from the spot where she was standing.

When she got back to the bivouac her lamp was out.

Patiently she relit it, only to find Kit Colenso staring up at her in what appeared to be full comprehension.

'You look as if you've seen a ghost,' he said.

She nodded. 'I've seen ghosts already on this trip, but tonight was worse. I saw a python as long as a river.'

He tried to sit up but found himself too weak and had to remain on his elbows for a minute, before falling back.

'You have a tendency to exaggerate,' he told her, after a while. 'Everything that comes out of your mouth is an hyperbole.'

'I saw the snake, you did not,' she replied firmly. 'If you would like to go looking for it to prove me wrong, you have my permission. If not you must accept what I say or be regarded as no gentleman, for you might as well call me a liar.'

He snorted in derision, but said nothing further.

She applied a cold compress to his head, but it was obvious that he was improving rapidly without such aids. It was around three o'clock in the morning and the rainforest was at its coolest and quietest. The waterfall could be clearly heard above the sound of frogs and crickets, which added to the impression of coolness within the glade. Occasionally, some nearby monkeys would squabble for a minute or two, but on the whole it was a good time of day to begin a recovery.

'I think you're getting better,' she told him. 'I shall leave you to your Dyak friends. They rather resented my presence in the first place.'

'You mustn't mind them. They're used to looking after me and get a little jealous.'

'Oh, I realize that.'

He stared at her in the lamplight.

'Stay a while,' he murmured. 'You look positively beautiful to me at the moment.'

She laughed a little. 'You mean, you've had a brush with death, so any woman would look lovely.'

'No,' he said seriously. 'Perhaps it's the lamplight, or the stars behind your head? It doesn't matter. It may be the soft tone of your voice and the way your hair falls over your brow. I have known so few women in my life. I have difficulty in talking to them, as I'm speaking to you now.'

'I'll take that as a compliment, but I have to tell you I don't believe it. While you were feverish you imagined I was any number of women. I think you've known quite a few.'

One of the Dyaks, Patan, came by and put some sago porridge on the fire to boil. He had seen his friend was now over the fever and it was time to feed him. Harry took this as a hint to go away, but she was still curious about certain aspects of Kit Colenso's life, and this was the closest she had been to the man since she had met him. There might not be another opportunity for the two of them to talk in the way they were now doing. She liked to get to the heart of people.

'You mean I thought you were . . .'

'You believed I was your mother, your sister, and certain other ladies. At one point I think you believed I was – was your wife.'

'My dead wife.'

He said it so plainly and dully the words seemed to swing at her ear like a lead plumb bob on the end of a line.

'Yes – I do believe so.'

He laughed out loud, huskily, and she thought he was making fun of her. What was it she had said that was so stupid? He was turning into the man she detested again.

'I really did – you should not be so coarse with your humour, sir.'

He turned the laughter to a chuckle. 'I'm sorry, but you see, my wife was as black and shiny as jet. You are absolutely nothing like her. How could I confuse the two of you? Ithuka

was a Bantu woman, with tight black curls, big dark eyes
and skin the colour of wet slate. You have nothing in common with her, you with your ivory skin and red lips.'

'I don't know how, but you did.'

He stared at her with lively eyes, trying to make her see
the funny side of it, but she refused to do so.

'Oh, don't look so hurt,' he said. 'If I did confuse you
with Ithuka you should be quite pleased, for she really was
a beautiful woman, in every way. She was lithe and supple
and she danced as if her bones were made of willow wands.
Her complexion was like satin and her teeth as white as
bone china. Though her hands should have been rough,
with all the work she did, they were as smooth and soft as
leopard fur. And she had a good sense of fun.'

'Which I do not?'

'You seem to take everything so seriously.'

In spite of herself she found she was flattered by his
remarks. If this woman, who sounded like some dark
Cleopatra of the Bantu world, was so beautiful, then to be
compared with her was indeed a great compliment.

'Did you leave her behind, when you left Africa?'

He looked so shocked at this question she wanted to bite
her tongue immediately. She knew at once she had committed, in his eyes, a terrible sin.

'I'm sorry,' she murmured, miserably, going to a nearby
fire and stirring it with a stick. 'You said your wife was
dead, didn't you? I don't know what I meant by that. I'm not
very wise in the ways of men, you know, despite my pretence
at worldliness. I have known too few of them in my time and
my judgement is impaired. I know there are men who marry
Oriental women, then leave them behind in Hong Kong and
Siam, and places like that, when they go back to Britain. I
thought – I thought . . .' But she knew that if she finished
that sentence she would compound her felony.

'You thought I might be one of those men?'

'Oh, I don't know – why do you always make me feel so awkward?'

He was quiet for a while, staring up at the stars.

'Yes, it is my fault,' he said. 'You know nothing of me and why should you? In fact I loved my wife very much. I would never have taken her to England, but not because I would have been ashamed of her. Because there she would not have been treated well by other members of my class. In any case, the place would have made her miserable, with its cold winters and drizzle and grey skies. She was Africa, Ithuka. In Britain she would have curled up in a ball and shut out the world.'

'What happened to her?'

'She was killed in an elephant stampede. The kraal where we lived at the time was surrounded by a thorn fence, but it was not strong enough to keep out the larger beasts. Rhinos and elephants, if they are going somewhere, are very difficult to deter. They came crashing through the kraal and she fell under the feet of a big bull. I shot him dead, a few minutes later. I never ever shot another elephant.'

'You miss her.'

It was not a question, but he took it as one. 'Of course I miss her. I miss her like the very devil. But that was some time ago. I'm a different man, in a different country. You know how it is.'

But she did not know how it was and, when she could, she crept away from the bivouac and went to lie down. Her feelings were akin to those of a woman who has been to church and has been unjustly harangued from the pulpit. Once on her sapling-sprung bed, she lay there with her mind reeling. Luckily, she could not remain awake for long, and fell into a deep sleep. All her troubles slipped from her in her unconscious state.

She slept for at least six hours. In the morning she was woken by Jack, who gave her something to drink and then said they should be on their way.

'Colenso seems to have recovered, thanks to you. You make a very fine nurse, Harry. Very fine.'

'Thank you, Jack.'

'Your face is dirty,' he said pleasantly, and smiled.

'Is it? I've forgotten what it's like to be really clean. I could do with a bath.'

'Why don't you go and bathe in the waterfall pool. I'll keep the men away. Go and have a jolly good splash around. Do your hair.'

'Does it look such a mess?' she asked, ruefully.

'It looks fine, but I know women like to wash their hair a lot.'

She was grateful for this opportunity, not just to cleanse herself from top to bottom, but to be away from men. Whether or not it was *safe* to be alone did not cross her mind. She was just fed up with being in the company of men, whoever they were. Lidah could bathe with her and the two of them could chatter without Harry being worried about whether she was saying something the men would regard as silly.

While they were bathing, a large red-haired creature came to feed on ginger stems, figs, durians and anything else she could get in the nearby trees. It was an orang-utan mother, with an infant clinging to its red fur. A crashing higher up in the trees revealed a fully adult male complete with cheek pads and throat sac, swinging leisurely from branch to branch. This creature was massive. Harry guessed he was somewhere near or above two hundred pounds in weight. He was like a broad red fire in the sunlight, long-haired, shaggy, and limber.

'Don't worry, missy,' whispered Lidah. 'He won't hurt us.'

The orang-utan mother, just above their heads, was raining pink and white petals into the pool, as she fed on the fruit and mast. She did not seem to have anything to do with the male, who may or may not have been the father of her infant. They seemed uninterested in one another. She looked down, from a short height above Harry, and suddenly stared into the woman's eyes. Harry felt a thrill go through her as their eyes locked.

We're just two females crossing paths in the vast rainforest, thought Harry. Deep down, we know one another as well as any two creatures can.

Then the mother swung past, long arm over long arm, her baby hanging on for grim death. It looked painfully thin next to its mother, but it would appear to be not long born and had yet to put flesh on to its skeleton.

When the male passed overhead, bending a tree with his weight, Harry could see he had deep gashes in his leathery shoulder. He had been fighting, probably with another male orang-utan. A bigger one, since this ape appeared to have suffered several wounds.

Then the visitors were gone, off up into the canopy, drifting their separate ways in a yellow-fire sunset. Harry somehow felt fulfilled. This chance meeting between two sets of naked beings had instilled in her an appreciation of the Borneo rainforest and its myriad diverse lifeforms. The apes had been beautiful, in their way, and Harry had been privileged to witness their passing. An inspiring moment amongst many difficult and tedious moments on a hard journey through the rainforest.

They had a fine bathe, the pair of them, and managed to return to the camp sparkling, ready for the next phase of the long journey into the Ulu

# PART FIVE

# Kingdom in the Sky

# 1

Baldwin, one of Keller's party, had refused to sleep up in the trees. He had become a ship's cook when he was nineteen, not because he had a calling for the work, but because he had dizzy spells and was likely to fall from the rigging. When Keller's party came to the edge of a swampland, which seemed to stretch out for ever in front of them, Baldwin had categorically refused to sleep up in the walkways that some tree-top clan had erected in the canopy. They were more than just walkways really.

These catwalks formed a network of paths high up in the trees. There was evidence that people lived there on a semipermanent basis. The group could see houses built of rattan, and walled and thatched with sago palm leaves, some 150 feet off the ground. These had a lacework of dizzying ladders going up to them from the mossy earth beneath. Keller shook his head in amazement at this new sight.

'Why would the beggars want to live up there?' he asked Raki. 'What's the point? Protection from other clans?'

'They can see mountains, and forest birds, and maybe waterfall from their window. They move close to the sky, tuan. And safe from sorcerer there. Everyone knows the sorcerer not like to climb up high. Sorcerer hate ladder to lofty place.'

'Is that a fact? You must be a sorcerer, Baldwin.'

'I'll come up there when we cross it in the morning,' Baldwin promised, 'but I can't sleep there. It'd be like sleepin' in the crow's nest. I'd be afeared of fallin' out of my cot in the night and droppin' to the ground.'

So Baldwin alone remained on the ground, sleeping on the edge of the swamp in a nest of his own making. He never woke in the morning. They found him with nearly a dozen giant leeches – horrible pale creatures each a foot long and distended to balloon-like proportions with Baldwin's blood – having been sucked dry in his sleep. Several ringed his neck like some grotesque wobbly Elizabethan ruff. Others had fastened themselves to the arteries inside his thighs, around his crotch. He had not felt a thing, simply having fallen asleep and been drained of blood gradually as the night passed, leaving a shrivelled husk for the morning light to show.

Standing in the low drifting mists of the marshland, Keller looked down with disgust on the shrunken corpse. One of the leech late-comers to the body, not yet fully satisfied with its quota of blood, reared towards the body heat it could feel coming from Keller. Keller swiped at it with a parang. The leech burst and covered the corpse of Baldwin with his own blood.

Johnson, standing by him, shivered. The seaman stared at his former shipmate's body. The eyes now protruded from the skull, stretching through the lids. Sunken cheeks and bared teeth gave the face a death's-head appearance. Limbs had collapsed in on themselves and the ribs showed stark through the cotton shirt. Baldwin was a ghastly parody of a man, a scarecrow, a corpse dredged up from a forgotten grave.

'Them's monsters, they are, Keller. Look at the ugly brutes. They sucked old Baldy dry, they did.' Johnson suddenly lashed out with a boot, in anger and distaste, splattering another of the bloated creatures. Blood splashed on boots and canvas pants. 'What kind of country is this?' he yelled, the revulsion and fear evident in his voice. 'Things just come up out of nowhere and drain you dry.'

'It's these damn swamps,' said Keller. 'You won't get these monsters all over the place. We'll just have to stick to the trees.'

'They'll be snakes up there,' warned Johnson. He buttoned his shirt at the neck and sleeves as if it were armour able to keep out these horrible intruders. 'I saw a green whip-snake when I woke this morning. This is a godforsaken place, Keller. I've a mind to go back to civilization, where things is normal.'

Keller's eyes narrowed. 'And how are you going to get there?'

'You could lend me one of the Dyaks,' Johnson said, hopefully.

'No Dyaks. They all stay with me. I need 'em. You want to go back, you go. I'm likely to shoot you, though, if you try. I need all the men I've got, including you. I never thought you'd turn against me, Johnson, after all we've been through.'

Johnson whined, 'I'm not turnin' against you, Keller. It's just this place. It's as spooky as hell. I think I'm goin' mad. We're all sick – all of us, even you. Everybody's got that grey fungus growing atween their legs, under their arms. It goes red raw when you try to scrape it off. Chivers's got some kind of gut worm, that's eatin' faster than he can get his food down. It must be longer'n a snake curled round inside his stomick, 'cause he looks like a skeletin.

'There's these damn leeches, every day, wantin' to suck us

all as dry as Baldwin here. There's bees an' hornets, that sting you without a by-your-leave. Mosquitoes? They're bigger than bloody birds in this place. I tell you, it's driving us all crazy. If it wasn't for the money . . .'

'Riches, beyond our wildest dreams, Johnson. You think that kind of money comes easy? We have to make sacrifices for it. Yes, some of us ain't going back. Some of us will die in here. But them that don't will be rich. We're going to find them heads, an' that's flat.'

Johnson, seeing it was useless to argue with Keller, started back up the vine ladder to the walkways above. He was afraid of the unpredictable and savage Keller. Johnson knew he was as likely to lose his blood through a cut throat in the middle of the night as he was to giant leeches.

Keller, on the other hand, had not been completely telling the truth. He *was* afraid of dying in this green abyss of swamps, malaria, orang-utans and crocodiles. It filled him with terror to think that his soul would be set adrift in this dank and sweaty tangle of vegetation. Keller was a firm believer in an afterlife. He did not so much mind going to hell, but he wanted it to be a Christian hell, not some weird native idea of one. Keller was not so sure his soul could find its way out of this dark forested island to an English afterworld.

Keller would never tell Johnson about such things, however, for he was man who kept his weaknesses close to himself.

'Please, tuan,' said a voice near him, as he began to gather up the equipment, 'can you tell me the kiblah?'

It was Budrudeen. Every day the young Moslem boy came to Keller with the same question. Keller was the only member of the party with a compass. Being unable to see the sun through the canopy, Budrudeen needed to know the direction in which to pray, the direction of Mecca. Keller would consult his compass, cupped in his hand and out of Budrudeen's sight, and would point this way, or that way, and leave the young man to genuflect.

'That way,' said Keller, arm outstretched. 'Dead on north-west.'

Budrudeen looked puzzled.

'What's the matter?' asked Keller.

'We've been walking in that direction and since we're going south . . .'

'You know as well as I do, boy, that you can't walk through the jungle in a straight line. The path twists and turns, first this way, then that way. I expect we walk towards all the points of the compass at some time during the day.'

'Oh – oh, yes – I understand.'

Keller smiled when Budrudeen went down on his knees and began muttering his prayers, working through the prayer beads which he wore as a necklace. Verses of the Koran drifted out over the mist-covered swamp. The Dyaks had long since ceased to be curious about Budrudeen's prayers, but the Europeans were always fascinated. They wondered why the Malay youth did not get struck by lightning, or become the victim of some other accident of God, for Keller always gave him the *wrong* direction.

Some days Keller had pointed to the bearing opposite to the one required by the boy, so that Budrudeen had his back towards the holy city. It was one of Keller's running jokes, to entertain his men on the long hard journey. They grinned and nodded, as the absorbed young man intoned his prayers, completely unaware of the ugly jest. Mayok saw how Keller's friends giggled and nudged each other at such times, but he was not familiar enough with their culture to make sense of it all. He thought they were amused simply because Budrudeen took his prayers seriously.

After Budrudeen's prayers, the group set out along the swaying walkways, held up by thick vines and strips of bark, high above the swampland. Twin-barred snakes and paradise snakes glided from tree to tree as they were disturbed by the men. Flying foxes dropped from fruit trees and flapped their leathern wings on the party's approach. Forest eagles swerved through the canopy and eyed the hunters suspiciously. There was as much life amongst the branches of the rainforest as below it, especially if you counted the ubiquitous monkeys.

At noon Keller was out in front, crossing one of the enormous swaying bridges, when he saw shadowy figures ahead. These mysterious-looking people must have been the owners of the walkways in the sky. Going closer, Keller noticed they were carrying shields and spears. They appeared hostile, shouting at him and his party, waving parangs. He called up his Iban.

'What do they want, Raki? Do you know 'em?'

'I do not know the name of this tribe, tuan.'

One of the intruders had now ventured forward, yelling and dancing, brandishing his weapons. He was quite an elderly warrior, but his muscles stood out in ridges on his legs and arms. His limbs and shoulders were covered with blue tattoos. On his head was a hornbill-feather war bonnet and hanging from his back was a cloak of long-haired monkey fur. An abalone shell, its mother-of-pearl interior shining in the midday light, hung from his neck.

'What's he sayin', Raki – can you make it out?'

'Yes, tuan. Though this is not my language it is very like the speaking of the Ukit, which I know. This man is challenging you to fight him. He says he will take your ball-holder,' here Raki pointed to Keller's scrotum, 'as purse for his wife's beads. He says, from the colour of your hair your mother was an orang-utan and your father was a bearded hog. He calls you a girl. He says he will take the skin from your back and make himself jacket, using your hair as a lace for his buttons . . .'

'I think he's said enough,' muttered Keller. The seaman loaded his weapon with dry powder from a jar and rammed a ball home with the rod in less than twenty seconds. He then levelled his musket at the figure prancing before him.

Raki put a hand on the stock of the firelock.

'No, tuan,' said the Iban, quietly. 'You must fight this man one against one, with parang or maybe knife. If you do not, you will have to kill all his tribe. They make big war against us. They fight us until they all die.'

Keller, at first annoyed with Raki, but then seeing the point he had to make, lowered the musket.

'You mean single combat? If I beat him, will they let us go through?'

'Maybe they send one or two more warriors for same, but they not start us a big war with them.'

Keller was loath to risk single combat, but he saw no other way out of it. He told Johnson and Blake what he was going to do. They informed him he was mad and why not send one of the Dyaks in, rather than go himself.

'It was me he insulted,' snarled Keller. 'I'm the one to sort him out. Raki,' he added, turning to the Iban, 'tell that son of a river leech that I'm going to cut out his eyes and eat them in just a short while. Tell him he is less than the slime which sticks to turtle shit. Oh, and say his mother mated with a cockroach when his father was out hunting and then gave birth to something that crawled in moonrat dung.'

Raki took great delight in yelling these insults back at the warrior waiting on the end of the bridge. The tribesman screeched. He had been affronted by a worm. He had been insulted by a slug. It was time to exact revenge for such a verbal attack. The warrior invited Keller to meet him at the halfway point between their two positions. In order to confirm this invitation the Dyak moved to the middle of the bridge.

His friends stayed where they were, amongst the tree tops at the other end of the walkway.

Keller, now stripped to the waist, drew a parang from his belt and marched towards the elderly warrior.

There was not much room to manoeuvre on the walkway. The two figures stood off from one another at first. Keller looked down through the flimsy bamboos slats which made the floor and sides of the bridge. Far below was a waterway forcing a path amongst some boulders. If either man fell, there would be no soft landing. But Keller was used to fighting in the rigging of a ship. This was his home territory. And his adversary was not looking at all confident.

The Dyak stared at his opponent, whom he had taken to be a tree demon when he had first issued his challenge. He had not expected this strange creature with its leech-pale skin to take him at his word. Demons were supposed to disappear like a puff of smoke when they were confronted with the threat of earthly battle. Now there was no choice but to fight this offspring of orang-utan, whose chest grew the same colour hair as his head. What sorcery was this, which sent such a creature against him? And there seemed to be more of them, waiting on the other side, with skins just as sickly-white. The Santang Sisters were surely testing his courage and that of his tribe.

'What are you looking at, you painted savage?' growled Keller. 'Come on, let's have you.'

To the warrior these words were just the grunts and growls of a demon. They meant nothing. He fidgeted with his sword, wondering whether to make the first swing. He was a warrior who owned five heads. Once upon a time he had been the tribe's champion, but he knew those days were past. Still, this big man-of-the-forest before him looked to be flesh and blood. Flesh will cut and blood will flow. If he was of this world, this fungus-coloured man, then he would die as any other.

'Arrrghhh!' With his short sword the warrior suddenly lunged at Keller from behind his shield. It went through the flesh of Keller's abdomen, just above the hip, and struck bone. The walkway rocked violently with the attack. It continued to do so, as the triumphant tribesman attempted to retrieve his weapon. But the sword point was stuck in Keller's pelvis. Keller ground his teeth as waves of sickening pain swept through him.

The seaman staggered forward instinctively and gripped the top part of the warrior's shield to wrench it downwards. This exposed the man's head and chest. Keller swung at him with the parang. But the old man was wiry and agile and he dodged the blow. He danced away on his bare feet. Keller's next wild cut sliced through the bamboo wall of the walkway. A gap appeared. Keller could see a rocky torrent below. Seeing this drop, the Dyak jumped back from the edge instinctively.

Keller's wound was pouring blood and he felt giddy. Nevertheless, he took advantage of this momentary distraction on the part of his foe. Keller had the benefit of heavy seaman's boots. He raked his right boot heel down on the leg of the warrior, driving the kneecap down the shin bone. The old man screamed in agony and let go of his sword. Keller then struck with the parang at his opponent's head. He missed, but the blow fell on the man's shoulder, between the collar bone and neck. An artery was severed, the blood spurting sideways.

The tribesman now fell to the floor, writhing and convulsing. Keller gripped the edge of the bridge to support himself and trampled on his victim with his boots. The walkway swayed, this way and that, with the violence of the kicks and stamps. Soon it was obvious that the Dyak warrior was a dead man and Keller, veteran of many tavern fights, stepped back, breathing heavily. He gripped the sword in his side and wrenched it free, tossing the weapon over the edge of the walkway. It fell, spinning like a sycamore leaf, to the marshy floor of the rainforest below.

'Bastard!' he growled at the dead twisted body, while gripping his weeping wound. 'You nearly had me there.'

As Keller spoke the words, there was the sound of swift wings. Something swept close to Keller's chest, fell on the corpse, and then took off again. It was so fast, Keller had only time to glimpse what he believed to be the shadow of a hawk. It left with something in its claws. After it had gone, Keller wondered whether he had been seeing things. Perhaps his loss of blood was making him faint and liable to visions?

He staunched the flow of blood from his side with his fingers. Then he was aware that Raki was yelling at him.

'Head – take his head.'

Keller saw that other warriors of his adversary's tribe were clustering at the far end, probably wondering whether to try an attack. He let go of his side, grasped the warrior's head by the hair and chopped through the neck with two swift strikes. Then he held the severed head up by the hair and shook it at the warriors milling under the tree tops.

'Here he is!' cried Keller. 'He's mine! I took him fair and square. You want some more of me? Come on, let's have you. I'll chop off all your bloody heads . . .'

Keller put the head down and picked up the body. He threw it over the side of the walkway. It plummeted to earth, splatting on the rocks below. Within a few minutes insects were settling on the gory stump of the neck. Keller left the head on the slats of the bridge. He knew that he was supposed to keep this part of the warrior's body.

There was a muttering and murmuring amongst the attacking tribe, who finally melted into the tree tops, leaving the way clear.

Raki came to offer his congratulations to Keller. The Iban was always impressed by good fighting men. Keller was not someone Raki would have chosen for a friend, but the Englishman undoubtedly had great courage. It was not easy to face a man in single combat. Those who were able to do so were to be praised and admired. Raki picked up the severed head and put it into a sack, which he tied to his waist.

'I look after trophy,' he told Keller, who was having his wound bound by Johnson. 'I give you later.'

The party continued their progress through the tree tops, hoping to get beyond the marsh country by nightfall. Keller and his men felt vulnerable up in the canopy. Keller had been lucky to win his fight with the Dyak warrior. Next time it might be different. This tree-top tribe obviously knew their territory better than the visitors, even though the seamen were quite at home several dozen feet above solid ground.

Evening came in with a great flow of redness, like a tide of blood across the sky. They saw a bearded hog wandering the marshes below the trees and managed to shoot it from the walkway. The pig provided them with much needed meat. Johnson went down with two Dyaks to bring up the hog. While down there he filled the goatskin containers with water and drank directly from a narrow stream. When he came up they asked him where he had got his whiskers. Johnson did not know what they were talking about until he felt his lips. He had thread leeches hanging from all around his mouth.

'You look like a bloody walrus, Johnson,' cried Blake,

laughing like a madman. 'If I throw you a fish or two, will you catch 'em and oink?'

Johnson glowered, removing the leeches one by one with a pair of twigs, so as not to get them stuck to his fingers.

Later, Raki spoke quietly with Keller, as they roasted the boar meat on some stones they had gathered from below.

'How is your wound?' asked Raki. 'I put some leaves on it in a minute.'

Keller knew that Raki was familiar with basir ways. The Iban always carried certain herbs, which he would apply to wounds, rashes and sores of various kinds. Keller appreciated this kind of attention. Men did not usually bother with his welfare. Raki was quickly becoming the closest thing to a friend that Keller would ever know.

'Thanks,' he said, gruffly. Then he remembered the strange phenomenon which had occurred just after he had killed the Dyak warrior. 'Listen, Raki. I saw something after I topped that bugger out on the bridge . . .'

Raki looked up quickly, and nodded. 'I see it too.'

'What did you see? What was it?'

'I see fleeting shadow drop on to dead man. Quick, quick, then it fly away. It is Antang, hawk of Mahatara. Spirit of warrior not quick enough to hide from Antang, because he have fight you. Warrior think you demon. Is make slow. Not quick enough to hide from Antang. Antang rip out dead man's spirit from his breast and take it to God.'

'Is that what you think happens?'

'Yes – God sends his hawk for the soul.'

And what does this – who? Matahara – what does he do with a man's spirit?'

'Mah-at-ara. He is divine god of all things. He eat souls for his food. He send hawk, like man uses hawk for hunting, to snatch up the dead warrior's spirit if it not know which way to run. Quick soul can get into hollow tree, or in hole in ground, to hide from Antang. Mahatara need to feast on men's souls, to make him strong. One day he eat Raki's spirit and I become part of god.'

Keller shuddered. 'He's not going to get mine. He can't have mine. I'm a white man.' He touched the wound on his side. It was tender, but the pain made him feel more alive.

'Mahatara eat whatever his hawk brings.'

'Well, he's not going to have me.'

Keller thought about all this later, when he lay in his bed, the wound pulsing angrily and keeping him awake. He had been listening to the stories told by one of the Dyaks, a penglipur lara, or 'dispeller of worries'. Raki had translated the tales for him as best he could with his limited English. There had been the tale of the 'thumb boy', who had been eaten by a giant; stories of stupid ordinary men and women, and stories of handsome, bright and artistic princes and princesses; stories of Pa Bilalang, the 'old grasshopper' who always won through no matter what tangles he got himself into or who was trying to thwart him.

That's all this hawk thing is, thought Keller. It's just another of those strange tales they tell. There's nothing to it really.

Keller could not lie to himself though. He had been a victim of Jata. He had seen the omang. He was chasing after a legend which he hoped would make him rich. These things existed. Antang, the supreme being's hawk, was as real as any of the fairy-tale creatures he had come upon thus far.

So, though he told himself these things in a very firm inner voice, he actually found it hard to reject the actuality of Mahatara and his hawk, Antang. After all, *something* had happened out there on the walkway, and Raki had described what he had seen, which matched what Keller had witnessed and experienced. The horror he felt, when he thought of his soul being torn from his corpse and carried away to be eaten by an alien god, was deep. Keller did not want such a fate for his spirit. If his soul was going anywhere, he wanted it to be a Christian place, heaven or hell, it mattered not which.

## 2

Keller used a crutch cut from a tree branch for a while, the loss of blood having weakened him.

Beyond the marshes, Keller's party came across another hostile tribe of head-hunters, who attacked them on sight. However, before any real damage could be done with poisonous darts, one of the attacking warriors noticed the head which now hung from Keller's backpack by its hair. This man yelled for the fighting to cease forthwith and then went forward and embraced Keller, inviting him and his men back to the longhouse, where they were greeted enthusiastically.

It turned out that the people of this particular tribe, the Bahau, were enemies of the tree-top clan. The man Keller had killed was a paramount chieftain of the Bahau's fiercest foes. This local tuai rumah had been past his best at combat, but the Bahau were still impressed. The owner of the face that stared out from Keller's backpack had been personally responsible for several deaths in the Bahau longhouse. He was a hated man and there were those who were prepared to show their appreciation to his killer.

Keller knew what it was like to be hated himself. On board ship he had caused all sorts of mayhem for the officers. He had influenced his shipmates and taken them with him, but not because they liked him. Keller had been more feared than loved. In his time he had been flogged and had been as close as any man to being hanged from the yardarm. Now he was a hero. It was not surprising that he was enjoying the feeling, despite the pain he was still experiencing.

'Blake, Johnson, we'd be best making the most of this, for I don't think we're going to see its like again,' he told his two cronies.

The tuak began to flow freely as the evening wore on: an evening of dancing, songs and storytelling. One of the stories told was the fight between the man with hair like the orang-utan and an enemy chief. Once more Raki translated as best as he could, bearing in mind that neither language was his first tongue.

During the singing, a young woman came and sat beside Keller. He, being the hero of the hour, was subject to much attention from the women of the longhouse, especially the unmarried ones. This one, who sat very close to Keller, wore a heavy and elaborate necklace of several tiers which hung between her small breasts. The end of the necklace was weighted with wild boar tusks and seashells. There were heavy brass rings hanging from her stretched earlobes. On her head she wore a tiara of the ubiquitous hornbill's feathers.

'Hello,' said Keller, unused to the attentions of young women. 'What's your name?'

He noticed that the other women had moved away, seemingly unwilling to be close to this girl and her touch. They glared at her and curled their lips in sneers. Some of the men seemed hostile towards her too. Keller did not understand why, because she was quite a pretty young woman. She ignored the stares and rebukes, however, reserving her attention for Keller. Seeing the blood on his shirt which had seeped from his wound, she tutted, but made gestures which implied that Keller was a hero.

She said something and giggled. Raki then asked her name in her own tongue and she told him.

'They call her Usang, tuan,' he told Keller.

'Usang, eh? That's a pretty name.'

Keller was not a ladies' man. He had paid for whores in back alleys and dirty bedrooms, and had taken the odd tavern girl, too drunk to be choosy, but he had never in his life had a pretty young woman tell him she was fond of him. When this one whispered in his ear he understood immediately that she wanted him to sleep with her. He needed no translation. It shocked and delighted him. She was a desirable woman.

Keller was sensible enough to ask Raki, 'If I take this girl into one of those rooms at the back, am I going to get attacked by the men of the tribe?'

'No, tuan. So long as you do not take her by force. If she likes you she is free to give you favours. But for some reason they do not like this girl here. Maybe you should not go with her. She may be cursed with demons.'

'Oh, I can handle a demon-girl,' Keller said, smugly. 'I've been with Liverpool harlots who spit and claw like cats with hot coals in their bellies. A demon or two don't deter the likes of John Keller. And I think she likes me all right, so that's fine and dandy, ain't it? I prefer they carry demons to diseases, an' these girls out here in the Ulu are clean as a bosun's whistle. No poxy sailor's been out here to dirty 'em up yet.'

Keller and the woman slipped away, into a room which was bare but for a stool and a broom. But there was reed matting on the floor. Keller helped the girl out of her skirt, then took off his pants. Usang stared at his penis, her hand going to her mouth, and gave a little giggle. Anger suddenly flooded through him and he almost exploded in wrath.

'What're you laughing at?'

Then, just in time, he remembered. The men she knew would probably have a palang. Also, he supposed, she would not be used to such a pale specimen as he owned. Being a red-headed man, Keller was whiter-skinned even than most Englishmen and covered in freckles from head to toe. All this would be new to her. He laughed with her then, pulling her down on to the mats.

'You think it's funny do you?' he growled, running his hands over her breasts. The dark hair of her head smelled strongly of coconut oil. Her body scent was some kind of musk. These feminine perfumes coupled with her nakedness was beginning to excite Keller a great deal: 'I haven't got one of them bamboo sticks through the end of it, have I? Well, I'm no rhino, but don't need one of them things to give you the pleasure you need. Have your little laugh, missy, then we'll get down to some certain business.'

She gripped him tightly when he entered her and he yelled in pain, her fingers finding his wound.

'Don't touch me there,' he said. 'Not there!'

She understood and looked contrite, letting him manage the love-making in his own detached way.

After they had finished, Keller had a rest. In his condition, such activity took its toll. Later, he woke and they went back to the singing and dancing on the ruai. Keller sat down amongst the men now and they nudged him with their shoulders.

'You old dog,' whispered Johnson. 'I wouldn't mind havin' a stab at her meself.'

'Be my guest,' Keller said, airily, as if he now owned the young woman.

One of the tribal elders called to Keller across the circle, while a dance was in progress. The women had taken the floor now and were swaying and describing elegant movements with their arms and hands. Keller looked to Raki for a translation of the elder's words.

'He asks if you like his daughter.'

'Oh,' said Keller, wondering if a fight was coming anyway. 'Yes, she's a fine young filly, tell him. She knows how to please a man . . .' Keller turned to Johnson. 'Can I help it if his daughter's a loose woman?'

Budrudeen, overhearing this, said, 'Mr Keller, tuan, the woman is not of loose morals. This is their way for all their ladies before marriage. They may sleep with which man they please, in order to find the right one for a husband.'

'Well that's all right then,' said Keller with heavy sarcasm, 'they're all tarts, are they?'

The seamen laughed uproariously at this joke and caused such consternation in their hosts that the dancing stopped for at least twenty minutes. It soon resumed however. Guests were invited to dance after the warriors and women had shown their skill, with the usual hilarious results. Mariners stamped around the communal verandah with about as much grace as rhino. These men could dance a jig with the best of them, and did so to prove their worth to their hosts, but they could not copy the sinewy movements of the warriors' hornbill dance.

Raki, Mayok and many of the other Dyaks with Keller went to bed, sleeping at the far end of the ruai. The seamen, however, had not had so much fun since they left the taverns behind and they were not willing to give it up early. Keller sat on one side of Usang's father, while his daughter sat on the other. She kept giving Keller sly glances and secret little smiles. Some of the men joked about it, but Keller shrugged it off.

'I'm leaving port tomorrow, lads,' he jibed. 'And this one's staying behind on the quay.'

Usang's father was drinking from a bamboo cup, which he then handed to his daughter to sip from, then to Keller. Although Keller had his own cup of tuak, he saw some sort of ritual in this act and not wanting to offend his hosts he drank from the proffered cup. After this had happened three times, in about the space of one hour, a great shout went up from the Bahau. They crowded around the three cup-sharers, smiling and laughing, and nodding towards Keller and Usang.

Keller's hand went towards his pistol. 'What's going on here, lads? Something's afoot.'

The noise had woken Raki, who now came running down the verandah, to talk with the Bahau. These people were not at all hostile, but they chattered in high excited voices. Raki shook his head sagely, first staring at the happy-looking Usang, and then at her father, before saying to Keller, 'You say you will marry this young girl?'

'What?' exploded Keller.

'You take cup three times after she has drink. This mean you want to wed her. Her father say you agree to take her in this marriage. You have to give her the head of your enemy as present for your bride.'

Keller looked down at the fly-covered head and then stared at the faces of the Bahau. They were still smiling at him. They had no idea that he had not the least intention of marrying anyone. However, Keller realized that to cause a fuss now, while they were in the midst of the Bahau, would be a big mistake. He quickly came to the conclusion that it was better to brazen it out for a while.

'Tell him I did not mean to ask for his daughter.'

Raki shook his head. 'Not wise words, tuan. You say you no like the girl and they insulted. They kill us.'

'All right,' Keller said slowly, forcing a smile on to his craggy features, 'say I am pleased by all this.'

Raki spoke haltingly to the young woman's father and his grin broadened to cover his whole face. He seemed delighted to get an orang-utan for his son-in-law. Raki later explained that the girl had been rejected by the young men of the tribe because of some incident involving the basir, who had accidentally dripped sacrificial chicken's blood on to her when she was still an infant. She was regarded by eligible bachelors as tainted and possibly carrying one or more demons in her breast.

Raki explained.

'The basir chase a demon out of sick man into a chicken, then he slit the chicken throat, so the demon die with the bird. But the blood fly out of chicken and land on this girl. Maybe demon still in blood of chicken and go into girl.'

'Why not do the same trick with the wench?'

'She no get sick,' said Raki, simply. 'Demon stay in her, but not make her ill. No one can get a demon out who hides deep down inside where no one can find him.'

'So I've got second-hand goods, have I? So be it. We'll take the girl along with us.'

'They want you to stay with the tribe.'

'Then we're going to have trouble, Raki, 'cause you know I ain't going to do that. Better persuade 'em that our tribe is moving on in the morning. She can come with us or she can stay. Tell the father I'll come back for her, and marry her when we go north again. Otherwise, we'll take her with us and we'll do the ceremony on the run.'

Raki looked doubtful, but spoke at length to the father, with the rest of the tribe looking on. The girl had plenty to say about this too. She gabbled away the whole time, sometimes yelling at her father, sometimes yelling even louder at the ring of warriors around her. Finally, Raki said to Keller, 'They not want to keep her here. They afraid of her demon. She come with us in the morning.'

Johnson looked relieved, his hand falling away from the pistol in his belt. 'That's more like it, matey. By God I thought we were goin' to have to blast our way out of here, Keller. You do choose the damnedest women.'

'I didn't choose her, she chose me,' replied the groom. 'We'll dump her later. In the meantime, she's to be left alone by the rest of you, you understand, all of you? I won't have none of you touching my goods.'

'Suit yourself,' said Blake with a shrug.

They went to bed then, on the verandah, Usang and Keller disappearing back into the room they had shared earlier. He gave her the severed head and she hung it outside the door by its hair, complete with buzzing flies. This was a symbol of their marriage.

In the morning, the party rose early. One of the seamen, a drifter who had jumped ship in Hong Kong, was desperately sick. Keller decided to leave the man behind.

'These people will look to him,' he said.

Blake said, 'They'll likely cut a chicken over him and then what?'

'Where's the choice? You don't know, it may help him get better. You want to carry him? We can't all stay here. Time's runnin' short. You can see he's going to die anyway. His piss is black with blood. I'll put a bullet in his brain, if it'll make you feel better.'

Blake stared down at the yellow-faced seaman whose staring eyes revealed that they alighted on no one familiar to him. He was beyond even recognizing his closest friend. His fingers clutched and plucked at his own clothes, as if he saw insects crawling all over them, and the sweat ran from him on to the bamboo floor of the ruai. It was true there was nothing they could do for him. He would be dead within a day or two.

'Better to leave him here,' said Blake, who could be squeamish about certain things. 'I just pray to God that I don't fall sick too, with you leadin' the pack, Keller. You can be a cold-hearted bastard.'

'That's true enough,' agreed the leader, 'and you'd be too – if you had to.'

Before they set off into the rainforest again, Keller called Mayok to his side.

'Listen, boy, I'm putting this wench in your hands,' he indicated Usang. 'You look after her, feed her and such. Help her if she needs it, when we're back on the trail. You can see I'm not fit yet, with this damn cut in my side. I can hardly walk myself, let alone help her along. Tell me if any of the other men bother her. Understand?'

Mayok, whose English was still limited, managed to grasp the gist of this rattled-out speech.

'Tuan, I no want look after this one girl.'

'You'll do as you're told,' growled Keller. 'I'm not askin' any favours, I'm handing out orders.'

With that, the big red-headed seaman turned and limped away, leaving Mayok with Usang. Mayok was unhappy with the arrangement, but there was little he could do about it.

## 3

Mayok felt that looking after Usang was demeaning work. Others went out to hunt gibbons, or wild pigs, while he had to stay and guard a woman. It was not that she chattered all the time, as he thought she would, but she was silent and uncommunicative. Twice he had asked tuan Keller to be relieved of the duty, but each time permission to hand her over to someone else was refused. Mayok was in despair, thinking that the other Dyaks would reject him as a woman-watcher. It was worse than being a nursemaid to the babies of a longhouse.

Two days after she had joined the party, the rest of the men were out hunting while Budrudeen had remained behind to do the cooking. Mayok was also there, with his charge, who had gone to sit with her feet in a forest pool. He knew she was unhappy and eventually he went and sat with her.

'Why did you come on this walk,' he asked her in the words common to both, 'if you are so miserable?'

She picked up a pebble and threw it into a pool of water, reddish-brown from the minerals in the soil. The stone sank, sending ripples towards her toes. She let the water gently lap her feet then, surprisingly, she answered him.

'I was flattered by the red man's attentions. So would you be if you had spent your life being abused as I have, just because some clumsy basir splashed you with chicken's blood. Anyway, my people did not want me to stay with them, not even my father. They are all afraid I will bring them bad luck.'

'You have brought *me* bad luck,' said Mayok, bitterly.

She hugged her knees and turned her head and looked at him with damp eyes.

'I am sorry for that. It must be hard to see the others go hunting while you look after a girl.'

She was so understanding of his position that Mayok felt ashamed of his feelings of resentment towards her. True, it was not her fault that he had been assigned as her body-guard. That was down to the tuan.

Some monkeys were swishing about in the trees over-head, making a noise with the branches. These creatures rained shells on the pair below, as they ate their nuts. To hide his confusion, Mayok picked up some stones and drove the monkeys further into the trees, away from the pool. They shrieked and cursed him in monkey language, possibly oaths well known to Mayok if he could but under-stand the tongue, for everyone knew that the souls of head-hunters often hid in the bodies of monkeys at the point of death. This was to avoid Antang's talons. Once inside the monkey, there the soul stayed, until the death of that creature.

'Do you like this man?' asked Mayok, at length, carefully avoiding the word 'love'. 'His skin is so pale and his hair has been stolen from the orang-utan.'

'It is not for me to like or dislike. I have been given to him.'

'You took him to your bed before that.'

'I told you, he looked at me in that way. No one had done so before. I am a woman with a woman's needs. Do you think I should go the rest of my life without knowing love? Was I supposed to become a dried-up fig, never knowing what it felt like to have the sharp bamboo pierce my fruit? I have been accursed all my days. When I was young, they fed me with the chickens and pigs, under the longhouse. Then, when I was older, they made me sleep in a room on my own and used to glare and spit at me when I came out on to the ruai. I was so lonely I wanted to die. Even my own brothers would kick me when they saw me, telling me I was not fit company for a family.'

Even as she spoke, Mayok had some sympathy with her family members. To have a sister or daughter who was cursed with demons was no light matter. While she remained with the tribe she would be a constant fear and embarrassment to her close relatives. It is some wonder that one of the brothers did not slit her throat one night, knowing that few questions would be asked in the morning. If she had been Mayok's sister, he would have been just as cold as her brothers had been towards her.

'What does the demon feel like, inside you?' he asked, curiously.'

'You would like to know? It is a small pain which moves around my body. I hardly know it's there.'

'Everyone has small pains.'

'Then you all have demons like me. My demon does not bother me much at all. I think he is a friendly demon.'

'There is no such thing,' said Mayok. 'All demons are bad.'

'Then I am bad,' she said, her eyes filling with tears again. 'Why don't you go away from me? Aren't you afraid I will contaminate you?'

She looked so helpless at this point that Mayok felt the need to touch her cheek.

'I am sorry for you,' he said, sympathetically. 'You don't *look* bad. You have a soft skin and very beautiful eyes. Why would a demon leave you looking so pretty? A really bad demon would shrivel you up and dry your skin hard and wrinkled, to make you look like a hag. Perhaps he is not so bad?'

This brought a smile through the tears. He guessed she had had so few soft words spoken to her during her lifetime that any such gentle water which fell on her brow was welcome. At that moment a bee came buzzing around her head, before settling on some flowers close to the pool. Usang watched the bee then take off with full pollen sacs on its legs, towards a hollow tree.

'Honey,' she said, getting to her feet. 'Let's go and find some honey.'

'I shall get you some,' Mayok said, to make amends for all his questions.

They went to the tree together and saw the hive up high in the dead branches. Mayok gave his blow-pipe and darts to Usang to hold, then began the climb. It was not easy work, since he had to test each step in case a rotten bough cracked and fell away under him. All the while he climbed he sang the traditional honey-tree song, first sung by the legendary hero Sibauk, who climbed an upside-down tree with its roots on the moon, where he met the souls of dead moon-people in the form of bees.

Once he reached the hive Mayok blew gently on the opening until the guard bees retreated further inside. Then he quickly put a hand in and scooped out a fistful of honey. He swiftly shinned down the tree again, now knowing where the safe holds were to be found. Once on the ground the pair of them ran laughing to where Budrudeen was cooking with his earth-oven. They were pursued and stung by some of the bees, but not seriously. Mayok had grown up enduring many bee, and some hornet, stings. He was used to their attacks, for no Dyak would pass a hive without securing some of its contents.

Mayok let the girl lap her half of the honey from his open palm. It felt strange, feeling her tongue licking his skin. He simply stood there with her warm mouth close to his hand, her moist breath on his fingertips. The attention of her lips and tongue on his skin made Mayok tingle from head to toe. He let out a soft sound of delight. Then he became aware that Budrudeen was staring at the pair of them.

Mayok whipped his hand away. 'We found some honey,' he told the Malay. 'That's all it was.'

Budrudeen shrugged and went back to his pots.

Just after noon, a wind began to rise in the foothills of some distant mountains. It grew steadily stronger, drawing breath from the mountaintops and sweeping down through the many-layered green foliage below. Steadily, steadily, it increased, developing twists and turns as it wound its path through the forest's trees, straightening crooked vines and whipping tree tops to a frenzy of movement. Its howl began to grow with its strength as it found its voice amongst the branches.

The three people in the camp felt it coming. There was little they could do about the bivouacs, which in any case could be remade, but they did their best to weigh down any loose equipment with heavy stones from the pool. Then they tried to find some shelter for themselves. Many trees would come crashing down in such a typhoon. Many branches would be hurled through the air. It was best at such times to be amongst rocks.

'Over there,' cried Budrudeen, as the howling reached its highest pitch. 'In between those two big boulders.'

They found a spot on the moss, sandwiched between two big flat rocks up on their ends like standing stones. They needed to squeeze in there together and keep their hands and feet from the entrance. Already there was debris whirling about in the atmosphere, some pieces large enough to knock a man cold. They sat in a row facing one way, as if in a canoe, with Usang between Mayok's legs and Mayok between Budrudeen's. Here they remained, conscious of each other's proximity, while the storm raged around them.

Mayok was wondering if Keller and his men had found shelter.

Rajah Angin, king of the wind, was very pleased with himself. He was enjoying the freedom to demonstrate his powers to the watching sangiang, who had parted the sky to witness the typhoon. Mahatara had called Rajah Angin forth, to devastate that part of the rainforest which at that moment housed both questing parties. Rajah Angin tore leaves in plenty from the branches of the trees and flung them far and wide. He uprooted the weaker trees and bent low the stronger. He caused waves to grow on the lakes and rivers to rage through their path.

'I am the mightiest of the elements,' he howled to any who would listen. 'I am the greatest of the few.'

Fire, of course, would not have agreed with this assessment, nor indeed would water. Earth said nothing. No one ever knew how the earth felt, for it was not given to demonstrative behaviour quite so often as the others. For every earthquake there were a dozen tsunami. For every rockslide there were a hundred forest fires. For every volcanic eruption there were typhoons aplenty, sweeping over the surface of the world.

Although he bragged unnecessarily, Rajah Angin was capable of great force. Among other things, he blew the supernatural creatures around the rainforest like so many semangat. When he had finished, there were good souls hanging like wet rags from the branches of trees and bad spirits scattered up and down the riverbanks like ruffled parrots.

Also, after a great wind has passed, the trees have new shadows. These have to introduce themselves to each other. One might say 'I am Kelana the pirate,' while another might say, 'I *used* to be Kelana the pirate, but now I am Kala the eater of men.' Those beings of the shadow world all have their grand names and titles. There is Rama, the demon-king and the beautiful Sita, and many others, who now enjoy a new locale, since the wind has reshaped the trees which give them their silhouettes.

The three survivors of the wind crept out of the crevice in between the two rocks. The earth, one of the rivals of the wind, had protected them and kept them safe. Some while later the hunting party entered the camp again. They had been savaged by the typhoon, flung asunder, wrenched from handholds and tossed around the forest. There were broken limbs to set and cracked skulls to patch. One man had died, being torn from the ground and thrown at a tree, the forked branch of which caught his head in a lock, and there he hung until the storm abated.

'What a mess,' growled Keller, looking around the glade at a tangle of torn boughs and leafy branches. 'I would've thought you could batten down the equipment.'

'We put heavy rocks and logs on things, tuan,' replied Budrudeen. 'If you lift some of the branches you will find your supplies buried underneath them. I even managed to save a pot of stew, which is still warm. I shall make it hotter on the fire, once we have it going again.'

Usang, Mayok and Budrudeen had in fact done well to protect the equipment, which was indeed found under the debris of the storm. Boughs the size of small ships were heaved away by those men still capable of heavy work. The ground was a lattice work of litter where the smaller branches had criss-crossed and knitted with each other. These all had to be gathered in armfuls, and dumped on the edge of the camp site. There, underneath it all, protected by stones, were the precious stores.

Keller had the good grace to apologize to the three who had remained in the camp. He praised them for their efforts. That night, once the fire was going strong, and the tuak was flowing, he called for a toast to Budrudeen, saying he was a pious Moslem and a good cook. There was general laughter which Budrudeen did not understand, though he was pleased to be recognized as a man who took his god and his duties seriously.

'No one knows that I am a murderer,' he whispered to Mayok after the toast, 'otherwise they would not be so free with their toasts and praises.'

'These people would not care if you were a murderer or not, for I think half of them have killed men illegally,' replied Mayok, who had grown in worldliness since knowing Keller. 'These are scoundrels and scallywags from taverns, not decent men.'

'Then what are we doing here with them?'

Mayok answered practically, 'Because they are going somewhere. We are both looking for new homes, you and I, and we need to share the journey to make it less dangerous.'

That evening, Mayok was surprised to find a sharp dart entering his heart when he saw Keller leading Usang to his bivouac in the forest, away from the other men.

'Why am I stabbed thus?' he whispered to a black owl, who sat staring with love-sick eyes at the moon. 'She is nothing to me – nothing at all – I swear.'

# 4

Prince Kalim was twenty-seven years of age and now the most active in the snakes' nest of plotting princes. He was the youngest brother of Muda Hassim, the rajah's grand vizier and closest adviser. Being young, his blood was fiery and his character not yet tempered by age or wisdom. Among his peers he raged against the 'white rajah' and swore that his kris would enter the rajah's heart one moonless night. 'Then I shall make my eldest brother, Muda Hassim, the rajah,' he told his friends. Though wisdom was not yet upon him he had common sense enough to know that he was too young to be considered for the sultanate. If his older brother took the throne, however, he stood a reasonable expectation of inheriting the position on his brother's death.

He could tell his brother none of this. Muda Hassim was the rajah's man, through and through. The grand vizier wanted nothing to do with plots and schemes to murder the rajah. Wisdom *had* come upon the older brother of Kalim. More than that, while Muda Hassim would have preferred a rajah from amongst the Malay princes, and himself in particular, he was a rare thing amongst princes and prelates of all races. He was an honourable man. His former master had bequeathed the sultanate to a foreigner for good reasons and Muda Hassim accepted this. Besides, he had now come to admire and respect Rajah Starke and could see that he was managing the country with justice and mercy.

So Kalim turned in a new direction. There was another old man he could use, if he was clever enough. Issam, the bomoh prince, could be manipulated, if one used the right tools. Kalim met with a minor Ilanun pirate who went by the self-chosen name of Ruwakruwak (the invisible heron) whose base was in the mouth of Long Datling. After receiving gold and instructions from Prince Kalim, Ruwakruwak sailed to Sabah, where Issam's son-in-law lived with Issam's daughter. Here Ruwakruwak kidnapped the eldest child, a boy of ten, Issam's grandson. Word was sent back to Prince Kalim who then met with the bomoh prince on the terrace of a small palace just outside Kuching. Issam was staring out over a splendid garden of fig trees and frangipanis when Kalim swept on to the terrace, a hunting hawk on his wrist.

Issam turned to face the young prince, insulted by the fact that Kalim had not the good manners to receive him without his playmate. A man with good social graces would have put such distractions as the hawk aside, while he sat and gave his whole attention to his guest. The prince saw by Issam's face that he had upset him. That object having been achieved, he called for one of his retainers to take the hawk. He then offered Prince Issam a silk cushion and sat on one himself.

Issam said, coldly, 'What is it you want, Prince Kalim? Are you ill? Do you wish to see into the future? Shall I change you into a nightjar so that you may visit your lover when the moon is full?'

The last sentence was spoken in a mocking tone and Kalim decided to cut to the quick.

'I have your grandson,' he said, simply. 'You will do as I say or the boy's throat will be cut. Please, do not even think of using your magic. A man sits by the bed of the infant. This man has a sharp knife in his hand, poised, ready to slit the boy from ear to ear. Even should you use your magic to locate the child, at the first hint of rescue he will die.'

To Issam this was not totally unexpected. He knew his grandson had been kidnapped by pirates even before his daughter had come to him in her great distress and told him that the boy had gone. The bomoh prince was even now trying to organize a rescue. His powers as a bomoh had led him to the belief that at least one of the Malay princes was involved in the deed, but not until now was that belief confirmed.

'So, it was you,' said Issam. 'Are you alone in this?'

'I have one or two others I can rely on, from amongst our brothers and cousins, but for the most part, yes, this was my devising.'

'You know that once my grandson is safe or, Allah forbid, harmed in any way, I shall have you sliced into a thousand pieces and fed to sewer rats?'

Prince Kalim frowned. 'That will not be necessary, for if you do as I say, you will eventually thank me.'

'I cannot see that day ever arriving, but go on, you obviously have something to tell me.'

The sweet scents of giant blooms wafted over the terrace. Kalim sat in a white wicker chair and motioned for the older man to do the same. Issam took the seat he was offered while Kalim ordered tea to be brought to the terrace. Issam was thinking that the world was a beautiful place, with its slow, winding rivers, palms and beautiful lawns, its white palaces and pavilions, its floating birds and jewelled dragonflies – yet his grandson was down in the dank dark hold of some stinking pirate prahu, lonely utterly miserable and terrified, thinking he was never going to see his family again. Issam could not banish this picture from his mind as he stared into the eyes of Prince Kalim, who had now begun to talk animatedly.

'You are now one of the white rajah's advisers,' said Kalim, 'and it is in this capacity I want you to assist me. I understand the rajah asks you to follow his cousin's journey through the Ulu. You let him see how she is progressing, is that not so?'

'That is so,' replied Issam, carefully.

'The next time you are called to the rajah's bungalow, you will show him that his cousin Harriet is in trouble – alone and undefended – having somehow become detached from the main party.'

'Alone and undefended,' repeated Issam, thinking, just like my grandson.

'You will then suggest he leads a party into the Ulu in search of his cousin, in order to rescue her.'

Issam stared into the dark-brown eyes of Kalim. When all this was over and his grandson was safe, a polong would creep from a bottle in Kalim's bedchamber and stab each of those eyes with a sharp needle, while the young prince was laying awake in the darkness, too terrified to move. Then, in his blindness, Kalim would stagger from his bed, screaming for assistance, while the bottle imp crawled up his nostrils, found a passage into his mouth, and sank its sharp teeth into the gums and tongue, leaving poisonous bites all along the inside of his cheeks and around his teeth. These would swell over the next few hours of life remaining to Prince Kalim, gradually restricting his breathing, until finally his disfigurement resulted in his slow death.

Kalim was saying, '. . . you understand what you must do?'

Issam jerked himself out of his reverie. 'Yes, yes, the rajah must think his cousin is in such trouble that he organizes an expedition and goes to rescue her himself.'

'Exactly. While he is in the rainforest, from which he will of course never return, we shall crown a new rajah – my brother, Muda Hassim.'

Prince Issam leaned forward, a jolt of surprise going through him. 'Prince Muda Hassim knows of this plot?'

Kalim looked uncomfortable. 'No – no, not yet. But he will, once the white rajah is out of the way. He will be ruling in his stead at that time in any case, for who else would the white rajah leave in charge but his grand vizier?'

Prince Issam left the young Prince Kalim and made his way down to the river where his boatman was waiting patiently with his barge. The boatman, a Malay boy of sixteen years, helped the elderly Issam clamber aboard, but saw that his master was deep in thought, so he said nothing. If no instructions were forthcoming the boy knew he was to row the craft home. Issam lived on the eastern bank of Long Sarawak, an easy journey downriver.

Issam was indeed greatly troubled. As a Malay prince he had no deep-seated love of foreigners, especially those imported to rule his country, but he saw the wisdom of the dead rajah's thinking. And, all other things being equal, he was quite fond of Rajah Starke as a man and saw that he was doing the best job he could of ruling a turbulent land.

On the other hand, Muda Hassim would indeed make as good a ruler as Starke, though undoubtedly the Chinese would suffer under his overlordship, for Muda Hassim hated the Chinese. The grand vizier's youngest child had been abducted by Chinese bandits and had never been seen again. No doubt the girl had been raped several times, to rid her of any vestige of honour and thus prevent her from running away and trying to return to her family again. Once she had been taken forcibly by several men she would consider herself unworthy and submit to the most base indignities life forced upon her. Although his own society was partially responsible for the beliefs of poor, wretched girls in such circumstances, the grand vizier blamed the Chinese. All he knew was that certain foreigners had sold his child into slavery and he hated the whole race for the actions of a few.

For Issam there was also the problem of who would follow Muda Hassim. Without a doubt Kalim believed it would be him. If Prince Kalim ever ascended to the sultanate there would be a wholesale slaughter of certain Dyak tribes, against whom Kalim had a grudge, especially the Iban and the Kayan.

Prince Issam sighed heavily. Just then, on recognizing his barge, a huge crowd of young children playing on the bank rushed noisily into the shallows of the river. They yelled and screeched at him, waving their arms. He reached into a pot which he kept on the bows. It was full of small coinage. He tossed a handful of the coins into the air. They fell like silver rain on to the surface of the river. The delighted children dived and swam for the bright disks of metal, their babbling voices reminding Issam of the his poor grandson's plight.

An ox suddenly surfaced from feeding on the bottom of the river, startling the bomoh prince. The animals had a habit of wandering into the shallows and disappearing for a few moments beneath the surface, feeding on the green weed of the riverbed. They sometimes surprised you when they came up close to the craft, like some guardian behemoth from the underwater palace of Rajah Naga. The prince stared the creature full in the eyes, before it dipped its horned head below the surface again, its body sliding down with it for a few moments.

Issam's son-in-law, the father of the grandson, had just

arrived from Sabah with his wife. On learning that Prince
Kalim was responsible for the kidnapping the young man
went into a terrible rage, followed by weeping and tearing
of his raiment. Issam did what he could to comfort his son-
in-law and then left the two young people to talk over
matters between them. Issam was the grandfather, but any
action on his part would have to have the assent of the
son-in-law.

Prince Issam then went to the room of his first wife,
Selina, whom he loved and respected above all the other
wives in his harem. There had been a time when the lust of
youth had made him forgetful of his first wife, as new
young beautiful wives, still with the bloom of innocence on
their cheeks, came to his bed each night. In those days sex
had seemed more important than finer feelings. However,
with age he came to realize that his deepest feelings were for
the wife who had grown old with him, shared the most
years with him, and – despite his temporary neglect of her –
remained loyal to him.

Now he honoured her above all people and always
sought her wise counsel in matters of importance. She ran
that part of his household which was her province with
efficiency and no nonsense. His younger wives, purchased
after his career as a bomoh had brought him wealth enough
for a large harem, listened to his first wife and followed her
instructions without question. It had never been necessary
for him to confirm her orders, since her personality was
reinforcement enough.

Issam certainly regretted those years when he had passed
by her room without a glance at the shadowy figure behind
the chiffon curtains billowing in the evening breezes.

'My dear,' he said, taking her hands in his own wrinkled
palms, 'once more I come to you for advice.'

'Husband, that is your privilege,' she replied, and as

always, he was not quite sure of her true meaning. She would never openly mock him, but there was always a teasing tone behind such words.

'Yours is probably the one level head in this affair of my grandson, the one head I can trust.'

He said 'my grandson' for the child was not the grandchild of his first wife, but of his third wife, who had died of the cholera some years ago. Selina grieved for the boy, of course, but as one not connected to her by blood. Her ideas were not confused by those other destructive emotions: hatred and revenge. She was concerned only with getting the boy back to his mother and father again, safe and sound, without any permanent inner scars.

Prince Issam told Selina everything. Her eyes went cold when she heard that it was Prince Kalim, not some distant potentiate or bandit, who was responsible for the kidnapping. Prince Kalim was a cousin of hers. She begged forgiveness for the family connection first of all and, when this was waved aside by her husband, she gave him her thoughts on the matter.

'My first consideration is for the boy,' she said, once he had finished his tale. 'This is quite natural, for I am a woman and not given to following the petty political wranglings of men. Yet, on the other hand, I am sensible enough to foresee that if Muda Hassim is ever made rajah or, Allah forbid, Prince Kalim after him, Sarawak will be plunged instantly into civil war. How many of your grandsons will die then? Some of them will also be *my* grandsons. Mothers all over the land will lose their sons. Wives will lose husbands. Daughters will lose brothers and fathers.'

'This is true,' murmured the bomoh prince.

'So, what we are faced with here is risking one boy's life in the hope that we can save many. You, my lord, have an anguishing decision to make. The choices are: to give in to

Prince Kalim's demands and go along with his devious scheme, or to hatch a counterplot and hope that the child is still alive and that we have him returned to us unharmed. I have already spoken about what would happen if Kalim's plans were to reach fruition. However, if he discovers that a counterplot is in motion, we will surely never see your grandson again.'

'Everything you say makes sense, as usual, and confirms my own fears on the subject.'

She laid a hand on her husband's wrist. 'I am sure at this very moment you would like to poison Kalim, so that his face produces growths like dried figs and his head swells and blackens before throwing pus all down his chest and back, but these are thoughts for a later time. Now you must consider your alternatives carefully, without emotion clouding your mind's eye. I am sure, whichever path you choose to follow, your arguments will have been weighed and balanced and the best will prevail.'

Issam thanked Selina for her counsel and then went to see his son-in-law and daughter. They, having expended their burst of fury and sorrow, were now rational enough to listen and speak with him on the matter. He sat down and talked with them for a long time. Finally, between them, they came to a decision. It was not a perfect solution, for there was no such thing in these cases, but Issam felt it was right one.

# PART SIX

# The Glass
# Mountain

# 1

Now it was Harry who was sick.

She had picked up some sort of fever from the swamps. She lay in a state of semi-consciousness in a place where Kilir, the green one who turned deserts to meadows, had left his footprints. There was lush grassland, in a wide clearing which reached to the foot of some tangled mountains, but few trees. What trees there were seemed to be dwarves, indicating that the depth of the soil was shallow, since this was no rainshadow plain.

There were grazing animals in the far distance, which meant meat for the pot, and the insects were surprisingly few. A lone rhinoceros with its palang had been seen running from east to west, which was a good omen for the Land Dyaks in the party. The Sea Dyaks had never seen a rhino before and they were as impressed as the Europeans in the group.

It was a good place to camp, to allow Harry to recover, though Singapore Jack was clearly anxious to be getting on. They had come across a body – a white man's – on the last trail. The body's head was missing, which indicated that some hostile tribe of Dyaks was around. Hostile to Keller, at least, but Jack was no fool. If Keller had upset someone, Jack's party would be blamed too. It was necessary to remain alert.

Keller's group was still ahead of him and seemed to be going strong, despite losing several men to the harsh culling meted out by the rainforest, rivers and mountains.

Since Jack was continually busy with problems which arose in the camp, and gathering specimens and information about the local flora and fauna, it was Lidah and Kit Colenso who shared the brunt of sitting with Harry, making sure there was someone there when her scrambled faculties cleared for short periods. Lidah and Colenso sat in the doorway of her bivouac and talked quietly, while Harry tossed and turned, muttering and groaning.

'I knew she would be sick,' said Lidah. 'I see a bajang go to her in the night.'

Lidah believed that an evil spirit had entered Harry, causing her sickness. The bajang would have stolen Harry's soul and this was even now being tortured by ghosts in some remote mythical land, causing its owner such great distress. Colenso, who was well-used to the myths and beliefs of the Dyaks, did not scorn this view of illness.

'What form did the bajang take?'

'It was a polecat. I saw it with my own eyes. I rush in to chase it away, but by then it gone with missy's soul in its mouth.'

'I see. And what do we have to do to make the bajang return the soul?'

Lidah sighed. 'We need a basir to sing magic hymns to the sangiang. They will help us if they hear the songs. But we have no basir with us.'

'What if we were to sing, you and I?'

Lidah shook her head. 'I do not know the magic hymns.'

'I have seen a basir chase a demon from a woman by cutting the throat of a chicken.'

'That is when the demon is still inside, twisting the soul, trying to pull it out by the roots. Then you can chase the demon into the chicken, kill the chicken, and so kill the demon.'

Colenso nodded. 'But how do you know the demon is not in her still?'

'Because I see the bajang come and go.'

There was no answer to that. Lidah was an eyewitness. She had been there when the soul had been stolen.

Singapore Jack came by the bivouac shortly after that. Jack had been gathering local plants, including several varieties of orchid. In the process of gathering wildflowers, the Dyaks had also been collecting wild fruit: sweet rambutans and the durian with its foul-smelling flesh. They had also caught a flying frog, with similar gliding equipment to the flying snakes, with which Jack had been very pleased. He liked oddities.

But he had come to Harry's bivouac now to discuss another piece of urgent camp business with Colenso.

'I've got one Dyak out of action,' said Jack. 'You remember the man whose foot was pulped in the overspill while we were shooting that last set of rapids? The injury has turned gangrenous. It'll have to come off. He's terrified of course – would you come and help?'

'What do you want me to do?'

'Help hold him down, while we cut. I'm afraid his friends will listen to him when he starts screaming to be released and let him go at the crucial moment. I need reliable people. I've got Kitts and Ferguson. I need someone to press down on his shoulders.'

Colenso hated this kind of thing. He was no more immune to a man's cries of agony than were the Dyaks.

However, he knew it was something he was going to have to do.

'If I must,' he said, getting to his feet. 'Who's going to do the cutting?'

'I am. Someone's heating up a parang in the fire right now. By the way,' Jack turned to peer into the bivouac, 'how is she? Any improvement?'

'Still feverish, still in some dark place.'

'Kaseteran,' mumbled Lidah.

Jack looked puzzled and Colenso explained, 'The kingdom of the ghosts – Lidah believes . . . Well, never mind, let's get this over with.'

The two men left Harry for their unpleasant task.

Harry was indeed in another place, perhaps another time. But, far from being tortured, she was walking through a pleasant part of the rainforest. The sun was filtering down through the green canopy, adding a sparkle to the spider's webs and turning the air dust to gold. An orang-utan was high above her, hanging from a sapling which bent like a bow under his great weight. He was a massive, heavily built fellow with a magnificent red-ochre coat. He stared down tat he woman curiously, while munching a banana, but showed no aggressiveness towards her.

She felt an intruder in this quiet world of birds and mammals as she paused to drink cool rainwater from a pitcher plant. There were rhododendron bushes flowering on all sides, their copper-coloured blooms twisting from the buds. A pale-faced bulbul bird flew out suddenly from the middle of these shrubs, startling her and making her back into a tree.

Almost instantly, after touching the tree, a tall, very handsome man appeared by her side. He was completely naked, which should have shocked a woman of Harry's class and culture, but somehow it seemed natural. She studied his physique and found the proportions perfect. He was beautiful in every sense of the word and she was charmed by his presence.

'Where did you come from?' she asked.

'From the tree,' he replied.

She believed he meant the forest, for the Dyaks often used the singular where they should have used the plural.

'What tribe are you? Where is your longhouse?'

'The forest is my longhouse and I am a pampahilep.'

'Pampahilep,' she murmured. So many of the Dyak words were alliterative, musical, and deserved repetition. 'Pampahilep? I don't think I know that tribe. I know the Ukit and the Iban and the Kenyah . . .'

He stopped her there, with a finger to her lips.

'I am none of those. I am from the spirit world. A tree spirit. You must lie with me.'

Harry knew then that she was in one of her dreams, like the time she had been taken to Kaseteran by Rajah Hantuen. The pampahilep was stroking her hair, murmuring in her ear that she had to lie with him on a mossy bank. Even though this was a dream, Harry could not do as the tree-spirit asked. She had been raised in the Victorian manner and such casual love-making was as unacceptable to her as cutting off one of her fingers.

'You may not lie with me. I will only do such a thing with the man I love.'

The pampahilep looked shocked. 'Do you not realize what I am? Do you not know you are close to the river of death, Long Bali Matei, which flows between life and the hereafter? If you do not accept me, then you will surely slip into the dark waters and be carried to Kaseteran.'

'I have been there as a guest of Rajah Hantuen. I am not afraid. If I must die, then I must.'

The tree-spirit was impressed, both by her courage and by her experiences.

'You have been to the land of the dead, the kingdom of ghosts, and survived? Yes, yes, now I can see the marks of the ghosts on your feet. This is truly a great honour for me, to meet one of Rajah Hantuen's favourite people. One day there will be a korwar erected which will bear your face. Your semengat will be exalted! I see now why you are here, in the magical forest. You are seeking Bukit Kaca, the great mountain.'

'Am I?'

'Yes, of course you are. If you find it you shall live. If you do not, you will die. Good luck in your quest.'

With that the pampahilep left her alone again, disappearing into his tree. She saw that the tree was a mango and she picked one of the fruits, intending to eat it later. Strangely, she felt no hunger as yet, though she had not eaten for days.

Bukit Kaca! A mountain! How fortunate for her that she now knew why she was here and what she was looking for. She continued walking through the rainforest, weaving between the vines that hung sometimes as thick as curtains. Paradise snakes glided between the branches of trees. Black eagles and crested serpent eagles wound invisible clocks in the sky. Spinetailed swifts cut through the lower regions of the air.

She came to a raging torrent which swept and roared down a narrow rock gorge. Instinctively she knew this was not Long Bali Matei, nor any of the other rivers of the land of the dead – Long Julan which flowed into the lake of blood, where those who die in battle spend their eternities, Long Malan, behind the high mountains – but a river with the force of life still thundering through it. Without hesitating, she threw herself into the white waters and was carried, hurtled, down the channel. Her body struck no rocks, nor was scraped on the bottom, but eventually finished in a shallow pool far from the source.

Harry picked herself up out of the pool and began walking again. A moonrat scuttled along the path ahead of her and she followed this creature when she came to thickets and thorn bushes, letting it lead her through them. With the moonrat as her guide she crossed harsh country, which tore her boots to ribbons, but left her miraculous feet untouched. Eventually she came to the shores of a great lake. This was Bawang Gala, the mythical lake which harboured a monster known as Ku.

Harry fashioned a coracle from reeds and set off in this craft after caulking it with river clay. When she reached the middle of the lake, Ku rose to the surface, intent on swallowing her whole. When Ku opened his dragon mouth, with its teeth like shaven trees, she tossed inside the mango from the pampahilep's tree. The great leviathan swallowed and his eyes widened.

'You have tricked me,' he roared, the blast of his fish-stinking breath causing Harry to gag. 'I have eaten of soul-food and must not taste live flesh for a year.'

Harry laughed and paddled her small vessel towards the distant shore. Here she was met by a range of forbidding dark mountains, with sheer black sides. She began to scale them, one by one, and each time she crested a mountain, an even taller one lay in wait on the far side. But Harry did not despair, and finally she was on the highest peak, looking into a circle of mountains, within which was a singular feature.

Here at last was Bukit Kaca, the immense mountain of glass, its peak piercing the highest level of the sky. Here it shone amber, red and orange where it touched the bottom edge of the sun. Glorious rays of coloured light were reflected into Harry's body and she began to feel revitalized, a new strength surging through her arteries. The pampahilep had been right. This was the end of her search. She had found the source of life.

While she stood there, imbibing the rays of light, a bird began to sing in high sweet tones. Once its song was over she knew the danger of her illness had passed. She felt ready to return to the world of the living.

At that moment an eagle left his eyrie at the top of Bukit Kaca and swept down towards her. The eagle had the head of a handsome man . . .

Harry opened her eyes. The man-eagle had kissed her on the lips. A face hovered above her, then retreated into the dimness of the bivouac. She blinked, recovering her faculties, knowing she was now out of danger. The fever had passed, leaving her feeling exhausted but alive. Her eyes focused on Kit Colenso.

'Did you just kiss me?' she asked, her own voice sounding strangely weak to her ears.

'I – I – I'm sorry – I don't know what came over me,' he said, covered in confusion. 'It was an impulse.'

'You kissed me,' she said, matter of factly.

Harry supposed she should be annoyed with him, even angry, but she could not bring herself to any pitch of fury. Instead, she found herself smiling into his eyes.

'I – I thought you were about to die,' he confessed, 'that's why I did it. I felt that someone, even me, should be saying goodbye, and since you could not hear me I hoped you would be able to feel the – the touch of my lips on your own, and know that someone cared a life was passing on. I'm glad I was wrong, for you immediately rallied, and seemed to be through it.'

'How lovely,' she murmured. 'What a beautiful thing to

do. You might have caught my fever, you know. You risked it in spite of that, didn't you, simply to say goodbye.'

Colenso seemed uncomfortable then. His mood had changed suddenly. He began wrapping things up in a towel, a shaving brush and razor, to take out of the bivouac with him. A leather-bound book on birds went in with his washing kit. She wondered how long he had been with her to need such items. Once his bits were together, he took his leave of her.

'Don't make too much of it. It was just a gesture.'

'Is that all it was?' She found herself feeling disappointed.

His tone was gruff. 'Yes, nothing more. Now I expect you will want Jack. I'll fetch him for you. Lidah is just outside, asleep. She's been watching over you night and day. The rest of us have been too busy with other things. It's her you should save your gratitude for, you know. The rest of us, well, we had important matters to attend to.'

'Oh?'

He melted a little and his face showed the strain of the last few hours. 'I had to help Jack hack off a conscious man's leg at the knee. It wasn't very entertaining.'

'I had to cut off a man's head.'

He had forgotten that. The man stripped of his flesh by ants. It was easy, when he looked at her, to forget that she was actually a very capable woman. She looked fragile and delicate, and would have been better placed in a schoolroom or the drawing-room of an English country house, but in fact she was tough underneath: tougher than many men he knew.

'Yes, you had to kill a man, didn't you? It had gone from my mind. You will suspect purposely. Forgive me. I shall stop complaining and get about my business.'

He left her then. Shortly afterwards Jack came, lifting back the side of the bivouac with a strong hand and smiling into her eyes. She could see the sunlight glinting on the sweat which clung to the sun-bleached hairs on his tanned arm. Oh, he was a tall handsome man, this Singapore Jack. He made the blood sing in her veins.

'Jack,' she said. 'I'm better.'

'Good. Good. We must be on our way soon. Can you get up? Are you able to walk? I can have a litter made.'

'Give me some soup and an hour to get used to my legs.'

He seemed relieved, then she saw his nose visibly twitching. He said, 'That's my girl. I'll send Lidah in to you. You'll probably want a wash down . . .'

Jack then left abruptly, letting the flap of the bivouac fall back on its own. My God, she thought, I stink! She had been sweating pounds over the last forty-eight hours. The odour of the air inside the bivouac would have made a wild pig wrinkle its nose in distaste. Poor Jack. Poor Lidah! Then she remembered, Kit Colenso had actually kissed her. She smelled worse than one of those swamps they had crossed and he had bent down and kissed her. That made her wonder a great deal about him.

Lidah came into the bivouac with some water from the river. She helped Harry strip down and wash every part of herself. Then they attended to her hair, which was encrusted with dry sweat, tangled and matted. When it was all over, Harry felt ten times better. It was marvellous how a simple outer wash could revitalize the inner Harry. She was ready for anything.

'Tell me what happen in your dream,' said Lidah, as they both ate some stew together. 'Tell me how you come home again.'

Harry did her best to recount the dream accurately. When she had finished, Lidah looked triumphant.

'Indera Bayu,' she said, emphatically.

'What?'

'The bird who sing to you. The Malay peoples call it Indera Bayu, which means sacred wind. This is a bird of Princess Chaya Bulan, which can sing away the sickness from people.'

'You mean it cures illness with its song?'

'Yes, yes, and it sing to you, so you are chosen of the gods, missy. I think you marry tuan Jack and have many golden children. You are very lucky lady to have tuan Jack love you. I think you will be very happy.'

Harry surprised herself by expressing doubts. 'Yes. But it was tuan Colenso who came to me while I was sick, wasn't it?'

Lidah snorted. 'Oh, *him*,' she said, with a dismissive wave of her hand. 'He do nothing really. He just sit here while I have to sleep. Tuan Jack is out getting food for us, making us all together safe, watching over all the camp. Tuan Colenso, he just stare at you like a frog watches a fly . . .'

'Or the owl watches the moon?'

An elaborate shrug from Lidah. 'Maybe.'

In fact Harry was not fit enough to move that day. Also the man whose leg had been amputated had died in the night and it seemed appropriate to allow a respectable gap before surging on. It was not until the following morning that they broke camp. There were some mountains on the far side of the grassy plain which needed to be crossed. Standing at the foot of these dark beasts, Colenso and Jack could see no obvious passes. It was Patan and his friend – the Ngaju Dyaks – who were leading the group now. They were the only members of the party who had been remotely near this part of Borneo, and here even they were strangers.

'Isn't that a track, up there?' Colenso asked of Jack, who was studying the terrain with his spyglass. 'Snaking up to that col?' He pointed.

Jack swung his brass telescope and found the track.

'It looks like a dry water course. We could try that. Won't be easy. I'm worried about flash floods. We're moving into the rainy season.'

'Is there any alternative?'

Jack felt a sting of annoyance. Colenso was one of those men who liked to be definite about things all the time. He ~anted quick decisions. There were no moments of com- ~ble vagueness about the man. *This* or *this* – no fiddling ~ound. Jack had been raised to mull over things, turn them around, look at them from all sides. In short, he liked to take his time with problems, before making a decision.

'We could go round them,' he suggested.

Colenso had already looked at the length of the range of mountains. It disappeared into a haze on both sides.

'It would take us weeks, Jack, and you know it.'

It did not help Singapore Jack to know that Colenso was right. He said nothing in reply to Colenso's last statement, but studied the water course again. It was steep, with a lot of loose scree around, but it was the only possible route over. He did not know how the Dyaks felt about climbing up high. When he spoke to them about it, they looked upset.

'We must be careful, tuan,' said one. 'There are many spirits in the mountains, many demons. We must wait for right time to cross over, or gods will be angry.'

'Wait? How long?'

The Dyak was non-committal. 'I do not know. Maybe if we see a hawk tomorrow, we can go? Yesterday was two snakes. This is not good for a journey.'

Jack had seen the snakes too, a green whip-snake and a mangrove cat-snake. They were ordinary creatures, going about their reptilian business. He did not understand why the Dyaks put such superstitious significance on ordinary creatures. They saw something every day of their lives and seemed, arbitrarily to an outsider, to decide on the spot whether it was good luck or inauspicious. He could not have it. He would not have it.

'We are going to cross the mountains tomorrow,' he stated firmly, 'whether there is a hawk or not.'

However, it happened that a rhinoceros wandered closer to the camp than usual. The humans were downwind of the beast, which was quite short-sighted, and so it was unaware of their presence behind a large clump of boulders. Jack asked Colenso to shoot the rhino, so that he could take its two horns. Colenso shook his head.

'I've had enough of shooting pachyderms just for the sport of it, Jack.'

Jack was irritated by this reply. 'What do you mean?'

'I used to be an ivory hunter, in Africa. One day something happened and I swore I would never shoot another elephant unless there was a danger to life. The same goes for rhinos, I'm afraid. I don't kill creatures for sport or money any longer.'

'But this is for scientific purposes.'

'Those horns will never reach the British Museum. Some Chinese merchant will steal them from you and turn them to powder to sell as an aphrodisiac.'

Jack was incensed with Colenso for a while. He stopped short of ordering the hunter to shoot the beast, because he knew Colenso would refuse to carry out the command. Instead, he took a musket and two Dyaks and went out to do the job himself. Keeping downwind of the creature, Jack crawled through the long grasses, using them as a screen, praying he would not put his hand on a pit viper, or any other dangerous snake. Even before he had gone a hundred yards he had collected boar ticks in the creases of his body, and leeches on the exposed parts of his skin.

The rhinoceros was a fine beast, with dark wiry hair. Close to, it was a smaller animal than Jack had anticipated. He had seen African rhinos and they were a good deal bigger than this creature. It was grazing quietly about two hundred yards from where Jack and the two Dyaks lay. The musket was loaded and ready and Jack went up on one knee. His movement, however, was enough to put up a cloud of fly-catchers that had been clinging to the reeds of a pool. They had been tensing themselves with the approach of the three men, their legs constricting like small springs and, when Jack showed his head above the grass, they took off.

The rhino turned immediately, its head pointing at the spot where the birds had risen. Its eyes peered in Jack's direction, as if it were trying to make out the figure. Just then, the wind changed, carrying the scent of the three men to the beast. It snorted again and began lumbering forward. This soon developed into a full charge when it was sure of the presence of an enemy.

The two Dyaks were on their feet in a second and running for some nearby trees. They yelled at Jack to join them, not pausing to see if he was taking their advice. Jack now stood up and planted his feet firmly in the ground. He sighted down the long barrel of the musket, taking careful aim. The weapon fired, going off rather sooner than he had anticipated, and he knew immediately it was not a good shot. The ball struck the enraged beast on the left shoulder, merely wounding it.

'Damn!'

Hurriedly, Jack began to load the musket again. This required taking a cartridge from his shirt pocket, biting off the end, dropping powder and ball into the barrel, drawing the ramrod, ramming down, returning the ramrod, taking out a percussion cap from the opposite shirt pocket, placing it on the nipple of the hammer, and, finally, cocking the hammer. The weapon, one with a modern rifled barrel, was then ready to fire.

He was only halfway through this series of actions, an operation at which he was not greatly proficient, when he fumbled and dropped the percussion cap into the grass. If he had been a soldier he might have performed the procedure in twenty seconds, but he had never been trained to that degree of cool efficiency under stress. In that moment he knew he was not going to have the weapon loaded in time. He stood there, staring at the rhino, which was now only twenty yards away.

Another man might have turned and run. Colenso might have. Keller certainly would have. But Jack was, of course, Lord Randolph Braiks, raised firmly in the belief that a gentleman does not make a fool of himself, even in dire circumstances, *especially* in dire circumstances. Colonels and generals of Jack's class had been decorated for bravery, for remaining still, firm and erect in the face of overwhelming odds, when all they had been doing was standing on their own dignity.

He could not run. A gentleman. It would make him look ridiculous in the eyes of the watching Dyaks. He simply stood and waited for the crashing, killing blow of two thousand pounds of hard flesh bearing down on him. His musket was in his hand and he used it as a staff, standing like some biblical character awaiting the wrath of God to descend upon his person.

Just as it was almost over, when the rhino was less than ten feet away, there was a booming in Jack's ear. He reeled sideways, clutching his head, the monstrous sound painful to him. An anger flared within his previously peaceful spirit. It was an automatic reaction to a sudden very loud noise.

'What on earth . . .?' he cried.

When Jack had recovered his wits he saw that the rhino

was lying on its side, its head almost at his feet. He then turned to see Colenso, standing just behind him, a smoking musket in his hands and another two loaded muskets by his side. It was then he knew that Colenso had saved his life and for some unfathomable reason Jack hated him for it. He was, of course, too much the gentleman to show such an emotion. Instead, he thanked the hunter in a cool, calm voice, adding, 'Colenso, how fortunate you followed me. I should have been a dead man but for that fine shot.'

'I told you. I only kill when life is threatened. You were in grave trouble there, Jack.'

'I know, I know. The beast would have gored me had you not killed it.'

They inspected the carcass. Colenso's shot had gone through its right eye and penetrated the brain. It was a brilliant piece of sharpshooting. The Sea Dyaks came up, all excitement. They assisted Jack in removing the horns from the animal with a bow saw. Then they slit open the torso to remove the soft meats, saying there would be feasting that night in the camp.

The Land Dyaks, the Ngaju in particular, were not so happy about the kill. They muttered amongst themselves that it was bad luck to destroy such a magnificent creature of the forest. There was certain specified game which they were permitted, by their own unwritten rules, to hunt for the pot. The rhino was not one of them. Its meat was too tough and, in any case, the rhinoceros was a mystical creature, not common game like bearded hog.

Singapore Jack went to his bivouac. He was followed there by Harry, shortly afterwards.

'I'm so glad you're not hurt,' she told him. 'You aren't, are you?'

'Not physically,' he replied, quietly, from within the half-darkness at the rear of the bivouac. 'But I am mortified.'

She was puzzled. 'Why should you be?'

'I was made to look foolish. Well,' he was more generous than that, 'perhaps not *made*. I put myself in the position. What a figure! Standing there, waiting to be trampled, while a beast thundered down on me. How ridiculous I must have looked. Yet it would have been even worse to have been gored in the back while running away. What a story that would have made for my enemies in the Geographical Society to repeat to one another! "Have you heard? Braiks got it in the rump while running away! Always knew the chap was a damned funk!"'

'It was not your fault, surely?'

'That doesn't matter. I should never have put myself in that position. I fumbled. I dropped the percussion cap. It was a stupid mistake that should have cost me my life. A man in my position should not make such errors.'

'Good heavens, Jack, it could have happened to anyone.'

'No, it would never have happened to Colenso.'

She made no reply to this and he knew that what he said was correct. A man as experienced as Colenso would not just have taken a single musket, hoping that one shot would be sufficient. Colenso had had three loaded muskets with him, all of them primed and ready to use in an emergency. Jack should have thought of that. Jack should have prepared himself for the eventuality. He had not. Therefore he felt himself to be a foolish man. The thought was agony to him. He bore it with difficulty.

Harry could see he was in torment. 'Jack, I don't think any less of you for this. I'm sure Kit doesn't either. Whatever your feelings on the matter, you can be sure that no one here regards you as anything but unlucky in this respect.'

But Jack remained convinced of his own stupidity.

The morning after the incident with the rhinoceros, the party were again on the move. Luckily for Jack, the Dyaks had seen some good omens in the sky. They were ready to climb up to the col. They were still fearful of mountain spirits, but they did not let this fear rule their progress.

Colenso went up the water course first, playing out lengths of rope behind him. He started out in the darkness, before dawn, in order to make the most of the day. It was a dangerous business but the party did not want to be caught having to spend the night on the col. Neither Jack nor Colenso had any idea whether there were ledges up there which they could use as platforms on which to sleep. From below the col looked like a sharp ridge.

Ferguson went up next, some way behind Colenso, securing one rope to provide handholds for those who were to follow. Kitts remained at the bottom to fasten the equipment to the hemp, so that it could be hauled up. The rest of the party made their way up the steep escarpment, using the jagged rocks bared by the rushing water, when it used that path.

Both Jack and Colenso continually looked up to the sky, wary of any cloud they saw forming in the blue. The last thing they wanted at that moment was for it to rain. A monsoon downpour would wash them off the side of the mountain. Happily, the sky remained bright and clear. They were able to make progress.

As with most ranges this one was not a single line of mountains. That would have been too neat for the gods. Instead, once Colenso made the col he saw that they would have to cross at least two more like it. It was apparent that they could not cross the range in one day. They would have to spend the night in a high valley.

Once the party was together on the col they descended down a slope a great deal less steep than their ascent. On their right they had a seemingly bottomless gully, hopelessly tangled with thick jungle foliage. They remained on the edge of this, working their way down to a wide ledge which overlooked the gully. Once they reached the flatness of the ledge, they made camp and produced a meal. After this, most of the party fell asleep, wrapping themselves in blankets in preparation for the cold they knew the night would bring with it.

Again they rose early, before the sun was up, and set off for a pass which had appeared during their previous day's trek. This was a difficult journey over rugged ground. All the while the Dyaks in the group were nervous and unhappy, expecting to be visited by demons, or mischievous spirits at the very least. It was to be expected that they were not disappointed. When a man believes in something so thoroughly, it may be manifested out of his very fears.

On their third night in the mountains a strange sound was heard, much like the whine of a mosquito, only many times louder. On hearing this the Dyaks rose almost as one man and clustered around the base of a rock hang. The Europeans came out of their bivouacs and stared up into the blackness, wonderingly. There was fear in every person's heart. The sound was so insistent, so penetrating, it caused the listeners pain.

'What is it?' cried Harry, her hands over her ears. 'I've never heard anything like it before.'

Neither Colenso nor Jack could answer her, despite their greater experience of foreign climes. Since the sound came from the air and was moving rapidly over their heads, they guessed it was some kind of flying creature. An unusual bird. Or a bat the like of which they had not encountered before now.

Lidah, who had remained with Harry, called to the men under the rock hang. They answered her.

Lidah turned to Harry in hysterics. 'They say it is a woman, missy. A woman like a giant insect. She flies in the night with a terrible sting. She stays in the mountains, waiting for people to come . . .'

Jack said calmly, 'I've heard of such a mythical creature, from my Dyaks. They say she picks up her victims, injects them with poison using this huge sting in her tail, then cocoons them. Normally she lives on pigs and deer, but she has been known to take humans, when she's hungry enough.'

The Dyaks in question were now crouched under the protection of their shelter, staring at the night sky. The firelight glinted in their wide eyes. Occasionally, the creature circling the camp swept just inside the hemisphere of light thrown out by the fire, but the creature flew so fast it was a fleeting blur of transluscent wings swishing through the red glow. None of the Europeans could make out any further details.

All they knew was that this rainforest eccentricity was larger than any bird they had ever encountered on their various travels. The mariners amongst them were not difficult to convince that this was some unnatural monster. They had seen things rise from the depths of the sea which had men's hair standing on end. In the misty spray and spume of the ocean, they had personally witnessed the shapes of mermaids diving from sight, and the dark shadows of great leviathans cruising in the depths. That which could rise to the surface from the ocean floor could also hide in unexplored jungles. The world still had many great areas of mystery and magic yet to be unfolded.

'You don't believe that do you?' questioned Harry, quickly. 'That's simply invention.'

Jack did not answer her. Instead he fetched a musket from his bivouac. The next time the high-pitched drone went low overhead, he fired in its direction. A foot-long tongue of flame came from the end of his musket barrel and lit the darkness for an instant. The sound of the shot echoed in the night around them and the creature's note turned to one of alarm. Now it sounded like an angry insect, as it continued to remain above the camp, swooping in a threatening dive ever so often.

Lidah and Harry joined the Dyak men under the rock hang, while Colenso and Jack fired several more shots into the air. The flashes from the muzzles of the muskets were bright to see. Each time they fired the hills reverberated with the sound of the shot. Eventually, the angry drone drifted away from their area and went off somewhere deeper into the mountain range, until finally they could not longer hear it. Certain imaginations allowed them to picture some awful monster lurking there, awaiting its opportunity to attack the camp again.

After much chatter, in which the Dyaks reiterated their belief that the creature had been the 'insect woman', they all retired to bed once again. The following day they were up and preparing to go when Ferguson went to wash in a rock basin. A shadow kept drifting across the surface of his bathing water. He looked up, high above his head, to discover a body.

The corpse was hanging from the broken branch of a dead mountain tree. It was in the form of a huge pupa dangling by means of a silken cord. The dead creature, wrapped in its sticky silken bonds, was half the size of a man, but unidentifiable due to the thickness of its bonds. Its blood had seeped through and stained the outside of the pupa scarlet and black. There were also signs of dripped blood on the face of the rock.

'No wonder that creature was angry last night. It thought we were after the contents of its larder,' said Jack on being summoned by the worried boatswain. 'Keep this quiet from the others. We don't want any panic.'

He stared at the object, swinging like a bloody side of beef in the mountain winds.

'At least we know that's not a man up there. It has to be a pig – or possibly a tapir. I think we should leave it alone. Whatever it was that fashioned that pupa, it's best we don't meet it again. No sense in alarming the others. I hope you understand that, Ferguson. Men like you and I are able to bear the idea of such knowledge without falling into a funk.'

Ferguson nodded doubtfully, crossed himself, and finally muttered a fervent prayer, before going with Jack to rejoin the main party.

# 2

Jack's attempts at thwarting a general panic were in vain. The following evening at dusk, as the group were preparing for camp, the horrible curiosity which the Dyaks called the 'insect woman' decided to harass them further. The group had been travelling along a hanging valley all day. The ground had been rough and stony beneath a carpet of creepers. Ankles and calves were sore with stumbling. Sweat bees swarmed over them, irritating and maddening. Biting flies came out of the creepers and attacked exposed areas of skin. The group was looking forward to a good meal and a restful night.

Kit Colenso had lit a scented candle in the dusk to keep the mosquitoes at bay. He and his Dyak, Patan, had settled down to a game of chess. Iguina, the other Ngaju, sat alongside to watch them. Since teaching them both chess on their journeys around the coast of Borneo, both the Dyaks had become skilled players and Colenso was having to fight hard to win any games at all.

The two Dyaks were hunters who often had to second-guess the moves any prey might make over two or three days. They were used to applying their minds to such problems. A group of gibbons might have several possible routes, depending on their needs at the time, whether it was for water, for food, for rest, for recreation, for breeding, and so on. The Dyaks were used to sitting in deep thought, their stomachs dependent upon the next move they made.

The idea of many of their hunts was to force their quarry into a corner from which it could not escape. Doing the same to a king with various knights, rooks, bishops and pawns became just as exciting to them. It would not have surprised Colenso to hear that, since having learned the game of chess, they shouted 'Checkmate' at some poor pig which had been tracked, harried, and finally trapped in some cave or hollow.

Their dispositions certainly allowed for such a thing. Dyaks, and the Ngaju were no exception, had a great sense of humour. The difference between them and Occidentals like Kit Colenso was that when they were going to laugh they lay down first, so they could split their sides without falling over. This cultural difference had astonished Harry, who now lost no opportunity in amusing the Dyaks, just to see them put down their weapons and lay on their backs to roar with laughter.

However, Patan and Iguina also liked the 'war' aspect of chess, which made them keen to win at the game. The board and pieces were old and stained with fungal growths, as well as having the usual scratches and worn patches. Colenso often had difficulty in recognizing the edges of the squares and the colours of the pieces. The Dyaks played with the utmost concentration however, making very few mistakes.

'Check,' said Colenso, quietly, as he became aware of a shadow over him.

Patan grinned, waited for a moment so that his watching friend Iguina could appreciate and savour the moment with him, then quietly took Colenso's queen with a white knight which had been lurking in the vicinity of a black rook.

'Damn,' muttered the South African, annoyed with himself. 'I'd forgotten that was there.' He looked up to see Harry standing over him. 'You distracted me,' he protested. 'Your shadow on the board! I was one move away from checkmate.'

'Patan has got you boxed in and you know it,' she replied.

It was true. Three moves later and it was all over. The delighted Dyak slapped him on the shoulder. Colenso left the board then, so that the two experts could play a game, while he talked to Harry.

Harry led him off to the water source, a thin stream dropping in a veil of mist from a high crag. There she confronted him. 'Look,' she said, 'Jack is very upset with himself over that rhino business.'

'So he should be,' replied Colenso, unable to stop his lips from tightening. 'I'm very upset with him too.'

'No, I don't mean he regrets killing the beast. I mean he still feels he was made to look a fool. Can't you go to him and persuade him that this just isn't true?'

Colenso stiffened. 'I don't think that's my place.'

She became exasperated with him. 'You are such an obstinate man, Kit. Is this too much to ask, that you should go to your friend and ease his mind a little? Surely you can see this is for the good of the expedition? A leader who has lost confidence in himself is liable to make errors.'

Kit Colenso stared at Harry. In the dusk she looked warmly attractive, soft and yielding. At that moment he would have given everything he owned just to kiss her on the mouth again. The thought of making love to her made his mind reel and his heart race. Harry, he thought, can't you see how in love with you I am?

His fondness for her had grown into something a great deal stronger over the long trek across the Ulu. One day the journey would come to an end and he would have lost his chance to impress her. It was childish, he knew, to *want* to impress her, but he was aware that she was Jack's. If Kit Colenso was to win this lady from her very brave, handsome and well bred gentleman, he would have to do something fairly spectacular. So far he had done nothing but bungle his chances. It was a game he was likely to lose: worse than playing Patan and Iguina at chess.

He was about to plunge his chances even further into the pit he kept digging for himself.

'Firstly, Jack is not my friend, never has been, never will be. I respect him as a man, he has many good qualities, but it is not my job to act as nanny to him. He would not want it. He would resent it. And if he feels his qualities of leadership are impaired, he should hand over to me.'

He walked away from her, knowing he was provoking a storm.

'Don't be so pompous!' she called. 'If you respect him, tell him so. I'm sure that's all it will take.'

Colenso shook his head wondering how these impossible thoughts ever entered a woman's head.

He stopped and turned. 'My dear Harry . . .'

'I am not your *dear*.'

'Harry, then – plain Harry – I could no more march up to Lord Randolph Braiks and say, "Sir, I respect you!" than I could pick up that boulder over there with my bare hands. What's more, he would not like it. It would worsen any discomfort he feels about himself and his abilities. You really don't understand men, do you, Harry? We do not like that sort of interference from other men. We like to work out our own problems, privately. Jack would regard anything I said to him in that vein as an affront. He is a proud man, pure aristocrat, through and through.'

'Nonsense. You would become closer to each other – like – like brothers.'

Colenso shuddered at the thought.

'I'm afraid it's you who is speaking nonsense.'

It was getting quite dark now. While there was no canopy overshading the valley there were some lone giant trees. Harry was standing in the buttress roots of one such cathedral-tall tree when Colenso thought he saw a shape detach itself from the foliage at the top. There followed that ugly whining sound from the skies. A short while later a fusillade of shots was heard coming from the camp area. Colenso and Harry ran back towards the camp, just in time to see one of the Dyaks struggling with some hideous creature which appeared, in the absence of good light, to be half winged-insect, half-human.

No fires had yet been lit and the single lamp burning was sputtering and flickering. It was therefore difficult to ascertain the true shape of the monster. All one could see was that it was indeed larger than a man, and that it had crisp wings which rasped while it struggled with its prey. Colenso could think of no known winged creature of that size which had yet been discovered. It was, of course, possible there were such creatures, for the world was not fully explored, nor all its creatures classified.

The beast's tail curved beneath its body, between its legs. The end of this tail seemed to be buried in the stomach of the writhing man. It was like witnessing some strange mating dance, as the pair moved back and forth, their desperate combat turning horror into dark comedy. The man seemed to have his thumbs hooked into the monster's eyes, gouging, plunging deep, making its whine high enough to shatter glass.

The rest of the men were standing off, looking on in absolute terror. All except for Singapore Jack, who weaved around the fighting pair, wielding a parang. Colenso could see that Jack was trying to get a clean swing at the monster, to hack her without hurting the Dyak. The man's eyes were wide with terror and a peculiarly thin scream was coming from his lips, building like a whistle reaching its top note, then dying again. He was covered in some sticky substance, which came from the insect woman's mouth, as her several pairs of thorny legs tried to subdue her victim.

'Cut the tail, Jack,' yelled Colenso, grabbing another parang. 'Sever the sting!'

Jack saw his chance and swept the blade of the parang between the monster and the Dyak. The creature suddenly flew off in an instant, astonishingly swift. One moment it was gripping the Dyak, the next it was somewhere up in the evening sky. Kitts and Ferguson fired their weapons. Their shots were hopelessly wide, for one moment she hovered in one spot, the next somewhere else. She darted about the sky at eye-defeating speeds, filling a space here, then there, then here again. It was impossible to get a bead on her with a musket. Her grating whine got louder as the shots hummed through the air around her.

'Light a torch,' cried Jack. 'Someone get a brand going. If she comes down again, we'll blind her with fire. Quickly, move yourselves . . .'

Kitts and Patan sprang into action, using the lighted lamp to fire a brand. Others then scrambled about in the poor light of the lamp, gathering bracken and grasses, lighting their own torches. All eyes looked fearfully to the heavens, waiting for that creature to dive again.

It seemed she had had enough for the night. Either that or

the firebrands frightened her away. The whining ceased, there was a crackling of wings against a crispy carapace, and she was gone into the night. Many doubted she had gone for good, but at least there was a respite from her attacks.

'Bring the injured man over here,' cried Jack, putting his brand to a fire at last. 'Let's have a look at him.'

'He's unconscious,' replied Colenso, helping to carry the limp figure into the light, where he could be studied more closely. 'I can still feel a pulse, but it's very weak. Wait, wait, it's flickering – he's not going to last much longer. I sense him going. Bring a mirror, quickly.'

Jack brought the mirror and held it to the man's mouth. It did not mist over. He was gone. When they inspected his body they found a foot-long barb in his gut. It was the grotesque tail-end from the insect woman. Some flesh was still attached to the blunt end. The point of this sharp, curved object, looking like the black sting of a massive scorpion, brought forth the Dyaks innards when wrenched from his abdomen. Since he was dead, it hardly mattered to him, but it had a profound effect on the morale of the living.

'That's disgusting – that's horrible,' said Harry, turning away. 'Are you sure he's dead? You may have hurt him.'

'Stone dead,' muttered Jack. 'No feeling there.'

He took the sting and cleaned off the sharp point, leaving the larger end with the insect woman's flesh still attached. He wrapped the whole thing in damp muslim. It was Jack's intention to take this curio with him. If the legend of the Punan heads came to nothing, he would be able to sell artifacts like the sting and the rhino horns to finance some other expedition. He had to think of the future, even as he was dealing with the present. Then he held a conference with Colenso and Harry.

'We must push on as soon as it gets light tomorrow,' he began.

'Agreed,' replied Colenso.

Harry looked from one man to the other. 'There's no urgency now, is there?' she said. 'That – that *thing* is like a bee. It will surely die now that its sting has been cut from it.'

'We can't be sure of that,' answered Jack. 'The sting may regrow, the creature repair itself, don't you agree, Colenso.'

'Yes, I'm afraid I do. I must agree with Jack, Harry. We know nothing about this creature. Who's to say there is only one in the district? There might be more.'

Singapore Jack nodded. 'Thank you, Colenso. It is precisely for that reason that I intend leaving the body of the Dyak where it is. If this local horror wants it, she can come and get it, rather than attack *us* again.'

Horrified, Harry rounded on her fiancé.

'But – but you can't. We must bury him.'

'I agree, we ought to, but we can't. Don't concern yourself about the other Dyaks. He was the only Christian amongst them, recently converted by that new fiery Scottish Presbyterian minister who arrived in Kuching not long before we left. The majority of the Land and Sea Dyaks are heathens. They look on the missionaries as witchdoctors and sorcerers. If we tell them this is how to deal with Christian dead after an attack by a supernatural creature, they will believe us. They know nothing else.'

If Harry had been upset with Jack before this moment, she was trebly so now.

'We can't lie to them like that,' she said, aghast. 'What if – what if someone attempts to convert them later?'

Jack snapped, 'They should bloody well mind their own business. These people are all right as they are. Why stuff their head with *more* nonsense than they already carry?

Leave a pagan as he is, I say. Don't these priests have enough to do already, ministering to their own flocks, without trying to turn wolves into sheep? I'm firm on this, Harry. We will leave the Dyak where he is when we move on in the morning.'

Thus Mahatara's hawk, Antang, found his talons busy again, stooping on a lost flimsy soul and carrying it to his master to be devoured.

## 3

Prince Kalim was summoned to the palace. It was here that Rajah Starke held court every morning except for Islamic and Christian holy days, and those days in the Chinese and Dyak calendars which were inauspicious or unlucky. This meant there were sometimes gaps of three or four days, but eventually a morning arrived in which business could take place and the rajah made sure he stayed until suppliants, accusers and accused were satisfied that justice and mercy had been fairly meted out. Of course, there were those who went away unhappy, but what judge in history has been able to satisfy all parties, whatever the dispute, and carry out the laws of the land to the letter?

Kalim was apprehensive as he made his way down the river by his barge to the magnificent gardens in which the old rajah's palace stood. The gravity of the building, as he approached the white portals, did nothing to allay his worries. He knew this was about the rajah's cousin, Harriet Glendenning, and that his schemes and dreams were about to reach a head. He tried to look serious and concerned, without showing the fear he felt inside, as he climbed the marble steps to the iron gates.

In the courtroom he found Rajah Starke, seated high above everyone else on a judge's throne. On a stool below the rajah's imposing figure, sat Muda Hassim. Lower still, amongst the benches which faced the imperious rajah, was the bomoh prince, Issam. There were various other dignitaries and court officials, scattered about the floors and seated on chairs: some were whispering to their neighbours, others stood quietly, awaiting the next piece of business for the day.

'Ah, Prince Kalim,' said Rajah Starke, as the prince strode with noisy steps across the marble floor. 'Kind of you to come at short notice . . .'

'You sent word you wished to see me, my lord. I thought it only fitting to heed the call at once. By the messenger's tone it sounded an urgent business.'

Kalim was irritatingly aware that Prince Issam's eyes were on him the whole time he spoke, as were Muda Hassim's. He felt as if he were being prodded by spears from the front and the flanks. However, he dared not look backwards to see if his rear was blocked also. Though he could flick his eyes left and right, it would be too obvious a move to glance behind.

Starke said, 'I have been consulting Prince Issam on the progress of my cousin, Harriet Glendenning, and the prince has informed me that she is unfortunately in dire straits. It was suggested that a party of Dyaks be sent to attempt a rescue, before it is too late. Of course, she being most precious to me, I made ready to lead these men, to go at once into the Ulu to find her and bring her back to Kuching, where she will be safe . . .'

Prince Kalim smiled inwardly, revealing nothing on his smooth, unlined countenance. He was a man well able to hide his true feelings, having practised deceit his whole life. The rajah was now continuing to speak on the subject.

'However, my grand vizier and your older brother, Muda Hassim, has persuaded me after much discussion and argument, that my place is here, at the head of my kingdom. You may imagine how desperate I became as I searched my mind for someone I could trust to carry out this mission in my stead, someone who would not hesitate to lay down their life for my cousin's sake, and could find no names there.

'Then Muda Hassim told me of you, his younger brother. He speaks of you as an honourable, courageous young man – strong in body and heart – for whom the Ulu would hold no fears. I have called you here then, to plead with you to assist me in this matter. Will you go in search of my cousin and bring her back safely? You will be rewarded most handsomely, I promise, both in wealth and in status. Someone must be grand vizier when your older brother retires or, God forbid, leaves this world. Do this task for me and you will earn my eternal gratitude.'

Despite his resolve to show nothing on his features, a shock wave went through the young prince which must have registered on his face. He looked quickly at Prince Issam, to divine whether some sort of counterplot was in progress, but he quickly decided that the bomoh prince was as distressed by this turn of events as he was himself. It was true that Kalim had not brought his older brother, Muda Hassim, into the plot, for he would have disapproved and forbidden such a scheme. It was therefore entirely possible, given Muda Hassim's dedication to his duties and his country, that his older brother had indeed persuaded the rajah not to go after his cousin himself, but to send a reliable and trustworthy substitute. If he had not been in the thick of a plot of his own making, Prince Kalim would have been flattered and proud to be chosen for such a deed.

'My brother is most kind in his regard for me, but, my lord, are you certain I am the right man to head this expedition?'

Kalim could definitely feel a pair of eyes boring into the back of his head. He knew, he could *feel* someone behind him in the courtroom, who, if this person did not wish him ill, was not a friend. It was maddening, not being able to turn around and see who this person was, though a faint whiff of perfumed oil came to the prince on a gentle draught. He had smelt this particular scent somewhere before and his mind raced to remember time and place, and therefore pinpoint the character of his watcher. Smell, as everyone knows, is the most potent trigger of memories, but the identification of this certain fragrance remained a mystery to the prince.

'I *know* you are the right man!' came the reply.

Kalim's mind twisted and wheeled in its attempts to turn this situation to his advantage. Very quickly, for he was a bright and cunning individual, the solution came to him. He gave the rajah and his court an easy smile.

'Then of course I shall go. I shall carry out this task for my lord, with great pleasure and, hopefully, with equal courage. What is the nature of your cousin's plight, my lord, that I might know best how to form my expedition?'

'She has been captured by Olo Dusun tribesmen and is being held hostage. According to Prince Issam, her protectors have all been killed and she alone survives. The Olo Dusun are preparing to marry her to one of the minor chiefs. If she refuses to take him, as I am sure she will, she is to be put to death. If we are unable to save her, Miss Glendenning will be thrown to the crocodiles and eaten alive.'

'For such an expedition I shall require many warriors,' Prince Kalim said, thinking quickly. 'A small army. They must be placed under my sole command, with instructions to obey my orders to the letter. I must have sturdy men to cut a path if we move away from the rivers. This is the only way we will be able to progress through the jungle at speed.

'We shall sweep down through the Ulu, carrying all before us, and be on the Olo Dusun people before the end of the month, which is the next auspicious day for a wedding. Nothing will happen to her before the full moon, by which time me and my soldiers will have destroyed their longhouses and rescued your cousin from any further harm.'

'You have at your disposal,' replied the rajah, 'my whole army if necessary. My cousin is the dearest person in the world to me. I will do anything to rescue her.'

Kalim was satisfied. With a large body of men under his sole command he would be strong enough to take Sarawak by force. It meant he would have to go into the jungle for a while, acclimatize the troops to his command. Once he had bonded with them, made promises to the officers, won them to his cause, he would attack Kuching and depose the rajah. It was a better plan than his original scheme, for it meant that he could kill his brother, Muda Hassim, in the attack, and therefore take the sultanate for his own. There would be no waiting around for his older brother to die of a great age.

'In that case, my lord, I accept the commission.'

'Good. Some of my personal guard will take you into the forest to a place of my choosing. The troops will follow at sunrise tomorrow. May you be successful in your mission.'

Kalim bowed, then turned to walk out of the court, at last being able to see the person who had been standing behind him.

It was a bare-chested, muscled Dyak with a red kerchief

tied around his head in a swashbuckling style. His right hand was on his sword hilt. His left around the shoulders of a boy.

'You!' gasped Kalim, as he recognized the pirate he had employed to kidnap Issam's grandson. This was the boy by his side.

Prince Kalim did not turn and look at the rajah. Nor did he glance at the faces of his older brother or Prince Issam. He knew he had been beaten. Walking forward, his head held high, he whispered to Ruwakruwak, 'Why?'

The pirate shrugged and gave him a little smile. 'For gold, naturally. They offered more . . .'

Outside the court, Prince Kalim was silently accompanied by a dozen Dyaks from the rajah's personal guard. They took him to the river where a boat was waiting. From there Kalim was transported south until they came to a particular longhouse. Here it was indicated that he should disembark. Two of the head-hunters remained with him. They took him into the longhouse. The first thing Kalim noticed was the fishing net full of severed heads which hung from the ceiling above the ruai. Their grisly faces, the fresh ones with eyes still staring, teeth bared in grimaces formed at the moment of death, seemed to mock him.

He turned to one of his guards. 'Am I to be imprisoned here?'

'You are to stay until the rajah sends for you,' came the reply. 'If you try to escape our orders are to kill you.'

'So, the rajah is not going to have me executed?'

There was no reply to this question and Prince Kalim believed that his life was safe. On worrying the matter further in his own mind, he could see that the rajah would have problems if he were to order his death. There would be great unease amongst the other Malay princes if one of their number were to be summarily executed. It was true that Rajah Starke had killed princes on the battlefield, but that was an entirely different matter. To have one hung or decapitated like a common criminal, why that would not have been acceptable to the princes. Thus, for the moment, Kalim believed he was safe.

'I shall settle down and enjoy my sojourn here in the rainforest, as best as I can,' he told the heads, clustered like rotting balls in the net above him. 'It will not be as pleasant as my pavilion, but it will give me time to devise new plots, new ways of ridding our land of this white rajah.'

That night, one of Prince Kalim's household retainers arrived at the longhouse, with a few of his creature comforts. The young boy had brought salves, sweet-smelling ointments, oils, and various other lotions for care of the hair and body. The prince was glad of this. Already he was horrified at the thought of having to bathe in river water, which might carry all sorts of filth in its currents. The boy could now cleanse him with oils and rub balm into any sores he had caught from these unclean creatures of the rainforest, his new companions.

'You will attend very closely to my armpits and crotch,' said the prince to the boy, as the latter undressed his lord. 'The sweat in those two areas in particular has grown stale and unwholesome during my time here.'

The boy nodded and said he would make sure the prince smelled as sweet as a flower.

'The maidens here will fight amongst themselves to sit next to you at supper, master.'

The prince shuddered. 'Those unsavoury creatures . . .'

But actually, after he had been bathed in oil, and anointed with various balms and ointments – always a sensual and arousing experience – he found himself staring at their primitive beauty and admiring their natural, unpretentious looks. They were handsome women, rather than pretty, with strong bones, clear eyes and rounded happy faces. He joined the circle of men and women for supper, sitting between two young females who giggled when he touched them as he squeezed his chubby body between theirs.

They sniffed his skin and laughed, their small brown-tipped breasts quivering temptingly before his eyes. One of them fed him from a leaf with her hand and let him lick her fingers clean of honey. Once the meal was over however, a great weariness descended up on him. It had been a long day, with many tensions. He decided to retire to the room given him on the end of the ruai. One of the guards slept by the door on the inside of the room, the other remained awake on the outside. His body servant seemed to have disappeared into the night.

The close scrutiny by his Dyak jailers infuriated the prince. He had not been subjected to such treatment in his life before. It pierced the very core of his arrogance. As he lay down on the rush matting which was his only bed, he told himself he was a proud man, a man with an impeccable blood line. To be exposed to such indignities was humiliating and degrading. Someone, sometime would pay dearly for these affronts to his person.

As he fell asleep, he became aware of the fragrance of the ointment with which he had been smeared. It was not a scent familiar to him, nor one he would have chosen from his vast store of such cosmetics. The perfume was musky, rather than sweet, with a rather earthy undersmell. Not one he would have picked for himself at all. Still, he had not been there to guide the hand of his retainers and so had to make do with what had been chosen for him. Yet one more inconvenience!

He dreamed he was alone on a boat being carried forward by a great rushing river. The water spirits leapt and pranced around his prahu, delighting him with their sinuous movements, while at the same time he was terrified by the thundering, tumbling of the water beneath the boat. Rajah Angin, the king of the wind, was partly responsible for the turbulence of the river and this deity sent someone to keep the lonely prince company.

This 'company' was a body bobbing in the water, being swept along by the same force which carried the boat. The corpse spoke to Kalim, telling him she was Kin Tambuhan, the 'unknown maiden', who had been lifted from her palace garden by an eagle. The geruda had carried her over the seas and had dropped her in the forest of the King of Kuripan. The king's son found her and wed her, but his mother was desperately angry over the match. The queen had the new princess murdered and her corpse thrown into the river. Her husband was bathing in the waters with some friends as her body was swept past him and the young man killed himself with his own kris, stabbing himself in the throat.

Kalim sympathized with the babbling corpse, saying if he had his kris, he too would cut his own throat. A nobleman's wavy-bladed kris was his most sacred possession. The first kris had been given to King Jamajaya by the goddess Durga. Prince Kalim explained to the corpse of the princess that he had left his kris behind, at his house in Kuching, and therefore could not carry out the honourable act of suicide. Kin Tambuhan called him a coward and accused him of leaving his dagger behind on purpose.

'No, no, I had to go to court – one cannot enter the court armed. Afterwards I was taken against my will to a longhouse deep in the rainforest. I had no opportunity to retrieve my kris.'

'In your heart you are glad you left it behind.'

He had to allow this was true but he was not going to

admit this to a dead body, even if it was that of Kin Rambuhan. When she continued to argue with him, he left her to be washed away with the current. He landed on the shore and was just beaching his boat when something came charging out of the jungle.

Kalim was terrified to see that what approached him was Gerjis, the giant man-eating tiger. It was said that Gerjis had been buried by Kanchil, the mousedeer, and that the elephant had later crushed Gerjis's skull with a tree trunk. Yet, here he was, in all his ferociousness, ready to devour the unsuspecting Prince Kalim. The prince immediately set off in his prahu again, to follow the less dangerous river.

He soon caught up with Kin Rambuhan's corpse and she began berating him. For the rest of the dream he listened to her reprimands. After a while he grew intensely hungry and the only thing to eat was the carcass of the woman. He began feeding on her rotten flesh, tearing chunks from her limbs and torso with his teeth, and swallowing the foul meat with revulsion in his heart, if not in the buds of his taste.

When his belly was full and her torn body attested to his greed, he said, 'Now let us hear your nagging, woman!' and laughed.

Prince Kalim woke with a start in the early hours of the morning. The sweat poured from his body, soaking his silk nightgown. This garment stuck to him uncomfortably and he removed it, throwing it petulantly across the room. Once he had got rid of his nightgown he became increasingly aware that his skin itched. He began scratching, which seemed to make it worse. In the end it was driving him insane, so he arose and walked to the door, only to have a Dyak guard leap up in front of him, sword unsheathed and ready to cut off his head.

'All right, all right,' grumbled Kalim, returning to his bed. 'I was only going for a cool walk by the river.'

The rest of the night was spent in extreme discomfort. In the morning light he inspected his skin and found he was covered in tiny spots. He called his body servant in a great panic and asked him what they could do about this defilement.

'I have come upon some infection in this flea-ridden paradise,' he said with heavy sarcasm. 'Have we any balms or salves for such a condition?'

The boy searched the various bottles and jars. Eventually he came to the prince with a jar of ointment. The prince allowed the boy to smear it all over his body and rub it in.

'Ah, that's better – more soothing,' murmured Kalim.

Yet, by the evening the condition was as bad as ever. The prince's scratching had opened the spots to sores. These formed black scabs over the wounds. Thereafter, no matter how much irritation the prince received from these wounds, he now refrained from scratching. He continued to chide the boy and insist that the youth find something which would ease the irritation and cure the condition.

Over the next two days something very strange happened. The black scabs turned a greenish colour. This frightened the prince very much. He was now convinced he was the subject of sorcery, but he did not know how it had occurred. In the longhouse was a basir, a priest-shaman who was dressed as a woman. Kalim called this person to his room and asked him to exorcise it.

'There is something in here which is troubling me. Perhaps the fingernail parings of a bewitched woman? Or the hairs from the head of a sorcerer. I want you to find it, to root it out, to burn it on the longhouse fires.

The basir said he would do his best over the next few days, and set to work.

By the time the basir had found the offending substance, Kalim's skin had begun to harden into what appeared to be small green scales. The young Dyak maidens no longer fought to sit beside him, but positively avoided him. There was horror on their faces as he approached and passed them by. To the prince, who had always been very handsome and used to the attention of women, this was devastating. He wept great tears in the privacy of his room and even his guards felt sorry for him.

'What is it?' he cried to the basir. 'What causes my distress?'

'This is to blame. This jar of ointment. It has been bewitched by a sorcerer. It contains a magic formula, for which we have other words, but in your language is called *tiang maleh rupa*, the shapechanging spell.'

The basir held up one of those items which had come upriver with Kalim's body servant.

He called his retainer to his side then and asked him where the jar had come from, for it was that ointment which had been unfamiliar to him on the first evening at the longhouse. The one which had a strong undersmell of earth and with which the young man had smeared his whole body.

'Why, that is a gift from Prince Issam, my lord,' said the retainer, brightly. 'He said to be sure to cover you with it the first evening in the rainforest, to protect you from fungal infections and jungle sores.'

Prince Kalim screamed and threw the jar from the longhouse into the river. He began tearing at his body with his nails, trying to remove the scaly substance which had replaced his skin. Over the next week the Dyaks quietly witnessed the prince's legs and arms shrivel to half their size. Claws grew in place of fingers and toes. The prince's jaws began to grow, sprouting outwards, until he had a long snout.

His mouth shed its old teeth and he grew new pointed

ones, all along the rim of his mandible and upper jaw. His eyes turned yellow, with black slits for pupils. His belly changed colour. Worst of all, from the base of his backbone, a growth began which did not finish until it was a long reptilian tail, thick at the rump and pointed at the very tip. It swished from side to side, in a sweeping motion, when he walked.

And how he walked now! Not on two legs, but on all four, a scuttling motion, which frightened the Dyaks so much they locked him in his room. In this place of half-darkness, he snapped his jaws in anger, and scuttled around trying to tear holes in the walls with his strong, sharp teeth. Eventually he was successful and managed to rip through the bamboo slats, to let the daylight in. Once the hole had been fashioned he slipped through it and made his way down to the river, to enter its waters.

This was where he now belonged, battling with the other crocodiles for fish and meat, at times resting on the river-bank to warm his cold blood, at others thrashing and twisting with his ugly jaws, to wrench a piece of rotten flesh from the carcass of some dead animal washed down-river with the broken branches.

And the only thing he now feared was the giant Gerjis, that fabulous tiger-creature made of sunlight and shadow, who might sneak up one day and come out of the rainforest so fast it was impossible to escape, to tear him limb from limb.

# PART SEVEN

# King of the Fairies

# 1

Rajah Jinn Peri, the king of the fairies, had just heard of the altercation between the omang and Keller's group. When he learned that the humans had caused some deaths amongst the gnomes, he was very disturbed. Rajah Jinn Peri was not particularly fond of the omang himself – they were a troublesome tribe of half-wits and were not easy to discipline – but he felt every fairy death quite sharply. If such things were permitted to happen on a regular basis, his kingdom would be whittled down to nothing before a few centuries were out. The fairy population, unlike that of mortals, was slow to regenerate.

Rajah Jinn Peri consulted the Santang Sisters, they with the golden brooms, for it was the seven sisters who were ultimately responsible for the fate of the mortals. Rajah Jinn Peri put it to the sisters that they should encourage Bujang Sembelih, the throat-cutting demon, to pay the mortals a visit. The Santang goddesses would not countenance this approach. They said their brother Jata, he with the red-faced head of a crocodile, wanted the mortals to die slowly. Bujang Sembelih tended to dispense with his victims in one swift movement, careless of the mess he caused, oblivious of the sweeter side of revenge.

'Better,' said the sisters, 'that we persuade Hantu Kuang, the ghost with a hundred eyes, to harass their leader, get him to lose his way and sense of purpose.'

Once again the Santang Sisters had the perfect answer. Rajah Jinn Peri was satisfied. He would ask Hantu Kuang to work his madness on the group's leader. This particular demon enjoyed tinkering with the minds of men, corrupting their thoughts, turning them against themselves. It would be satisfying to watch this process, from the high trees of his mountain home.

The wound Keller had received from the warrior on the bridge had festered and he was constantly in a half-fever. When the group discovered the ruined temple, covered in vines and creepers, and surrounded by strange korwar, he ordered a halt. The rambling place of many rooms, built from roughly hewn blocks of local stone, was cool within and to Keller it had a touch of civilization. The Dyaks were not afraid to enter the inner darkness of the temple, but they did hold the place in some awe.

'Iskander,' they said. 'He has built this place many, many years ago, with the help of the green one, the half-god Kilir, the immortal teacher, whose touch could turn wastes into verdant pastures.'

Keller, though without a formal education, was not an uninformed man. He had learned much about Alexander the Great from a clerk who had been pressed into the navy. Keller admired the ancient Macedonian king a great deal. However, his knowledge was not complete and it did not seem incongruous to him that he had found one of Alexander's waystations, here in the middle of the Borneo jungle, where only primitive tribes dwelt.

Keller found a separate chamber for himself and Usang in the vast temple. In the next room, acting as a buffer between him and the more disgruntled of the men, were Raki and Mayok. They had with them Budrudeen. Raki had formed an attachment to Keller which had been strengthened by the defeat of the warrior on the bridge. Raki admired men who were warriors through and through, and the cultural differences between him and the group's leader served to mask the flaws in the man he had chosen to follow to the death.

In truth, the Europeans in the party, and many of the Dyaks, had had enough. They wanted to go back. Raki told them they were getting close to the Kingdom of the Sun Bear, the land where the Punan held the seven heads. But they were exhausted. The rainforest had knocked all the desire for gold out of them and now all they wanted was a friendly tavern and civilization. The five Europeans – Smith, Aldous, Chivers, Blake and Johnson – held a meeting in Keller's absence and voted that once they had rested they would return to Sarawak.

The party elected Johnson and Blake, Keller's closest cronies, to tell him of their decision. Johnson was wise enough to go to Keller's room with a loaded pistol in his belt. Blake decided that the sight of a weapon might antagonize Keller and left his firearms by his bed space.

The pair entered the room accompanied by a suspicious Raki, who quietly ordered Mayok to stand with him, behind the two men. Keller was sitting up, his back against the damp cool stone wall of the chamber. Usang was down at the stream with two of the other Dyaks, washing herself and her clothes. Keller's blanket, now moth-eaten and mouldy, was laid out on the floor in front of him. On it were his pistols, his compass, and various other personal items which he was in the process of cleaning and oiling.

Keller stared with bleary, bloodshot eyes at Johnson. There was a poultice of moss and clay strapped to the wound on Keller's side. Blood had seeped through this and had clotted and turned black, forming a crust. It was clear that the wound was festering badly, but Keller would let no one touch it but Raki, who simply changed the moss and clay dressing once the poultice had dried and begun cracking.

'What do you want?' asked Keller in a surly manner.

'Listen,' began Johnson, uneasy now that he faced the man who had appointed himself their leader, 'we've been shipmates a long time, right? I don't want no part of no mutiny here, but the lads have had enough. They want to go back.'

'We're going on,' snapped Keller, returning to cleaning one of his pistols.

Blake suddenly exploded. 'Who the bloody hell do you think you are? You're just a seaman, like any of us. If we want to go back, we don't need your permission.'

The heavy, red-haired eyebrows on Keller's face lowered, as he squinted at his 'shipmate'.

'You think you don't, eh? You namby-pamby. Listen, I've been through a thousand times worse that what we're goin' through here. You think this is bad? I've seen men killed and eaten by blackies in the Pacific and got away to tell the tale. I've been on a man o' war which was sunk and spent two days in the sea, while men was took by sharks not an arm's length away from where I trod water. I've been flogged, keel-hauled and half-hung. I've run the gauntlet and spat in the face of them who beat me.

'There's nothin' you can show me worse than what I've been through before. The same goes for the likes of you. You've seen men squashed by buckin' cannons, ain't you, their arms and legs still wriggling while the gun crushed 'em to death? You've seen men fall from frozen riggin' rounding the Horn, so cold they might have shattered like glass beakers on the deck. You've seen men drop from scurvy and be thrown overboard like so much rotten meat. Why, this what we've got here,' Keller waved a free hand, 'is luxury. We've got food, we're not cold, and we're like to make ourselves the richest men in the world.'

'You don't understand,' said Johnson, his hand on his pistol, 'the lads are dead weary. There's only six of us left now, countin' you in too, and the other three don't want to go on. You can't look to the Dyaks. This bloody jungle's their home. They live here. But we don't.'

Blake said, 'We're goin' to get bit by snakes or scorpions in this place,' he looked around the walls where there were indeed scorpions lurking in the cracks. 'And it's worse out there in the jungle. We've lost four of the lads already. If we don't go back now, we're all goin' to die, and that's a fact . . .'

While Johnson and Blake had been talking, Keller had been deliberately loading his pistol. He had rammed the powder and wadding down, but his ammunition was in his backpack, which was just out of his reach. Instead, he left the ramrod in the barrel, ready to be fired like a small harpoon. Johnson stared at the pistol uneasily. Blake, the unarmed one of the pair, edged backwards until he was half-shielded by the bulky Johnson.

'Are you going to use that firearm?' asked Keller quietly, his eyes glaring yellow in the light of a lamp.

Johnson's hand dropped from his pistol butt. 'Why, Johnny me lad, would I shoot a shipmate what's been with me all these years?'

'Then why'd you wear it in here in the first place?' snapped Keller.

'For protection. You've been damn testy of late, Johnny.

Now don't say you ain't. I think that wound's poisonin' your mind. No one of us can tell what you're goin' to be up to next. Ain't that right, Blake?'

Blake blurted, 'He's tellin' the truth, Keller.'

'There's nothing wrong with my mind,' Keller said slowly. 'I'm fine. You go back to them others and tell them who's in charge, you hear? Me, I'm in charge. I say what goes and what don't go around here. You lily-livered bastards. We're that close to being the richest men in the world and you all want to run back to Kuching to soft beds. You make me sick.'

The two seamen began to edge towards the doorway, nodding.

'All right, Johnny,' said Johnson, 'we'll tell them what you said. They won't be none too happy, but we'll tell them. I can't speak for what they'll do though, you know that. Me an' Blake, we'll steer clear of any mutiny. But I warn you, they're in a bad mood. I can't answer for their actions.'

'You just tell 'em what I said.'

'All right.'

Throughout this whole encounter Mayok had been standing by Raki's side. Mayok had stared dispassionately at the confrontation, not really caring who won and who lost the argument. Raki's hand had been on his Dyak short sword. He was clearly ready to leap forward and give Keller any assistance needed, had fighting broken out between the Europeans. Budrudeen had remained in the shadows of the adjoining room. He carried no weapon and would not have taken sides had a fight started.

Keller grunted, shifting the poultice on his wound with his left hand. He laid the pistol down carefully, by his side. It was still loaded with the ramrod, which poked out an inch or two beyond the end of the muzzle.

'Ungrateful bastards,' he said, gesturing towards the

door. 'You take 'em along with you, to make 'em rich men, and the first sign of trouble they turn on you. Watch my back, eh? Well I might just get in first. Raki, Mayok, you take turns in guarding the door tonight. If someone tries to get in, you chop their bloody heads off, understand?'

His fever running high, the leader of the expedition tried to get some sleep. He drifted in and out of a light doze all night, but he was too unwell to obtain the kind of refreshing sleep a man needs to recharge his energy. In the middle of the night he woke with a terrible thirst. The waterskins were to hand. He reached over the snoring form of Usang to grasp one, nudging her in the process.

Usang stirred slightly, her rounded form uncurling like one of those furry caterpillers Keller frequently squashed between two pinched fingers. He could smell the sleep-sweat wafting up from her warm body. Keller stroked her breast. She did not wake and he did not bother her further. He was in no mood to talk to her anyway and had only bumped her simply because she was in the way of his elbow.

As he drank, he felt he was being watched. His eyes went to the doorway first, only to see the solid back and head of Raki. The Iban was sitting, presumably wide awake, staring down a long dark hallway in the direction of the room where the other Europeans slept.

Then there was a slight movement in one of the corners of the room. Keller's attention switched to this spot. Now he saw it. A dark figure in the shadows at the rear. It seemed to be hovering somewhere near the Malay cook. Somehow Keller knew that what he was looking at was an apparition of some kind.

He thought it was not surprising to find such a creature in an ancient ruin. Spectres, he knew, inhabited old dwellings and this was a crumbling temple. It would have been unusual not to find a legion of ghosts in here. Strangely enough he did not feel menaced by it. He was only curious. It seemed to him that this was a special ghost, one quite powerful in its own world. Keller felt that power as he would feel the hot glow from a bonfire. It burned into him, making him sweat. He picked up the lamp and lifted it, to get a better view of the shape.

The flicker, the changing light, alerted Raki, who swung round to see what was going on. The Iban then let out a great cry and fell forward, laying prone on the floor. His arms were outstretched in the manner of Budrudeen, when the Malay boy was praying. If Keller had been reflective before, this action now alarmed him. Raki was clearly terrified by the figure at the back of the room.

'What is it?' whispered Keller. 'Is it a ghost?'

Usang opened her eyes, stared at the creature not two feet from him, and screamed. Mayok woke and scuttled in from the next room. He too fell down on seeing the spectre and sat hugging his knees and shivering violently. Only Keller remained calm, still fascinated by the supernatural being. Ordinarily, he might have been afraid, but his feverish brain seemed to accept the intruder, and he was only excited by the reactions of the others.

The ghost then spoke inside Keller's head, telling him what he must do if he was to be successful in his mission. Keller listened, enthralled. How was it that the ghost spoke English? Was it the spirit of a Briton who had come looking for a fortune and had found death in the jungle? Perhaps it was a ghost with a universal tongue, who could speak to any manner of man? Keller stood up, intending to ask the ghost a question.

Just at that moment the phantom disappeared into the ancient stones. One moment it was there, threateningly close to Budrudeen, the next it was gone. Keller felt almost exalted, as if he had been chosen by angels. His blood was running hot in his veins, pounding through his head in great rivers. It seemed to him this was a good omen. Perhaps the ghost had come to lead them to the Kingdom of the Sun Bear.

'You saw that?' he said to Raki and the others. 'You saw that creature? It spoke to me.'

Usang cried, 'It was Hantu Kuang! We are lost, tuan.'

'No, no, it told me how to go on,' said Keller, excitedly. 'I'm sure it wants us to find the treasure. Don't you worry about that. I'm not proud. I'll deal with ghosts if they know the way to a fortune in gold and diamonds, no matter what they was called in real life. Raki, go and wake the others. There's somethin' we've got to do – and it's to be done *now*.'

Before settling down for the night, Johnson, Blake and the three other mariners had made a plan. The scheme did not include the four Dyaks who preferred to sleep outside the temple. Nor, of course, were Raki, Budrudeen or Mayok brought into the plot. The five seamen wanted to keep this to those they could trust implicitly. They planned to kill Keller in the morning, by shooting him in the back as he walked through the forest ahead of them. They would have attacked him in his bed, in the night, if it were not for the fact that Raki and Mayok guarded him.

Johnson was the first to be woken. He sat up. The dawn's rays were filtering through holes in the roof and fell into the room, carrying a grey light. Johnson blinked, seeing shadowy figures in the room. 'What's goin' on?' he mumbled.

'Get 'em up,' said Keller. 'Get 'em all up.'

Budrudeen, who was nervously carrying one of Keller's pistols, began poking the sleeping men with the muzzle.

'You be careful o' that,' muttered Johnson, needing some time to gather his thoughts. 'You watch it don't go off.'

'Never mind that.' Keller's voice sounded thick and

husky, as if he were coming down with a head cold. 'If it does it'll save me a lot of trouble. I'm going to shoot one of you anyway. It's just a matter of which one. I want you all up. Line up against the wall at the back. Quickly, quickly.'

Johnson now saw that besides Budrudeen, Raki and Mayok also had firearms pointed at the men.

He objected. 'What's goin' on, Keller. Why're you doing this? We're just trying to get some civilizing sleep, enough to turn us back into human beings.'

'Satan came to me in the night,' replied Keller, his face flushed. 'He told me to kill one of you as an example to the others. That's what I'm goin' to do. One of you is going to die while the others watch on. We'll see how much mutiny there is in the air after that. Maybe then I can sleep safe.'

Blake, who had woken last, believed their plot had been discovered somehow.

'It wasn't me,' he said, shivering. 'It was Johnson. I heard 'em say it was going to be in the morning. He's the one who made up the plan.'

'Plan?' Keller said.

Blake said, 'The plan to . . .' But he stopped there, aware that Johnson's eyes were trying to tell him something.

'The plan to *what*?' screamed Keller into his face. The leader struck Blake over the side of the head with a pistol. Blake fell on the floor, clutching his wound. It hurt and he was bleeding badly. Blake let out a yell of despair and pain.

'They was going to kill you.'

Keller nodded his head slowly. 'Was they now?'

Raki and Mayok lined the men up, their backs to the wall. Keller was leering at them, as if he had some sexual interest in their bodies, looking them up and down. 'Right,' he said at last, 'you'll have to draw lots. The loser will be shot.'

Johnson cried, 'You can't do this. It's not human.'

'You were going to do the same to me. If I had a con-science about it before, I don't have one since Blake spoke his piece. You all signed your death warrants last night. But I'm a generous man, I'm only going to turn one of you off, just as an example to the others. The ghost said it was best.'

'Ghost?' shrieked Smith, a little wiry man with a harelip. 'What's a ghost got to do with it, Keller? You're stark starin' mad. Can't you see that? You should be in Bedlam. It's that wound. The pus has got into your blood and found its way to your brain. For God's sake man, let us be. Have a little mercy.'

'Too late. If it's mad I am, more's the pity for the rest of you.'

Keller made them draw straws while the two Dyaks and Budrudeen pointed loaded firelocks at them. Smith was beginning to buckle at the knees in terror, when he drew a long straw. He changed his tune immediately, sneering at the others, telling them they had been wrong to plan against Keller. Chivers called him a coward and punched him on the head. Aldous yelled at both of them, saying they should stick together, and rush the weapons pointed at them. Johnson told him not to be a fool. Only Blake was silent, starting at the short straw in his hand.

'Blake it is then,' Keller said, quietly. 'Blake's the one to hang.'

Blake shrieked, 'You said you were goin' to shoot the one with the short straw, not hang 'im.'

Keller, hot-eyed, shrugged. 'What does it matter. I changed my mind while you were all arguin'. You'll dangle from the nearest high tree, like you would from the yardarm if you was at sea. Johnson will do it, along with Smith.'

Johnson stepped forward, the palms of his hands open

placatingly. 'Johnny, he's my shipmate, just like you – don't make me do this.'

'You'll do it, or hang alongside him.'

The other Dyaks had come in now and were looking on in puzzlement. They did not have enough English to work out exactly what was happening, but they knew something ugly was going on amongst the white men. Budrudeen had beads of sweat standing proud from his forehead. Raki and Mayok were impassive. Both these Dyaks knew vaguely what was happening, but since it did not involve them directly, they were not concerned. Keller and his men came from another world, a place where things went on quite differently from life and death in Borneo. They were simply observers, witnessing a foreign scene.

Usang had no idea what was going on and was quietly singing to herself, while she picked out a twig which had caught in her hair during the previous day's march.

'Oh God,' sobbed Blake, white with fear, 'don't let him do this boys. He's gone quite mad. Don't let him kill me.'

A shot suddenly boomed in the confines of the room, shocking everyone but the man who had pulled the trigger. Usang, terrified by the sound, scuttled away like a cockroach caught in a light, trying to climb the wall inside the room, gibbering all the while. Mayok went to her and put his arm around her neck and shoulders, holding her tightly until she stopped struggling.

The smoking musket belonged to Keller. It rested in the crook of his arm. It was he who had fired the shot. He nodded in approval at the gaping hole he had put in Blake's chest, while the shot man stood swaying on his feet, a pained expression in his eyes. 'You bugger,' he choked.

'I told you,' Keller said. 'I warned you, didn't I?'

Budrudeen dropped his pistol and began running, fell over, scrambled to his feet, and ran again, out of the room and down the hallway. The other men had parted and were staring at Blake, whose mouth now began dribbling blood and spouting red bubbles. The fatally wounded man then drifted backwards, falling, falling slowly, as one does in a bad dream. He grabbed a vine which had forced its way through the stonework. It held his weight for a moment, then gave way. Blake crashed to the floor on his back, gave one last cry of recrimination, and was then still.

Aldous said in surprise, 'You shot 'im!'

'I changed my mind again,' growled Keller. 'You was all takin' too long. Now, Raki, gather up their weapons. I don't want no hero putting a ball in my back. Parangs too. I'll kill every one of you if I have to. Mutiny, would you? I'll shoot every man jack of you – one a day until you learn to behave. I'm the captain on this voyage. You hear that?'

'We hear you,' said Johnson, calmly. 'We hear you, Johnny.'

**2**

Mayok had not been particularly shocked by the execution of Blake. One of the reasons was that he hardly comprehended what was going on. When tuans started shouting at one another he could not understand what was being said. Mayok also had no real understanding of the relationships between the seamen. He did not know that Blake and Keller had sailed on many ships together and were once good friends. He did not know that Keller and Blake were of equal status in the outside world: to Mayok it seemed that Keller was a chieftain and Blake was an underling. Chieftains are, of course, permitted to kill underlings, if the latter break the laws of the tribe. And who knew what laws governed these pale-skinned creatures?

Of more concern to him was his own relationship with Raki, the Iban. Traditionally, the Ibans and Kayans were hostile to one another, but like many of these traditional enmities it was on a tribal basis, not amongst individuals. When a Kayan like him met an Iban like Raki they tended to make the best of it. Sometimes they ended up being fast friends.

In this case, Raki and Mayok were not 'good friends' but they tolerated each other. Raki held a privileged position as Keller's closest Dyak. This meant he was the one to hand out orders and, while he did not victimize Mayok, he did treat him with the same sort of mild contempt that one might show towards a callow youth with no experience of life. Mayok resented this, feeling he had achieved his manhood and deserved to be dealt with on an equal footing with other men, Raki included.

'I wish to go hunting today,' he told Raki. 'I wish to go with the others on the monkey hunt.'

Raki shook his head. 'You are to stay with the woman. The woman is your responsibility. Tuan Keller has made it so.'

Mayok began to get angry. 'I am not a grandmother, to be put in charge of minors. Three times the hunt has gone out in the last few days and each time I am left behind. Someone else can look after the woman today. I am going on the hunt.'

Raki's eyes narrowed. 'You will do as you are told.'

'Who are you to tell me what to do?' said Mayok, stepping backwards and putting his hand on his sword. 'I have taken as many heads as you. You are not my master. You are not my tuai rumah . . .'

Keller came by as the two men squared up to one another, under the shade of a giant tree.

'Here, here, what's all this?' growled Keller, his yellowy eyes regarding the two men with disfavour. 'Raki, what's this about?'

'This man refuses to do his work.'

Mayok drew a deep breath. His English was still faulty and he wanted to put his case succinctly.

'I no want to look after woman today. I want to go on monkey hunt.'

Keller said, 'You are the guardian of my woman. It is special work I gave you because I trust you.'

'It is grandmother's work.'

Keller stood, fuming for a moment. He was irritated that these two Dyaks were drawing on his limited energy for the sake of a stupid argument. Yet he was also disturbed that the unrest between the Europeans should be spreading to the Dyaks as well. He could not afford to have a rebellion from that quarter, not while he had to watch his back with his own people. It was best this was all settled amicably.

He said, 'Usang has been with us long enough to look after herself now. You can go on the hunt.'

Mayok was elated. 'Thank you, tuan.'

'Just make sure you don't come back empty-handed.'

Raki stood for a while looking at Mayok. It had clearly not pleased the Iban that Mayok had gone over his head. He had been overruled. It was not something he was going to forget in a hurry. The seeds of hatred were now sown. The poisonous plants were small and needed nurturing, but men are good at growing such ragweed crops in their breasts, and feeding them from their minds.

So, Mayok joined the hunt. It was a while since he had used his blow-pipe, so he practised for half an hour before the hunt went out. The skill was in holding an eight-foot-long pipe still enough to be able to hit the target. Being made of hardwood, the blow-pipe was quite heavy. It had to be pressed against the mouth and there was no support at the far end, or even in the middle of the long pipe. Yet it had to be held absolutely unwavering for the shot. It took immense strength to perform this act, though, as with all things, there was a knack to it.

Out in the forest they found a family of orang-utans, feeding high above the ground. There was a baby in the family, which clung to its mother. Chivers, who had been sent out on the hunt, wanted to kill the baby for the pot. He had been given a musket and ammunition by Keller, which was to be handed back when he returned to camp. Chivers was the least likely of the seamen to attempt to assassinate Keller, and he knew that if he attempted it he would be cut down by the Dyaks.

Thus Chivers was armed and ready to shoot the baby orang-utan. However, when he raised the weapon, Raki waved it down. Dyaks rarely hunted the man-of-the-forest, or his offspring. Orang-utans were not exactly sacred, but they were regarded with respect. Adult males were over five feet tall. Since they were large man-like vegetarians the Dyaks were not altogether comfortable hunting such animals.

'We leave this one,' said Raki, to Chivers. 'We get him on our way back if we not catch something else.'

Chivers was clearly disappointed, but he knew better than to cross Raki, especially when they were out in the rainforest, miles from any landmarks recognizable to Chivers. It was certain he did not want to be abandoned in a place where he would instantly be lost. Chivers nodded and said, 'You know best.'

They moved on, to a spot where a beautiful waterfall dropped from mossy crags to a shining pool beneath. Some small freshwater turtles were found in the pool, but not enough to feed a dozen or so hungry people. They moved on to a place where the foliage was low in height, with few large trees. Here, as they crept forward, they heard a scrabbling sound in the bushes. There was no wind and the scent of the creature did not reach their nostrils, but the sounds were those of a wild hog, rooting around in the undergrowth.

'Maybe pig,' whispered Raki to Chivers.

The seaman's eyes lit up. If there was one meat which the

sailors enjoyed it was fresh pork. He nodded enthusiastically and lifted his musket to his shoulder. Raki pressed the stock down and shook his head. Instead, the Iban pointed to Mayok, and then out into a clearing. Mayok was to go out there and chase the wild hog towards the hunters. They would need to put two or three darts into the creature to get it to drop within a few paces. Hogs had a habit of running off screeching into the rainforest and hiding somewhere in order to die.

Mayok wondered whether the Iban was trying to put him into a vulnerable position, where a stray dart might 'accidentally' be used to end the animosity between them. However, he could not argue with the Iban in front of the other Dyaks while a precious quarry was just a few yards away. It behove him to get out there and beat the pig towards the hunters. This he did, slipping around in a short semi-circle, so that he was on the far side of the prey.

Almost as soon as he was in position he knew the quarry had scented him, despite the still air. A Dyak's nose is more sensitive than a European's, but his sense of smell is still nothing like as sharp as that of a wild animal. The snuffling sounds stopped as the animal paused to listen, to sniff, to use its eyes. All its senses were now primed, trying to decide what its next move should be – freeze or run.

Mayok stood up and made a loud noise, to drive the pig towards the line of hunters.

There another pause, then a crashing sound, as the creature broke cover in front of Mayok.

It was not a wild hog.

It was an adult sun bear, four feet long, with sharp teeth and even sharper claws.

The sun bear ran straight at Mayok, clearly intent on inflicting injury, severe if possible. Mayok's eyes widened and he yelled for assistance. The hunters came rushing forward, knowing from his shouts that something was wrong. They reached the clearing when the sun bear was three feet from Mayok, charging him down, its claws ready to slash.

Mayok stood his ground, his empty blow-pipe now a spear, pointing at the sun bear's breast. The bear came on, possibly because it was now blind with fear and fury. The weapon was end-on and difficult to see from the front. The sun bear roared its displeasure at being interrupted at a ter-mites' nest, where it had been feeding itself. It wanted to clamp its jaws around some part of the man's anatomy and rake his guts from his belly with claws quite adequate for the task.

The spearpoint entered the bear's breast. Mayok fell on to his back. The other end of the blow-pipe was buried in the dirt. Mayok used the spear as a pole to propel the sun bear over his head. The creature did indeed go sailing over Mayok's supine form, a black short-haired creature venting its wrath on thin air. When it hit the ground on the other side however, it was still full of fight, despite its chest wound.

Two or three darts struck the bear, as it gathered itself for another quick run at Mayok. The Kayan now scrambled away, leaving his pipe-spear buried in the bear's chest. The sun bear cried out in pain and anger. It came forward again, shedding the spear as it did so. It reached the line of Dyaks and lashed out, catching one of the men on the calf of his right leg. The Dyak went down like a felled tree, screaming, as the others rammed their spears into the already dying bear.

The sun bear struggled for a few moments, then its eyes milked over, and it was gone.

Chivers stared at the dead creature wide-eyed. He had not managed even to aim his musket, let alone shoot it. The speed at which the whole episode had happened had been far too quick for any action on his part. And, as bears went, the sun bear was not a big animal, being much the same height as a female orang-utan and half the weight. Beside a grizzly, the sun bear is an infant. But like many creatures interrupted at meal times, the sun bear's rage was bigger than the sum of his dimensions. With one single swipe from his dying form he had laid a man's leg open to the bone, muscle and sinew torn beyond any permanent healing. That Dyak would now and for ever walk with a severe limp.

'Better get it up on a pole, for carrying,' said Chivers, attempting to take command again. 'Are these things good to eat, or not?'

'We eat it,' said Raki, which told the European nothing.

The injured Dyak's calf was bound with leaves and plaited grasses. Mayok felt it his duty to help carry the hunter back to the camp area, where he could be treated properly. There was an obvious fear in the Dyak's mind that he would be left behind in the morning, when the group set off again. He mentioned this to Mayok, who told the man, 'I will stay with you, whatever happens. It was my fault you were hurt. I should have killed the bear.'

'You had no time. We should have known it was a bear. Then we would have prepared for bear instead of hog.'

'This also is true,' said Mayok.

Back at the camp the bear was skinned and cut up, then put into a pot for boiling. Its meat needed to be well cooked in order to soften it. Keller listened to the story of the hunt with only half a mind, as Raki changed the dressings on his wound. Mayok could see that the leader of their expedition was still in a bad way. Due to Keller's anxious concern over details of the trek and the people on it, leaving him few spare moments for personal care, the leader had stupidly not taken the time to have his wound sewn up. Maggots fell out when the Iban opened an end of the cut which had sealed itself with pus.

'Clean it up, Raki, then Smith can sew it this time,' gasped Keller, as the pain washed through him. 'Smith? Sew it up nice and tight like a good piece of sail. Should have done this before, but I hoped it would heal without.'

If there was one thing the seamen were good at, it was sewing, and Mayok watched as the bright needle, with a piece of thread pulled from the tail of a shirt, punctured the blackened, swollen skin around the area of Keller's wound. Smith did his needlework with the detached air of a young woman sewing the seam of a dress. He had done it many times before. At least Keller was quiet during the operation. There had been times when wounded men, men in great pain, had been screaming in Smith's ear, calling him all the obscene names that came to mind, while he quietly stitched flesh to flesh.

He tied a knot and bit the end off the cotton.

'There you be, as nice a neat row of stitching as you'll see on the altar cloth at Canterbury Cathedral, which is where I'd like to be right now . . .'

'They wouldn't have a heathen like you anywhere near their cathedral,' growled Keller. 'Thank you, for that, shipmate. I won't shoot you today, at least.'

The remark was only half in jest. Smith and the other seamen, including Chivers again, remained unarmed. They were all at the mercy of a man whose brain was addling with poisons from his wound. Johnson had sworn at Chivers when that man returned his musket to Keller, but really Chivers had little choice in the matter. If he had attempted an assassination he would have been cut down after firing the first shot. Raki had ensured that the Dyaks were loyal to Keller and no one else.

The morning after the hunt, Keller had them up early and

ready to go. It was a sultry day, the sweltering atmosphere bringing in a mist which clogged the forest ahead of them. Birds called to each other from hidden positions. Such poor visibility was dangerous, since wild animals might be surprised suddenly, at close range, and snakes might be trodden on before they were seen.

The mighty trees of the forest, some like the tualang which rose to two hundred and fifty feet tall, became dangerous in such poor visibility. The tualang has a base ten feet in diameter and several of them together form a solid wall of trunks and buttress roots. But it was their habit of falling which was the great danger. A tree fall is a relatively frequent occurrence in a place of thousands, where insects eat away the bases. And when a giant like a tualang dropped, it tore the branches of other trees, some having boughs the size of young English oaks, which fell as debris from the sky. Since they were in a thick mist, none could tell from which direction a tree was coming down. There was great panic when, around midday, the creaking of falling giant was heard.

Fortunately, none of the men were struck by the many tons of wood falling from the sky, though the forest floor shook with the impact. Keller called a halt to the march. The men rested, drinking fresh water from a river. One of the Dyaks came to Keller and told him in an excited voice that this was the river he had been looking for. Keller had been moving purely on the compass at this time, but knew that if they walked south they would hit the river they were seeking at some point, since it crossed the wide trail laterally. It was somewhere along the bank of this waterway that the Punan longhouse was situated.

Keller knew then that they were now at last in the heart of Kalimantan.

'The Kingdom of the Sun Bear,' he said, with great satisfaction in his voice. 'Here at last!'

Raki ordered the Dyaks to fashion shapes of certain creatures out of ferns and reeds, and hang them from the trees around the perimeter of the camp. These told the local people that the newcomers had peaceful intentions. They were the equivalent of flags flown from the masts of ships.

The Dyaks had told him that the secret of the exact location of the seven heads was held by only one person, the basir of a Punan longhouse. First they had to find the longhouse. Once they knew they had the right village, then Keller could go about persuading the basir to part with his secret. He had brought with him a variety of gifts: beads, parangs, knives, scissors.

'The mist is too thick to go on at the moment,' Keller said. 'We'll stay here till it lifts.'

They set up the camp on the banks of the muddy waterway. Once the Dyaks had raised his tent, Keller went inside with Usang. A short while later two Dyaks in a canoe came by. They seemed astonished to see strangers and fetched up on the far bank. There they stood, staring across at the seamen and their Dyak porters. After a while one of Keller's Dyaks began calling to them. He told them they had come in peace.

The two Punan men yelled back, asking what were the strange men with pale skins doing with them? Were they demons? Were they shrunken giants from the mountains, trying to disguise themselves as mortals? Were they sorcerers?

Keller's Dyak yelled back that they were none of these. They were ordinary men, but from a different forest. He invited the two Punan to come over and meet the white men. After some discussion and dithering, the Punan got in their canoe and paddled across the river. They beached their craft and walked warily towards the group awaiting them.

Here they spoke some more with Keller's Dyak and then one of them went forward and touched Johnson on the cheek. Johnson smiled. The Punan grinned back, then the man lay down on a mossy bank to have a good laugh, while his friend stood guard over him. Finally, there was animated conversation between the Punan speakers. Keller came out of his tent to find out what all the fuss was about.

'Are these men from the longhouse we're looking for?' he asked Raki.

'Not from that one.'

Johnson heard this exchange and his heart sank. He envisaged still more days, perhaps weeks, searching the rainforest for the longhouse. Perhaps it did not even exist? Maybe it was a mythical place, like the land of the dead which the Dyaks talked about. Johnson spoke with the other seamen out of earshot of Keller and Raki.

'I've had enough of this,' he said. 'What say we take that canoe and go? It'll carry the four of us. We can just follow the flow to the sea. Once we're on the coast, we can work our way north, back to Sarawak. What say?'

'We need our muskets,' said Smith. 'If we don't have 'em, how are we goin' to feed ourselves?'

'There's nets in the bottom of that canoe. I've seen them,' said Johnson. 'We'll fish the river. Mudfish are easy to catch. And turtles. I've seen the Dyaks catch turtles – it don't look too hard to me. We can get our hands on parangs and knives. There's fruit and sago, nuts and roots in the forest. We're not idiots . . .'

'Let's do it,' muttered Aldous. 'Me, I ain't stopping till I get to the sea. I'd like to cut that bastard Keller's throat before I leave though.'

Johnson shook his head. 'His Dyaks will chop you to bits.'

The four men, agreed on their desertion, then slipped down to the riverbank, where the canoe was moored. They leapt in it and began paddling downriver before their intentions were recognized. It was Raki who shouted the alarm, pointing at the defectors. The two local Dyaks let out cries of despair, seeing their precious canoe shooting down the river.

Keller, his musket loaded and ready to hand, fired a shot after the deserters. It splashed harmlessly behind the canoe, which was well out of range. Aldous stood up and shook his fist, yelling an oath at Keller. His sudden action was a foolish one and he almost overturned the craft. Johnson yelled at him and, in trying to regain his seat, Aldous tipped overboard.

He fell into the rapidly moving flow and was swept alongside the canoe for a while. His face was white and lined with fear. Johnson and Chivers back-paddled, but they were in the centre of a very fast young river, which resisted attempts to slow the canoe. Smith stretched out a hand but could not reach the panicking Aldous, who finally struck a log or rock just below the surface. The seaman disappeared under the water and the other men were carried off on their long journey to the sea.

Keller saw the body come up a short while later, caught in the branches of a dead tree which had fallen into the river. Aldous had drowned or had been battered to death. The angle of his broken body attested to the fact that he was gone.

'Good bloody riddance,' snarled Keller, infuriated that the seamen had managed to escape. 'Leave him to rot.'

The local Dyaks were now angry, shouting at Keller's Dyaks. The others tried to calm them, saying the people who had stolen the canoe were rogues and thieves, not friends of the men who remained. Raki sat down and invited the angry fishermen to do the same. He managed to placate them after a while, by offering them compensation. The two men were given parangs, metal spearheads, and knives. After a while their grumbling ceased and though they still appeared aggrieved they were not angry.

They even agreed to take Keller and show him the way to the longhouse he had come so far to find.

# 3

Rajah Starke had been on another spiritual journey with Prince Issam, floating high above the forests and coming to land as delicately as any butterfly. He had marvelled at the winding muddy rivers below him, sometimes spreading wide into brown-and-green mangrove swamps. He had seen his own lodge high up in Peninjau, his summer holiday residence, perched like an eagle's nest on a hill above a plain. There were ladders and stone steps to climb to reach this retreat: bamboo bridges from high boulder to high boulder, gullies to cross and chasms to negotiate.

When he arrived at the spot where his cousin was camped, he looked down on her from afar, marvelling at how well she looked. There she was, striding about, helping the men to strike camp, tending an injured Dyak, sketching, painting, writing. There was Colenso too, always watching her, pretending to be thoroughly engrossed with marking the stores and supervising the loading of the canoes. Singapore Jack was also not far off, deep in thought, busy with his maps, his cataloguing, his labelling, his classifying of species of insects and plants.

'They seem to be well enough,' said the rajah to the bomoh prince. 'They seem to be in good health.'

'They are well enough,' confirmed the prince, though he noticed that there were one or two men missing from amongst the Dyaks and Malays of the party. 'Lord Randolph has managed to hold his people together. That in itself is an achievement. Do not be fooled, however, for there is a lack of harmony in that pleasant scene below us, though it is not evident to our distant eyes.'

'A lack of harmony?'

'They are drifting apart down there.'

The bomoh prince then took the rajah not far away, over trees full of monkeys, along rivers where kingfishers were as numerous as dragonflies, through valleys where the rhinoceros roamed and the leopard stalked. Here the rajah was shown a different picture. Some white men were desperately fording a rapids. Their clothes were in tatters, their boots in ribbons, their skin lacerated and covered in sores. Not far beyond them, perhaps thirty miles as the heron flies, was the rest of that party, limping towards a longhouse hanging over a river.

'These too are faring, though they are not thriving,' said the bomoh prince to the rajah, 'yet they are near the end of their journey, while the other group still have a way to go.'

The rajah was satisfied. He had seen his cousin, alive and well, and needed no more than that. Time took him home again, over layered cliffs which threw their ochre colours back at the sunset, over peaks buried in clouds where gods had their residences, into the jasmine scented air of Kuching, to his own lawns which swept green and sleek down from the bungalow to the Sarawak River where the boats were moored.

When he came to, he was in his own bed, the soft sunlight

from the windows falling on his face, making him blink with its brightness. A servant bearing a silver tray opened a door and the scent of Indian tea wafted pleasantly into the room. A brown bird-dog bounded in through the open doorway and leapt on the bed to lick his face.

'Down, Ranee, down,' ordered the rajah. 'You'll get your walk after breakfast.'

The rajah then rose, showered and dressed, and went to find his guest.

The bomoh prince was out on the terrace, enjoying a light breakfast of fruit. Rajah Starke joined him for coffee. 'Thank you,' said Starke, 'for another startling flight through the night.'

'You are welcome.'

'Tell me, if my cousin was in trouble, and I wished to intervene – would that be possible?'

'You may observe, nothing more.'

Starke nodded, pouring himself a second cup. He could not let this thought go without further investigation. It was horribly intriguing and he was a curious man. His own imagination was his worst enemy. It was not cowards who died many times, but men with creative minds, men who could visualize possibilities.

'It would be hard to witness, say, a fall from a cliff, or a charge from some wild beast, yet be unable to do nothing.'

Prince Issam agreed. 'You would live with the guilt to the end of your days. It is one of the drawbacks of this kind of journey.'

'You say it is impossible to assist, physically, in any way?'

'Not impossible, but it would take more magic than I can wield. There is one who could perhaps do it – who could carry you there in the flesh as well as spirit – but you would get no help from him.'

The rajah was puzzled. 'Why not?'

'Because he does not like you. He holds you in contempt. You would have to win his friendship and under present circumstances this is not possible. The man I speak of is Chin Hua, the Chinese sorcerer who lives at the mouth of Long Rajang. His people are very unhappy with you. I do not think Chin Hua would actively support any rebellion, but he would not assist you to defeat it in any way.'

The rajah, in the act of patting Ranee, was shocked by the language Prince Issam was using.

'You speak of a rebellion? But not from the Chinese, surely? They are happy with my rule. I have heard nothing to make me think they are dissatisfied in any way.'

The prince smiled grimly at this credulous Englishman.

'Did you not receive a deputation from their communities south of Kuching just over two months ago?'

Starke thought back and remembered. Yes, there had been a group of Chinese, from the gold and antimony mines worked by the immigrant Chinese population. The owners of these mines were rich and powerful men, extremely nationalistic. Prince Issam had said previously that the Chinese felt they were not getting the respect they deserved. They felt they were being taxed too highly, while the other races in Sarawak were not paying their way.

'They simply grumbled about their taxes.'

'Grumbled? They are incensed. Even now they gather at the mines to discuss rebellion.'

'There are only a few thousand Chinese, most of them merchants who would lose by rebellion. Civil war brings chaos with it – looting, burning, random violence – their bazaars and shops would be plundered, perhaps razed to the ground.'

The bomoh prince shook his head. 'You underestimate the power of fear. The immigrant Chinese brought with them several secret societies, whose members rule their communities. There have been many murders not reported, where men have been found stripped of their skin, or cut in a thousand places. The worst of these secret societies is the Tien Ti Hueh, feared throughout the Orient. This group has been smuggling guns into Sarawak and arming the Chinese for months now. They incite the traders and miners to violence. It is just a matter of time.'

The rajah felt hopelessly out of his depth. 'But what can they hope to gain in the long run? There are two hundred thousand Malays and Dyaks who would never consent to be ruled by less than ten thousand Chinese.'

'This is not a logical thing, it is emotional.'

Not for the first time Rajah Starke felt inadequate in the face of Oriental reasoning. It was true they did not understand him much of the time, his motives and desires for a peaceful kingdom, but neither did he understand them. Of course he knew that the Chinese resented paying taxes. They were the only race of people in Sarawak who earned substantial amounts of money. Naturally, since their income was so high, they paid the most tax. But the rates were not exorbitant

'Everyone grumbles about paying tax – they don't usually go to war over it.'

'I told you, rajah, it is not about money, it is about *respect*. If there is one thing the Chinese can't bear it is not being shown the proper respect. They feel that, even though they contribute a great deal to the state coffers, they are regarded as second class citizens. Malays look down their noses at them. Dyaks steal from them. Englishmen treat them all like coolies. They see all these slights as faults of your government. You are being blamed for the culture of the masses.'

'I can't change the culture of the masses overnight, no matter how much I disapprove of it.'

Prince Issam shrugged. 'Then you must face the consequences. But I warn you, rebellion is brewing. Muda Hassim is going to speak to you about it, which is why I have been so reticent. It is really up to him to explain the situation to you, being your vizier. I think he wants to gather more evidence first, before putting it before you.'

The rajah now recalled that Muda Hassim *had* tried to talk to him about a subject to do with the Chinese a few days ago, but Starke had been worried about something else at the time, a personal matter.

'I can't believe it. I've been told that as long as he has his tea, tobacco and opium – and can gamble now and then – your average Chinaman is happy. I deny them none of these things. I will go down to see the Chinese leaders at the weekend. I'll talk to them and find out what's on their minds.'

Later that day, the rajah walked down to the markets and the bazaars and made himself known amongst the Chinese traders and merchants. They greeted him with smiles and bows, exchanged pleasantries, and showed no animosity towards him. He bought one or two things: a gold ornament for his collection, some silk brocade for Harry, a carved chair for his study. To outward show the bargaining was mutually satisfying.

Starke could not think that, for all their supposed inscrutability, the Chinese would hide their true feelings so deeply. He had seen them cry at funerals, jump for joy at on the moonday of a newly born child. They were not *that* impenetrable. Surely if they were unhappy with him they would reveal it in certain expressions and in their demeanour, if not in their words? It was the rajah's opinion that Prince Issam was exaggerating the feeling of discontent amongst them. Issam was a Malay after all. There was no reason why he should understand the Chinese mentality any better than an Englishman.

Starke made a mental note to send for Chin Hua, the Chinese sorcerer.

The next Friday night there was no moon. On such nights Sarawak was plunged into darkness. Lamps were lit, it was true, but they merely glowed. For the most part, the rivers and forests around the town were hidden in blackness.

Starke was playing cards, late into the evening, with a circle of friends. They were all British. Since he had become rajah many British men, and some women, had come to Sarawak to settle in this pleasant land where the sun always shone and the warm night air was perfumed with the scent of blossoms. There were the jewelled lizards on the banks of the river, clouds of butterflies over the lawns and birds of many colours in the trees. There was discomfort, it was true, but the benefits of the land far outweighed any of its disadvantages.

On the far side of the table was the bishop, a Scot by the name of Alexander Kinley. To his right was William Devoy, a Welsh surveyor. On his left was Sir John Inchcape. These four men were deeply locked in a game of bridge when there came a heavy rap on the French doors. The rajah looked up, annoyed because he had a good hand. Bridge needed all his concentration and he hated being interrupted.

'See who that is, please, Devoy. It's probably one of the guards worried about something.'

'Certainly.'

They were in the library, adjoining the living-room, but the rajah could see the French doors through an archway between the two rooms. Devoy got up and walked through the living-room to the French doors beyond. He opened one and stepped outside. There was a sharp cry which caused the rajah to look up from studying his hand. He was just in time to see Devoy's head being taken from his shoulders by the sweep of a parang.

Instantly, the rajah was on his feet. There was a gun closet behind him. To the astonishment of his other guests, who had seen nothing, he smashed the glass panel with his elbow and snatched out a shotgun. It was one he kept loaded in case game wandered on to the lawn outside the library window. He fired one barrel towards the French doors, shattering the living-room lamp in the process, and then another at the lamp in the library, above the heads of the two remaining bridge players.

'Knock out the candles,' he yelled. 'Here, Bishop, a revolver. He tossed the weapon towards the bishop, who caught it deftly. Sir John, an elderly man, blundered around knocking over the candles and thus dousing their flames. Sir John had been a soldier, a colonel in a foot regiment, and he knew an emergency when he saw one. Once they were in darkness, listening for any entry into the house, the rajah spoke again.

'Devoy is dead,' he whispered. 'I saw his head roll.'

'Who's out there?' asked a shocked Sir John. 'Those blasted pirates again?'

'I've no idea,' replied the rajah.

They could see lights now, on the lawn beyond the library windows. The three men went to the windows to look out. The grass outside was thronging with Chinese men, their faces lit by the brands they carried. They had Devoy's head on a spear and were gesticulating towards it, dancing around it and yelling triumphantly. Clearly they believed they had someone important on that spear. Then, one of them, a man who appeared in a more sober mood than the rest, pointed to the house. The mob turned and began walking towards the library windows.

'They've seen us,' whispered the bishop.

'No,' replied Sir John Inchcape, 'they're coming to set fire to the house. They'll probably ransack and loot it first. Do you want us to try to defend it, Starke? Quickly man, we need to know.'

A great fear was in the rajah's heart. He knew now that Prince Issam's warning had been timely. Only he had not heeded the prince's words. Now he knew he was faced with a dangerous rebellion. Not just a few pirates. A whole community of Chinese, who in killing at least one Englishman had burned their bridges and had nothing to lose by further murders.

'That mob is too large. We'd get one or two, then we'd be overpowered. My guards are obviously all dead. God knows where the servants are – I hope they're safe. We'd best try to get out the back way and down to the river. Sir John, you'd better arm yourself from my gun closet . . .'

It took but a minute to snatch cartridges and more weapons from the closet. The rajah knew his own house, even in the darkness, and led the other two men out to the back porch. There the way was clear to the forest. Running through the darkness is a dangerous game, but somehow the three men managed to reach the edge of the rainforest without injury. They then skirted the trees and worked their way across to the river. Starke and Inchcape were all right, but the bishop was breathless. They let him rest for a minute, assessing the situation.

The river was brilliant with the reflections of lights. There were boats full of Chinese coming along the Sarawak, torches ablaze. These mobs were waving weapons and yelling, clearly highly worked up. In the streets of the town there were already some shops on fire. The silhouettes of figures could be seen running here and there, some carrying objects obviously looted from the burning buildings.

'It's started,' said the rajah in despair.

'Can we get across there?' asked Inchcape.

The rajah shook his head. 'I had a pinnace moored here, but it's gone. Someone's either stolen it or cut it adrift.'

'I shouldn't wonder that the rioters are using it now,' remarked the bishop, having regained his breath. 'Well Starke, what do we do? We can't stay here.'

'There's one of my forts half a mile along the bank. Let's make our way there. I've left a young Irishman in charge there – Michael O'Malley. He's a good man. He's got half a dozen Malays with him. If we can reach him we can help defend the fort.'

Inchcape said, 'Well, that's better than sitting on our arses doing nothing. Come on, which way?'

The rajah led the other two men cautiously along the bank. At one point they came across two Chinese men trying to launch a boat belonging to a British family. The boat was full of furniture from the house. There was the body of a servant on the bank, one of the gardeners, a Malay boy of about twelve. Another body lay on the lawn, further up, nearer the house. There was no sign of the family. The bishop shot both looters dead with his revolver. He was a good shot for a man of God: he might have been born with a pistol in his hand.

Then he and the rajah took over where the looters had left off, trying to launch the boat.

Inchcape ran up to the house, which was in complete darkness. He wanted to see if anyone else was alive within. Windows had been smashed, doors broken open. A torn curtain decorated a garden statue.

'Anyone in here?' cried Sir John. 'Call out now, for we can't stay too long.'

A muffled sound came from one side of the porch. Inchcape went to that area but could see no one.

'Where are you?' he said. 'I can't see you.'

'In here . . .' A head appeared out of the neck of a large Chinese vase. It was that of Mrs Williams, one of the owners of the house. She looked pale and very frightened.

'Are you hurt?' questioned Inchcape

'No – no – not hurt.'

He helped her climb from the urn. She was shaking and unsteady on her feet. Inchcape held her for a moment in his arms, more to support her than anything else. In a minute or two she was ready to walk. Starke was calling out softly from the middle of the lawn, saying they should be on their way.

'We can't shift the boat, Sir John, it's stuck in the river mud . . .'

Inchcape took Mrs Williams' hand and led her down to the river's edge. She explained on the way that her husband was in Singapore on business. Their two sons were at school in England. Three Chinese men had entered the house and had begun turning it over, looking for valuable items. The cook, ironically also Chinese, killed one of the looters with a meat cleaver, but the other two stabbed him to death. His body was on the hallway floor. Mrs Williams had then run out on to the porch and had climbed into the giant vase.

'Chang saved my life,' she said in hard tones. 'If he had not attacked them, they would have – have . . .'

'There, there,' puffed Inchcape, patting her hand. 'He was a good man, but he's gone. We must get you to safety.'

Now numbering four, they made their way along the bank to the fort. When they were two or three hundred yards from the wooden stockade, they saw they were not going to get in. The fort was surrounded by ferocious Chinese rebels. Even as the four paused in the darkness beyond the waving torches, a gun boomed out from fort. Grapeshot whistled just ahead of the group.

At that moment someone climbed over the wall of the fort, between the spiked stakes of the battlements, and dropped to the ground thirty feet below. Whoever it was seemed unhurt, for the figure got to its feet and, after a moment's indecision, began running down towards the river. Torches borne by Chinese rebels flowed after him, like the tails of comets. Although the runner was fast he could not outrun a horde ready to cut him off from his bid for freedom. The Chinese closed in on his flanks and cut him down with parangs and hand axes. He disappeared from the view of the watching British, under a welter of blows.

Then there came a ragged cheer and the man's attackers went running back up to the fort, carrying bits of the victim's body to show those still surrounding the wooden stockade.

The response from the fort was another set of blasts from the fort's two six-pounders. This time O'Malley had used deadly canister shot – shells filled with musket balls – and many of the attackers went down wounded or dead. The mob was infuriated. Torches were flung over the walls of the fort. A tiny decorative cannon which had stood outside the gates of a Kuching home, was wheeled up to great cheers from the rebels. They managed to fire one shot with it, which cracked a spar over the gate. Then it blew up in the users' faces.

More and more rebels came up from the river, until there were about four hundred Chinese surrounding the fort. They settled down now and began to pour musket fire into the walls. Finally, one of the balls found a chink and hit the fort's magazine. There was a tremendous explosion. The gates flew open and acrid smoke and dust billowed out of the small stockade.

Incredibly, O'Malley and two of his Malays had survived

the blast. They came running out, their uniforms in tatters. Just outside the fort they paused to empty their firearms into the mass of rebels. Then they were cut down in a withering hail of fire.

The rajah let out a short sob as he saw O'Malley and his men die. There was little the watchers could do to help. They might have intervened with one or two shots of their own, but the rebels would have discovered them and killed them too. All they could do was lay in the long grass on the edge of the riverbank and witness the destruction of the fort. In a short while the stockade was in flames, with gleeful rebels caught in the light of the fire, dancing around their handiwork.

Once the stockade had been taken the rebels lost interest in it and began to drift towards the town, where there was loot and plunder to be had. Many buildings were alight in the town now and the streets were full of wailing victims and cheering victors.

'Let's make our way to the church,' whispered the bishop. 'I don't think the rebels will go in there and at least it's something we can try to defend.'

The rajah agreed and the four of them crept along the bank until the reached the large wooden church and mission house. Going inside they found a number of people already there, but no Chinese rebels. As the bishop had intimated, the Chinese were a superstitious group of people. If they entered the church it would be reluctantly, expecting divine retribution for their lawless attack on the town and its inhabitants.

Talking to those in the church, the rajah learned that many of the residents' houses outside the town had been attacked and burned. Dozens of Europeans and Malay, and many Dyaks, had lost their lives. Some children had been murdered along with their parents. It was a terrible night.

The rajah went paler by the minute as he listened to the accounts of atrocities. Finally, he sat down in a pew and covered his face with his hands.

'This is all my fault,' he whispered. 'I should have acted on Prince Issam's advice.'

The bishop and Inchcape assured him that he could not have foreseen such a massacre, but the rajah knew it was complacency and a lack of real understanding on his part which had led to the night's terrible events.

'Even so,' conceded the bishop at last, 'there is nothing to be done about that now. What we have to do is find a way to survive this slaughter and put some reason back into the heads of the Chinese miners.'

The rajah rallied and agreed. There would be plenty of time for regret later. Now was the time for action. Outside, the grey dawn was slipping down from the hills and into the town. The sounds of rioting and battle continued for a while afterwards. But such activity begins to pall with the light of the day. By eight o'clock the rajah was in the bell-tower of the church, looking out over the town, and he could see groups of desultory rebels moving through the charred remains of the streets. They had quietened now, exhausted by their night's destruction.

There was no standing army in Kuching at this time. There was a small garrison of Malays in the town, and there were the little wooden forts which were not much more than local prisons, but these would have been over-whelmed by the sudden surprise onslaught of the Chinese rebels. There would be Malay and Dyak guards still alive, but the rajah expected them to be scattered and disorga-nized. He had no doubt they would have fought bravely and he had no doubt that somewhere Muda Hassim and the princes loyal to him would be working to retrieve the situation.

However, the majority of the rajah's fighting men were head-hunters who lived in their longhouses along the Sarawak, Skrang and Rajang rivers. The rajah could call on ten thousand well trained warriors, but the news had to get to them first. He had no doubt word was reaching them now, by river, that there was trouble in the town.

Once the day had come the Chinese rebels began to get nervous. Some started to drift back towards the boats, which were piled high with loot, thinking to get back upriver to their homes before the Dyaks arrived. Others were high on opium and staggered about the streets bleary-eyed, still looking for trouble. Still more were intent on settling old scores, or discovering plunder they knew to be there. Even Chinese shops had not survived the fury of the night's events.

At nine thirty, Muda Hassim arrived at the church with about thirty Malay soldiers.

'Rajah Starke,' said the old man, 'the city is in ruins.'

'I know,' groaned the rajah. 'It is my fault. But once my Dyaks arrive . . .'

'. . . there will be a second massacre,' finished the grand vizier. 'Rajah, we must control the Dyaks or they will go on a wanton slaughter throughout the country. Once they start taking heads it will become a fever with them. The innocent will suffer along with the guilty. You must be ready for their arrival and personally take command of their forces.'

Starke saw the truth in this warning. He did not want to be guilty of allowing a second great blood bath. It was necessary to forestall the Dyak army and keep them under tight control.

'Thank God I have men like you,' he told Muda Hassim, 'or I would be a completely useless ruler of this country.'

'Mistakes will be made, Rajah, no matter how we prepare for them. This was indeed a mistake, but we must now lick our wounds and put things right. The Dyaks will be in a bloodthirsty mood when they see the havoc the Chinese have wrought on the town. I suggest you make myself, Prince Issam, the bishop and Sir John your generals, to command your forces. Ten thousand Dyaks cannot be watched over by one man alone.'

The rajah agreed to this. 'First we must round up all the surviving women and children. Put them into any boats you can find and get them down river, to where my yacht is moored. Once under the protection of the *Monarch* they'll be safe enough.'

This instruction was carried out without interference from the rebels. These were now beginning to disperse. The Chinese captains in and around the town had now called for a halt in the killing. They believed the rajah to be dead and they felt they had dealt a blow to the ruling body of the country. They had decided that whoever became rajah next would think again before taxing the Chinese too heavily.

At noon the Dyak army cruised downriver in the form of a great armada. They were fully aware, through messengers from the town, what had happened. Those Chinese who had set off back to their houses upriver, met the flotilla head on. The rebels panicked and rowed desperately for the shore, leaving most of their plunder behind in the boats. Dyak warriors pursued them, caught them, decapitated them, leaving a trail of headless bodies along the rainforest paths.

The Dyak war prahus then proceeded further downriver. The majority of the Chinese rebels, some three and a half thousand men, saw them coming. They wisely took to their boats and fled in the opposite direction, towards Sambas. The rajah and his generals managed to get aboard the Dyak prahus and were therefore part of the pursuit, though it was difficult to command when no formal chain of authority had been previously set up. Desperate struggles took place all along the rivers and backwaters. Chinese boats went down under ferocious attacks from the Dyaks.

About a thousand rebels were killed in the flight towards the border between Sarawak and Sambas. Sometimes the Chinese took to the land, fighting furiously to survive, forming squares which went down under a hail of poisoned darts. They slapped at their necks and faces as the darts flew into them like swarms of deadly insects. Much to the dismay of the rajah there followed a welter of beheadings, which the Dyak warriors would not be denied.

Two thousand Chinese rebels managed to escape over the border into Sambas, where they were immediately arrested by the forces of the Sultan of Sambas. All heart had gone out of the rebels and they capitulated immediately, allowing themselves to be led off to a hastily erected prison camp on the edge of the Sambas jungle.

Chin Hua, the Chinese sorcerer, contacted the rajah, to speak to him on behalf of the rebels now in Sambas.

'Please, you will not allow the Sultan of Sambas to send the rebels back? Your Dyaks will treat them as fair game and none will survive. Already the Dyak warriors clean the heads of those they have killed in front of us. I can recognize the faces of many of those dead men.'

Starke knew this was happening. The Dyaks were behaving in a triumphant manner. It was difficult to stop them.

'Those rebels sacked my city and killed many of my personal friends,' said the rajah. 'Some of them were women and children. They went on a trail of murder and destruction, with dubious cause. Yet you ask for leniency?'

'I ask for a favour,' said Chin Hua. 'There has been enough killing. I know justice should be done. If these men are not allowed to return they will lose everything they have ever worked for – diamond mines, land, businesses, antimony mines, gold mines – for some it will be *worse* than death.

'I am only concerned about preventing further hatred, further bloodshed. Ask the sultan to send them back to China, where they can do no more harm. They will be returning to the homeland of their ancestors in disgrace. They will have lost face in front of relatives, friends and enemies. This is a terrible punishment for a man born of China, as you well know, and it will keep any further carnage from our chosen land, the country we both hold dear, Rajah – Sarawak.'

The rajah saw the sense in Chin Hua's words and agreed to do as he had requested.

'I will not forget this favour,' said the sorcerer. 'You will have need of my services one day.'

Rajah Starke learned a terrible lesson from not heeding the early and timely warnings from his Malay advisers. He was a more sober and sadder man after the Chinese rebellion, and needed even more the comfort he knew his cousin Harry would give him, had she been there to do so.

# PART EIGHT

# The Kingdom of the Sun Bear

# 1

The three seamen, Chivers, Johnson and Smith, were crammed into their craft. They had to resort to portage when they came upon rapids. The canoe was a dug-out, extremely heavy, and lugging it up steep slopes was a difficult task. Even after two days away from Keller's expeditionary group, they were ragged, exhausted and close to madness.

'Up there?' groaned Smith, viewing the rocky ascent with dismay. 'I'll never make it.'

'Do you want to die in this godforsaken jungle?' asked Johnson, looking round at the dense foliage beyond the river. 'Do you want . . .?'

He never managed to finish his sentence. The was a tremendous rustling of the undergrowth at that point and a creature came hurtling out of the greenery. It ran on two legs but it was not human. It swerved out of the shadows and attacked the three unsuspecting men before they knew what was happening. Smith, who had been staring at Johnson and wondering why he said nothing more, had his back to the monster. He was given no time to turn and look. His head was taken from his shoulders in one swift, clean sweep and snap of the jaws.

Johnson was amazed by a momentary change of expression on Smith's features. The head was in Jata's mouth at this time, teeth buried in both temples. Then Smith's face was distorted, as the strong jaws bore down on it.

The headless body fell sideways, against Chivers, who cried out in terror. Chivers turned and ran into the jungle. Johnson was rooted to the spot. He could not move. He simply watched as Jata crushed and swallowed Smith's head, then stooped and gripped the limp corpse in his enormous mouth. The red-faced lord of the crocodiles shook the headless cadaver angrily, just as a dog will shake a rag. Then he tossed the human meat aside as if it were a piece of rubbish.

Johnson waited no longer. He turned and ran for the canoe. Jumping into the dug-out, he pushed off, into the rapids. As soon as he was in the flow the tumbling whitewater current took the canoe, shooting it downriver. White-faced and anxious, Johnson clung to the gunwhales. He pressed himself down into the crude, hollow-log craft, resigning himself to the inevitable. Better death by drowning, he had decided, than be swallowed by that monster with a man's body and a crocodile's head.

Unknown to Johnson, a demon of the waterfall lurked in expectation. His jug of eyes was not yet full, there being few humans in this part of the forest. This demon was a manyheaded dragon that waited just under the foam at the bottom of the falls. It could see the dark canoe above, bouncing and bumping down through the rocks, and it opened its several mouths in anticipation.

Back on the bank of the river, Jata was triumphant! His enemies, the enemies of the forest, had returned to the river, had been delivered to him! Now he could take his time and destroy them, one by one. His father, Mahatara, had said it would be so. His sisters, the Santang goddesses, had promised to act as his eyes and ears, to signal him when this happened.

However, just at that moment the goddess Mang decided to turn day into night. It was probably spite on her part: she had little love for the red-faced Jata. To her he was a petty little half-god who played with men like a cat with mice, while she was a full goddess yet was less feared or revered than Jata and the other demi-gods. So, on rare occasions, she did something like this, simply as a show of power, to make herself noticed in the world. She *could* do it, therefore let no one remain complacent. Just because the sun had arisen as usual did not mean that Mang could not remove its light if she chose to do so.

Mang took the moon and put it in front of the sun.

Jata screamed at her, 'Leave the sky alone!'

But Mang took no notice of the lord of the crocodiles. This was *her* business. If it ruined Jata's day, let him complain to the pitcher plants, let him whine to the orchids. Darkness was hers to give or withhold. No other god, not even Mahatara, would dream of telling her what she could or could not do with darkness.

When Mang removed the moon from in front of the sun, Jata had missed his opportunity. Chivers was now deep in the jungle, sobbing, falling, cut to ribbons by thorns, but well away from the river. Johnson had miraculously missed the jaws of the Naga, who had been just as surprised as Jata by the darkness. His canoe had bounded along on the rapids and shot out into a wide lake on the far side. Johnson was not stupid enough to remain on or near water. He too abandoned the river for the interior.

By the time Mang's next period of darkness came around naturally, at the end of the day, Chivers was stark staring mad. What clothes had been hanging from his frame in ribbons were now completely gone. He was naked and bleeding from a thousand cuts. Insects came down to feast on him. Leeches clung to him, marvelling at their luck in finding a walking larder. Even in the darkness he kept moving, stumbling forwards, moaning and swearing.

There are some demons of the forest who appear when an oath is uttered, which is why there are few swear words in the Dyak language. Curse words are secret keys for such demons, opening the doors between their world and the world of mortals. So it is with the junips, tiny hairy little men with enormous genitals, who float through the air. They have mouths full of razor-sharp teeth, which they use to tear at the flesh of their victims.

When the junips heard the curses which came from the mouth of the lost, pale-skinned traveller in their ancient land, they came through the holes between the real and spiritual world in their swarms. At first, Chivers thought they were bees and he tried to beat them off with his hands. But soon he realized that the pain they brought was not from stings, but from bites, as little chunks of flesh began to disappear from his arms and legs, from his chest, from his abdomen.

When he squashed one of the creatures between his finger and thumb, he saw that it had a head like a human, and that its body was almost all penis and scrotum. He cried out in horror and fear as more and more of these ugly little parasites converged on him, until he was a mass of raw nerve-live flesh, and sank to the forest floor, to bleed to death on the soaked moss. His last word on this earth was, like his first word, a scream for help, a cry for his mother. No one heard him, least of all his parent. Even had there been someone within earshot, the sound of his pathetic cry would have been lost in the screaming of the junips, as they repeated the curse words they had heard from his lips, over and over and over again.

In the meantime, Johnson was making his way through the forest. He still had his parang, with which he hacked himself a path. He ate the moss off the side of trees, the roots he had seen the Dyaks eat, and any living thing he could lay his fingers on: slugs, snails, frogs, lizards. He ate them uncooked. Some were still alive when he put them in his mouth. Johnson was beyond caring. His hunger dictated to him. Desperation was in every pore of his body, as he chopped at the thick undergrowth which seemed to gather like a green wall before him.

Finally, he ate something acidic which burned his mouth with an unbearable fiery pain. When he spat it out his tongue went with it, burned away at the roots. Now dumb, as well as starving, he continued on until he could go no further. Then, like Chivers, he sank to the ground, moaning incoherently.

He was found by two Dyaks. Johnson thought at first they were going to decapitate him and he was ready for it, but when he spoke to them they looked at him in fascination and fear. Eventually they took him back to their longhouse on a backwater of one of the great interior rivers.

He was taken before the basir and much discussion took place concerning his strange way of speaking. Finally, the basir forced his teeth apart with a knife and looked into his mouth. The basir smiled and spoke to the other Dyaks, who then lay down on their backs and started laughing, having discovered the reason for his unusual speech. They knew, of course, of the plant which had destroyed his tongue and, though they laughed from relief, they felt sorry for him. The two Dyaks who had found Johnson gave him to the basir as a present, and he became the priest-shaman's slave.

Johnson had no escape from the longhouse. He wanted none. Even if he could speak he had no way of conveying to the Dyaks that they would be rewarded if they led him out of that place to the coast. In any case they would have gone by river, which was the only safe way to travel long distances. And Johnson knew that he would have stood no chance of survival on the river, not with Jata still hunting for him. So he decided to spend the rest of his days amongst these hunter-gatherers in the forest.

Though Johnson did not know it, it was the intention of the basir to shrink this pale-skinned marvel down to the size of a polong, a bottle imp. He tried various ways of doing this, experimenting with something he had never tried before. Each time he gave Johnson some special food to eat, or fluid to drink, Johnson would become violently sick, but he remained the same size.

It was true he did become shorter, closer to the ground, but this was due to the painful effects of the basir's cruel experiments. His stomach muscles contracted, resulting in the same sort of bending of the spine as old age might induce, making him stoop down. And his joints weakened so that his knees had difficulty in bearing his weight. They remained permanently crooked. So much so that the knuckles of his hands brushed the ground when he walked. They began to call him the 'monkey man' and the children treated him like a pet.

One day an experiment by the basir shrivelled Johnson's head, so that it was half its original size, and then other smaller heads began to grow up his arms, over his torso, down his legs. These tiny heads had little mouths which screamed all day and night, until the Dyaks could stand it no longer. Finally, they put Johnson out of his misery and buried his body under the chicken coop. They kept his head, the original one that had rested on his shoulders, sticking it on the prow of the tuai rumah's canoe, as a kind of ornament.

It was bitten off by a crocodile the first time the chief took his boat out on the river.

## 2

They were in the Kingdom of the Sun Bear.

The longhouse of the Punan sun bear clan had a brooding atmosphere about it which Keller had not encountered before. The men looked sullen and aggressive. The women timid and frightened. At first, Keller thought the place must have an oppressive tuai rumah, but on meeting the man he observed that the chief was a mild individual with a nervous tic. His eyes constantly darted about the place, as if he were expecting an assassin's knife in his back at any moment. He said, through interpreters, that he was happy to offer the hospitality of his longhouse to the pale-skinned traveller and his porters.

'Thank you,' Keller said. 'Please tell your people to take one gift each. You may take three, as the chief of this fine longhouse, and your wife may take two.'

Budrudeen had spread out a blanket and had arranged there various gifts for the tribe. Keller obviously had to limit the number of presents he handed out, for they were his only means of leverage. Now he was in the sun bear longhouse, he had to bide his time, seek out the information he required. This might necessitate handing out more gifts later.

The women came first and chose a necklace of beads, or a mirror, or a small cooking pot. Then the men trooped by, taking knives, iron spearheads and parangs. The mood of the longhouse lightened a little during this parade, with some of the women chattering to each other, but it was nothing like the normal easy, friendly atmosphere of a rumah. Again, Keller wondered if some event had befallen the place, like the death of an important person.

While he was standing thus, musing on the possibilities, he studied the Punan store of heads, gathered in a fishing net which hung from the palm-leaf ceiling of the longhouse. They did not look particularly old heads. That was to be expected. Keller did not suppose they would keep the seven ancient heads mixed in with those of common enemies. The magical heads had to be hidden somewhere else, somewhere difficult to find.

When all the members of the tribe had a gift each – one or two had tried for a second one but had been recognized by an alert Raki – one more figure emerged from a room at the far end of the ruai. Keller was a little taken aback by this person's appearance. The face was old and lined but stained with red berry juice on the cheeks, as if he or she were wearing rouge. Indeed, it was difficult to decide on the gender of this hunched creature for, though dressed like a woman, he or she had the movements and stumbling gait of an old man.

On his back the old man had a cloak of sun bear skin and around his throat a necklace of sun bear teeth. He carried a staff with the paw of a sun bear as its head, the claws extended. There was a tattoo of a sun bear on his forehead.

'The basir,' whispered Mayok.

This explained the androgenous nature of the creature, for in many longhouses the basir was a man dressed as a woman. This one had long grey hair tied up at the nape of the neck like a female. Besides the decorations on the cheeks and a set of bright blue lips, charcoal liner emphasized a pair of small glittering eyes. The basir's fingernails and toenails were long and sharp, like the claws of some wild beast. His tattoos were extraordinary. Instead of the usual symbols there were bears etched on his chest, legs and shoulders. When this wrinkled old man moved down the ruai the Punan parted to give him free passage. They seemed nervous, perhaps even afraid, of this shambling creature. Clearly here was the true ruler of this remote longhouse.

When the basir drew opposite Keller he turned and stared with a long penetrating look. Keller remained unflinching, looking back, trying not to antagonize but at the same time refusing to be intimidated. Finally the basir's gaze switched to the gifts laid out on the blanket.

'Tell the basir he may take five presents – any that take his fancy,' said Keller quickly, to Raki.

Raki did as he was bid. He received a sharp reply.

Raki said to Keller, 'He wants pirogue. Two.' Raki held up two fingers.

'Canoes?' murmured Keller. 'We have no canoes. Tell him we came on foot.'

'He say you steal one canoe from his cousin who live in next longhouse downriver.'

'Oh, *that* canoe. I didn't steal it. Bloody Johnson and his mates did. You saw it, Raki.'

Keller knew this was not going to wash with the basir. The men who took the canoe were white skinned. Keller was a white man. Therefore, he was responsible for the theft, whether he actually did the stealing or not. This was not going to be easy. A single word from the basir and

Keller would have one of his own parangs buried in his back or chest. For once in his life he dug deep into himself and searched for some diplomacy.

'Tell him when we leave here I will catch the thieves and personally hang them from the nearest tree.'

After more conversation Raki said, 'The basir tells me they are already dead, tuan, but he is interested in how to hang a man. I tell him this is how white men kill other men who have done wrong. The basir has never heard of this method before. He want for you to explain it to him. He knows many ways to kill a man but this is the first time he hear of someone hanging by the neck from a tree.'

Grisly old bastard, thought Keller. He's a damn tyrant, a despot. He likes killing people.

Keller explained about hanging. He told the basir it could either be quick, or very slow. A man might have his neck broken instantly if he were dropped from a height. But if a man were hauled aloft then he would probably strangle over a period of time. It was difficult to say how long such a strangling would take, but men had been known to live an hour or more. In general, they were usually dead after half an hour.

The basir did not understand such precise measurements of time, but Raki was able to give him some idea of the length. The old man seemed pleased with the information. He came up to Keller and gripped him by the wrists, staring into his face with those pig-like eyes. Keller remained impassive, hating the basir's touch but allowing it for the sake of amity. They then sat down and drank tuak together, while the tribe crowded round them, watching in an interested but sullen fashion.

'How did you come here?' asked the basir.

'My dreams guided me,' replied Keller, using a Dyak phrase he had heard many times.

The seaman knew he had to woo the old man, for if there was a secret here this man would be the bearer of it.

The basir smiled. 'Are you sure you did not follow a "stinking shrew"?'

The reference was to the moonrat, which had an offensive odour.

Neither Keller nor Raki knew what the basir meant by this remark so Keller said there had been no moonrat in his dream. The old man smiled at this, but did not elucidate any further. He simply waited for Keller to open the conversation again.

'What is your name? Mine is Keller.'

'I am Skallag,' replied the basir. 'I am a great magician.'

'I too can work magic,' said Keller. 'I have blow-pipes which spout fire and noise.'

He showed the basir one of his muskets.

'I have heard of these thunder-and-lightning blow-pipes. Birds bring me messages from the sea. They have told me of such wonders. I wish you will show me how the thunder and lightning comes from the pipe.'

Keller was pleased to do so. He enjoyed impressing these ignorant natives. He opened a fresh jar of dry gunpowder. Then he carefully loaded the musket in view of the watching men, women and children. Taking aim at a chicken in the yard below, he squeezed the trigger. The bang was followed by shrieks and screams of fear from many of the Punan, some of whom leapt up and ran a few paces, looking for somewhere to hide. The basir had not moved a fraction though, and he called the tribespeople back in curt tones, telling them not to act like infants.

The basir walked to the edge of the ruai and stared down at the dead chicken, whose feathers fluttered in the breezes which came up from the river below. He could see the hole in the bird and the blood oozing from it. He nodded thoughtfully, before turning to stroke Keller's musket with brown, wrinkled hand, his long nails catching on the iron-work of the stock. Then he chuckled and sat down facing Keller on a reed mat.

Firing the musket had caused Keller's inflamed wound to give him trouble. He drank more tuak to attempt to dull the pain. In his exhausted state this had the effect of making him very tired. He explained to the basir that he needed rest and if the basir would like they could talk again later. The old man agreed and called the chief to give Keller and his Dyaks rooms. As usual, Raki, Mayok, Usang, Budrudeen and Keller had one room, while Keller's other Dyaks shared a separate smaller room.

In the middle of the night, Keller and his companions were woken by an disturbance outside. It seemed to be coming from the room next door. There were shouts and the sound of scuffling, followed by the rasping tones of the basir's voice. Keller made ready to get up, but Raki put his hand on his tuan's shoulder and shook his head. Keller then understood it was best not to investigate the cause of the noise. He lay back down, between Raki and a wide-eyed Usang. Mayok, in the far corner, was awake with his hand on his sword. Only Budrudeen had not stirred. Even when there was a scream, cut horrifyingly short, the Malay youth did not wake from his deep sleep.

Later, when all was quiet, Keller spoke to Raki.

'I'm going out there. My side's giving me hell.'

He rose and went out on to the ruai and stood in the cool breezes. The sound of a barking deer came to him faintly on the night air. Looking along the ruai he could see nothing unusual and wondered what all the fuss had been about earlier.

Then he happened to glance towards the chicken coop. There was something there, swaying in the moonlight. A shadow was drifting back and forth amongst the trees. Staring hard, he saw that there was a plumbline there, weighted by a long shape. It was a body, the body of a hanging man. Skallag had executed someone in the dark hours, using the method he had learned only that evening, from Keller.

'That damned old goat,' murmured Keller.

He padded to the steps and went down to ground level, heading for the swinging corpse. When he reached it and looked up, he saw that the face was that of one of his own Dyaks. The basir had murdered one of Keller's men. This disturbed Keller in a number of ways. It meant that he, Keller, was not safe. If the basir could kill one of them, he could destroy them all. Yet it was necessary that Keller remain friendly with the old man, in order to learn the secret whereabouts of the heads. That or kidnap him and force the location from his lips. Keller was not unwilling to resort to torture, not after this hanging.

While he was standing there, Raki came down the steps.

'Other ones, they go.'

'What's that?' asked Keller, not understanding.

'Our men. They have run away. Only Mayok and the boy still here.'

Keller nodded at the hanged man. 'That's not surprising – they didn't want to end up like this. Why did he do it, d'you think? Skallag. Why did he hang this man?'

'Someone have to be punished for stealing canoe.'

'He didn't want to punish me, so he chose one of my men?'

'Yes, tuan.'

Keller shrugged. 'Well, at least we know he values me, for the moment anyway. I don't trust that old goat though. We'll have to watch our backs. When he gets tired of me, I'll wager he'll have me turned off quick enough.'

They went back to bed, but Keller arranged watches. Raki took the first two hours, followed by Mayok. By that time the dawn was coming. Keller hardly slept a wink anyway and kept two loaded muskets close at hand. In the morning, when they went out on to the ruai, the hanged man was gone. There was a fresh head in the ceiling net. No one spoke of it again. Even the missing Dyaks were not mentioned. There was no point.

Skallag did not appear during the day. Keller spent the time idly. He cleaned his firelocks and oiled his knives. Usang washed out his wound once again, but it was clear to the seaman that it was not going to heal properly while he remained in the jungle. He knew he needed to get to a good doctor and a bed with clean linen.

Later in the morning a local warrior approached him. This man had been out on a night hunt when Keller had arrived at the rumah. He appeared to be in an aggressive mood. Keller was prodded in the back by the harpoon head on the tip of the man's blow-pipe. Keller stood up and angrily knocked the pipe away. Usang let out a gasp and backed off a few paces.

'Listen you,' he growled at the head-hunter, 'I'm a guest here, but I won't be pushed – understand? Don't push me again, or I'll break that silly pipe over your thick skull.'

The Dyak warrior glared at him and went to poke him again, this time in the chest. Keller snatched the pipe out of the man's hands and threw it off the ruai, into the yard below. The warrior let out a yell and reached for the short sword at his waist. Keller's musket was leaning against the bamboo wall at the end of the longhouse. It was within reach. He snatched it up and struck the warrior with the butt, catching the man behind the ear. The warrior went down like a felled tree.

Suddenly, Keller was surrounded by the Punan men. They

were jabbering at him. He quickly gauged the situation and decided they were not aggressive. They seemed to be trying to tell him something about the fallen man.

'Raki,' he yelled. 'Get over here!'

Raki came at the run, with Mayok close behind him.

'What are they yelling about?'

Raki said, 'This is son of Skallag. They say you have killed the basir's son.'

'He ain't dead,' snarled Keller. 'The fool started in at me. Tell them he's just knocked cold. Tell them they'd better keep him away from me or I will kill the beggar. Tell them that.'

Even as Raki began translating, the body on the floor stirred and a sigh went through the crowd. The warrior sat up, groggily, and felt a bump like an egg behind his ear. He looked up at Keller then. Keller decided he had better warn this hothead off here and now. He pointed the muzzle of the musket at the warrior's chest, then turned the gun and fired at a clay pot in the yard. Once again the booming sound of the shot in a confined space had women screaming and a few of the men dashing away in fright. Down in the yard the clay pot had shattered.

The warrior visibly jumped and stared at the shards of the cooking pot.

'See that?' barked Keller. 'That's your head, you stupid beggar. You brace me again and I'll put a ball in you, you understand? Tell him, Raki.'

The son of Skallag slunk away. Later, when the night came, Skallag himself appeared again. He seemed not in the least disturbed by the incident. Keller got the idea that Skallag was actually only really interested in one person: himself. His son was not an appendage of him, but a detached entity. No mention was made of the hanging. That was now no longer an issue. Keller set to work on ingratiating himself with the basir.

One thing was troubling him: if the seven heads revealed the secret to untold wealth, why were the Punan not rich?

The answer seemed to be that the secret was passed down from basir to basir. Thus, only one person in the longhouse held the secret. That person was already the most powerful creature in the world of the head-hunters. What did the basir need of untold riches? Diamonds, gold, money – these meant little to rainforest hunters – and any discovery and disposal of such riches would have to include the whole tribe. The basir would lose his status immediately and would be just one of the crowd.

So, as bearer of the secret, the basir was powerful. Once it had been released, his power would drain away. The basir was a crafty old man in women's garb, decided Keller, and he knew how to hold on to power. It was not going to be easy to prise the information from him, but Keller was determined to do so.

Mayok was just glad the journey was over at last. Of course there was the return trip, back to Kuching, but he knew instinctively that the worst was over. It had not been the travelling which had made the trip a nightmare, but the people who composed the party. The white men had been the biggest problem. Their mistakes had brought the wrath of the rainforest gods down on the group. Now, most of the white men had gone. Only one remained and though this man had a foul temper and was subject to dangerous moods, he had come to respect the Dyak beliefs, even if he did not follow them himself.

There was still a troubling aspect to the situation. Mayok was now hopelessly in love with Usang. Her firm plump body was before his eyes most of the day and his heart ached when Keller took her into his bed at night. Although Usang had said nothing, Mayok was certain she had feelings for him. He caught her looking at him in a certain way. Of course, it would be courting death for either of them to confirm their love, for Keller would just as soon shoot them both as not.

'I am going fishing,' Mayok said to Usang on the second morning. 'You will have to come with me.'

'Why do I have to?'

'Because I have been told to look after you. How can I look after you if you are not by my side? You may help me with the net. I shall show you why a Kayan man is the best river fisherman in the whole world.'

'Huh!' she said. 'I do not see how the Kayan men can be the best fishermen, when Bahau men are twice as good. Bahau men are also the best hunters. I am a Bahau woman and we are the best—'

'Lovers?' interrupted Mayok, unable to help himself.

She stared hard at him, then smiled. 'Yes, we are.'

'I can believe that. You are a lovely woman. Your skin is taut and unblemished. You have strong eyes.'

She nodded, briskly. 'I think I shall go fishing with you.'

Mayok gathered up his net and they began to walk down the path towards the river. The track was narrow and it was necessary for them to go single file, but Usang seemed to be right on Mayok's heels. Her swinging arm kept brushing his thigh and before they reached the water Mayok was entirely aroused. He was embarrassed by this because he had only a loincloth covering his privates and his erection was very obvious.

Usang stared down at the spot below his waist and the faintest of smiles hovered in the corners of her mouth.

'We have come down to the river to fish, have we not?' she murmured. 'But I should like to wash first.'

'Yes, yes,' cried the flustered Mayok. 'You must wash – I mean – you *can* wash if you want to. I shall stay here, on the bank, and watch for crocodiles. We must be very careful after the stupidity of the white men. Jata must know it is they who are responsible for the tragic death of one of his servants but, as porters and guides for the white men, Jata may feel that we need punishing too. I shall stay up here, high up where I can see ripples in the water.'

She ventured out into the shallows and proceeded to bathe, paying particular attention to her firm breasts. Mayok stood on the bank, hopping from one foot to the other, his mouth dry and his eyes moist. He could not stand it. He loved this woman with every ounce of his being. If he could never have her he would rather die. He might even die of misery if given enough time.

His attention was at first on the river. The Punan said there were no crocodiles in this part of the river but, when Jata has been annoyed, anything could happen. So Mayok began by watching intently for any sign of a ripple on the surface. However, when Usang started to wash the lower part of her body, Mayok's good intentions flew away like birds. When she had finished she came out on to the bank, wet and gleaming.

'The – there are no crocodiles here,' Mayok said, huskily. 'I watched particularly well.'

'I saw you watching particularly well,' she said, nodding. 'You did not take your eyes from looking at me.'

'I was looking at the river.'

'You were looking at *me*,' she said, and came, bare-breasted, and stood right in front of him, her nipples lightly touching his naked chest.

Mayok let out a groan of despair and before he knew it he was running his hands over her body and babbling about how much he loved her. He knew it was wrong, but he could not help himself. She too was crying about the passion she felt for him. Her hands were also everywhere.

The pair were feverish, frantic to touch each other wherever they could, seeking the rounded places, the secret crevices, the flat and ridged muscles. They ran fingers through each other's long black hair, kissed each other's palms and eyelids, licked the salt from each other's eyebrows. When he stroked her vagina she shivered in delight. When she touched his penis, and fingered with wonder his cross-spar palang, he almost exploded with the rush of passion which followed.

Finally he entered her. His palang excited her beyond any feelings she had experienced with Keller. Mayok's palang rippled up and down the walls of her vagina, gently stimulating the nerves that gave her such pleasure. The pair thrashed around in the undergrowth, making love for the first time with each other, oblivious of the outside world. They made love in a very natural way, as two creatures of the wild might make love. There was no fumbling, no hesitation on either side. Nor was there any refinement. They knew nothing about what they were doing and they did it in splendid ignorance.

Their explorations were all into unknown territory. Even though Usang was no longer a virgin, her forays with Keller under the blanket had required only that she lay still and be penetrated for a minute or two. There had been none of this flood of passion, these high pitches of ecstasy, which now came on, wave after wave. She thought she was going to expire with the intensity of the feeling. Mayok believed he almost did, his heart was beating so fast in his chest. The blood was pounding through the pair of them, like a mountain torrent in full flood.

When it was all over they sat hugging each other.

'I love you,' he said. 'I love the smell of your hair, I love the feel of your skin on mine, I love everything about you.'

'What are we going to do?' she asked, unhappily. 'The tuan is my master – and yours – he will kill us both.'

'We must say nothing to him. He is a destructive man. I do not think he has long to live in any case. Death follows him around.'

'It follows him, but does not touch his person.'

'Then I must kill him,' said Mayok, simply.

She touched his lips with the tips of her fingers.

'No. To murder a man in cold blood for his wife will only bring us great misery. The gods would not allow happiness to come out of such an act. We must wait and see whether we are to be together for always. If it is to be, it will be.'

'Whatever you say. In the meantime we must show something for our trip to the river. I must fish.'

Given work to do, he was able to put love out of his mind for a period. He walked out into the river's shallows and whirled the net around his head. On seeing a fish below the surface, gliding, then poised to eat weed, he let fly the net, which fell with a gentle hiss into the water. The weights took it down, to encircle the fish. Mayok pulled it out of the water triumphantly, just as an owl ruffled its feathers as it sat on the broken branch of a tree hunched and interested, peering at this human activity. Mayok realized the owl had been there the whole time. He suspected such behaviour. Owls were night birds. Perhaps this one had been sent to spy on them by the basir.

'If I had my blow-pipe I would kill you,' Mayok told the owl. 'If I see you again, I will certainly do so.'

'Why are you talking to the owl that way?' asked his female companion, hugging her knees on the bank.

'It is a spy, sent to watch us.'

'By whom?'

'Perhaps the tuan, or the basir.'

Usang shook her head. 'We Bahau believe the owl to be the messenger of love.'

'I hope you are right.'

Mayok caught three more large fish, then left the water. Usang lovingly removed the leeches from his legs. He bled in a dozen places where they had bitten him. Then the pair of them walked back to the longhouse, to see Keller deep in conversation with the basir. This was good, for it not only kept Keller busy, but Raki too, for the Iban had to interpret for his master. In the darkened longhouse room Budrudeen was at evening prayer.

Mayok had seen in which direction the sun had gone down and noticed that the Malay boy was facing that way. He spoke to his friend after the prayers were over.

'I thought you said Mecca was in the opposite direction to the *morning* sun.'

Budrudeen was puzzled. 'So it is.'

'Did you not look at the sunset?'

The Malay boy shrugged. 'I have been asleep since noon. Besides, there is no need. I asked the tuan for the direction on his compass, as I always do. He pointed that way.'

'Come out into the yard,' said Mayok.

Budrudeen did as he was told and was shocked to see the faint light in the southeastern sky. In the dim room at the back of the longhouse, he had been facing the wrong direction for prayer.

'The tuan must have made a mistake,' he said in dismay. 'I shall repeat my verses again. This time in the direction of holy Mecca. How he could have made such an error I do not know, for I noted that he looked hard at his compass.'

Usang said, 'Perhaps it was not a mistake.'

Budrudeen shook his head, as if to clear it of flies.

'What do you mean?'

'I used to see the white men laughing at you behind your back when you went away to prayer.'

It took a little while for the implications of this to sink in. Once Budrudeen had realized what had been going on he was at first horrified. Then a cold anger crept through him. The tuan had been pointing him in the wrong direction all the time – every time he had asked for kiblah. There had been no purpose to this deception. It had been done purely for sport.

'I'm sorry,' said Mayok. 'It is important, yes?'

'Very important,' confirmed the Malay youth, dismally. 'Too important to allow to go unpunished.'

'But you stand no chance against the tuan. You are but a boy and he is a strong man. His strength comes from the orang-utans who gave him his hair. He will crush you like a beetle. You must not go against the tuan openly.'

'I shall bide my time,' promised Budrudeen. 'I have already killed one man. What will it matter that I kill another?'

Budrudeen gave no indication to Keller that he had discovered that man's duplicity. He cooked the evening meal as usual: rice and toucan meat served on a banana leaf. Mayok did not touch his meal. He feared that if it had been poisoned by Budrudeen, the Malay youth might not be in the mood to discriminate between wrongdoer and innocent bystander. However, Keller seemed to be merely tired once the evening came round. He certainly did not look in the humour to die.

In the morning, when they were alone, Mayok spoke to the boy again.

'Are you going to poison him? I hear Malays are good at that. Many of the princes tried to poison the rajah.'

'If they tried and failed, then they were not very good at it, were they? No, I will bury a kris between his shoulder blades,' said Budrudeen. 'I wish to see his blood. With poison all one sees is a change of complexion and then the victim rolls over in agony, or expires straight away. In either case they no longer care who has been responsible for their death. They selfishly concentrate on their pain. I want him to know who has killed him. I need the satisfaction of that. I want him to be sorry for his part in his own death.'

Mayok shook his head. 'I do not think tuan Keller will ever be sorry for anything.'

'We shall see. There is plenty of time. Now that I know I am going to do it, I am in no hurry. I wish to savour my revenge.'

'He is a strong man. He may kill you first.'

'God is with me. Allah is aware that I have been abused by this man. Tuan Keller prays to no god. He is an unbeliever. Where will he get his strength from, if he does not recognize a spiritual power greater than his own?'

'Men do not always rely on divine strength. He may get *his* from a devil. I think he does.'

Budrudeen was supremely confident. 'Good will always triumph over evil – right will conquer wrong.'

Mayok was not sure this was necessarily so.


In the middle of the night, Mayok was summoned by Keller to join the seaman outside. The young Kayan prepared himself for a fight to the death. He was sure from Keller's demeanour that his love-making with Usang had been discovered. Keller was in a vicious mood, muttering to Raki about something which had clearly driven him into a cold rage. Mayok was very afraid. He had seen enough of Keller's fury to know that should it come to a fight, Mayok would be in danger of losing his life. He kept his hand on his Dyak sword as he approached the two men.

'Yes, tuan,' he said.

They were standing under the moonshade of two trees. Keller turned and glared at Mayok. He was clearly very drunk. Then the white man's eyes turned moist, he shook his head and said in despair. 'She won't let me touch her.'

'Who?'

'Usang, of course, you blamed idiot,' snarled Keller. 'She refuses to let me take her.'

Mayok's heart began singing. 'Maybe it one bad time for woman, tuan?'

'No, she had that a week ago. I know what it is.'

Mayok's heart sank again. 'Yes?'

'Yes, damn you, I do.' He reached out and lifted up Mayok's longee. 'It's one of them things she wants.' He pointed to Mayok's penis. 'One of them yardarms you Dyaks have stuck through your mainmasts.' He then surprised both Iban and Kayan. 'I want one. If it's supposed to give her so much pleasure, then damn her, I'll have one too.'

'Tuan?' said Mayok.

Keller turned and snarled at him. 'Well, don't just stand there, make me one, *now*. A bamboo splinter, ain't it? Cut me one the right length and size . . .'

Mayok looked at Raki who shrugged and nodded. The Kayan youth then went to the edge of the rainforest and drew his sword, ironically not to kill Keller, but to assist him in his love-making with Usang. Mayok cut a sliver of bamboo from a live plant. He shaped the piece, cutting small wooden blades on either side of the sharpened rod. When it was finished he took it to Keller, who dropped his pants.

'Right,' said the seaman, looking quite pale now, 'stick it through me.'

Mayok's own palang had been inserted as a child, but only after the flesh had been treated with the juice from a medicinal plant, to numb it. He shook his head, vigorously. 'No, not me, tuan.'

Raki also shook his head and turned away.

'Damn you cowards, I'll do it myself,' growled Keller.

He knelt down with his penis resting on a moss-covered log. Then, positioning the organ with his left hand, he rammed down with the right, driving the bamboo spike through the gristle. Mayok saw the white man's eyes widen in pain. Keller let out a terrible gasp. Blood began seeping from the wound. Worst of all, the spike had not gone all the way through. It had failed to break the skin on the far side. Gritting his teeth, his eyes bugging, Keller forced the palang until it burst through.

Raki handed Keller some strips of cloth, which he hastily wrapped around the wound. Once it had been swaddled, Keller's penis looked like a ball of calico, the red staining through. Mayok was gratified to realize the white man would not be making love to Usang for quite a time. It was, however, horrifying to the youth that Keller obviously thought so much of her that he would undergo so much pain for her. Clearly, Keller was in love with Usang, which made things that much worse for the illicit lovers.

'I've mutilated myself for that bitch,' groaned Keller, hobbling towards the longhouse. 'I hope she appreciates what I've done for her.'

After that night Keller discarded his ragged European clothes and took to wearing native dress.

# 3

Harry was the last one to climb the steps up to the ruai of the Punan longhouse. When she reached the top she found Kit Colenso, Jack and the others staring at the far end of the verandah. To her amazement they were looking at another white person, a man in native dress with red hair.

'Keller,' muttered Jack in disgust. 'That piece of excrement has somehow found his way here.'

It was only then that she recognized Keller. She had seen him many times before, at her cousin's bungalow, but he was a changed man. He was much leaner. Gaunt, she decided. There were scabs on the backs of his hands, on his face, down those parts of his legs which were visible below his longee. He had a full beard, red streaked with white, and his wild hair was long and matted. In the middle of this sun-like profusion of hair were two glaring, feverish eyes.

Keller looked like some madman escaped from Bedlam.

When she looked around her, however, she realized that Jack, Kit and herself were not a great deal more presentable. The long journey through the Ulu had taken its toll on all of them. They were all yellow skinned with illness and their clothes were ragged and worn. The real difference between them was that Keller had started out with a party almost the same size as Jack's. It appeared he was now down to about two or three men.

At that moment the staring contest was broken by the arrival of the local basir, dressed in women's clothes, who came hobbling towards them with a big grin on his face.

He spoke at length, gabbling away like a turkey, while Jack's interpreter mumbled in his ear.

Lidah whispered to Harry, 'The basir say we are welcome, missy. He say the tuai rumah is honoured to have two visits from the pale-skinned people from outside. There is much talking to be done, much to discuss. Tonight there will be music and dancing – and drinking.'

Harry inwardly groaned. Every longhouse they stopped at the tuak flowed like bountiful streams. Out came the sakes – primitive guitars – and the keluri – little organs made of bamboo pipes – and the dancing would begin. A great deal of tuak would be drunk. The dancing would be followed by storytelling. Then more tuak would be drunk. Once everyone was thoroughly intoxicated, roosters would be fetched and the cockfights would start, with loud arguments which sometimes ended in brawling.

Neither Jack nor Kit Colenso walked the length of the ruai to speak to Keller. There was something in that man's stance which decided them against such an action. Instead, they found themselves spaces at their end of the long, roofed verandah, somewhat glad that there was a buffer zone full of Punan huntsmen and craftswomen between the two parties.

Harry noticed that Keller made no move towards their party either. He stood for a while, glaring at them, then sat down with his Dyaks. It seemed that trouble had been averted for a time.

Harry took out her sketchbook and crayons. It was coming on sunset and she wanted to draw the longhouse while the light was soft and yielding. Taking her equipment she went down the steps and sat on the far side of the yard. There she concentrated on her work. Her sketchbook was full of drawings and paintings: of trees, birds, butterflies, insects, mammals, landscape scenes, almost everything she had encountered while on the great trek through the Ulu. She was proud of what they were doing, the gathering of scientific knowledge. Jack had acquired many specimens of unknown creatures and plant life during the expedition, as well as making maps. She wondered what Keller had been doing with his time, apart from going native.

She had not long to wonder, for he appeared beside her in the gloaming like a phantom from hell.

'Miss Glendennin',' he murmured from behind her, making her jump. 'What are you doing here?'

'What am I doing?' she replied, flustered. 'I'm with Lord Randolph Braik's expedition.'

'And what would our Singapore Jack be doing then?'

'I don't know why you should ask *me* this, when he is up there on the ruai. I'm sure he would be pleased to answer any questions you may wish to put to him.'

'I don't think he would, see? I think he's here after the same thing I'm after, only I got here first. The seven heads are mine. I've earned them. I've gone through hell to get 'em and I won't give 'em up. I won't share any of what I get either. You tell him that. If he tries to take it, I'll kill him. I'll kill you too. I'll kill every blamed one of you. I'll burn all your damn drawing books and paintings and kill all your animals. I'll hunt down your Dyaks. I can do it as well. I've killed men for giving me the wrong breakfast, so it don't think I won't. You tell him that Miss Glendennin' . . .'

With that, Keller was gone, in amongst the trees. Jack came down from the ruai a few moments later.

'Was that Keller? Was he bothering you?"

Harry said, 'He came to tell me he would kill you if you tried to take whatever it is that's here.'

Jack's eyes narrowed and he stared into the rainforest. 'Did he, blast his eyes?'

'He spoke about the seven heads. He surely hasn't come all this way to prove a myth? He must be crazy, Jack.'

'Crazy? Of course he is.'

Harry put down the crayon she was holding.

'*You* don't believe that story, do you? Tell me that's not why we've come to this longhouse.'

Jack turned and stared at her now. In the red light of the fading sun he looked as mad as Keller had seemed. There was a strange gleam in the eyes of the tall, handsome aristocrat.

'It is my duty as an explorer,' he said, 'to investigate all such legendary claims, to discover whether they are true or false. I don't need to explain myself to you. You would not understand in any case. You're a woman. Women have no imagination. Their heads are full of practical matters, like raising children and sewing dresses.'

'Thank you, Jack,' she said, with faint sarcasm, 'my father once told me women's heads were full of fripperies, that I was totally impractical. You men will have to get together to make up your minds about what it is that we women lack.'

Jack stiffened a little and stared at Harry.

'I'm sorry if I offended you,' he said, in a very formal voice. 'That was not my intention. Let me explain myself. I do not believe in any hidden treasure. However, myths and legends need to be documented and their authenticity investigated. Someone clearly believes there *is* a treasure or the myth would not exist in the first place. Perhaps they do have some heads, which they believe talk to them. I have seen a creature, an insect woman, which will be difficult to talk about once outside this environment. People will scoff at the idea. They will laugh. The world is full of bankers and businessmen out there, men who are natural sceptics . . .'

'And also women with no imagination.'

He shrugged. 'You sound very bitter, Harry. That is not like you. I was merely making a point.'

'I am not so much bitter, as bitterly disappointed. I thought you were different – different from the man you are. I see I was wrong about that and I'm sorry for it.'

With that, Harry gathered up her sketching materials and walked slowly back to the longhouse. Jack watched her go. Although he had been civil to her, and had been successful in appearing cool and detached, inside he was seething. More recently he had noticed a change in Harry. She no longer had that light of adoration in her eyes when she looked at him. Jack was fairly sure why this was so. It was Colenso who was the problem.

'That man has been poisoning her against me,' muttered Jack to himself. 'He wants her for himself. Well, he shan't have her. He doesn't know who he's dealing with here. I shall win back the girl's approval of me and marry her.'

Jack had never cared that much about women. Some men believed it was because he was keen on young boys, but that was not the case either. He had a lack of interest in the physical side of any relationship. Yes, he had visited brothels in Singapore, and other countries, but in the company of men who had been, like himself, inebriated. Had the suggestion been quail shooting or horse racing, both of which equally failed to engage him, he would have gone along with them. It was a question of being a good sport, running with the pack occasionally, letting one's inhibitions drop for a few drunken hours.

He could not imagine himself making love to Harry, in the physical sense. In Jack's experience respectable ladies were as revolted or indifferent to that side of things as himself. Even low-class women did not always like it. On the odd occasion when he had taken a whore, or some girl sent to his room by his host, he had sensed their loathing of the act. Those who had not been disgusted by it had definitely been bored with it all.

There had been chambermaids who seemed to enjoy it, but of course a lady was different from a maid. Especially a lady like Harry.

Women of Harry's class had finer sensitivities.

There were one or two of course, like the notorious Lady Jane Fitzwilliam of Highgate, who went to bed with every other lord or earl. But they were doing it for reasons other than a delight in the act. In Lady Jane's case, her husband had married her for her money, then lost it all at cards. She was paying him back, not in spades but in hearts, by destroying his reputation as a husband, lover and respectable aristocrat. It was all a set of games, everywhere, to which Jack did not subscribe.

No, Jack was not so much interested in a romantic relationship with Harry, as having her as a good companion for the rest of their lives. It would, among other things, enable him to cry off from those visits to whorehouses after a night at the club. A man was entitled to protect his wife against venereal diseases without appearing a coward. And he could certainly picture a life of harmony with her. They would set up house together in England, travel abroad when the fancy took them, and she would be the perfect associate. She was intelligent and could paint and draw well. She would be invaluable to him on his many expeditions.

Jack, however, was not a fool. He could recognize love blossoming when even the participants themselves were all at sea. Colenso was clearly enamoured of Harry. And the lady herself, though desperately trying to ignore her own feelings, was undoubtedly falling for Colenso. Singapore Jack was aware that the two had not yet admitted to themselves that they were falling in love, but such a state was often more evident to onlookers. Jack could see it happening. So could Lidah. Jack, therefore, intended to get rid of Colenso before any declarations were made.

Jack made his way back to the longhouse. Kit Colenso was in the process of cleaning his firelocks. Jack confronted him.

'Colenso, I think you should take half the party, including Lidah, Ferguson and Kitts, and go on ahead. Harriet and myself, and two Dyaks, will follow in three days' time.'

Colenso looked up from cleaning his rifle.

'Why? What's brought this on?'

'I don't really have to explain myself,' Jack said, pompously. 'I'm the leader of this expedition.'

Colenso stood up. He frowned. Then he said, 'Look, Starke sent me on this expedition mainly in order to watch over his cousin. I can hardly do that if I'm three days ahead of her, now can I?'

Jack became imperious. 'Are you suggesting that *I* am incapable of seeing that Harriet is safe? I'm as responsible for her as anyone on this expedition, especially since she is now my fiancée. In fact, you could say I have taken over the guardian's role from Starke. I am her husband-to-be. You need have no worries about Miss Glendenning, Colenso. I shall look after her.'

Colenso, shorter and more rugged than Jack, squared himself for an argument.

Harry, who had been listening in from her room, now came out.

'I do not need a guardian of any kind,' she stated, emphatically. 'I have long since been over age. I can look after myself.'

Jack turned to her. 'No, you cannot, not in the Ulu. I'm sorry, you are all under my orders here. I do not want to have to exert my authority, but believe me I shall do so.'

'People are free to do as they choose, Jack,' Harry said.

'No they are not. Before setting out on this expedition you agreed, did you not, to obey my orders? That was your promise and it was only under such conditions you were permitted to join the expedition. Colenso, you know that as leader of this expedition I am in the same position as a captain at sea. You are my crew. I must work individuals as I see fit, for the good of the whole. You will take the rest of the men ahead. Harriet will remain here with me, to assist in some details.'

Colenso said, 'I would still like to know why.'

Jack nodded. 'We are now over two thirds of the way to the south coast. We have reached rivers flowing down towards the southern part of the ocean. Our progress from now on will be fairly rapid, since we do not have to battle upriver against the direction of the flow. I have a few things to sort out here, then I shall join you in your forward camp.'

'I still don't understand.'

Jack began to lose patience. 'You do not have to understand. It is for *me* to understand. I wish you would not argue with me. You will leave tomorrow morning.'

After which Jack turned on his heel and went to speak with the basir, who was sitting halfway along the ruai. Jack had no intention of joining Colenso at the forward camp. There were many waterways going south. His intention was take a different waterway and go all the way to Bandjarmasin without the South African. As soon as he and Harry were back in the real world, Jack would marry her and Colenso could make whatever fuss he liked once he realized he had been duped. It would not matter then. Nothing would matter. Jack would have won.

Through an interpreter, Jack discussed several aspects of life in the longhouse with the basir, before he broached the main subject.

'Basir, has the red-headed man been asking you about seven heads of ancient chieftains of the Punan?'

'The offspring of the orang-utans has been asking many questions about the seven heads.'

'And have you told him where they are to be found?'

'I tell no one. I am the guardian of the heads. I am permitted only to pass on the knowledge of the heads to my apprentice. This I have not yet done, nor will do so until I lie on my deathbed.'

Jack nodded. He was satisfied that the basir was telling the truth. Treasure or no treasure, it would not do to go home without sight of the heads or knowledge of their whereabouts if a common sailor had managed to obtain the information. It would be embarrassing and humiliating to have Keller arrive in England, while Jack was engaged on a lecture tour, to state that he had seen the heads and knew where they were located. So long as Keller was unsuccessful in his attempt to find the heads, Jack was only mildly concerned.

'What would happen if you died before you passed on the knowledge to your apprentice?' he asked the basir.

Skallag smiled. 'Then I should come to him in his dreams. The barriers between death and life are thin, when there is important work to be done. My ancestors would assist me in this endeavour, have no fear.'

'Do not be fooled by this offspring of the orang-utan,' Jack warned the basir, nodding in the direction of Keller.

'He is a cunning man. He will discover your secret if he can.'

'I am not afraid of him. He is afraid of *me*.'

Jack was satisfied that Keller was no nearer to finding out the secret location of the heads than he was himself. This gave Jack hope that he would be able to work on the basir. If anyone could get information out of a reluctant old man who dressed like a woman, it would be Harry. Women were good at subterfuge, Jack decided. They were used to wheedling information from each other. He would set Harry to work on it.

The following morning, Kit Colenso set out with the main party, leaving just two Dyaks and Jack with Harry.

# 4

The jinn and natural wildlife of the rainforest were both in a great state of excitement. Mugar, the great dark boar, ran through the thickets and brakes at great speed, smashing all in his path. The parrots, who could talk with the tongues of men, carried the excitement to the lizard-women who lived along the secret rivers down which men did not go. Man-eating giants hid in deep caves. Little people, small as a man's thumb, took to mouseholes. Bezoar stones rattled in the bellies of climbing monkeys anxious to escape the chaos. Hawks and eagles gathered like dust clouds in the mountains. In the valleys, leopards, customarily lone, stalked the undergrowth in packs.

It was the Santang Sisters who were the cause of all this confusion, for all seven were flying on their golden brooms above the rainforest. All seven at once. This meant the fates of several men were being reworked, refashioned. The Santang goddesses were having to work hard to redirect the life-lines of their charges. Having to do so put them in a bad temper and just occasionally one of them would take the time to snipe at an animal or bird, demon or jinni, out of pure spite.

It was this activity which had put the creatures of the forest, natural and supernatural, in such a state of agitation.

Keller was getting nowhere with his efforts at prising the basir's secret from that man's lips. On the other hand, the seaman was pleased to see Kit Colenso and the others leave the longhouse. Only Singapore Jack and his woman had remained behind, along with a couple of Dyaks. This made things a lot simpler for Keller, who itched to confront the eccentric English aristocrat.

'In here, deep in the Ulu, it don't matter who your family is or was,' muttered Keller to a perplexed Raki. 'He might be a lord back home, but in here he's just another man. Now we're both in a place where his rank don't matter I'll cut him off at the knees. His kind have been stampin' on my kind for centuries. Well, we'll see how hard he can stamp now he ain't got the whole force of the law to protect him.'

Keller was certain that Singapore Jack was simply waiting for a chance to kill him. The seaman went nowhere now without Mayok and Raki to watch his back. Usang and Budrudeen being non-combatants, were left to their own devices. Keller had no time for such people at the moment. Later, when it was all over, he would find out why Budrudeen was acting so sullen. Also, more importantly, why Usang refused to let Keller into her bed. Things were not right with those two.

Thanks to the herbs given him by the basir, Keller's torso wound had healed somewhat. His rough surgery on his genitals had left his penis swollen and infected. It was still extremely painful, but a special moss was working even here. Keller was determined to keep the palang. If these Dyaks could have one, so could he. Once his self-inflicted injury had healed a little more, he intended to put his palang to work.

Over the next two days Keller made his plans. Ostensibly he went off into the jungle each day to hunt with his two Dyaks. In fact, he sent Raki and Mayok on ahead and remained on the forest edge. Here he stayed, lodged high up in the fork of a tree, waiting and watching intently.

He kept a weather eye on the whereabouts of three people: Singapore Jack, Harriet Glendenning and Skallag. No movement, even just a walk to use the forest as a latrine, went unwitnessed. In the afternoon of the second day his spying bore fruit. The elderly basir left the long-house and began to hobble inland, following a little-used rainforest path. Korwar lined the track, which gave Keller hope that this was an important byway to the Dyaks in the Kingdom of the Sun Bear.

Skallag had never worried about being followed by members of his Punan longhouse. His reputation as a powerful wizard was such that no Land Dyak would dare stalk him. The basir therefore did little to disguise his direction, except occasionally to look back along the path. Keller knew that the way to track a man without being seen was to remain to the side and a little ahead of him, about fifty yards distant. In this way you can keep within sound and sight of your victim, who is constantly watching the path at his back for signs of pursuit.

Skallag eventually led Keller to a rock face on the side of a cliff. The cliff was covered in vegetation and vines and it was only when the basir actually disappeared that Keller knew he had struck lucky. On going immediately to a spot where a pine tree stood up against the rock face, he found a small opening. It was difficult, but a fully grown man could just slip between the trunk and the rock, into a two-foot wide fissure.

Keller had to divest himself of his musket and other equipment before he could squeeze through the gap and into the hole. Once he had done so he found himself in a cave which widened gradually, until he could stand erect. Inside the cave it was pitch black. Keller felt his way along, very slowly, mindful that the basir was somewhere ahead. He did not want to go blundering into the priest-shaman in the darkness. On reaching a sharp corner he was once again in a dim light, which came from crude oil lamps attached to the walls. He noticed these lamps were made of the skulls of sun bears. There were cave wall drawings of this very same creature, in various poses, lining the walls of the cave.

The basir was not a great one for washing and his odour was present in the atmosphere, mixed with the scent of the plant oil burning in the lamps. Deeper and deeper into the ground went Keller, smelling the old man's musty progress all the way. Finally, the cave turned yet another corner and Keller was faced with roughly hewn steps cut into the rock. These went down and like a spiral staircase. Again, he followed, refusing to allow any fear to stop him now he was so close to his goal. He could hear the old basir chanting, somewhere ahead.

There was a trap on the steps. As Keller turned a bend, a rise he expected to fall six inches actually dropped two feet down to the next step. Keller stepped out expectantly and then tumbled forward when he found nothing but air under his sole. He fell all the way to the bottom of the steps, another three or four yards, and sprawled on the dirt floor at the bottom.

The chanting stopped immediately. The basir had heard the fall. Keller was reluctant to confront the old man without a firearm in his hands. The basir might have stored weapons of any kind in the cave. Keller had no wish to end up with a blow-pipe dart in his neck. He retreated, hastily, back up the stairs and along the tunnel, to the cave's entrance. Once outside, he armed himself and sat in the tree line, aiming for the pine. When the basir showed himself, Keller meant to shoot him dead.

After several hours it became apparent that the basir was not coming or had found another exit. Keller then made his way back to the longhouse. Instead of marching up the longhouse stairs, Keller stood just inside the rainforest again, and watched. He saw the basir appear out of his room. The old man went to sit on the edge of the ruai, to look out into the jungle. Keller knew that Skallag was waiting for him to return. Well, the basir was going to get a shock. Keller was not going back into the longhouse until the night hours, when he intended to murder the old man.

# PART NINE

# Seven Sisters on Golden Brooms

# 1

After the riots the royal bungalow, being half-gutted by fire, could not be used as habitation. Rajah Starke moved into the palace, a grand building and a fine monument to Eastern architecture. It had a very impressive gateway, tinged with rose and gold, and the horseshoe archway was inlaid with coral and ivory. Seven imposing watchtowers were situated around the outer wall on which beacons as large as bonfires were lit on ceremonial occasions.

There were several inner courtyards, some of them so well hidden as to be almost secret. Around and within the courtyards were porticoes and gardens edged by myrtle bushes, covered walkways with slender supporting columns for their roofs, coupled latticework windows of arabesque design separated by mullions and surrounded by beautiful stucco decorations in white gypsum. On the tops of most walls were friezes in carved sandalwood and marble cornices by the dozen.

Of course there were pools too, and running water irected along teakwood channels, some of which was used to water the roses Harry had imported from her garden in England. The tiles on the roof of the palace were of red clay moulded over the thighs of young men and women into curved interlocking shapes. On the watchtowers the cupolas had lapis lazuli tips which glittered brightly in the sun and shone wetly on rainy days.

Rajah Starke had felt uncomfortable in such opulent surroundings when he had first come to Kuching, but had now grown more used to grandeur and was able to settle into the palace without too many qualms. In fact, he looked forward to using the courtyards and gardens as a retreat. He was a quiet man by nature, given to reflection, and the beauty of the courtyards was not just in their architecture, but also in their tranquility.

Prince Issam found him one morning walking in the Courtyard of the Leopards, breathing the scent of myrtle bushes. The prince quickly explained that he had received signs through dreams that Miss Harriet Glendenning was in mortal danger. He informed the rajah that only a supernatural intervention could prevent the young lady from the consequences of a horrible attack.

'I must go and help her,' said the agitated rajah. 'Please send Chin Hua to me at once.'

A boat was quickly dispatched to fetch the Chinese sorcerer to the palace. Chin Hua, tall and slim, with long flowing beard and moustaches and hair in a single braid which touched the ground, entered the palace and stood before the rajah. Starke noticed that his guards were clearly nervous with the sorcerer around. They unconsciously edged away from the man in the silk robes and small black hat.

Chin Hua was not an old man, but in his twenty-seventh year. His eyes were like those of a hawk in its prime. He looked into the rajah's face and nodded. Without being primed, the Chinese sorcerer, who owed the rajah a favour, knew where the problem lay and the solution to the rajah's troubles.

'You wish to join your cousin. I shall send you to her.'

'But will I be in time?' wailed the rajah. 'How can I reach her fast enough to save her?'

'I was not going to send you as a man,' replied Chin Hua with an enigmatic smile. 'Man travels too slowly on his two legs. You shall have two legs, but two wings also. I intend changing you into an owl – a black owl – and you will fly south to where there is chaos and murder. Remember, you will not be able to regain your human shape until you return here, to me, so anything you do will have to be as an owl.'

The rajah thought about this and nodded. Of course, he would have felt more useful as an eagle, with stronger weapons, but an eagle attracts attention. Dyak hunters would bother with an eagle, but not an owl. He saw that Chin Hua had made the right choice.

'Just a word of warning,' said Chin Hua, before he began the spell. 'Do not look up at the moon, whatever you do, or you will be distracted from your task. Owls cannot but help fall in love with the moon and it has been their downfall since the dawn of the world. Ignore the shining rays and stare straight ahead. You will not go wrong if you heed my advice on this matter.'

The rajah promised that he would not stare into the eyes of the beguiling moon.

Within an hour a black owl was flying southwards, over a forest of trees like a hundred thousand cathedral spires clustered together. Kites, buzzards and falcons wheeled above these giants, casting cross-shaped shadows on the top of the canopy. The black owl stayed low, weaving in and out of the tips of the spires, worrying to any predators who felt he was fair game. Only harrier hawks could manoeuvre as well as he and they were few and far between at that particular height.

The black owl marvelled at the towering individual giants which made up the forest. Each one had a base the size of a small house and flew upwards hundreds of feet to tips no larger than an ear of corn. They swayed several feet in either direction in the wind, with supple creaking and moaning. They swished like broomheads, sweeping the base of the clouds. They seemed as numberless as stars or grains of sand.

What a universe of wood and green we have here, thought the owl, as an ocean of foliage stretched out beneath him, undulating like the waves of the sea and no far shore in sight.

Occasionally, there were gaps and chasms which fell straight down to rocky outcrops or whiplash rivers deep below. These were like veins running through the forest, carrying brown rushing lifeblood to the roots of the trees. Along the rivers were small black oblongs, which were the longhouses of Land Dyaks. Here, children were playing in the bright sunlight, running amongst the chickens, chasing the dogs and hogs. Higher, but still far below the black owl, were the creatures of the branches: orang-utans, several varieties of monkeys, brightly coloured birds, monitor lizards, flying snakes and flying foxes. Fruit hung thick and pendulous from the tips of boughs and vines entangled all in their weaving and interweaving threads.

Over smoking volcanoes flew the black owl, through sulphurous yellow clouds of gas, into regions where the mountains suddenly burst through the forest canopy with a slow but ancient energy, to dwarf even the mighty trees. Between these mountains were gullies, cryptic in their depth, able to swallow whole tribes of men without a trac

Somewhere, down within those brooding gullies, choked with thick vines, dead trees and fallen boulders, ran new water from the tops of the mountains: becks which fed and grew prairie-wide lawns of moss and lichen that hardly saw the light of day from one century to the next.

Eventually, the black owl came to the central region of Kalimantan, deep in the heart of Borneo, where men were so few they hardly mattered at all. Thus to the Kingdom of the Sun Bear. Here the bird found a river, flew along between its banks, wafting past the silent stork-billed king-fishers and little green herons waiting for silver meals to flash from beneath the shadows of overhanging boughs.

Finally the black owl reached the longhouse of the Punans, there to settle on a branch and watch events.

Keller saw the bird land on a dead branch. It quickly dis-appeared into the foliage, its dark feathers a perfect camouflage at night. The seaman took a bead on the spot where the bird sat, now just a shadow, and knew that given normal circumstances he could have killed it dead. Tonight, however, he was watching and waiting for his chance to enter the longhouse from the rear, in order to cut the throat of the basir, while that man slept and dreamed of his absolute regional power.

Before Keller was ready to enter the longhouse, he saw the legs of someone appear, coming down the steps at the front of the ruai. He knew from the garment covering the legs that this was either Singapore Jack or the woman. It became evident within a few moments that it was the latter, for the figure was short and shapely in the moonlight. Keller saw that Harriet Glendenning was heading down to the river, probably to get some cool air, for the longhouse became hot and sultry with so many sleeping bodies in so confined a space.

'Hello,' he murmured to himself, 'this lass is tempting fate a bit, with a red-blooded seaman in hailing distance.'

Usang had still not let Keller anywhere near her body and Keller was feeling grieved about that. The wound he had made in his penis with the palang had not yet healed completely, but the pain of the erection fired his lechery rather than dampened it. On Raki's advice he had shortened and rounded the ends of the palang, so that now there were wooden knobs projecting from both sides of the blood-encrusted gland. Keller felt that the palang gave him sexual power. He felt immensely strong, with a great driving force of lust deep in his groin. This contained energy needed release and Keller now saw a way of relieving it.

'We'll see how stuck up you are now, missy,' he whispered to himself, 'with John Keller between your legs.'

The moon was behind a cloud. Keller used the starlight to see by as he slipped into the shadows of the trees and drifted silently down to the bank of the river. There he made his way along, over the fallen trunks of smaller trees, under the archways created by bigger ones, to within a short distance of Harriet Glendenning.

She had opened her shirt and was washing her chest in the cool water of the river. Keller was disappointed by the size of her breasts. He liked women who were well endowed, but he told himself beggars could not be choosers. Then she turned her back on him and he saw gleaming white shoulders, smooth as ivory, with slender arms and a trim neat waist. He was going to jump her there and then, take her while the fright was freezing her to the spot, but he decided to play a little game instead.

Keller crept between Harriet and the longhouse, to cut off her escape, then rustled a high branch. He did this several times, at infrequent intervals, until finally she looked up, alarm registering in her features.

Now, he thought, she will be wondering whether it's monkeys or something more dangerous, like a clouded leopard or a sun bear. She will move along the bank, rather than cross under this particular tree, and try to find a circuitous route back to the longhouse. After one or two more rustles she did indeed start to move along the bank, away from the usual path to the longhouse. Keller followed her, rustling his way in the thick undergrowth, like a big cat stalking its quarry.

He heard her whisper, 'Oh, God,' to herself, just once, before she opened up into a quick walk.

At that moment, the moon came out from behind the cloud, dazzling in its splendour. All creatures, including Keller and Harriet, looked up. The great yellow disc was like a huge lantern, illuminating all, attracting attention.

Keller ran forward, snarling and spitting as if he really were a wild cat. On reaching her he ripped the flapping shirt from her back, pulling her to the ground in the process. With a small cry she immediately jumped up and tried to run as he scratched her white skin with his dirty nails. Then he grabbed her by the neck with two hands and threw her to the ground, knocking all the breath out of her body, rendering her helpless.

Turning her over quickly, he rammed a wad of moss in her open mouth before she could scream. Her eyes bugged in fright as he stared down into her face, pinning her body to the bank of the river with his own weight, his knees on her upper arms. With his free hand he reached down and whipped away his loincloth, revealing in the moonlight the ugliness of his mutilation, which projected like the gnarled stump of a broken branch.

Harriet Glendenning's eyes started from her face.

'Oh, dear God, no, please no . . .' she choked, having llowed half the moss he had crammed into her mouth.

He forced another thick clod of moss between her teeth.

'Nothing can help you now, missy,' he snarled in delight. 'I'm goin' to have my way with you, whether you enjoy it or not.'

She began to fight now, enraged by his words, kicking his back with her knees, making his teeth rattle. He laughed low and menacingly into her face, kissed her mouth with its wedge of moss, and then quickly slid down and reached with his hands to rip open the front flaps of her trousers. Standing up, he took the legs of the trousers and tipped her out, so that she now lay naked on the grass, legs and arms spread, firing the lust in his loins to furnace heat. He dropped down on her with all his weight, knocking the wind out of her chest. His hands grabbed at her small breasts, crushing them, kneading them.

Then he forced her legs apart as she began to choke again on the moss and earth in her mouth. Keller was at the point of driving his rigid palanged penis into her vagina when something came out of the forest at immense speed and clamped itself to his face, raking his cheeks and brow with razor talons, repeatedly pecking at his eyes with a sharp beak.

Keller stood up and shrieked with fury and pain, clawing at the black owl which was tearing his face to ribbons. He had instinctively screwed his eyes up tight, to try to protect his eyeballs from the assault, while his hands tore at the feathered creature which was turning his features into a mess of blood and shredded flesh. He could not get a good grip on the bird and, before his blood-slippery hands could grasp it and hold it, the owl had flown, back into the darkness of the forest.

'You bastard!' screamed Keller after the bird. 'I'll destroy you!'

He ran a few paces to where his musket lay and he

a useless shot crashing into the night. Shouts of alarm came from the longhouse. When Keller looked back he saw that Harriet Glendenning had disappeared, had run back to where protection was to be found. Keller went down to the river and bathed his face, crying oaths and calling down curses on owls and all birds of the air. He was in agony, as well as feeling furious at being thwarted from his prey. One of his eyes hurt like hell.

There was clearly no way he could go back to the longhouse now, with everyone awake, and Singapore Jack no doubt loading a musket. The English lord would be itching to discharge that firelock into Keller's breast at the first sight of him.

Keller decided that Jack would not, could not, let such a matter as attempted rape rest. If Keller did not return to the longhouse, then Singapore Jack would feel it necessary to hunt him down. That was good. Keller would be waiting for him. It was easier to shoot a man dead when you were expecting him to cross your path than it was to find a hidden quarry. Keller would discover for himself the perfect place for an ambush, then let the English lord walk up to the end of his musket.

## 2

The black owl instinctively knew that its work had
been done and flew north. It was bitterly disappointed with
itself. It had almost failed in the task. It should have flown
in earlier, saved her from the horrible struggle which took
place, the humiliating disrobing, the consequent naked
flight into the night. Had the owl attacked the man as he
ran forward to accost her, she might have escaped
unscathed except for a nasty fright.

The moon had been responsible for the owl's tardiness.

No, no, it told itself as it flew over rivers and lakes,
forests and mountains, the moon was *not* at fault. The owl
had been warned not to look into the face of the moon and
it, like every other creature at that moment, had been
stunned by the beauty of the moon as it came out from
behind a cloud. It had been impossible not to look up,
instinctively, at this object which had so suddenly bathed
the world in golden light.

Once the moon had caught the black owl's eyes, the owl
was lost in its glory and lustre. It had sat transfixed, its
heart full of desperate love for the distant orb. Oh, how

yearned to become the moon's mate, the lover of that perfectly rounded beauty of the night! The owl had sighed, had thought about stretching its wings and flying up into the ether, to attempt like many other owls before it, to reach for the impossible.

Luckily, since this black owl had another creature's persona nestling inside its body of beak, claw and feathers, it was able to be distracted. It heard the despairing cry of the woman as she was about to be violated by the madman. Suddenly it jerked itself out of its silly reverie and flew straight into the face of the man. Just in time! Another few minutes and irreparable damage would have been done. As it was, she had suffered dreadfully, and the black owl would never forgive itself for its lapse of concentration, its own fickle heart.

Harry had to run the gauntlet of amazed watchers as she struggled up the steps of the longhouse, naked, distressed, afraid, and befuddled. Jack reached her and bundled her into a room. He quickly found a blanket to cover her. Then he began to question her, shouting into her face.

'What happened? Who did this to you? Was it Keller?'

'Jack, please,' she moaned. 'Just hold me for a minute. I think I'm going to be sick . . .'

Then, much to his disgust, she vomited over him and the blanket. He pushed her out to arm's length, his face showing his revulsion. But then he quickly composed himself again. Going to the corner of the room he found a jug of water and washed the vomit from his arms and chest, then did the same for Harry. She stood there, swaying, confused and upset. Once more she reached out for him and this time he took her by the arms and sat her down on the floor, where she began to talk.

'Oh Jack – it – it was horrible. He tried to rape me. He's 1. I'm so angry with myself . . .'

He held her away from him again. 'Why? You, didn't encourage him did you?'

'What?' She could not believe what she was hearing.

He looked uncomfortable. 'I don't mean – well, I just thought you might have inadvertently – I don't know – that's why I'm asking the question. If he thought you – you were interested – he might have got the wrong idea.'

She said coldly, 'I was angry with myself for not fighting harder. The attack was sudden. It shocked me. I'm still feeling very unsteady.'

A Dyak woman came in then, carrying some tea in a bamboo cup. She spoke softly to Harry in her own language, made Harry drink some of the tea, then hugged her. The Dyak woman, indeed the whole longhouse, had guessed what had happened. They probably did not know who the perpetrator was, but they knew this white woman had been sexually attacked. Harry clung to the woman, finding solace in the warmth and firmness of her embrace.

Jack said, 'I am going to kill Keller.'

He started to leave the room, when Harry called him back.

'Jack, let's get out of here. Let's go on, to where Kit is waiting for us? Please?'

Jack frowned. 'You must be out of your mind. I'm not going to leave that maniac to roam the forest at will. He needs to be put down, for his good and for everyone else's benefit. Do you think I could live with myself if I just walked away from this? Don't you see, Harriet? I *have* to kill him. He's a wild animal. When a wild animal runs amok you have to shoot it. To do otherwise would be shirking responsibility.'

She pulled the blanket tighter around her body, forming a cocoon with it.

'He attacked *me*, Jack – *me*. Surely I should have so

say in what happens here. Leave him to the longhouse Dyaks. This is their country. They will have their own laws for dealing with such men. Let them handle it in their way.'

'These primitive people? They're not even Christians – they're a pagan people. They probably regard rape as a legitimate way of taking a woman.'

'Can't you see how this woman is trying to comfort me? It is just as abhorrent to them as it is to us. Leave it to them.'

Jack was adamant. 'No, I shall go out after Keller first thing in the morning. And I don't want any blasted Dyaks with me. This is between Keller and myself.'

With that, Jack left the room. Harry began to weep, soft, angry tears, wondering whether there was such a thing as a sane man in the world.

The following morning, Singapore Jack was up with the sun. He bathed in the river, shaved, and put on the cleanest clothes he owned. When an English aristocrat goes out to kill someone he has to look his very best. He also had to take his favourite musket, loaded and ready. A pistol in his belt might not go amiss. And a kris with a wavy, clean blade.

In point of fact, a gentleman has to look his best for *all* significant occasions, and killing a man can be considered a very weighty business. It was not a duty to be enjoyed, but being such a serious affair it had to be done properly and with gravity. In medieval times the importance of such a preparation had a phrase to cover it. It was called 'the arming of the hero' and while Jack did not see himself as a hero exactly, he did consider himself a legitimate judge and executioner in this godforsaken forest, hundreds of miles from any real law.

Jack left the longhouse and went down to the river, to the spot where last night's incident had taken place. It was logical to begin looking for the rogue seaman at this point.

However, though he found the signs of a struggle, and searched the forest area around that spot, Jack knew deep down that he had not a hope of finding someone who hid in the forest. It took only a short while to acknowledge this, then he returned to the longhouse to get his two Dyaks to join him.

'You must not interfere in this matter,' he told them, once he had found them. 'It is my place to carry out the execution, not yours.'

The two men promised they would not intervene and Jack then set out again, with these two expert trackers.

Starting at the river they were soon on Keller's trail. The seaman had made his way to a rocky outcrop in some hills to the east, presumably a position of strength, where he would be able to see anyone chasing him. Singapore Jack had to acknowledge Keller's cunning. Finding and killing this madman was not going to be an easy task. Not for a moment though did Jack doubt his own ability to bring Keller to book. Justice was on the side of the English gentleman. Justice did not protect waterfront riff-raff. It was similar to hunting a rat.

By noon, Jack knew that he was in the area where Keller was hiding. The Dyaks said they could smell the seaman. The noses of these forest hunters were sharp enough to pick up the scent of an outsider and they smelled him as surely as if he really were a wild animal. They led Jack to a glade on the edge of the forest, beyond which was a shallow hill with some rocks near the crest. They pointed to these rocks from the safety of the tree line and told Jack this was where Keller was hiding.

Jack told the two men to retire and leave him to it.

'Keller?' he called, after the Dyaks had melted into the trees. 'Come down here.'

'What for?' came the reply.

'To take your punishment.'

'Why don't you come up here?'

Jack felt this was a positive sign. Keller had not argued that he did not deserve punishment. He clearly knew he had done wrong in the eyes of any law.

'No – I think I will wait for you to come down. You will have to come down sometime you know. There is no water up there on the hill.'

'There's none down there, either.'

This was true. Jack had let the Dyaks go without thinking of supplies. He realized now that he should have made sure of a regular supply of water for himself. He had his own goatskin, but that would last only a day. Jack looked around him, for pitcher plants which would hold rainwater, but was disappointed to see none.

'I'm all right,' called Keller. 'I made sure of provisions before I came up here.'

Jack began to feel a little frustrated. Keller was in a position of strength. The moment Jack stepped outside the tree line, Keller would be able to shoot him down. Although he could not admit it to himself, it was a job Colenso would have carried out far more efficiently. Kit Colenso was the expert hunter, not Lord Randolph Braiks. It was an unsettling business.

'Tell you what,' called Keller. 'I'll come down there if you promise to give me an even chance.'

Jack pricked up his ears at this offer and crawled to the edge of the tree line, suspecting a trick.

'What do you mean?'

'Just what I said. An even chance. You an' me. Let's call it a duel. You toffs are used to duels, ain't you?'

Jack considered this offer coldly. 'Gentlemen do not ordinarily duel with scoundrels,' he called back. 'Duels are fought between two equals.'

'I'm a man, same as you,' came back the gruff reply. 'You won't deny that. I weren't born with no silver spoon between me teeth, but I walk on two legs and I'm as free as you are.'

All this was true. Yet still Jack felt entitled to stand on his rank and refused to have anything to do with a duel. But how long was it going to take to get that scum out from his hiding place, if he did not agree? For all he knew, Keller might have stashed a cache of stores away on that hill. The seaman had been in the region a lot longer than Jack and his party.

'You are a man,' he acknowledged, 'but I would deny you are the same kind of man as I am. You are trash, Keller. A freeman, yes, but a slave has more worth than you. I swore to Rajah Starke that I would protect his cousin. You have caused me to betray my trust. I have failed the rajah and it causes me more grief than you will ever know.'

'Choke on your failure,' growled the distant voice. 'I don't give a damn. Are you going to fight me or not? Say not if you're the blamed coward I think you are. All silk shirts and a piss-pot under the bed. I've been biting pieces out of men like you since I was born. You hide behind your rank and ain't got the courage to stand against real men like me. Get down off your cork-heeled shoes and face me, one to one.'

All the while they had been speaking, Jack had been gauging just where the voice was coming from. Keller's insinuations were making him furious. Finally, he could bear it no longer and fired a chance shot, up into the boulders, hoping to hit his opponent.

The ball ricocheted uselessly off a rock, sending up chips and sparks. Keller laughed delightedly.

'I knew it! Afraid to face me, man to man. Why, I sailed with men in the fo'c'sle who were twice your weight in bravery. They ate like pigs, got drunker than a bishop in port and disgraced themselves, farted and belched in company, but they had spines of steel. You lily-livered loon. Thought you could catch me unawares with your sneak shots? I've spit on better.'

Jack could have screamed in frustration. This man's madness was catching. He felt it surging through his own brain. He reloaded and fired up into the rocks twice more, without any replies in kind from Keller. Every time, his wild firing was mocked by Keller, who called him filthy names and maligned his family, especially his mother, and yet he had to stay there and take the abuse, unless he was to accept Keller's offer.

'All right!' cried Jack, finally. 'We'll meet in single combat, in the glade.'

He refused to call it a duel. It was simply a battle between two men. Once he had Keller in the open, he was confident of killing him. Jack was a very good shot. He had already mortally wounded a Greek nobleman in a duel with pistols.

'You sure you won't shoot me when I come out?' called Keller, mockingly.

'You have my word.'

'I never thought the word of a gentleman added up to much,' came the reply, 'but you can be positive that if you try anything, I'll get you with a shot before I die. He'll make sure I receive decent justice in the hands of men. You remember that. There's eyes on us – eyes lookin' down from another place.'

Surely the man is not talking of God's justice? Jack thought. Was Keller seriously thinking he had the same moral rights as other men? To deserve moral rights one had to have morals in the first place. Keller was a miscreant and a cur. A tiger shark had more morals than Keller. Did he even believe in God? Surely he was thinking of Satan? Eyes from below?

'Keller, do you honestly believe God cares about a sewer rat like you?'

'You keep your mouth shut. God cares about all of us, whoever we are. I'm a Christian, same as you. God follows us in here, don't he? Into the Ulu? That's so we don't fall foul of some heathen god. I don't want no boogey-god takin' my soul when I'm dead, but the missionaries tell us that won't happen, if we believe in Jesus and the holy Church.'

Jack was incredulous. There was even a faint note of panic in Keller's voice. The man actually *needed* to believe that he was safe in the hands of the Lord.

'You will go to hell, Keller.'

'Well, that's all right then, if I deserve it. I don't mind going to hell so long as it's a Christian one.' A little chuckle came drifting down the slope, followed by the words, 'I'll see the likes of you there, won't I? Your lot have been bleeding us ordinary folk dry since the beginnin' of time. You let us die in the gutter of starvation and don't even turn your heads. Back home I've seen the wheels of coaches with crests on 'em run over a body in the street and those inside complain to the driver about the bump. Oh, I'll see you in hell all right, Mr Aristocrat, don't you worry about that none.'

'Are you coming down?' asked Jack, coldly. 'I'm ready to show myself.'

'Step out front.'

Jack did so, warily. Then he saw a figure rise up out of the rocks and begin walking down towards him. It was Keller, but the first sight of the man's appearance shocked the English lord to the core. Apart from being almost naked and filthy, exposing a hideous scar on his side, Keller's face was a mass of deep red scratches and one eye was still weeping blood. His features had been ripped from brow to neck. He looked gruesome.

'Good God, did she do that to you?' he said, without being able to help himself.

Keller stopped, reached up and touched his face, then shook his head.

'She didn't do it. Some bird from hell did it. I've had a gutful of this Ulu, I can tell you. It's full of devils – foreign devils – that tear the flesh from your very bones. I've seen enough horrors in here to last a lifetime. This black demon with feathers on came out of the night and tore my face to bits. Blinded me too, in my left eye. But that's all right, because the other's my shooting eye. I can still kill you, Singapore Jack. Make no mistake.'

To Jack it was Keller who looked the demon. The man's hair was matted and long, covering his head and face. His good eye burned out of this dirty tangle of red mane. His body was covered in sores and pocks. And he stank. He stank to high heaven. That Harry should have been subjected to an attack from this creature made the bile rise in Jack's throat.

'Do you have a pistol?'

Keller drew a large sailor's flintlock from the belt which supported his loincloth.

'I have – primed and ready.'

Jack drew a slimmer, much lighter weapon from his own belt.

'And I have mine.'

'Back to back, ten paces, then turn and fire,' Keller said. 'I've seen how it's done.'

The two men laid their other weapons on the grass. Then they assumed the duelling positions, standing with their backs against each other. There was not a great deal of difference in their respective heights, but Keller was broader than his opponent, especially at the shoulders. He made a larger target. But he bragged that he was going to blow Jack's head from his shoulders 'with my little cannon'.

Jack was quietly confident, saying nothing, concentrating his mind on the task ahead. The important thing was to remain calm and steady. A cold rage was more useful than a hot one. He could do that. Gentlemen were trained at birth to control their anger. Like the Chinese, your blue-blooded Englishman loses face when he falls into a public display of rage. Jack was imperious, outwardly composed, his hand steady, unwavering.

'We will both call the numbers,' he said to Keller. 'Ten paces, turn, fire.'

'Like I said.'

They began to walk away from each other.

'One, two, three, four . . .'

At that moment there was a disturbance. Four Dyaks arrived in the clearing. Two of them were Mayok and Raki. They were followed closely by the two guides who had led Singapore Jack to Keller's hideout. Clearly the first pair had tracked the white men down, while the second two had dogged their steps, worried perhaps that Raki and Mayok were going to interfere with the single combat between the two Occidentals.

All four Dyaks looked on in bewilderment to see the two white men walking away from each other, poker-backed and with stiff determined looks on their faces, their right hands holding pistols in a set manner.

One white man was dressed in clean jungle trousers, a grey shirt open at the neck, and brown knee-length boots. His hair was long but clean and brushed. He appeared as if he had been out for a stroll and had come upon an interesting game.

The other man looked like a wounded orang-utan.

The sudden arrival of the Dyaks had interrupted the counting.

Jack stopped pacing and said, 'Ah, the tardy seconds have arrived at last.'

'Never mind your gentlemen's jokes,' growled Keller. 'Let's get to it again.'

'Gladly.'

They returned to their former positions, back to back, and ignoring their audience, started pacing again.

'One, two, three, four, five, six, seven, eight, nine, *ten* – turn – fire.'

A brace of pistols blasted in the clearing. One man went down like a felled tree, on his back, in the grass. He had a surprised looked on his face. His hands still gripped the butt of the pistol and a Dyak, who went immediately to his side, had difficulty in prising the weapon loose. The fallen man had a dark hole in his chest, from which a stain was spreading through his grey shirt. Singapore Jack lay dying.

Keller strode over to him and looked down on the English lord.

'What happened?' whispered Jack, his eyes staring, as if peering into a dark place.

'I've killed you, that's what happened,' replied an elated Keller. 'I said I would, and I have.'

'All my work here,' gasped Jack, as the Dyak propped up his head with a knee. 'I wanted to take it back. To England. My maps. My catalogues. My drawings. All the new species of flowers, insects, birds . . .'

'Well, you're dyin' and that's that,' said Keller. 'No one can help you now. You would come up against me. I warned you what would happen. All those things you talk about will have to stay here, to rot. The woman's mine now. I won her.'

'Christ man,' gasped the dying lord, 'we weren't fighting to see who owned her. I was fighting to avenge her honour. Leave her alone, damn you.'

'You ain't got no say. You're dead.'

And shortly afterwards these words became true. Jack was gone. His Dyaks saw that they were in an dangerous position. The victor of the duel stood over the dead body and stared at them, his eyes challenging them to do something about the death of their party's leader. A tuan was dead. While he had been alive he had been their paymaster. Now he was gone, he was nothing to them. They drifted away, into the forest.

Keller turned to his own Dyaks.

'If you want to cut his head off, that's up to you,' said Keller to Mayok and Raki. 'I don't want nothing to do with that sort of thing no more. I'm a Christian see. We don't take heads, usually. Afterwards, though, you can bury him.'

Both Mayok and Raki saw no need to take the head. It was not theirs to own. They had had no part in the killing. Neither of the two men had any intention of burying the tuan either. Digging was hard work in a place where the ground was networked with strong roots. They decided to leave the English lord for the wild animals and the crawling, wriggling creatures that infest the dead. They would soon clean the flesh from the bones. They took his weapons though, passing on his firearms to Keller. Mayok kept the kris and Raki the parang.

Keller was quietly triumphant. He could not imagine who they could send against him. He was invincible. There was still the man they called Kit Colenso, out there in the rainforest, who would undoubtedly come looking for him once the news reached the forward camp. But Keller was not afraid of Colenso, any more than he had been afraid of Singapore Jack, a man he had beaten in a duel and with only one good eye.

Keller was a charmed man.

He touched the place where Singapore Jack's bullet had gone through his upper left arm. A clean hole. You could poke a stick through and waggle it. No bone or ligament touched. Simply torn muscle, just a little painful. Something was watching over him – angel or devil – and was protecting him from all who came against him. Let the contenders come then, at their own peril, and Keller would swiftly dispose of them.

When the Dyaks took the news of Jack's death to Harry, she did not panic. In fact, she had expected this outcome for some reason unknown to her. She calmly considered her position, then quickly packed a few things together.

'Can you take me to tuan Colenso?' she asked the two Dyaks.

They nodded briskly, looking towards the rainforest all the time, expecting no doubt that the red devil would hurl himself from its greenery and kill them all.

At that moment the basir came up to them and began chattering away. The Dyaks shook their heads.

'What's he saying?' she asked them.

'Basir say he will protect you.'

'I think not. I wish to leave. Will the basir prevent us?'

'No.'

'Then let us be on our way.'

Harry walked down the steps of the ruai and made her way towards the river. The Dyaks went one in front and one behind, to protect her from any new attack. They were scared themselves. They believed the red tuan had found and had eaten a badang's vomit. Badangs, or 'forest ghosts', were notorious for overeating, especially on dead fish. When they did so they were often sick. The man that ate a badang's vomit immediately became immensely strong. No mortal man could stand against him.

Harry found one of their canoes and threw in her pack. The two Dyaks followed her example. Soon they were shooting down the river, putting miles between them and the madman. Harry was still nervous, still very unsettled by the attack on her. Now that she could relax a little she began to grieve for Jack. It was true that she could never have married him. He was not the man she had first supposed him to be. But she had loved him, for a short time, and she was sorry he was gone.

'You are certain tuan Jack was dead?' she said to the Dyaks. 'Perhaps he was just wounded?'

'He have one big hole in chest, here,' said the one paddling behind her. The other was squatting on the bows, watching intently for any river obstacles. 'I think he is very dead. Mahatara send his hawk, Antang, for tuan Jack's soul. I see Antang's shadow come. He fly in, fly out, gone.'

There was a wistful note to the Dyak's words.

'Ah well, if you're sure,' she said, sadly.

'We very sure. He make last breath. Him eyes go glass and him breath stop.'

'What did tuan Keller do with him?'

'I think, nothing. Tuan Keller very proud. Tuan Keller say he is king of the forest.'

'It seems tuan Keller is untouchable,' she murmured, bitterly. 'He seems to win every time.

The other Dyak, the one looking for dead trees and rocks, heard this and shouted something back to his companion. The Dyak in the bows was not as good at speaking English as his comrade, who quickly translated for Harry.

'My friend say he saw a great god stand behind tuan Keller. This god breath on him neck.'

'You think this forest god is protecting him?'

'No, no. Other way,' grinned the Dyak, simply having to steer the canoe in the fast water. 'God who stand behind was Hantu Kuang, ghost with hundred eyes. Hantu Kuang protect no man. Ghost with hundred eyes use men for tricks. Him play with people like baby with – with . . .'

'With toys?'

'Yes. Him make mischief for men. Him make great muddle with tuan Keller. Tuan Keller is kill tuan Jack, but soon the other way. When Hantu Kuang is finished with play, then tuan Keller, him die bad. This always happen when forest gods do things with men. Always end with sad time.'

'There will be no sadness in my heart when Keller dies,' she said, mortified by her own savage thoughts. 'No sadness at all.'

'I think so, missy. I think so,' came the enigmatic reply.

# 3

Usang was praying to Hantu Uri, the placenta spirit, who is always responsible for trouble after a birth. It was never too early to placate Hantu Uri. Better to start buttering him up while the child was but a thought in the mind. Usang believed she was pregnant with Mayok's child. It was really too early to tell but she felt it in her blood. So she asked Hantu Uri to be kind to her and her child, even though the child was smaller than a tree frog inside her.

The hantus – ghosts or spirits who intervened in the lives of mortals – had been adopted from the Malays by some Dyaks. There was Hantu Air, the sea spirit; Hantu Ayer, the freshwater spirit; Hantu Puteri, the beautiful ghost. The latter was especially useful to young men who strayed from their loved ones. Hantu Puteri, in the form of a lovely young girl, had bewitched them (they said) and it was not their fault they had been unfaithful. Their wives, when they found illicit love, could equally blame the pampahilep, the tree spirits.

Then, of course, there was the mighty Hantu Kuang, ghost with a hundred eyes, who had chosen to dog Keller's footsteps. It was this spirit which finally caused Raki to leave silently, in the middle of the night. He had been aware for a long time that Hantu Kuang had been playing games with Keller.

Now he felt things were coming to a head and he did not want to be around when Hantu Kuang finally became bored with it all. The attempted rape of the white woman was the last grain of rice for Raki. He was a determined man, fiercely devoted when he chose to be, but once he had decided to break the cord, there was nothing that would hold him. There were few shades of grey in his spirit. It was dark or it was light.

'I am leaving,' he told Mayok. 'You would be wise to leave too.'

'You? Going? But you are the most loyal to tuan Keller.'

'Things are bad now. They will become worse. We have been enemies, you and I, but that is now behind us. We are all that is left.'

Mayok shook his head. 'No, I have been banished by my people. I have nowhere to go. Tuan Keller has promised me riches. I must stay until I have been paid. What about you? If you leave now you will have made this journey for nothing.'

The older man smiled grimly. 'I have made such journeys before and returned with nothing. All life is experience. I am still alive, I am no worse than when I started. This in itself would be enough, to have lived through it all, and to return unscathed. Once I am rid of tuan Keller, then Jata will not come looking for me. It is tuan Keller, the orang-utan, he hates.'

'So you will go back to Kuching with nothing?'

Raki patted a leather pouch on his belt. 'I have many bezoar stones, from the monkeys, to sell to the Chinese medicine men. This whole journey I have been collecting them. It will give me enough to buy many goods for myself and my longhouse.'

Mayok felt disappointed. 'I did not know about bezoar stones.'

'You are a Kayan, from deep in the forest. You would not know such things. I am an Iban. We live on the coast and know the Chinese well. You must not think badly of yourself.'

'That is the difference between us Land Dyaks and you Sea Dyaks – you know how to get rich from the Chinese.'

Raki shrugged. 'It is the way of the world. Goodbye my friend. I hope you and Usang survive beside this crazy white man. He is a great warrior. We have seen him take many heads. Some he has left on their bodies, but they were his heads. I admire him for his ferociousness. But there is also something bad in him, which sometimes you will find in any man.'

'He is not a good man,' agreed Mayok, 'but he is all I have got for now.'

Usang then said goodbye to Raki and he left, slipping away into the night. Budrudeen saw him go too, but the Malay boy and the Iban had never been at all close.

'He is gone then?' said Budrudeen.

'We are now three. Once tuan Keller has found what he is looking for we shall get our pay. Then you can go to Kinabalu, where you will be safe from the law. Here, I have a gift for you.'

Mayok gave Budrudeen the kris he had taken from Singapore Jack's corpse.

In the morning, Keller arrived back at the longhouse.

Budrudeen was shocked by his appearance, but Keller seemed oblivious of the fact that he looked ghastly. He asked for the white woman and was told she had gone. A glint of anger showed in his eyes. Then Mayok informed

him about Raki's desertion. Keller took this defection more
philosophically.

'They're all running away, are they?' he said, drinking
from a goatskin bag. 'Well so much the better. It's just us
three, my lads.' He put one arm around Mayok and the
other around Budrudeen. 'We'll find the treasure and share
it between us. I've never been a greedy man. You won't
find me bein' selfish when the share-out comes. It don't
even matter to me that you're not white. We've been
through a lot together. Let's drink . . .'

From Keller's stinking breath Mayok knew that there
was tuak in the goatskin. Keller was definitely maudlin.
Budrudeen did not touch alcohol, for religious reasons.
Mayok was not one to drink during the day. They left
Keller to it, knowing he probably needed the alcohol for a
painkiller. Once he had drunk his fill, Keller went to sleep
on one of the mats. While he slept the basir came

'The orang-utan sleeps?'

'He sleeps,' agreed Mayok.

'I could kill him now,' said the basir, 'before he wakes. He
has brought nothing but death to the longhouse.'

'There was death here before we came,' argued Mayok.
'You hanged a man the first night we were here.'

The basir said nothing. His eyes gleamed darkly in the
half-light of the room. Finally, he turned on his heel and left
the room, his bone-and-shell necklaces rattling. Keller
opened his eyes. Mayok now saw that Keller had his hand
on a pistol, no doubt ready to fire. Keller stared after the
basir, then winked at Mayok, before rolling over again to
sleep. Mayok realized the white man had been awake the
whole time. He was a demon, or something close to one.

In the morning, Keller felt a transformed man. He was
king of the rainforest. His enemies had been vanquished
and the site of the ancient heads of the Punan was known to

him. There was the basir, it was true, but the old man was afraid of him. If he had not been he would have killed Keller in the night. Keller knew the Dyaks believed him to be some sort of demi-god of the orang-utans, half-man, half-beast. No one here would move against him. He was free to do as he pleased.

He rose, washed himself in the river, then dressed in European clothes left by Singapore Jack's party. Usang trimmed his beard and hair for him. Once he had finished his ablutions he looked almost civilized again. There were the hideous lacerations on his face, of course, but he could do nothing about those except apply some balm. When he was ready he loaded two muskets and slung one over each shoulder. He stuck Singapore Jack's slim pistol in his belt, giving his own more cumbersome seaman's weapon to the basir as a gift.

'You can have that, you ugly old man,' he smiled, grinning at the basir, knowing he could not understand, 'for without the powder and ball it is useless to you. Hang it on the wall. A trophy from the man-of-the-forest.'

The basir was delighted with the weapon. Even if he could not get it to make thunder and kill things at a distance, it was a prized magical talisman. It would add to his already great power and standing within the tribe. The Punan themselves would not know he could not make it do its wizardry. If ever they got uppity, he would simply produce the strange weapon and they would fall on their knees and beg his forgiveness.

Keller left the longhouse with Budrudeen, Usang and Mayok. Mayok carried his blow-pipe and parang. Budrudeen had the kris. They took the path to the cavern. The entrance to the cave system was found and Keller entered, taking Mayok with him. Budrudeen and Usang remained outside. With flaming brands they searched the inner realm of the limestone caves – and found nothing. Keller began to get more and more angry, as each tunnel revealed nothing of the heads.

'That old bastard tricked me,' he snarled. 'I'll cut his damned liver out.' He began to despair. 'I must find those heads. I must find them.'

Eventually, after trailing through the system for more than four hours, Keller gave up. He and Mayok returned to the other two, waiting for them outside. Keller sat down on the grass, refusing to accept defeat. He ran his mind back over the events of that day when he had followed the basir into the rainforest. Obviously, the old man had realized he was being followed and had led Keller along a false trail. However, the basir would not have known right from the beginning. Therefore he had changed direction halfway along the route.

'Somewhere back there the path divides,' Keller muttered. 'There's another trail which leads to the heads.' He turned to the other three. He could have used Raki at a time like this, but the Sea Dyak had run out on him. 'Mayok, we go back. You look for new trail, understand?' He pointed to his eyes with two fingers of his right hand, then trotted the fingers along his forearm. 'You look-see new path, back in rainforest.'

'Yes, tuan. I look to other path.'

'That's right, that's right.'

Keller retraced his steps. About two-thirds of the way back to the longhouse, Mayok suddenly stopped and pointed. Keller stared but could not see what the Dyak had seen. Then he moved back and forth, changing his perspective, catching the area in different lights, and finally he saw it. A faint trail through the grass and roots, which led under an archway of vines.

'Good boy, Mayok. Eyes of the hawk, eh?'

Keller was not exactly elated. This new path could lead anywhere, not necessarily to the ancient heads. But he sensed he was on the right track now. A path had to lead somewhere. The basir would not visit the heads often. Even though the Punan held the old wizard in deep awe, he would still fear for his secret. He would go only when he needed their advice badly. Like when a party of strange white men, one endowed with the colouring of orang-utans, descended upon the longhouse? Thus it would indeed be a little used trail, not like the well-trodden path to the limestone cave system.

'Let's go. You lead, Mayok. You go first.'

The Land Dyak did as he was told, following the faint signs in the grass, on the leaves of the undergrowth. Mayok was very afraid. Terrified. They were going to enter the forbidden place and he was not sure his spirit was pure enough. Would the gods let him live? Would they let Usang out alive, being a woman possessed of a demon? Mayok knew that Usang trusted his judgement implicitly. She was going simply because he was going. Was she right to trust him so completely?

These thoughts worried him. Yet Mayok felt compelled to go on. He felt it was inevitable, a part of his destiny, written in the sky for him by the Santang Sisters. He could not have turned back, refused to go further. Something was drawing him on, pulling him forward. He hoped it was the gods who wished him to proceed. He hoped he had not been bewitched by the basir or by Usang's demon. His fate was now to lead a bad man into the forbidden place.

This was truly the rainforest primeval. In here was the usual jungle undergrowth and there, two hundred feet above, the overgrowth. Epiphytes, mostly bromalids, formed lacy patterns for the tree tops. There was a dark world between. Great tualang and merbau trees, the pillars of this world, rose upward from the forest floor in massive columns of wood covered in parasitic plant-hair. Around the buttress-rooted trunks were palm fronds, rattan, figs, suckers, creepers. Smaller trees like the red-fruited baccaurea, were bending under the weight of the canopy foliage.

The humidity was overwhelming. Before long the party were covered in sweat-bees. Keller continually brushed them off, but as soon as his hand stopped sweeping, they swarmed back over him again. Black leeches transferred themselves from leaves to his armpits and he cursed them with his usual venom. Whistles, loud buzzes and shrieks accompanied them with every step. It was an impossibly noisy world, swirling with mists and vapours, where hot damp air was the only kind to be breathed.

They walked for the whole day and still the path continued. That night they camped in a place which was rife with dragonflies, though there were lizards enough around to feed on the colourful creatures. Singapore Jack, and Harry, would have been in their element, trying to classify and label the insects, but to Keller they were simply a nuisance. Usang tended his sores and cuts, which – if they were not cleaned – would fester from fungoid infections and would ripen overnight.

The following morning, they were on their way again. All day they walked, until they came at last to a clearing. Stepping out into this welcome space where the sunlight was not filtered through a green haze, there stood a magnificent mountain before them. Keller named it the Black Mountain, because it looked like a spearhead carved out of jet. There were streams dropping like flimsy veils from its heights and caves were in evidence.

'This is more like it,' murmured Keller, as if the Punan hiding-place needed to have a dramatic setting. 'This is where we'll find the heads.'

The trail led to one of these caves, up on the second tier of the mountainside. Keller made camp down below, in the clearing, where there was fresh water and good air. Again, he left Budrudeen and Usang in the camp, while he and Mayok ascended the side of the mountain. They reached the entrance to the cave at nightfall. Mayok refused to enter the place at night, even though Keller said it did not make sense. There was darkness inside, whatever time of day they entered.

Mayok told Keller that it was good manners to remain outside for a while. They should not rush in, get what they wanted, and rush out again. The mountain gods would take a poor view of such behaviour. This was a special mountain, awesome in its aspect, and the proper calm respect was needed. A few rituals were to be observed, which Mayok had learned from his father.

He made a meal of plantain and cereals, over a slow-burning fire, and showed Keller what they must do. These caves were not like those they had entered earlier. The previous cave system had been part of a limestone hill, worm-holed by fast-running water. This cave was much older, part of the ancient mountain itself. 'This one gunung,' said Mayok, using the Malay word for mountain, 'is home of other-peoples from clouds. Us ones must make honour for these special peoples.'

'The mountain gods, you mean? I'm all for that, Mayok. I'm not one of your whites who don't respect the gods. We'll stay out here till you think it's right to go in.'

That night, Keller felt at peace with himself. He sat over a campfire and stared into its flames. Mayok sat with him, also looking into the fire. Each saw different things in there.

'You know what I can see?' said Keller, with sudden insight. 'You know what I see in those yellow and red flames? Gold. Gold beyond our wildest dreams. And rubies.

Great rubies larger than hens' eggs . . .' And now the logs flared white and green, as trapped gases hissed into heat. 'And diamonds too, and emeralds. What do you see, friend?'

Mayok was lost in his own dreams.

'I? I see yellow deer run. I see white horns of antelope, red eyes of great bull. I see green turtle and lizard. I see . . . life.'

Keller laughed, and said, 'More fool you,' before stirring his gold and gems with a stick

Mayok was right about the 'other-peoples' from the clouds. Supernatural creatures from the sky did indeed use the Black Mountain. The sangiang were able to step down on to it, because the clouds where they lived brushed its peak. This mountain was where they strolled to get exercise for their limbs and bodies. This was their 'park', where they walked and talked, greeted each other, gazed upon the flowers of their world: the forest trees below. Here they passed their leisure hours.

The most supreme of the sangiang demi-gods was Mahatara himself, whose heavenly name was Sangiang Dewata. On the day that the small party of humans had arrived at the cave entrance, Mahatara had been resting on the mountain peak. He was not overly pleased at having his rest disturbed by mortals. Their presence tainted the atmosphere of the mountain, especially since one of them was so consumed by greed as to be almost unrecognizable as a mortal of any worth.

Mahatara also noticed that Hantu Kuang, the ghost with a hundred eyes, was dogging the group. Mahatara retreated from the foul atmosphere with his hawk, Antang, on his wrist, to the fragrance of the clouds above. He sent messengers to Hantu Kuang, to tell that infant deity to desist from following the mortals. Mahatara knew they were close to their individual destinies. His daughters, swishing about the night sky on their golden brooms, had now finished weaving their fates.

Membang Kuning, the spirit of the sunset, and Rajah Jinn Hitam, king of the black jinn, were the messengers sent down to Hantu Kuang, to tell him to desist. These two deities wore fitting colours for such a task – red and black – to symbolize the end envisaged for the most violent visitor the forests had ever known since Kilir had guided Iskander, that great but bloody-minded warrior of the West, into the rainforests many years ago.

'You must leave now,' said Rajah Jinn Hitam, 'the supreme one desires your retirement.'

'Ah, things have come to a head?'

'This is the way of things.'

The three chatted for a while, passing eternity in idle talk, then said goodbye and went their separate ways. Keller woke with a start, the moment they had gone. He felt a great deal lighter. Some of his madness had gone from him. Violence was part of him, deeply engrained in his spirit, but the bloody state of mind he had been in of late was gone. He felt some relief at his refreshed state. He would be going into the cave in the morning with a clear head. That was good.

When he turned, to go back to sleep, he saw that Mayok was awake too. The Dyak's eyes were on him. There was no trust in those eyes.

'What's the matter with you?' Keller asked, sharply.

'No matter, no matter,' replied Mayok, not moving his head, but not closing his eyes either.

'You just mind your own.'

With that, Keller lay down his head once more and dreamed his last few dreams on this earth.

# PART TEN

# Mahatara's Hawk

# 1

Kit Colenso was feeding ginger stems to a tame monkey when Harry came running up to the camp from the river.

'Kit! Kit!'

He stood up and, because she continued to run straight at him, instinctively opened his arms. She fell into them, sobbing, and began to kiss his mouth and cheeks. Taken completely by surprise, the South African remained passive. It was not that he did not enjoy what she was doing, but that she seemed somewhat hysterical. He looked over her shoulder for Singapore Jack, but the tall dark aristocrat was nowhere to be seen. Only the two Dyaks who had remained with him and Harry came strolling up from the canoe, carrying very few goods.

'What's happened?' asked Colenso, when there was a respite in the furious affection. 'Where's Jack?'

She slumped now, still in his arms. Her whole body went limp.

'Dead,' she murmured.

'Dead? How?'

'Keller shot him. There was a duel. I didn't see it but the two Dyaks did. They said the two men had pistols and stood back to back, walked away from each, then turned and fired. Jack fell with a bullet in his chest. He lived for a minute or two, then he was gone. Keller was not seriously wounded.'

'All right. You'd better come and sit down. Lidah?' he called the last word loudly.

Lidah came out of a tent and, when she saw Harry, she rushed forward and hugged her, only to begin laughing as loudly as her mistress had been sobbing.

'You come home safe, missy.'

'Safe and sound.'

The way she said it made Kit Colenso look at her sharply.

'Keller didn't try anything? After he had killed Jack?'

'No,' replied Harry. 'He didn't have time. I left before he returned to the longhouse.' She did not want to tell him about the attempted rape at this time. Harry did not want Kit to go chasing after Keller the way Jack had done.

Colenso went and spoke with the Dyaks and found Harry's account to have been accurate. He then regretted asking them. What right had he to check on Harry's version of the events? He was simply her official protector. Admittedly, ladies did not rush at men and begin kissing them when there was nothing between them, but Colenso believed she had just been overwrought at that moment. She had been through a lot. Her fiancé had been violently slain and then she had fled his killer. She had lived with the knowledge for three days on the river, before arriving at the camp. It was no wonder she had been distraught.

Going down to the canoe, he found that Harry had left in such a hurry she had forgotten to bring her sketches and notes. None of Jack's boxes were in the canoe either. Somewhere there were packages and crates of specimens,

newly drawn maps and charts and copious notes and drawings. True, Colenso had some with him, but the bulk had
remained with Singapore Jack, who would not let the
results of his gathering out of his sight.

That evening, once Harry had rested, he went to see her
in her tent.

'I'm going back,' he told her.

She leapt up and frantically grabbed him by the shirt.

'No!' she cried. 'Kit – he'll kill you. You can't go back
there. We must go on to the coast now. Let us go on?' she
ended up pleading with him.

Colenso shook his head.

'It's unthinkable. I'm not going back after Keller. The
law, or the jungle, will have to take care of him. I have to go
back to make sure Jack's dead for one thing. Trustworthy as
they may be, the authorities back in England will censure us
if we go by the word of a couple of Dyaks. They, and Jack's
relations, will want definite proof of his death. I have to see
a body.

'Apart from that, we have to retrieve the results of Jack's
work. It's impossible to leave it there, Harry. The whole
expedition was formed to gather that material. Can you
imagine what the Geographical Society will say to the news-
papers and everyone else if we do not take back all Jack's
work? I shall take half a dozen Dyaks – including Patan and
Iguina, my Ngaju's – and collect all the packages and crates
before the Punan decided they are theirs and begin opening
them and ruining the contents.'

She flung herself at him again. 'No – Kit, he's dangerous.
He'll lay in wait for you. He'll shoot you as soon as look at
you. He's an evil, evil man . . .'

'Nevertheless, he has no quarrel with me.'

'All right!' she shrieked. 'He tried to rape me. He'll kill
any white man he sees. Send the Dyaks for the equipment

and material. Tell them to bring Jack's head back, so you can see he's well and truly dead. But don't go – don't go,' she groaned the last request. 'I – I love you, Kit. I love you with all my heart and soul. I thought it was Jack, but that was simply infatuation. A handsome man with a dark reputation. I want you. I've wanted you for a long time now.'

Colenso's heart soared at these words. He kissed the tears trickling down her cheeks as she kept her arms locked around the back of his head. There was not much in height between them. She was as tall as he was. A dark-haired woman and a blond-haired man, locked in embrace. Lidah giggled when she came in and saw them, putting her hand over her mouth the way Oriental people do, but she did not lie down to laugh.

While Harry clung to him, he said, 'I still have to go, Harry. It has to be me.'

'Oh, *please*.'

'I can take care of myself. The bastard tried to rape you, did he? Did he hurt you? Were you hurt in any way?'

'No, not seriously. I will have nightmares about it, I suppose, for some time to come, but I'm not physically hurt. He was though,' she added with grim satisfaction. 'As he was assaulting me an owl attacked him, tearing his face to ribbons with its claws and blinding him in one eye. It was the most extraordinary thing. I'm sure it was God's doing.'

'An owl?'

'A strange black owl, which seemed so hostile to Keller it was as if Keller had done something to it in the past.'

She raised her round face and looked Colenso in the eyes. 'I love you, Kit.'

'Yes. I love you too, Harry. I too have felt something deeper than mere fondness for you, for some time now. But you were Jack's. You told me you were Jack's . . .'

'Well, you were so annoying sometimes. You used to put

me in a temper. But I knew the engagement with Jack was a mistake, almost from the beginning. He was not the sort of man I wanted for a husband.' She laughed and released him. 'Listen to me, picking and choosing. Back home, where there are elegible ladies aplenty, not many men would even bother to look at *me*. I'm hardly a beauty, am I? Plain Jane. I expect when we get back to real society, you'll find yourself a nonpareil, a rare beauty. You'll have the pick of the bunch then, Kit, when you return a hero, having saved all your friend's collection.'

'That's not why I'm doing it and you know it,' he said, fiercely. 'Harry Glendenning, you are a witch sometimes. I am going back for Jack's stuff because it's right. And as for all that other claptrap, I have no interest in other women. Do you think I could not have been married to one before now? I loved my wife, before she was so tragically taken from me, but you and her are so different from one another you need never be jealous of her, Harry. You would have been great friends.'

Harry's eyes misted over. 'Oh, Kit, I'm sorry I say such horrible things. Of course you loved Ithuka. I could never be jealous of her. A little envious, that she knew you in the days when you were not so cynical, but never jealous.'

'You remembered her name.'

'I remember everything you told me about yourself.'

Kit Colenso felt as if a new life had opened up before him. Indeed, it had. 'Listen, Harry, don't ever call yourself a plain Jane again. When we are back in society – you won't believe me now, here in the rainforest – I shall tell you how beautiful I find you – to gaze upon, and in your spirit. Now, I must go. I *must*, darling. You have to be with me on this.'

'I am with you, my dearest – always.'

Colenso was satisfied. He began issuing orders to his Dyaks. They responded with alacrity. They liked Kit

Colenso. Men back in civilization were not that fond of him. His brusqueness and impatience with their frivolous ways did not endear him to men from his own part of the world. They thought him rough and ill-mannered, though many admired his hunting skills.

'We'll get married in South Africa, by my older brother,' he said. 'How would you like to be married by a bishop?'

'I would get married by a barber if it pleased you.'

'Well, plenty of time for talking that over later.'

He kissed her goodbye and then set off upriver. It would be a long and arduous journey, but he was determined to make it as quickly as possible. He had no idea what the Punan thought of the collection of writings, paintings and specimens that the expedition had gathered. They might ignore them, they might throw them away with the rubbish, or they might share them out amongst themselves.

Then there was the question of John Keller. What was to be done with him? He had the crime of attempted rape to answer for now. It would be difficult to take him into custody and transport him back to civilization where the due process of the law could deal with his case. Keller was not the sort of man to walk placidly by his captor. Then again Colenso balked at executing the man out of hand. He *wanted* to kill him. But equally, Colenso did not want to found his marriage to Harry on blood.

'I shall arrest him,' murmured Colenso, 'and attempt to take him back alive. If he tries to run, *then* I shall shoot him.'

Keller and Mayok entered the cave just after dawn. Mayok left his blow-pipe with Usang, but Keller kept his weapons. Keller was still grumbling about Mayok's fear of going in at night, yet the Englishman had not gone in on his own. Deep down, Keller also had a healthy respect for the night hours, and the gods.

This cave, unlike the limestone caves he had entered earlier, was simply a crack in the creation of the mountain. There were no stalagmites or stalactites, no folded curtains of limestone, no pillars or pools. It was a straight, dry cave which went in only about a quarter of a mile.

Although it was narrow, the ceiling was high, the whole cave being the shape of an axe head. There were bats flying around, making their high-pitched *cheer-reeps* as they flew past. The torchlight also illuminated moving clusters of shiny eyes – the eyes of huntsman spiders with poisonous bites. These creatures were as large as a man's hand and very swift moving. They, and the cave scorpions, made Keller's flesh crawl, as he ducked and weaved under razor-sharp shelves of rock.

Keller's heart was beating fast. He was both anxious and excited. What if this was another false trail? What if the heads were somewhere else? In which case, he told himself, he would go back to the longhouse and drag that basir out into the rainforest, force him to reveal the hiding place. Torture was the best way of obtaining such information. Keller had been to enough different countries to have learned a few tricks in that direction. Hanging by the thumbs would do for a start.

But he need not have worried. When he turned the next corner, there they were, lit by sunlight shafting in through an overhead fissure. Seven heads on seven poles, arranged in the shape of a dagger. They were grisly objects, skulls with dank hair which hung down to the ground. There was a slight breeze in the cave, from the fissures which were letting in light, and this gently lifted the hair, giving the heads a certain animation.

'Here they are,' Keller whispered, the hand holding the torch shaking. 'The seven heads. These are ancient chieftains, Mayok. Punan chieftains. Sorcerers, yes?'

'In old time, all chieftain was sorcerer,' agreed Mayok, hanging back in awe and fear. 'Very strong magic.'

Very strong magic! Keller could feel magic in the air, like electricity before a storm. His skin was tingling with it. Dust started to cling to his skin. The hairs on his body crawled upright. He noticed there were no snakes, spiders or scorpions in this part of the cave. Nor even bats. It was like a holy building or hallowed place: quiet, expectant, and carrying an atmosphere which was charged with supernatural energy.

'Come up here beside me,' Keller ordered Mayok.

Mayok seemed rooted to the spot.

'No, tuan. I stay here.'

'Suit yourself.'

Keller had been advised by Raki to sit and wait. When in the presence of demi-gods, it was as well to be patient. And the question did not need to be spoken aloud. The heads would know what the visitor wanted. Even if they had not the power to divine the visitor's request, there was usually only one question: 'Where can I find untold riches?' One man might wish to rule the world, to have unlimited power, while another might want a dying relative or friend made healthy again. But the heads did not grant wishes, they merely told the truth. They could not convey power or heal the sick, but they could tell a man where to look for wealth.

Keller guessed that the visitors had all been Chinese or Japanese until now. Keller was the first European to step inside the cave, unless Iskander, down from the Indus, had visited the cave himself. It occurred to Keller that there were two people present and therefore two possible answers to the question. Would this confuse the heads? He felt not, for what would a Dyak like Mayok do with gold and diamonds?

So Keller sat in the half-light of the cave, facing the ancient heads of the Punan chieftains, and waited for his question to be answered. Mayok sat far behind him, near the corner. They both remained respectfully quiet and reflective, almost meditative, under seven pairs of sightless eyes. In the deep silence they could both hear the bats in the other parts of the cave, swishing and bleeping, catching their food.

One whole day went by before the heads spoke, but not for one moment did the seaman doubt. He had come too far to find a fraud. His faith remained firm. Keller was worried about Mayok when the night came, but the Dyak still remained with him. It seemed now they were settled the gods would accept the quiet passing of time inside their mountain.

Keller fought sleep like a tiger.

He was terrified he would not be awake when the sorcerer-chieftains made their reply. What a tragedy that would have been for the sailor, to have missed the most important lesson of his life, through dozing off. He was used to going without sleep on watches when storms raged, but he had never had to simply sit and wait in silence before now. Lethargy crept through him, weighing him down heavily, but he forced his one good eye to remain open, staring at various points around the cave, refusing to succumb to the weariness.

When they finally spoke, they did so as a chorus, which echoed throughout the cave. A wild chill went through Keller, as he listened to the strange words. These were dead men talking, ancient men from a world different to the one Keller knew, and their voices bore an unearthly tone. These were words from beyond death, from mouths with no tongues, whose jaws hung slack and whose sightless eyes were black sockets.

If a man did not feel fear at the sound of those voices, then that man was not mortal. Keller was petrified. If he had been called to repeat the words, even though he had promised to listen intently, he would have been unable. He was too distracted by the terror those sounds conjured from within him. Never before in his whole life had he been so utterly afraid.

The brief message was, of course, in the tongue of the Punan, which Keller was unable to understand. He turned quickly, as they chanted, to make sure Mayok was still awake and alert. To his relief the Kayan youth heard the intonation.

Afterwards, Keller was elated. He remained respectfully silent for some time after the delivery. Then he rose quietly and made his way out of that part of the cave. Mayok had preceded him, treading softly in the dust. Both men wished to be gone from that location as soon as possible. There remained that feeling that at any time conditions could change, that disembodied hands might reach out for them from the darkness of the walls, and drag them away to nightmare, in a place run by the mighty jinn.

Once they were out of the cave they did not pause to speak further. The pair raced back to the place where they had left Usang and Budrudeen. These two were waiting for them, Usang at least was standing anxiously in a clearing. When the two men appeared she rushed forward immediately and threw herself into Mayok's arms. The Kayan held her tightly, looking over her shoulder at Keller, who was staring with narrowed eye at the scene.

'So that's how it is,' said Keller. 'Well, well. Never mind then, have the bitch. Tell me what the heads said, Mayok, in the best English you can muster. Out with it boy. I have to know now . . .'

'Please, tuan,' interrupted Budrudeen, 'which way is Mecca? I must pray. You tell me which way to pray.'

Keller took no notice of this intrusion.

'Mayok, are you going to answer me?' growled the seaman.

Mayok remained silent, staring at Keller.

Budrudeen was whining, 'Tuan, please, I must pray.'

'Get the hell out my hair, boy!' Keller yelled furiously at Budrudeen. 'Can't you see I'm busy.'

'But tuan . . .'

'This way, that way,' shouted Keller, waving his arm arbitrarily. 'Any bloody way. Just shut your trap, boy. I don't care which way you point your arse. I never have. I don't give a damn, see.'

Keller had now unslung one of his muskets from his shoulder. He levelled it first at Mayok, then seemed to change his mind, and pointed the muzzle at Usang. His attention off Budrudeen, the Malay youth shuffled off to one side of the seaman and reached into his ragged tunic.

Keller tried to keep the rage out of his voice as he remained steadily aiming the musket at Usang.

'You better tell me quick, boy, what those heads said to you, or by Jesus Christ almighty I'm going to shoot her. You hear me? I'll kill her. And you'd better not lie to me. I'll know if you're lying. I can tell these things. If it sounds like a lie I'll kill her anyway, d'you hear?'

At that moment, Budrudeen came up on Keller's blind side and plunged his kris between Keller's shoulder blades.

## 2

Kit Colenso found the journey upriver desperately hard. He was still weak from malaria and he was at that part of a long journey through difficult terrain where the body becomes exhausted and needs rest. However, his Dyaks were superb, taking the greater share of the paddling. When they reached white water, which was fairly often, they resorted to portage and refused to allow him to help carry the canoes. He felt ashamed of his weakness and admired their strength.

When he finally reached the longhouse, he went immediately to see the basir, knowing the tuai rumah was an ineffectual character. When he found the basir he spoke to him, partly through an interpreter, though he understood a great deal of the Dyak tongue himself.

'The red-haired one – has he returned?'

The basir, still in woman's clothes and with cosmetically enhanced features, nodded.

'He came back to fetch his Kayan man and his wife. Oh, and their Malay cook. They went off into the jungle. He has a demon in his head, that one.'

'Which way did they go?'

The basir smiled. 'Why do you concern yourself about the orang-utan? He is not your friend. You want revenge perhaps, for what he did to the white woman? Be assured he will not come back. The gods will destroy him.'

'Just in case they don't, I want to take him back with me, to face our justice. Will you take me to him?'

The basir's false smile faded. 'You wish me to take you to the forbidden place? Only I can go there, alone.'

'I do not want to enter any place forbidden to me. I simply want to find the red-haired one. I have no interest in becoming rich. I am rich already, in my spirit. Ask Patan here, or Iguina. They know me as well as I know myself. We have travelled together for many years. Ask them if they believe I wish to enrich myself.'

Patan said, 'It is true – the tuan is already rich – he needs no more.'

This was not entirely true, though Patan believed it to be. In the eyes of his two Dyaks, Colenso was a wealthy man. He seemed to want for nothing – food, clothes, shelter, weapons – all those things which would make a Dyak rich. However, he did nothing to dispel this view of himself, hoping to persuade the basir to take him to Keller.

The basir said he would consult his ancestors and his gods before giving Colenso a definite answer.

Colenso then asked one of his other Dyaks to take him to where Singapore Jack's body lay. This man was one of Jack's own Dyaks, present at his death. He and his friend had fled the scene afterwards and had made their way to Colenso's camp downriver. They had described to Colenso what had happened, but the South African needed to see the body for himself. As he had told Harry, he could not go back without collecting personal evidence of the death.

The head-hunter led him to the spot where Jack had

fallen. Colenso saw that the English lord was indeed dead. His body had been ravaged by insects, worms and larger creatures of the forest. Since it was not near a river the crocodiles had not been near it, so it was, in a sense, still whole. The wound in the chest was clearly visible.

'You idiot,' murmured Colenso. 'Fighting a duel in the middle of the Borneo jungle? You should have mobilized the Punan and put him down like a dog, if that's the way you felt.'

Colenso removed Jack's jewelry – his ring, his pocket watch – and emptied his pockets of his personal effects. Then he had Patan and Iguina make a litter to carry the remains back to a place where there were few trees, so they could dig a grave. Singapore Jack was buried with very little pomp and ceremony. Colenso fashioned a cross for him, but how long that would remain on the grave was anybody's guess. Colenso thought that the termites would get rid of it in a couple of hours.

The party then returned to the longhouse, to find the basir waiting for them.

'I have consulted my ancestors,' said the basir, 'and they tell me you are to be trusted. You and I will go alone. Your friends will remain here.'

'Do not go with this man,' whispered Patan in English. 'He is one evil sorcerer. You not come home alive.'

'I appreciate your concern,' replied Colenso, 'but I think I must go with him. I shall be on my guard the whole time, be assured of that, my friend. And if you and Iguina should track us from a suitable distance, without him knowing, why that would reassure me even more.'

To Colenso's astonishment a shadow of fear passed over Patan's features. He had believed there was nothing on the earth which would frighten Patan or Iguina that much. He had seen them face almost certain death without flinching.

Suddenly he realized that the forbidden place which was under the control of the basir held great terrors for all Dyaks. They were not scared of dying, but this was not about death, it was about things preternatural. He did not wish to make them do something that would give them nightmares for the rest of their lives.

'On second thoughts,' he said, as if changing his mind, 'it might be better if you stayed here and made sure we were not followed by any of the Punan warriors. I don't trust the basir's son. He's a shifty-looking individual.'

'No,' said Patan, a determined look on his face. 'We follow you, tuan.'

Colenso told the basir he wanted to start out straight away and the old man agreed. So, laden with his backpack and carrying his musket, Colenso set forth, lead by a basir carrying a blow-pipe and wearing a Dyak sword. It was the first time Colenso had seen the basir carrying weapons. He felt it was significant.

With the kris still sticking out of Keller's back, the seaman spun round and instinctively fired his musket. A ball the size of a man's thumb hummed past Budrudeen's ear. Had it been a few inches to the right, it would have taken off the top of the Malay youth's head. Keller then swung the musket like a club, catching the young man on the shoulder. Budrudeen went sprawling over some tree roots.

There was a red mist before Keller's eyes. A numbness was spreading up one side of his body. He tried to reach back to withdraw the dagger. It was in an awkward place. Though he could get his fingers on the boss, he could not grip it firmly enough to pull it out. The dagger was deep, stuck between two ribs. Blood began to trickle out of the side of Keller's mouth. It felt like a lung had been punctured.

'You ungrateful bastard!' snarled Keller.

He stepped forward and prepared to crush Budrudeen's head with the butt of the musket. At that moment he was stung in the throat by what he thought was a hornet. He reached up with one hand and plucked out the sting. Gazing on it though, he saw that it was a small dart. In that second he realized what had happened and gave Mayok an aggrieved look. Mayok was holding his blow-pipe, staring back, a stiff expression on his face.

'Boy?' Keller croaked.

Then the big seaman buckled at the knees. It seemed as though he were praying. He dropped his musket and blinked, staring round him as the three people with him began to ripple. The trees too began to dissolve in warping air. Then the light began to go from the world. He knew he was dying. Mayok had hit him with a poisoned dart. Keller had seen other creatures, including men, similarly struck. They died within a couple of minutes.

'You done for me, boy. You turned me off,' he managed to say. Then, with a vestige of fear, 'Don't let that shadow thing get me . . .'

His body fell sideways, on to the soft moss. Even as he lay there, the life gone from his body, and his soul struggling to free itself from the dead flesh, he saw the raptor coming. It came down like a black bolt from the mountain above. Its talons were spread, its beak half-open in expectation. Antang, Mahatara's hunting hawk, fell on the soul before it could escape its mortal remains. Keller was ripped from his carcass and carried like a flapping rag aloft.

No! he screamed silently. Then, Why?

But Keller's soul knew why.

He had killed the crocodile, just as Jack had been responsible for the death of the rhino. On meting out death to forest creatures these two intruders had linked themselves with the land and its gods. They had entangled themselves in a world whose meshes enfolded all within it: trees, creatures, mountains, deities, rivers – and men. They had entered, perpetrated deeds, and had thus become enfolded in the vast rainforest region known as the Ulu.

Keller's soul now belonged to Mahatara.

It would be devoured by the supreme god and travel his gut for eternity.

Antang's claws were not kind. They gripped the tattered soul tightly. On the way up, Antang's beak tore small pieces from his prize. Just as a living hawk is entitled to the brains of the prey he takes for his master, so Antang was permitted the yielding parts of Keller's spirit. This was the god-hawk's reward for a swift and merciless retrieval.

Kit Colenso saw a jolt go through the basir. The old man stopped in his tracks. Colenso suspected a trick and called to his Dyaks. Patan and Iguina came out of the rainforest with their blow-pipes. The basir glanced over at the men and then held up his hands. He said something about death.

Patan translated: 'The old man say no need go on – the redbeard is dead.'

'How does he know that?'

Patan shrugged. 'He is one sorcerer. He say he see Antang go fly with red man's spirit, take to Mahatara.'

Colenso stopped and thought about this. The old man could have been lying, but to what purpose? And the basir had definitely looked shocked. It was also in the basir's interests that Keller be killed or captured, since the red-headed seaman was determined to violate the basir's secret. However, Colenso wanted to see the body. He had to be sure.

'Is the corpse in the place the basir does not want us to enter?'

More words were exchanged, then, 'No, tuan. It is outside that place.'

'Then tell him I wish to see the body, after which we will leave him alone.'

The basir nodded when this information was passed on to him and led the party forward. Eventually, after an hour or so, they reached the spot where Keller had been killed. Colenso saw the blood on the roots and grass at his feet, but there was no body.

'Where is he?' asked Colenso.

It was Patan who pointed upwards. Keller's naked corpse was jammed in amongst the branches of a tree, high above. The red hair on his chest and head were clearly visible, stark against the whiteness of his skin. The late afternoon sun had caught his body in its rays and gave it a fierce and fiery appearance. Keller looked as if he were sitting on a bough, malevolently glaring down on those who hated him.

'How did he get up there?' Colenso asked.

'He climbed there after death,' said the basir, matter of factly. 'He is a man-of-the-forest.'

Colenso wondered, but thought it more likely that orangutans had found him and carried him up there. Though he had no explanation as to their purpose. It was another of those mysteries of the Ulu, which doubtless would never be solved. There was little point in dwelling on it. Such problems whirled around in the brain and never found a conclusion.

Colenso thought about giving the grotesquely scarred body a burial, then decided against it. Time was passing and Harry would be worried. Keller was not worth the concern Harry would be feeling. He, Patan and Iguina left the basir standing there, looking up at the corpse. No doubt the old man had some ideas about what should happen to the remains.

On the trip back to the forward camp, Colenso thought about the basir. The old man was a tyrant, but there were probably many such longhouse despots in the rainforest. It was not up to outsiders like Colenso to come in and enforce changes. What could he do? Arrest the man? Kalimantan was outside the rajah's rule, which only extended over Sarawak, far to the north. No, such despots would only be thrown out when the people of the Ulu tribes decided to deal with their own situations.

Harry was waiting for him when he reached the camp. Dark haired, dark eyed, lovely to his eyes. She ran into his tired arms like an eager young girl. He too felt youthful again, when he saw her. Youthful and rather shy. Their love was new enough to bring out the child in them. The Dyaks smiled behind their hands when they saw them hug each other, both talking at once, both listening at once, both as happy as baby turtles.

## 3

Mayok, Usang and Budrudeen eventually made their way downriver to the coast on a raft fashioned from reeds. There, Budrudeen found a Chinese junk which was sailing east, round the coast, to Sabah in the northeast of Borneo. Budrudeen told the captain he would work his passage as the ship's cook. Once the Chinese crew had tasted Budrudeen's chicken-rice, they nodded their assent.

'I go to join my uncle,' said Budrudeen to the other two, before the junk set sail. 'I thank you for your friendship. You, Mayok, have saved my life many times, in many ways, and you will always be as a brother to me. I love you both. Allah loves you for looking after one of his children. Peace be with you, wherever you go. Goodbye, my brother and my sister.'

They waved to him from the dock and then prepared themselves for a long journey back into the Ulu, to find Mayok's longhouse. Mayok worked long enough to buy a canoe. Then, with a new wife and his hunting weapons, he started out northwards, along the snaking rivers, through the dense green world of the rainforest. He knew well enough now how to survive in the Ulu without rice and other domestic provisions. There were wild sago, nuts, fruits, roots and leaves they could eat, to supplement any game he managed to fish or shoot with his blow-pipe.

A baby girl was born on the trip. They called her Udren, after their Malay friend, a word close enough to his name which meant 'kingfisher bird' in their language. She had indeed been born amongst the kingfishers, which flew like coloured darts up and the down the rivers they navigated. Mayok was so proud of his child he was almost bursting and he sang songs for days after she had entered the world, while Usang laughed at his boyish exuberance.

Finally, after many adventures, the pair arrived at the Kayan longhouse. Danta was still the tuai rumah. Mayok met some of his own people fishing for turtles and sent word ahead that he was coming to take his rightful place as chief of the clan. Danta was waiting for him in the yard before the longhouse, dressed for combat, his Dyak sword and shield in his possession. There were several warriors standing with him, armed with blow-pipes and swords. Mayok too had dressed himself for war, in bright hornbill feathers, carrying a short sword and shield.

'You are not wanted here,' Danta called to Mayok, as that man approached. 'Go away. You are forbidden to approach.'

Mayok did not pause in his stride. There was a firmness in his tread. He looked utterly certain of himself.

He said, 'I have come to take your head.'

Fear sprang to the eyes of Danta. There was a new confidence in Mayok which was startling for all to see. Clearly this was not the callow youth who had left the longhouse several seasons ago. This man had seen much violence, much of the world beyond the Ulu, and he knew his own strength. He had lived alone in the rainforest, which, despite the longhouse being situated within it, was a daunting experience.

'My warriors will kill you where you stand!' he called.

'Then they would be fools to do so,' cried Usang from behind her husband. 'My man has been told by the seven heads of the ancient Punan chieftains where to find untold riches. If he were leader of this rumah, you would never go hungry again.'

'You shut up, you stranger to our longhouse!' screamed Danta. 'You do not belong here. You are only a woman. Keep your mouth closed.'

Ten paces before Danta and his men, Mayok stopped.

'It is true,' he said to them. 'I have secret knowledge. Look into my eyes. You can all see the truth. Moreover, you all know that men sent away from their longhouse usually die. I was sent out into the rainforest. I was alone and hunted by men and animals, attacked by demons. I have taken many heads. I survived because the gods wished it so, and because I am strong. I have crossed the world from sea to sea and returned unscathed. Even Jata has not managed to kill me, though he desired it.' He spoke slowly and carefully, so that even the old men and women would hear him.

He said to Danta, 'You think you can defeat such a man as I have become?'

The warriors looked at each other. They could see the truth in Mayok's eyes. Many of them had been friends of the two men as boys. Some of them had been rivals. They were confused by this upheaval in their lives. Finally, one of them spoke.

'What is it you want?' one elder asked Mayok.

'I wish to fight my childhood friend and now my enemy in single combat,' replied Mayok, with a hard look at Danta. 'He knows he has done me wrong. The gods will decide who of us should be chief. I know it will be me. I shall make a pouch of his scrotum, to carry my darts. I shall use his hair to decorate my sword. I will feed his tongue to my chickens . . .'

Mayok spoke quietly, but in the traditional way of a man offering to fight one on one. You intimidated your opponent with bragging words. You stared him hard in the eyes and fought him with your mind first, to weaken his resolve. You worried him with your determination and your speech.

Gradually, the warriors drifted back, widening the ring, leaving Danta standing alone. Finally, Mayok had his wish. It was to be between the two of them. Danta himself now cast off his fear. He allowed the rage to build within him. He began insulting Mayok in the same vein.

When the shouting and the abuse had run its course, the two men called prayers to Sengalang Burong, the war god of the head-hunters. Then they began with the graceful hornbill dance, on opposite sides of the natural ring of people, as the combatants displayed their skill and agility for the clan. They knew their ancestors would be watching and they both prayed for victory. Mayok's father was there, and his grandfather, standing by the longhouse corner post, watching with keen narrowed eyes.

The sun was a hard disc in the heavens. The air was clear and warm. It was a good day for going to war against a neighbour. Or for duelling with a friend turned foe. You could smell the wild blooms, the dust, the moss in the boles of the trees. Hawks and falcons threw themselves up into the sky, to come hurling down again on running or flying prey. It would be a hard day on which to die, leaving such things behind.

They circled each other, several times, before going in to hack and slice with their swords.

The fight was long and furious, with both men sustaining minor wounds, until finally Mayok's fitness began to lift him above Danta's efforts. Their fighting skills with the sword were more or less equal. However, Danta had led a relatively soft life in the longhouse, while Mayok had been toughened by long journeys and living rough in the rainforest. Mayok was a hardened man, in mind, spirit and body. He was as strong as a teak tree and his spirit was light within him.

Danta had heard the words Mayok had spoken. He too, in his heart of hearts, believed that Mayok was now a great warrior. This knowledge gradually ate away Danta's confidence. Desperate though he was to retain his position as tuai rumah, Danta was convinced of Mayok's superiority. Gradually, Mayok wore his opponent down, until Danta was so weary he could hardly lift his weapon to ward off the blows. Finally, a sweep of Mayok's sword, and it was all over. Danta's head bounced over the yard, raising a cloud of dust, then settled face down by the coop.

There was a short silence, followed by pandemonium. Some warriors cried out for Mayok's death. Some women shrieked for his head. No one moved against him. No one dared. Standing firm and steady on the earth, with blood and dust on his hard body, he looked invincible. Finally, the basir stepped forward. This was not Danta's father, for the old man had died a short while previously. This was a cousin of both men. However, one was dead and one alive. It made the choice simple for him.

'Can you not see the eyes of this man, Mayok? He has been to the land of the gods. He has been to the four edges of the Ulu. There will be songs written about Mayok,' he said. 'There will be stories and legends in the telling. We must make Mayok our tuai rumah, or we will perish as a clan.'

The basir's words sunk into the hearts of the people, especially when another cousin began to tell of Danta's treachery, how he connived to have Mayok exiled, and how he had even warned members of an enemy tribe that Mayok would be alone and helpless in the rainforest.

'I know this, because Danta told me himself,' said the cousin. 'His guilt forced him to reveal his secrets to me one day when we were out on a hunt. I have said nothing until now because I was afraid I would not be believed.'

There were no more arguments. Mayok was thus installed as the new tuai rumah. Before the longhouse could settle to this idea, Mayok announced that they would be leaving this particular location. He was going to lead them to a land where there were riches to be found. The arguments began again, but finally Mayok persuaded the elders that this journey was for the good of the tribe.

He led them forth, first to a high place, which then dropped down into a hidden valley. The valley was lush with fruit and nut trees. Game, in the form of deer, monkeys and pigs, birds and fish, abounded. There was cool fresh water from the mountains. There were river plains with rich volcanic soil, where crops could be grown aplenty. No other clans lived in this lost valley. It was a contained bounteous world. The seven heads had told the truth. Here indeed was a land where wealth abounded. Mayok had led his people to promised riches.

Kit and Harry were married, with the rajah's full approval, in Kuching by Bishop Kinley. After a short honeymoon in Kuching itself, they sailed to Britain with their treasures from the rainforests of Borneo. There they presented various organizations – the British Museum, the Geographical Society – with gifts from their incredible journey into the Ulu. They then went on a lecture tour together.

There was some resistance to a woman lecturer at first, but those who deliberately stayed away from Mrs Harriet

Colenso's lectures on the 'Myth and Reality of the Borneo Interior' discovered they were the poorer for it. Within a year, lectures by her and her husband were missed by no one but unfortunates who fell ill on the night of the event.

Back in Sarawak, Rajah Starke's rule continued into the century. He still made mistakes, but somehow the country thrived despite them. On a visit into the Ulu, which was becoming less inaccessible as the years passed, he visited a Land Dyak longhouse. There he noticed a large skull with red hair nestling incongruously amongst other, dark-haired severed heads, hanging from the ceiling of the ruai. He recognized the ravaged object.

Pointing it out to his companions he told them the head had, at a time in the not-so-distant past, belonged to a pugnacious seaman he had once hired as a hunter of men.